RAVES FOR NELSON DEMILLE AND *SPENCERVILLE*

"DeMILLE'S PLOTTING IS SOPHISTICATED."
—*New York Daily News*

"PURE ENTERTAINMENT."
—Los Angeles Features Syndicate

"ANOTHER WINNER FROM AN AUTHOR WHO NEVER DISAPPOINTS."
—*Buffalo News*

"PASSION AND POLITICS, MEMORY AND DESIRE…IMAGINATIVELY PLOTTED…*SPENCERVILLE* IS VERY MUCH CUT FROM THE DeMILLE MOLD."
—*Atlanta Journal-Constitution*

"ANOTHER THRILLER…DeMILLE IS AMONG OUR BEST WRITERS OF ADVENTURE TALES."
—*Winston-Salem Journal*

"A MASTER OF THE UNEXPECTED…AN ACCOMPLISHED AND INCREDIBLY VERSATILE STORYTELLER."
—*Cleveland Plain Dealer*

"HIS NOVELS ARE TIMELY, AUTHENTIC, AND FILLED WITH CONVINCING CHARACTERS. Nelson DeMille is one of the few writers who co tently takes chances and consistently succeeds."
—*Ba*

Spencerville

NOVELS BY NELSON DEMILLE

Nelson DeMille

A NOVEL

Spencerville

GRAND CENTRAL
PUBLISHING

NEW YORK   BOSTON

Copyright © 1994 by Nelson DeMille
Excerpt from *Radiant Angel* copyright © 2015 by Nelson DeMille
All rights reserved. In accordance with the U.S. Copyright Act of 1976, the scanning, uploading, and electronic sharing of any part of this book without the permission of the publisher constitutes unlawful piracy and theft of the author's intellectual property. If you would like to use material from the book (other than for review purposes), prior written permission must be obtained by contacting the publisher at permissions@hbgusa.com. Thank you for your support of the author's rights.

Grand Central Publishing
Hachette Book Group
1290 Avenue of the Americas
New York, NY 10104

www.HachetteBookGroup.com

Grand Central Publishing is a division of Hachette Book Group, Inc.
The Grand Central Publishing name and logo are trademarks of Hachette Book Group, Inc.

The Hachette Speakers Bureau provides a wide range of authors for speaking events. To find out more, go to www.hachettespeakersbureau.com or call (866) 376-6591.

The publisher is not responsible for websites (or their content) that are not owned by the publisher.

Printed in the United States of America

Originally published in hardcover by Hachette Book Group
First mass market edition: October 1995
Reissued: May 1998
First oversize mass market edition: July 2015

10 9 8 7 6 5 4 3 2 1
OPM

Acknowledgments

I'd like to thank three fellow authors for sharing with me their expertise: Pete Earley, Washington insider; Tom Block, retired airline captain and novelist; John Westermann, retired law enforcement officer and novelist.

The barbarians are to arrive today.
Why such inaction in the Senate?
Why do the Senators sit and pass no laws?
Because the barbarians are to arrive today.
What further laws can the Senators pass?

. . . . night is here but the barbarians have not come.
Some people arrived from the frontiers,
and they said that there are no longer any
*   barbarians.*
And now what shall become of us without any
*   barbarians?*
Those people were a kind of solution.

Cavafy
"Expecting the Barbarians" (1904)

CHAPTER ONE

Keith Landry was going home after twenty-five years at the front. He turned his Saab 900 off Pennsylvania Avenue onto Constitution and headed west, along the Mall toward Virginia, crossing the Potomac at the Theodore Roosevelt Bridge. He caught a glimpse of the Lincoln Memorial in his rearview mirror, gave a wave, and continued west on Route 66, away from Washington.

Western Ohio, eight P.M., daylight saving time, mid-August, and Keith Landry remarked to himself that the sun was still about fifteen degrees above the horizon. He had nearly forgotten how much light remained here at this hour, at the end of the eastern time zone, and had forgotten how big his country was.

The driving on the flat, straight road was easy and mindless, so Landry allowed himself some thinking that he'd been putting off: The Cold War was over, which was the good news. Many Cold Warriors had been given pink slips, which, for Keith Landry, was the bad news.

But God had taken pity at last, Landry thought, and with a puff of divine breath blew away the pall of nuclear Armageddon that had hung over the planet for nearly half a century. Rejoice. We are saved.

He reflected, *I will gladly beat my sword into a plowshare or pruning hook, and even my 9mm Glock pistol into a paperweight.* Well, perhaps not gladly. But what was his choice?

The Cold War, once a growth industry, had downsized, leaving its specialists, technicians, and middle management exploring other options. On an intellectual level, Landry knew this was the best thing to happen to humanity since the Gutenberg printing press put a lot of monks out of work. On a more personal level, he was annoyed that a government that had taken twenty-five years of his life couldn't have found enough peace dividend to keep him around for five more years and full retirement pay.

But okay, Washington was two days ago and six hundred miles behind him. Today was day three of life two. Whoever said that there were no second acts in American lives had never worked for the government.

He hummed a few bars of "Homeward Bound" but found his own voice grating and switched on the radio. The scanner locked on to a local station, and Landry listened to a live report from the county fair, followed by a community bulletin board announcing church activities, a 4-H meeting, a VFW picnic, and so forth, followed by crop and livestock prices, hot tips on where the fish were running, and an excruciatingly detailed weather report. There were tornadoes in southern Indiana. Landry shut off the radio, thinking he'd heard this very same news a quarter century ago.

But a lot had happened to him in those years, most of it dangerous. He was safe now, and alive, whereas for the past quarter century he'd felt that he had one foot in the grave and the other on a banana peel. He smiled. "Homeward bound."

Sure, he admitted, he had mixed emotions, and he had to sort them out. Two weeks ago he was in Belgrade exchanging threats with the minister of defense, and today he was in Ohio listening to a twangy voice speculating about hog prices. Yes, he was safe but not yet sound.

Landry settled back in his seat and paid attention to his driving. He liked the feel of the open road, and the Saab handled beautifully. The car's unusual shape attracted curious attention when Landry passed through the small towns and hamlets of western Ohio, and he thought he should probably trade it in for less of a conversation piece when he took up residence in Spencerville.

The cornfields stretched as far as the deep blue sky, and here and there a farmer had planted soybeans, or wheat, or alfalfa. But mostly it was corn: field corn to fatten livestock and sweet corn for the table. Corn. Corn syrup, cornstarch, cornflakes, cornmeal, corn, corn, corn, Landry thought, to fatten an already fat nation. Landry had been in a lot of famine areas over the years, so maybe that's why the sight of the heartland's bounty made him think of fat.

"For amber waves of grain," he said aloud. He noticed that the crops were good. He had no vested interest in the crops, neither as a farmer nor as a man who held crop futures. But he'd spent the first eighteen years of his life listening to everyone around him talk about the crops, so he noticed them wherever he was, in Russia, in China, in Somalia, and now, coming full circle, in western Ohio.

Landry saw the sign for Spencerville, downshifted, and took the turn without braking, causing the Ford Taurus behind him to try the same thing with less acceptable results.

On the horizon, he could see a water storage tower and grain silos, then later, he could make out the clock tower of the Spencer County courthouse, a sort of Gothic Victorian pile of red brick and sandstone built in a burst of turn-of-the-century enthusiasm and boosterism. The courthouse was a marvel when it was built, Landry reflected, and it was a marvel now—the marvel being that Spencer County had once been prosperous enough and populated enough to finance such a massive edifice.

As Landry drew closer, he could see most of the town's ten church spires, catching the light of the setting sun.

Landry did not enter the town but turned off onto a small farm road. A sign reminded him to watch out for slow-moving farm vehicles, and he eased off the accelerator. Within fifteen minutes, he could see the red barn of the Landry farm.

He had never driven all the way home before but had always flown to Toledo or Columbus and rented a car. This drive from the District of Columbia had been uneventful yet interesting. The interesting part, aside from the landscape, was the fact that he didn't know why he was driving to Spencerville to live after so long an absence. Interesting, too, was the sense of unhurried leisure, the absence of any future appointments in his daybook, the dangling wire where his government car phone had once sat, the unaccustomed feeling of being out of touch with the people who once needed to know on a daily basis if he was dead, alive, kidnapped, in jail, on the run, or on vacation. A provision of the National Security Act gave him thirty days from time of separation to notify them of a forwarding address. In fact, however, they wanted it before he left Washington. But Landry, in his first exercise of his rights as a civilian, told them tersely that he didn't know where he was going. He was gone but not forgotten, forcibly retired but of continuing interest to his superiors.

Landry passed a row of post-mounted mailboxes, noticing that the one with the Landry name had the red flag down, as it had been for about five years.

He pulled into the long gravel drive, overgrown with weeds.

The farmhouse was a classical white clapboard Victorian, with porch and gingerbread ornamentation, built in 1889 by Landry's great-grandfather. It was the third house to occupy the site, the first being a log cabin built in the 1820s when the Great Black Swamp was drained and cleared by his ancestors. The second house had been circa Civil War, and he'd seen a photo of it, a small shingled saltbox shape, sans porch or ornamentation. The better looking the farmhouse, according to local wisdom, the more the husband was henpecked. Apparently, Great-Grandpa Cyrus was totally pussy-whipped.

Landry pulled the Saab up to the porch and got out. The setting sun was still hot, but it was dusty dry, very unlike the Washington steam bath.

Landry stared at the house. There was no one on the porch to welcome him home, nor would there ever be. His parents had retired from farming and gone to Florida five years before. His sister, Barbara, unmarried, had gone to Cleveland to seek career fulfillment as an advertising executive. His brother, Paul, was a vice-president with Coca-Cola in Atlanta. Paul had been married to a nice lady named Carol who worked for CNN, and Paul had joint custody of his two sons, and his life was governed by his separation agreement and by Coca-Cola.

Keith Landry had never married, partly because of

the experience of his brother and of most of the people he knew, and partly because of his job, which was not conducive to a life of marital bliss.

Also, if he cared to be honest with himself, and he might as well be, he had never completely gotten over Annie Prentis, who lived about ten miles from where he was now parked in front of his family farm. Ten-point-three miles, to be exact.

Keith Landry got out of his Saab, stretched, and surveyed the old homestead. In the twilight, he saw himself as a young college grad on the porch, an overnight bag in his hand, kissing his mother and his sister, Barbara, shaking hands with little Paul. His father was standing beside the family Ford, where Landry stood now beside the Saab. It was sort of a Norman Rockwell scene, except that Keith Landry wasn't going off to make his way in the world; he was going to the county courthouse, where a bus waited in the parking lot to take that month's *levy* of young men from Spencer County to the induction center in Toledo.

Keith Landry recalled clearly the worried looks on the faces of his family but could not recall very well how he himself felt or acted.

He seemed to remember, however, that he felt awful, and at the same time, he was filled with a sense of adventure, an eagerness to leave, which made him feel guilty. He didn't understand then his mixed emotions, but now he did, and it could be summed up in a line from an old song: How you gonna keep them down on the farm, after they've seen Paree?

But it wasn't Paree, it was Vietnam, and the recruits hadn't mustered in the village square for a roll call and jolly send-off, nor had they returned marching up Main Street after what would have been called V-V Day. And yet, the net effect of the experience for Landry was the same: He never came back to the farm. He'd come back physically, of course, in one piece, but he'd never come back in mind or spirit, and the farm was never his home after that.

So here it was, a quarter century after he'd stepped off his front porch into the world, and he was standing at the steps of that porch again, and the images of his family faded away, leaving him with an unexpected sadness.

He said to himself, "Well, *I'm* home, even if no one else is."

He climbed the steps, found the key in his pocket, and entered.

CHAPTER TWO

On the north side of Spencerville, the better side of town, ten-point-three miles from the Landry farm, Annie Baxter, née Prentis, cleared the dinner dishes from the kitchen table.

Her husband, Cliff Baxter, finished his can of Coors, barely suppressed a belch, looked at his watch, and announced, "I got to go back to work."

Annie had gathered as much from the fact that Cliff had not changed into his usual jeans and T-shirt before dinner. He wore his tan police uniform and had shoved a dish towel in his collar to keep the beef gravy off his pleated shirt. Annie noted that his underarms and waist were wet with perspiration. His holster and pistol hung from a peg on the wall, and he'd left his hat in his police car.

Annie inquired, "When do you think you'll be home?"

"Oh, you know better than to ask me that, honey buns." He rose. "Who the hell knows? This job's gettin' crazy. Drugs and fucked-up kids." He strapped on his holster.

Annie noticed that the gun belt was at the last notch, and if she had been mean-spirited, she would have offered to fetch a leather awl and make a new hole for him.

Cliff Baxter noticed her looking at his girth and said, "You feed me too damn good."

Of course it was her fault. She remarked, "You might ease up on the beer."

"You might ease up on your mouth."

She didn't reply. She was in no mood for a fight, especially over something she didn't care about.

She looked at her husband. For all his extra weight, he was still a good-looking man in many ways, with tanned, rugged features, a full head of thick brown hair, and blue eyes that had a little sparkle left. It was his looks and his body that had attracted her to him some twenty years before, along with his bad-boy charm and cockiness. He had been a good lover, at least by the standards of those days and this place. He'd turned out to be a passable father, too, and a good provider, rising quickly to chief of police. But he was not a good husband, though if you asked him, he'd say he was.

Cliff Baxter opened the screen door and said, "Don't bolt the doors like you did last time."

Last time, she thought, was nearly a year ago, and she'd done it on purpose, so he'd have to ring and knock to wake her. She was looking for a fight then but had gotten more than she'd bargained for. He'd come home that time after four A.M., and since then and before then, it was always around four, once or twice a week.

Of course his job required odd hours, and that alone was no cause for suspicion. But through other means and other sources, she'd learned that her husband fooled around.

Cliff trundled down the back steps and howled at their four dogs in the backyard. The dogs broke into

excited barking and pawed at their chain-link enclo-
sure. Cliff howled again, then laughed. To his wife he
said, "Make sure you give them the scraps and let them
run awhile."

Annie didn't reply. She watched him get into his
chief's car and back out of the driveway. She closed the
kitchen door and locked it but did not bolt it.

In truth, she reflected, there was no reason to even
lock the door. Spencerville was a safe enough town,
though people certainly locked their doors at night.
The reason she didn't have to lock the door was that
her husband had assigned police cars, nearly around the
clock, to patrol Williams Street. His explanation: Criminals know where we live, and I don't want nobody
hurting you. The reality: Cliff Baxter was insanely jealous, possessive, and suspicious.

Annie Baxter was, in effect, a prisoner in her own
house. She could leave anytime, of course, but where
she went and whom she saw came to the attention of
her husband very quickly.

This was embarrassing and humiliating, to say the
least. The neighbors on the neat street of Victorian
homes—doctors, lawyers, businesspeople—accepted the
official explanation for the eternal police presence with
good grace. But they knew Cliff Baxter, so they knew
what this was all about. "Peter, Peter, pumpkin eater,"
Annie said aloud for the millionth time, "had a wife but
couldn't keep her. He put her in a pumpkin shell, and
there he kept her very well." She added, "You bastard."

She went to the front door and looked out the leaded
glass into the street. A Spencerville police cruiser rolled by
and she recognized the driver, a young man named Kevin
Ward, one of Cliff's favored fascists. She fantasized now
and then about inviting Kevin Ward in for coffee, then
seducing him. But maybe Cliff had someone watching

Kevin Ward, probably in an unmarked car. She smiled grimly at her own paranoia, which was becoming as bad as her husband's. But in her case, the paranoia was well founded. In Cliff's case, it was not. Annie Baxter was sexually faithful. True, she didn't have much choice, but beyond that, she took her marriage vows seriously, even if her husband didn't. There were times, however, when she had urges that would have made her mother blush. Cliff's lovemaking came in spurts, followed by longer intervals of indifference. Lately, she welcomed the indifference.

The patrol car moved up the street, and Annie walked into the large living room. She sat in an armchair and listened to the grandfather clock ticking. Her son, Tom, had gone back to Columbus early, ostensibly to find a part-time job before school started, but in reality because Spencerville, and Williams Street in particular, had nothing to offer him for the summer, or for the rest of his life, for that matter. Her daughter, Wendy, was up at Lake Michigan with the church youth group. Annie had volunteered to be one of the chaperons, but Cliff had remarked smilingly, "Who's gonna chaperon *you,* darlin'?"

She looked around at the room that she'd decorated with country antiques and family heirlooms. Cliff had been both proud and sarcastic regarding her taste. She came from a far better family than he did, and at first she'd tried to minimize the dissimilarities in their backgrounds. But he never let her forget their social differences, pointing out that her family was all brains and good manners and no money, and his family had money even if they were a little rough around the edges. And brainless, Annie thought.

Cliff liked to show off the furnishings, show off his stuffed and mounted animals in the basement, his shooting trophies, his press clippings, his guns, his trophy house, and his trophy wife. Look but don't touch. Admire me and my trophies. Cliff Baxter was the classic collector, Annie thought, an anal compulsive personality who couldn't differentiate between a wife and a mounted deer head.

Annie recalled with amazement how proud she'd once been of her husband and her house, and how much hope and optimism she'd had as a young bride, building a life and a marriage. Cliff Baxter had been an attentive and courtly fiancé, especially in the months preceding their marriage. If Annie had any second thoughts about the engagement—which, in fact, she had—Cliff had given her no reason to break it off. But early in her marriage, she'd noticed that her husband was just going through the motions of marriage, keying off her in what he did and said. One day she realized with a sinking feeling that Cliff Baxter was not a charming rogue who was eager to be domesticated by a good woman, but was in fact a borderline sociopath. Soon, however, he lost interest in his half-hearted attempt to become normal. The only thing that kept him in line, kept him from going completely over the edge, she knew, was his official capacity as guardian of law and order. Spencerville had made the bad boy the hall monitor, and it worked for Spencerville and for the bad boy, but Annie lived in fear of what might happen if Cliff became a private citizen, without the prestige and accountability of office. She swore that the day he retired or was asked to step down, she'd run.

She thought of his gun collection: rifles, shotguns, pistols. Each and every weapon was locked in a rack the way a good cop would do. Most cops, however, probably all cops, gave their wife a key just in case there was an intruder. Cliff Baxter, though, did not give his wife a key. She knew how he thought: Cliff feared his wife would shoot him at four A.M. one morning and claim she mistook him for an intruder. There were nights when she stared at the locked weapons and wondered if she would actually put a pistol to her head or his head and pull the trigger. Ninety-nine percent of the time, the answer was no; but there had been moments...

She tilted her head back in the chair and felt the tears roll down her cheeks. The phone rang, but she didn't answer it.

She gathered the dinner scraps in a piece of newspaper and took them out to the kennel. She opened the wire gate and threw the scraps inside. Three of the four dogs—the German shepherd, the Doberman pinscher, and the Rottweiler—attacked the food. The fourth dog, a small gray mongrel, ran to Annie. She let the dog run out of the kennel and closed the gate.

Annie walked back to the house, the gray mongrel following her.

In the kitchen, she fed the dog raw hamburger, then poured herself a glass of lemonade, then went out to the big wrap-around porch and sat in the swing seat, her legs tucked under her, the gray mongrel beside her. It was cooling off, and a soft breeze stirred the old trees on the street. The air smelled like rain. She felt better in the fresh air.

Surely, she thought, there was a way out, a way that didn't pass through the town cemetery. Now that her daughter was about to start college, Annie realized that she couldn't put off making a decision any longer. If she ran, she thought, he'd probably grab her before she got out of town, and if she did manage to slip away, he'd follow. If she went to a lawyer in Spencer County, he'd know about it before she even got home. Cliff

Baxter wasn't particularly liked or respected, but he was feared, and she could relate to that.

The patrol car passed again and Kevin Ward waved to her. She ignored him, and the dog barked at the police car.

Still, she thought, this was America, it was the twentieth century, and there were laws and protection. But instinctively, she knew that was irrelevant in her situation. She had to run, to leave her home, her community, and her family, and that made her angry. She would have preferred a solution more in keeping with her own standards of behavior, not his. She would like to tell him she wanted a divorce, and that she was moving in with her sister, and that they should contact lawyers. But Police Chief Baxter wasn't about to give up one of his trophies, wasn't about to be made a fool of in his town. He knew, without a word being said, that she wanted out, but he also knew, or thought he knew, that he had her safely under lock and key. *He put her in a pumpkin shell.* It was best to let him keep thinking that.

This summer night, sitting on the porch swing made her think of summer nights long ago when she was very happy and deeply in love with another man. There was a letter in her pocket and she pulled it out. By the light from the window behind her, she read the envelope again. She had addressed it to Keith Landry at his home address in Washington, and it had apparently been forwarded to someplace else where someone had put it in another envelope and mailed it back to her with a slip of paper that read: *Unable to forward.*

Keith had once written to her saying that if she ever received such a message, she should not try to write to him again. She would be contacted by someone in his office with a new address.

Annie Baxter was a simple country girl, but not that

simple. She knew what he was telling her: If a letter was ever returned to her, he was dead, and someone in Washington would call or write to her regarding the circumstances.

It had been two days since the letter had been returned to her sister's address in the next county, where Keith sent all his letters to Annie.

Since then, Annie Baxter had feared answering her phone and feared seeing her sister's car pull up again with another letter, an official letter from Washington with a line or two beginning with, "We regret to inform you..."

But on second thought, why would they even bother with that? What was she to Keith Landry? A long-ago girlfriend, a sometimes pen pal. She hadn't seen him in over twenty years and had no expectation that she'd ever see him again.

But perhaps he'd instructed his people, whoever they were, to tell her if he died. Probably he wanted to be buried here with the generations of his family. He might, at this moment, she suddenly realized, be lying in Gibbs Funeral Home. She tried to convince herself it didn't matter that much; she was sad, but really how did it affect her? An old lover died, you heard the news, you became nostalgic and dwelled on your own mortality, you thought of younger days, you said a prayer, and you went on with your life. Maybe you went to the funeral service if it was convenient. It struck her then that if Keith Landry was dead, and if he was going to be buried in Spencerville, she could not possibly go to the service, nor, she thought, could she expect to sneak off to his grave someday without being seen by her constant police chaperons.

She petted the dog beside her. This was her dog—the other three were Cliff's. The dog jumped on her lap and snuggled against her as Annie scratched behind its ears. She said, "He's not dead, Denise. I know he's not dead."

Annie Baxter put her head down on the arm of the swing seat and rocked gently. Heat lightning flashed in the western sky and thunder rolled across the open cornfields, into the town, just ahead of the hard rain. She found herself crying again and kept thinking, *We promised to meet again.*

CHAPTER THREE

Keith Landry walked through the quiet farmhouse. Distant relatives had looked after the place, and it wasn't in bad shape considering it had been empty for five years.

Keith had called ahead to announce his arrival and had spoken to a woman on a nearby farm whom he called Aunt Betty, though she wasn't actually his aunt, but was his mother's second cousin, or something like that. He'd just wanted her to know in case she saw a light in the house, or a strange car, and so forth. Keith had insisted that neither she nor any other ladies go through any bother, but of course that had been like a call to arms—or brooms and mops—and the place was spotless and smelled of pine disinfectant.

Bachelors, Keith reflected, got a lot of breaks from the local womenfolk, who took inordinate pity on men without wives. The goal of these good women in caring for bachelors, Keith suspected, was to demonstrate the advantage of having a wife and helpmate. Unfortunately, the free cleaning, cooking, apple pies, and jams often perpetuated what they sought to cure.

Keith went from room to room, finding everything pretty much as he remembered when he'd seen it last about six years before. He had a sense of the familiar, but, at the same time, the objects seemed surreal, as if he were having a dream about his childhood.

His parents had left behind most of their possessions, perhaps in anticipation of not liking Florida, or perhaps because the furniture, rugs, lamps, wall decorations, and such were as much a part of the house as the oak beams.

Some of the things in the house were nearly two centuries old, Keith knew, having been brought to America from England and Germany, where both sides of his family originated. Aside from a few legitimate antiques and some heirlooms, a good deal of the stuff was just old, and Keith reflected on the frugality, the hardscrabble existence, of a farm family over the centuries. He contrasted this with his friends and colleagues in Washington who contributed heavily to the gross national product. Their salaries, like his, were paid from the public coffers, and Keith, who had never successfully accepted the fact that you don't have to produce anything tangible to get paid, often wondered if too many people in Washington were eating too much of the farmers' corn. But he had dwelled on that many times, and if any of his colleagues thought about it at all, they'd kept it to themselves.

Keith Landry had felt good when he was a soldier, an understandable and honorable profession in Spencer County, but later, when he'd become involved in intelligence work, he began to question his occupation. He often disagreed with national policy, and recently, when he'd been elevated to a position of helping to formulate that policy, he realized that the government worked for itself and perpetuated itself. But he'd known that secret long before he was invited into the inner sanctum of the White House as a staff member of the National Security Council.

Keith stood at the window in the second-floor master bedroom and looked out into the night. A wind had come up and clouds were sailing quickly across the starlit sky. A nearly full moon had risen, casting a blue light on the ripening cornfields. Keith remembered these fields long ago when a drought had been followed by constant rain, and the wheat—they had planted mostly wheat in those days—wasn't ready for harvesting until late July. A bright summer moon had coincided with a dry spell, with a forecast for more rain, and the farmers and their families had harvested until the moon set, about three A.M. The following day was a Sunday, and half the kids were absent from Sunday school, and the ones who showed up slept at their desks. Keith still recalled this shared experience, this communal effort to pull sustenance out of the land, and he felt sorry for urban and suburban kids growing up without a clue as to the relationship between wheatfields and hamburger buns, between corn and cornflakes.

In fact, Keith thought, the further the nation traveled from its agrarian and small-town roots, the less it understood the cycles of nature, the relationships between the land and the people, the law of cause and effect, and ultimately, he reflected, the less we understood our essential selves.

Keith Landry realized the inconsistencies and incongruities of his thinking and his life. He had rejected the idea of becoming a farmer but had not rejected the ideal of farm life; he thrived on the excitement of Washington and foreign cities but was nostalgic for this rural county that had always bored him; he had become disenchanted with his job but was angry about being let go.

He thought he had better resolve these discrepancies, these big gaps between his thoughts and deeds, or he'd become emblematic of the lunatic place he'd just left.

The clouds obscured the moon and stars now, and he was struck by how totally dark and still the countryside was. He could barely see the old ghost of the kitchen garden twenty feet from the house, and beyond that the landscape was black except for the lights of the Muller farmhouse half a mile away.

He turned from the window, went downstairs, and carried his bags up to the second floor. He entered the room he had shared with his brother and threw his luggage on the bed.

The room had oak furniture, pine floors, and white plaster walls. A hooked rug, older than he was, lay on the floorboards. It was any farm boy's room from the last century until recent years when local people had started buying discount store junk.

Before he had left Washington, Keith had filled the Saab with the things he needed and wanted, which turned out to be not so many things after all. There were a few more boxes of odds and ends, mostly sporting gear, coming by UPS. He had given his furniture in his Georgetown apartment to a local church. He felt basically unencumbered by possessions.

The house had been built before closets were common, and in the room were two wardrobe cabinets, one his, one his brother's. He opened the one that had been Paul's and unpacked first his military gear, his uniforms, boots, a box of medals and citations, and finally his officer's sword. Then he unpacked some of the tools of his more recent trade: a bulletproof vest, an M-16 rifle, an attaché case with all sorts of nutty spy craft gizmos built in, and finally his Glock 9mm pistol and holster.

It felt good, he thought, putting this stuff away for the last time, a literal laying down of arms and armor.

He looked into the wardrobe cabinet and contemplated what, if any, significance there was in this moment.

In college, he'd been taken with the story of Cincinnatus, the Roman soldier, statesman, and farmer in the days before Rome became an Imperial power. This man, having saved the fledgling city from a hostile Army, accepted power only long enough to restore order, then returned to his farm. In Washington, Keith had often passed a building on Massachusetts Avenue, the stately Anderson Mansion, which housed the Society of the Cincinnati, and he imagined that its members had the same sort of experience as its Roman namesake, Cincinnatus. This, he thought, was the ideal, Roman or American, this was the essence of an agrarian republic: The call to arms came, the citizen militia were formed, the enemy was met and defeated, and everyone went home.

But that was not what happened in America after 1945, and for the last half century, war had become a way of life. This was the Washington he'd recently left: a city trying to cope with, and minimize, the effects of victory.

Keith closed the door of the cabinet and said, "It's finished." He opened the other wardrobe and unpacked the two handmade Italian suits he'd decided to hold on to. He hung up his tuxedo and smiled at the incongruity of the thing in this setting, then hung a few items of casual clothing, making a mental note to stop at Kmart for jeans and plaid shirts.

To continue the Roman theme, he reflected, like Caesar, he'd burned his bridges behind him, but he wasn't certain that the future included this farm. It depended on who Keith Landry had become.

In his mind, he still thought of himself as a farm boy, despite college, travel, custom-made suits, proficiency in foreign languages, and proficiency with exotic weapons and exotic women. Whether he was in Paris, London, Moscow, or Baghdad, he still imagined there was a residue of hayseed in his hair. Probably, however, this was not true; perhaps what he had become was who he was. And if that was true, he was in the wrong place. But he'd give Spencerville some time, and if he started enjoying trout fishing and church socials, the VFW Hall and small talk at the hardware store, then he'd stick around. If not...well, he could never go back to Washington. He'd spent over half his professional life on the road, and maybe that's where he belonged: everywhere and nowhere.

Keith noticed that the bed was made with fresh linen and a quilt blanket, compliments of Aunt Betty, and he realized that she remembered this was his room, and she hadn't upgraded him to the master bedroom. This had been his father's room as a boy, and his father's before him, so Aunt Betty probably figured he should sleep there until he grew up. He smiled.

Keith walked downstairs into the big country kitchen. The round table could seat ten: family, farmhands, and any kid who stopped by for a meal. Keith opened the refrigerator and saw it had been stocked with basic necessities, except beer. Many of the rural people around here were teetotalers, and the county, while not dry, wasn't awash in alcohol either. Keith, on his rare visits, had found this quaint, but as a resident, it might be a problem. Then again, this might be the least of his problems.

He went into the living room, removed a bottle of Scotch from one of his boxes, returned to the kitchen, and made himself a Scotch and water in a blue plastic glass that made the drink look green.

He sat at the big round table, in his chair, and looked

around at the empty places. Aside from his mother and father and Paul and Barbara, there had been Uncle Ned, his father's younger brother, who used to sit opposite Keith, and Keith could still see his uncle at breakfast, at lunch, at dinner, eating quietly, tired after a long day of farm work. Ned was a farmer through and through, a serious but not humorless man, a son of the soil who wanted only to marry, raise children, raise crops, fix broken things, and do a little fishing on Sunday, usually with his nephews, and someday with his yet-to-be-born sons.

Keith was about ten when Uncle Ned was drafted into the Army, and he remembered his uncle coming home one day in his uniform. A few weeks later, Ned left for the Korean War and never returned. They'd sent his things home, and they were stored in the attic. Keith had gone through the trunk when he was a boy and had even put on the olive drab uniform once.

A forgotten war, a forgotten man, a forgotten sacrifice. Keith recalled that his father had cried when they got the news, but oddly, Ned's name was never mentioned again.

Perhaps, Keith thought, the last man to die in World War II had made the last meaningful sacrifice; since then, it was all politics and power freaks playing with people's lives and families. Perhaps now, he thought, we're starting to figure it out. He looked at Uncle Ned's place, empty now for over forty years, and belatedly, but with sincerity, he said, "I miss you."

Keith finished his Scotch and made another. He looked out the screen door into the dark garden. The wind blew harder now, and in the west he saw lightning, followed by a clap of thunder.

He smelled the rain before he heard it, and heard it before he saw it. A lot of memory circuitry—sights, sounds, smells—were deeply imprinted before a person turned eighteen, Keith thought. A lot of who you were in middle age was determined before you had a chance to manipulate, control, or even understand the things around you. It was no mystery, he thought, why some old people's minds returned to their youth; the wonder of those years, the discoveries, the first experience with the dirty secret of death, and the first stirrings of lust and love were indelible, drawn in luminous colors on clean canvas. Indeed, the first sex act was so mind-boggling that most people could still remember it clearly twenty, thirty, sixty years later.

Annie.

So, he thought, his journey of discovery had led home. On the way he had seen castles and kings, golden cities and soaring cathedrals, wars and death, starvation and disease. Keith wondered if old Pastor Wilkes was still alive, because he wanted to tell him that he'd actually met the Four Horsemen of the Apocalypse and knew more about them than their names; he knew who they were, and obviously they were us.

But Keith had also seen love and compassion, decency and bravery. And here, alone with himself, sitting in his place at the table, he felt the journey was not ended, but was about to get interesting again.

So here it was, twenty-five years since he'd stepped off his front porch into the world, and he'd put a million miles on his trip meter since then, and he'd had so many women he couldn't remember half their names if his life depended on it. Yet, in the dark times, in the mornings and in the evenings, on long plane rides to scary places, in the jungles of Asia, in the back streets of Eastern Europe, and in those moments when he thought he was going to die, he remembered Annie.

CHAPTER FOUR

Annie Baxter lay sleepless on her bed. Brief, incandescent flashes of lightning lit the dark room, and thunder shook the house to its foundations. A burglar alarm, triggered by the storm, wailed somewhere, and dogs barked in the night.

The dream she'd had crept into her consciousness. It was a sexual dream, and it disturbed her because it was about Cliff, and it should have been about Keith. In the dream, she was standing naked in front of Cliff, who was fully dressed in his uniform. He was smiling—no, leering at her, and she was trying to cover her nakedness with her hands and arms.

The Cliff Baxter in her dream was younger and better built than the Cliff Baxter she was married to now. More disturbing still was that, in the dream, she was sexually aroused by Cliff's presence, and she'd awakened with the same feeling.

Keith Landry and the other men she'd been with before Cliff were more sensitive and better lovers in the sense that they were willing to experiment and to give her pleasure. Cliff, on the other hand, had been, and still was, into sexual dominance. She had been turned on by this initially, she admitted, like in the dream; but Cliff's rough sex and selfishness now left her feeling unsatisfied, used, and sometimes uneasy. Still, she remembered a time when she was a willing and aroused partner.

Annie felt guilty that she'd once enjoyed that sado-sexual relationship with Cliff and guilty that she still thought and dreamed about it with no revulsion or loathing. In fact, it was quite the opposite, like now, awakening from that dream, moist between her legs. She realized she had to kill that dream and those thoughts once and for all.

She looked at the clock beside the bed: 5:16 A.M. She rose, put on her robe, went down to the kitchen, and poured herself an iced tea. After some hesitation, she picked up the wall phone and called police headquarters.

"Sergeant Blake speaking, Mrs. Baxter."

She knew that her phone number, name, and address appeared on some sort of screen when she dialed, and that annoyed her. Cliff wasn't comfortable with a lot of new technology, but he intuitively recognized the possibilities of the most sinister, Orwellian gadgets available to the otherwise Stone Age police force of Spencerville.

"Everything okay, Mrs. Baxter?"

"Yes. I'd like to speak to my husband."

"Well . . . he's out making the rounds."

"Then I'll call him on the car phone. Thank you."

"Well, hold on, let's see, he might be . . . I had some trouble raising him before. The storm, you know? I'll try to get him on the radio and tell him to call you. Anything we can do?"

"No, you've done enough." She hung up and dialed his car phone. After four rings, a recorded voice said the call could not be completed. She hung up and went into the basement. Part of the basement was the laundry room, another part was Cliff's den, carpeted, and finished in pine paneling. On his escorted house tours, he liked to point to the laundry room and say, "Her office," then to his den and say, "My office."

She went into his office and turned on the lights. A dozen mounted animal heads stared down at her from the walls, glassy-eyed, with the trace of a smile around their mouths, as though they were happy to have been killed by Cliff Baxter. The taxidermist, or her husband, had a sick sense of humor; probably both of them did.

The police radio crackled on a countertop, and she heard a patrol car talking clearly to headquarters with not much storm static. She didn't hear Sergeant Blake inquiring about Chief Baxter.

She contemplated the wall-mounted gun rack. A braided metal cord ran through the trigger guards of the dozen rifles and shotguns, through an angle iron, and ended in a loop secured by a heavy padlock.

Annie went into the workshop, took a hacksaw, and returned to the gun rack. She pulled the metal cord taut and began sawing. The braided wire began to fray, then the cord separated, and she pulled it loose from the trigger guards. She chose a 12-gauge double-barreled Browning, found the boxes of shotgun shells in a drawer, and slid a heavy-load, steel-shot shell into each of the two chambers.

Annie shouldered the shotgun and went up the stairs into the kitchen. She put the shotgun on the kitchen table and poured herself another glass of iced tea.

The wall phone rang, and she answered it. "Hello."

"Hello, baby doll. You lookin' for me?"

"Yes."

"So, what's cookin', good-lookin'?"

She could tell by the static that he was calling from his car phone. She replied, "I couldn't sleep."

"Well, hell, time to rise and shine anyway. What's for breakfast?"

"I thought you'd stop at Park 'n' Eat for breakfast." She added, "Their eggs, bacon, potatoes, and coffee are better than mine."

"Where'd you get that idea?"

"From you and your mother."

He laughed. "Hey, I'm about five minutes away. Put on the coffee."

"Where were you tonight?"

There was a half-second pause, then he replied, "I don't *ever* want to hear that kind of question from you or nobody." He hung up.

She sat at the kitchen table and laid the shotgun in her lap. She sipped her iced tea and waited.

The minutes dragged by. She said aloud, "So, Mrs. Baxter, you thought it was an intruder?"

She replied, "Yes, that's right."

"But there was no forced entry, ma'am, and you knew the chief was on his way home. You had to have cut the cord, ma'am, long before you heard a noise at the door, so it kinda looks premeditated. Like you was layin' in wait for him."

"Nonsense. I loved my husband. Who didn't love him?"

"Well, ain't nobody I know who *did* love him. Least of all you."

Annie smiled grimly. "That's right. I waited for him and blew his fat ass into the next county. So what?"

Annie thought about Keith Landry, about the possibility of him being dead, laid out at Gibbs Funeral Home. *"Excuse me, Mrs. Baxter, that's Parlor B, a Mr. Landry. Mr. Baxter is in Parlor A, ma'am."*

But what if Keith wasn't dead? Did that make a difference? Maybe she should wait to hear for sure. And how about Tom and Wendy? This was their father. She vacillated and considered putting the shotgun back in the basement, and would have, except he'd see the cut cord and know why.

The police car pulled into the gravel drive, and she heard the car door open and shut, then his footsteps coming up the porch, and she saw him at the back door window, putting the key in the lock.

The door opened, and Cliff Baxter entered the dark kitchen, silhouetted by the back porch light. He was wiping his face and hands with a handkerchief, then sniffed at his fingers and turned toward the sink.

Annie said, "Good morning."

He swung around and peered into the dark alcove where she sat at the table. "Oh...there you are. Don't smell no coffee."

"I guess not, if you're smelling your fingers."

There was no reply.

Annie said, "Turn on the light."

Cliff went back to the door, found the switch, and the kitchen fluorescents flickered on. He said, "You got a problem, lady?"

"No, sir, you have the problem."

"I ain't got no problem."

"Where were you?"

"Cut the shit and put on the coffee." He walked a few steps toward the hallway.

Annie raised the shotgun from her lap and laid it on the table, pointed toward him. "Stop. Back up."

Cliff stared at the gun, then said softly, "Take your hand away from the trigger."

"Where were you tonight?"

"On the job. On the goddamn job, tryin' to earn a goddamn livin', which is more than you do."

"I'm not allowed to get a paying job. I have to do

volunteer work at the hospital thrift shop down the
street from the *police* station where you can keep an eye
on me. *Remember?*"

"You hand me that shotgun, and we'll just forget
this happened." He took a tentative step toward her
and reached out with his hand.

Annie stood and raised the gun to her shoulder,
cocking both hammers.

The loud metallic clicks caused Cliff to back up into
the door. "Hey! Hey!" He put his hands to his front
in a protective gesture. "Now sweetheart...that's...
that's dangerous. That's a hair trigger...you breathe
and that's gonna go off...you point that away—"

"Shut up. Where were you tonight?"

He took a deep breath and controlled his voice. "I
told you. Cars stuck and stalled, bridge over Hoop's
Creek is out, panicky old widows callin' all night—"

"Liar."

"Look...look at these wet clothes...see the mud
on my shoes...? I was helpin' people all night. Now,
come on, honey, you just got yourself all worked up."

Annie glanced at his wet cuffs and shoes and wondered if he was telling the truth this time.

Cliff went on in a soothing tone, using every term
of endearment he could think of. "Now, sweetheart,
darlin', that thing's gonna go off, baby, and I ain't done
nothin', sugar..."

Annie saw that he was truly frightened, but oddly,
she wasn't enjoying this reversal of roles. In fact, she
didn't want him to beg; she just wanted him dead. But
she couldn't just kill him in cold blood. The shotgun was
getting heavy. She said to him, "Go for your gun, Cliff."

He stopped speaking and stared at her.

"Go on. Do you want people to know you died with
your gun in your holster?"

Cliff took a shallow breath, and his tongue flicked across his dry lips. "Annie..."

"Coward! Coward! Coward!"

A clap of thunder exploded close by, startling Cliff Baxter, who jumped, then went for his gun.

Annie fired both barrels, and the recoil knocked her back against the wall.

The deafening blasts died away but still echoed in her ears. Annie dropped the shotgun. The room was filled with the acrid smell of gunpowder, and plaster dust floated down from the gaping hole in the ceiling above where Cliff lay on the floor.

Cliff Baxter got up slowly, on one knee, knocking chunks of plaster and wood lathing off his head and shoulders. Annie saw that he'd wet his pants.

He checked to see that his pistol was in his holster, then glanced up at the ceiling. Still brushing himself off, he stood and walked toward her. She noticed he was trembling, and she wondered what was going to happen next, but she didn't much care.

He walked right past her, picked up the wall phone, and dialed. "Yeah, Blake, it's me." He cleared his throat and tried to steady his voice. "Yeah, had a little accident cleaning a gun. If you get any calls from the neighbors, you explain...Yeah, everything's fine. See ya." He hung up and turned to Annie. "Well, now."

She had no trouble looking him right in the eye, but she noticed he had trouble maintaining eye contact. Also, she thought his order of priorities was interesting: control and contain the situation so as to protect himself, his image, his job. She had no delusions that he was protecting her from the wrath of the law. But that's what he'd say.

As if on cue, he said, "You tried to kill me. I could arrest you."

"Actually, I fired over your head and you know it. But go ahead and take me to jail."

"You bitch. You—" He made a threatening move toward her, and his face reddened, but Annie stood her ground, knowing that ironically it was his badge that kept her from a beating. He knew it, too, and she took a little pleasure in watching him bursting with impotent rage. But one day, she knew, he'd snap. Meanwhile, she hoped he would drop dead with a stroke.

He backed her into a corner, pulled open her robe, then put his hands on her shoulders and squeezed the spot where the shotgun had recoiled.

A blinding pain shot through her body, and her knees buckled. She found herself kneeling on the floor, and she could smell the urine on him. She closed her eyes and turned away, but he grabbed her by the hair and pulled her face toward him. "See what you done? You proud of yourself, bitch? I'll bet you are. Now, we're gonna even the score. We're gonna stay right here like this until you piss your pants, and I don't care if it takes all goddamn day. So, if you got it in you, get it over with. I'm waitin'."

Annie put her hands over her face and shook her head, tears coming to her eyes.

"I'm waitin'."

There was a sharp rap on the back door, and Cliff spun around. Officer Kevin Ward's face peered through the glass. Cliff bellowed, "Get the hell out of here!"

Ward turned quickly and left, but Annie thought he saw that his boss's pants were wet. For sure he saw the plaster dust covering Cliff's face and hair and her behind Cliff, kneeling on the floor. Good.

Cliff turned his attention back to his wife. "You satisfied now, bitch? You satisfied!"

She stood quickly. "Get away from me, or so help me God, I'll call the state police."

"You do, I'll kill you."

"I don't care." She fastened her robe around her.

Cliff Baxter stared at her, his thumbs hooked in his gun belt. From long experience, she knew it was time to end this confrontation, and she knew how to end it. She said nothing, just stood still, tears running down her face, then she dropped her head and looked at the floor, wondering why she hadn't blown a hole in him.

Cliff let a minute go by, then, satisfied that the pecking order was reestablished to his liking, that all was right with the world again, he put his finger under her chin and raised her head. "Okay, I'm gonna let you off easy, sweetie pie. You clean up this here mess, and you make me a nice breakfast. You got about half an hour."

He turned to leave, then came back, took the shotgun, and left.

She heard his footsteps going up the stairs, then a few minutes later, heard the shower running.

She found some aspirin in the cupboard and took two with a full glass of water, then washed her face and hands in the kitchen sink, then went down into the basement.

In his den, she stared at the rifles and shotguns, all unlocked now. She stood there a full minute, then turned away and went into the workshop. She found a push broom and shovel and went back up to the kitchen.

Annie made coffee, heated the frying pan, added bacon, swept up the plaster and put it out into the trash can, then washed the kitchen counter and floor.

Cliff came down, dressed in a clean uniform, and she noticed that he entered the kitchen carefully, his gun belt and holster slung over his shoulder and his hand casually on the pistol grip. He sat at the table, his gun belt looped over the chair instead of on the wall peg.

Before he could react, she grabbed the gun belt and put it on the peg. She said, "No guns at my table."

The moment was not lost on Cliff Baxter, and, after an initial look of panic, he forced a stupid grin.

Annie poured him juice and coffee, then fried his eggs with potatoes and bacon, and put the toast in. She served him his breakfast, and he said, "Sit down."

She sat across from him.

He smiled as he ate and said, "Lose your appetite?"

"I ate."

He spoke as he chewed. "I'm gonna leave the guns and the ammo and everything down there. More coffee."

She stood and poured him more coffee.

He continued, "Because I don't think you got it in you to kill me."

"If I did, I could buy a gun anywhere."

"Yeah, true. But you can keep buyin' guns and stealin' guns and borrowin' guns, and it don't matter. I'm not afraid of you, darlin'."

She knew he was trying to reclaim his manhood after the pants wetting. She let him do what he had to do so he'd just get out of the house.

He continued, "I went for my gun, didn't I? I didn't have a chance in hell, but I went for it."

"Yes." True, she thought, he was more stupid than she'd imagined. An intelligent man knew he had at least a fifty-fifty chance of talking his wife out of shooting him, and less than a million-to-one chance of drawing against a pointed and cocked shotgun. But Cliff Baxter was short on brains and long on ego. One day, she hoped, that would get him killed.

He said, "You're wonderin' if I'd of killed you."

"I don't really care."

"What do you mean, you don't care? Of course you care. You got kids. You got family." He smiled. "You got me." He patted her hand across the table. "Hey, I knew you wasn't gonna kill me. You know why? 'Cause you love me."

Annie took a breath and fought down a scream.

He tapped his fork on her nose, and continued, "You see, you're still jealous. Now, that means you still love me. Right?"

Annie was emotionally drained, exhausted, and her shoulder throbbed. She had nothing left in her except the presence of mind to say what he wanted to hear. She said, "Yes."

He smiled. "But you hate me, too. Now, I'm gonna tell you something—there's a thin line between love and hate."

She nodded, as though this were some new revelation to her. Cliff was always mouthing idiotic clichés and aphorisms, as if he'd just made them up, and it never occurred to him that these were not original insights into the human mind.

"Remember that next time you're pissed off at me."

She smiled, and he realized he'd used a bad choice of words. She said, "I'm going to the cleaners this morning. Do you have anything to go?"

He leaned toward her and said, "You watch yourself."

"Yes, sir."

"And cut the sir shit."

"Sorry."

He mopped up his yolks with his toast and said, "You call old Willie to fix up the ceiling."

"Yes."

He sat back and looked at her. "You know, I break my ass to give you things most people in this town ain't got. Now, what do you want me to do? Retire, hang around the house, pinch pennies, and help you with the chores all day?"

"No."

"I'm bustin' my hump, doin' a job for this town, and you think I'm out there floggin' my johnson all over the county."

She nodded in the appropriate places during the familiar lecture, and shook her head when it was called for.

Cliff stood, strapped on his pistol belt, and came around the table. He hugged her around the shoulders, and she winced in pain. He kissed her on the head and said, "We're gonna forget this. You tidy up a little more here and call Willie. I'll be home about six. I feel like steak tonight. Check the beer in the fridge. Feed the dogs." He added, "Wash my uniform."

He went to the back door, and, on his way out, said, "And don't you ever call me at work again unless somebody's dyin'." He left.

Annie stared across the kitchen at nothing in particular. Maybe, she thought, if she had let him get his gun out of his holster, she would have blown his head off. But maybe not, and maybe he would have shot her, which was okay, too. Maybe they'd hang him.

The only thing she knew for certain was that Cliff forgot nothing and forgave nothing. She'd literally scared the pee out of him, and there'd be hell to pay. Not that she'd notice much difference.

She stood and was surprised to find her legs were weak and there was a queasy feeling in her stomach. She went to the sink and opened the window. The sun was coming up, and a few storm clouds sailed away toward the east. Birds sang in the yard, and the hungry dogs were trying to get her attention with short, polite barks.

Life, she thought, could be lovely. No, she said to herself, life *was* lovely. Life was beautiful. Cliff Baxter couldn't make the sun stop rising or the birds stop singing, and he did not, could not, control her mind or her spirit. She hated him for dragging her down to his level, for making her contemplate murder or suicide.

She thought again of Keith Landry. In her mind, Cliff Baxter was always the black knight, and Keith Landry was the white knight. This image worked as long as Keith was a disembodied ideal. Her worst nightmare would be to discover that Keith Landry in person was not the Keith Landry she'd created out of short and infrequent letters and long-ago memories.

The returned letter, as well as the dream about Cliff, had been the catalyst for what just happened, she realized. She'd snapped. But now she felt better, and she promised herself that if Keith was alive, she'd find the means and the courage to see him, to speak to him, to see how much of him was her fantasy and how much of him was real.

CHAPTER FIVE

The drone of some sort of machinery began to register in Keith Landry's mind, and he opened his eyes. A breeze billowed the white lace curtains, and sunlight seeped into the gray dawn.

He could smell the rain-washed soil, the country air, a field of alfalfa somewhere. He lay awhile, his eyes darting around the room, his mind focusing. He'd had this recurring dream of waking up in his old room so often that actually waking up in his old room was eerie.

He sat up, stretched, and yawned. "Day four, life two, morning. Roll 'em." He jumped out of bed and made his way toward the bathroom down the hall.

Showered and dressed in khaki slacks and T-shirt, he examined the contents of the refrigerator. Whole milk, white bread, butter, bacon, and eggs. He hadn't eaten any of those things in years, but said, "Why not?" He made himself a big, artery-clogging breakfast. It tasted terrific. It tasted like home.

He walked out the back door and stood in the gravel drive. The air was cool and damp, and a ground mist lay over the fields. He walked around the farmyard.

The barn was in bad repair, he saw, and, as he explored what had once been a substantial farm, he noticed the debris of a past way of life: a rusted ax buried in a chopping block, the collapsed corncrib, the tilting silo, the ruined springhouse and chicken coop, the broken fences of the paddock and pigpen, the equipment shed filled with old hand tools—these all remained, unrecycled, uncollected, unwanted, contributing to the rural blight.

The kitchen garden and grape arbor, he noticed, were overgrown with vines and weeds, and he saw now that the house itself needed painting.

The nostalgia he'd been experiencing on the way here was at odds with the reality before him. The family farms of his boyhood were not so picturesque now, and the families who once worked them were, he knew from past visits, becoming fewer.

The young people went to the cities to find work, as his brother and sister had done, and the older people increasingly went south to escape the harsh winters, as his parents had done. Much of the surrounding land had been sold or contracted to big agribusinesses, and the remaining family holdings were as hard-pressed today as they had been when he was growing up. The difference now was not in the economics; it was in the will of the farmer to hang in there despite the bad odds. On the ride here, he'd thought about trying to farm, but now that he was here, he had second thoughts.

He found himself in the front of the farmhouse, and he focused on the front porch, remembering summer nights, rocking chairs and porch swings, lemonade, radios, family, and friends. He had a sudden urge to call his parents and his brother and sister and tell them he was home and suggest a reunion on the farm. But he thought he ought to wait until he got himself mentally settled, until he understood his mood and his motivations more clearly.

Keith got into his car and drove out onto the dusty farm road.

The four hundred acres of the Landry farm had been contracted out to the Muller family down the road, and his parents received a check every spring. Most of the Landry acres were in corn, according to his father, but the Muller family had put a hundred acres into soybean production to supply a nearby processing plant built by a Japanese company. The plant employed a good number of people, Keith knew, and bought a lot of soybeans. Nevertheless, xenophobia ran high and hot in Spencer County, and Keith was certain that the Japanese were as unwelcome as the Mexican migrants who showed up every summer. It was odd, Keith thought, perhaps portentous, that this rural county, deep in the heartland, had been discovered by Japanese, Mexicans, and more recently by people from India and Pakistan, many of whom were physicians at the county hospital.

The locals weren't happy about any of this, but the locals had no one to blame but themselves, Keith thought. The county's population was falling, the best and the brightest left, and many of the kids he'd seen on his visits, the ones who had stayed, looked aimless and unmotivated, unwilling to do farm work and unfit to do skilled labor.

Keith drove through the countryside. The roads were good but not great, and nearly all of them were laid out in a perfect grid from north to south, east to west, with few natural terrain features to inhibit the early surveyors, and, from the air, the northwestern counties looked like a sheet of graph paper, with the muddy Maumee River a wavy line of brownish ink meandering from the southwest into the big blue splotch of Lake Erie.

Keith drove until noon, crisscrossing the county, noting some abandoned farmhouses where people he once knew had lived, rusted railroad tracks, a few diminished villages, a defunct farm equipment dealership, boarded-up rural schools and grange houses, and the sense of emptiness.

There were a number of historical markers on the sides of the roads, and Keith recalled that Spencer County had been the site of some battles during the French and Indian Wars before the American Revolution, before his ancestors had arrived, and he had always marveled at the thought of a handful of Englishmen and Frenchmen navigating through the dark, primeval forests and swamps, surrounded by Indians, trying to kill one another so far from home. Surely, he'd thought as a schoolboy, those wars were the height of idiocy, but he hadn't been to Vietnam yet.

The territory became British, the Revolution had barely touched the inhabitants, and the growing population had incorporated as Spencer County in 1838. The Mexican War of 1846 had taken a fair number of militiamen, most of whom died of disease in Mexico, and the Civil War had nearly decimated the population of young men. The county recovered, grew and prospered, and reached its zenith around World War I. But after that war and the next world war, with their aftermaths of rapid change, a decay and decline had set in, imperceptible when he was young, but now obvious to him. He wondered again if he intended to live here, or had he come back only to finish up some old business?

At a crossroads outside the town, he pulled into a self-service gas station. It was a discount place with a brand of fuel he didn't recognize, and attached to it was a convenience store, an interesting marketing concept, he thought: high-priced, brand-name junk food, and cheap off-brand gasoline of suspicious quality. He figured the Saab, like himself, should get used to a different diet, so he got out and pumped.

The attendant, a man about ten years younger than Keith, ambled over.

The man eyed the car awhile as Keith pumped, then walked around the Saab and peered inside. He asked Keith, "What's this thing?"

"A car."

The attendant laughed and slapped his thigh. "Hell. I know that. What *kinda* car?"

"A Saab 900. Swedish."

"Say what?"

"Made in Sweden."

"No kiddin'?"

Keith replaced the gas cap and stuck the nozzle back in the pump.

The attendant read the license plate. "District of Columbia—The Nation's Capital. That where you from?"

"Yup."

"You a G-man? Tax collector? We just shot the last tax guy." He laughed.

Keith smiled. "Just a private citizen."

"Yeah? Passin' through?"

"Might stay awhile." He handed the man a twenty.

The attendant took his time making change and asked, "Stayin' where?"

"I've got family here."

"You from around here?"

"Long time ago. Landry."

"Oh, hell, yeah. Which one are you?"

"Keith Landry. My folks are George and Alma. Had the farm down by Overton."

"Sure. They retired now, right?"

"Florida."

The man stuck out his hand. "Bob Arles. My folks owned the old Texaco station in town."

"Right. Still twenty-two cents a gallon?"

Bob Arles laughed. "No, they's closed up now. No stations left in town. Property taxes too high, rents too high, big oil companies got you by the short hairs. I spot-buy from anybody who got to dump it cheap."

"What did I buy today?"

"Oh, you got lucky. About half Mobil in there, some Shell, a little Texaco."

"No corn squeezin's?"

Arles laughed again. "Little of that, too. Hey, it's a livin'."

"You sell beer?"

"Sure do."

Arles followed Keith into the convenience store and introduced him to a stern-looking woman behind the counter. "This here's my wife, Mary. This is Keith Landry, folks used to farm down by Overton."

The woman nodded.

Keith went to the refrigerator case and saw two imported beers, Heineken and Corona, but not wanting to seem like a total alien to Mr. Arles, he chose a six-pack of Coors and a six-pack of Rolling Rock, both in cans. He paid Mary for the beer as Bob Arles made small talk, then Arles followed him out.

Arles asked, "You lookin' for work?"

"Maybe."

"Real tight here. You still got the farm?"

"Yes, but the land's contracted."

"Good. Take the money and run. Farmin's the kind of job you got to save up for."

"That bad?"

"What do you got? Four hundred acres? That's breakeven. The guys with four thousand acres, mixed crops, and livestock is doin' okay. Seen one guy drivin' a Lincoln. He's tight with the Japs and the grain dealers in Maumee. Where you stayin'?"

"The farmhouse."

"Yeah? The missus from around here?"

Keith replied, "I'm here alone."

Arles, realizing his friendly chatter was on the verge of being nosy, said, "Well, I wish you luck."

"Thanks." Keith threw the beer in the passenger seat and got into the car.

Arles said, "Hey, welcome home."

"Thanks." Keith pulled back onto the two-lane road. He could see the south end of Spencerville, a row of warehouses and light industry where the old Wabash and Erie tracks came through, bordered by cornfields; the place where town utilities and taxes ended and rural life began.

Keith circled the town, not wanting to go into it yet, though he didn't know why. Maybe it was the idea of cruising up Main Street in the weird car, and maybe seeing people he knew and them seeing him, and he wasn't prepared for that.

He headed out toward St. James Church.

As he drove, Keith sort of blocked out the mobile homes, the aluminum sheds, and the abandoned vehicles. The countryside was still spectacular, with broad vistas of crops and fallow fields that ran to the horizons where ancient tree lines still divided the old surveys. Creeks and streams, sparkling clean, meandered among weeping willows and coursed beneath small trestle bridges.

The land had once lain beneath a prehistoric sea that had receded, and when Keith's ancestors arrived, most of what became northwestern Ohio had been swamp and forest. In a relatively short period of time, working with only hand tools and oxen, the swamp had been drained, the trees felled, houses built, the land contoured for farming, then planted with grains and vegetables. The results had been spectacular: An incredible bounty had sprung from the earth as if the soil had been waiting for ten million years to sprout rye and barley, wheat and oats, carrots and cabbages, and nearly anything that the first pioneers stuck in the ground.

After the Civil War, whatever money was to be made in farming was made in wheat, then came corn, easier, heartier, and now Keith saw more and more soy, the miracle bean, protein-rich for an exploding world population.

Spencer County, like it or not, was connected to the world now, and its future was in the balance. Keith could see two pictures in his mind: one, a rebirth of rural life brought about by city and suburban people looking for a safer and gentler existence; the other picture was of a county that was little more than a mega-plantation, owned and operated by absentee investors for the purpose of planting the money crop of the moment. Keith could see fields and farms where trees and hedgerows had been pulled up to make room for the gargantuan harvesters. As he reflected on all this, it struck him that perhaps the whole nation was out of balance, that if you got on the wrong train, none of the stops down the line could be the one you wanted.

Keith pulled onto the gravel shoulder of the road and got out.

The cemetery lay on a hill of about an acre, shaded

by old elms and surrounded by fields of corn. About fifty yards away sat St. James, the white clapboard church that he'd attended as a boy, and to the right of the church sat the small parsonage where Pastor and Mrs. Wilkes had lived, or perhaps still lived.

Keith went into the cemetery and walked among the short tombstones, many of them worn away by weather and covered with lichen.

He found his maternal and paternal grandparents, and their parents, and their sons and daughters, and so on, buried in an interesting chronological order that you had to know about, the oldest graves on the highest part of the rise, then the next oldest graves descending in concentric circles until you reached the edges of the cornfield; the oldest Landry grave went back to 1849, and the oldest Hoffmann grave, his German ancestors, went back to 1841. There were no large groupings of dates as a result of any of the earlier wars, because the bodies weren't shipped home in those days. But Korea and Vietnam were well represented, and Keith found his uncle's grave and stood beside it a moment, then moved on to the graves of the men killed in Vietnam. There were ten of them, a large number for a single small cemetery in a small county. Keith knew all of them, some casually, some well, and he could picture a face with each name. He thought he might experience some sort of survivor's guilt, standing here among his old classmates, but he hadn't experienced that at the Wall in Washington, and he didn't experience it now. What he felt, he supposed, was an unresolved anger at the waste. On a personal level, he had this thought, which had recurred with more frequency in the last few weeks: that despite all his success and accomplishments, his life would have been better if the war hadn't happened.

He sat beneath a willow tree, among the graves between the base of the hill and the cornfield, and chewed on a piece of grass. The sun was high overhead, the ground was still damp and cool from the storm. Chicken hawks circled close by, and barn swallows flew in and out of the church steeple. A feeling of peace came over him such as he hadn't known in many years; the quiet and solitude of home had already worked its way into his bones. He lay back and stared at the pale sky through the willow leaves. "Right. If I hadn't gone to war, Annie and I would have gotten married...who knows?" This cemetery, he thought, was as good a place as any to begin the journey back.

He drove to the north side of town and found where Williams Street began off the county road. He pulled over, hesitated, then turned onto the suburban street.

Some of the stately old Victorians looked restored, some were run-down. As a child, he'd always marveled at this section of town, the big houses on small plots that he now realized were not small at all, the huge trees that formed a dark green tunnel in the summer, the fact that people could live so close together and see into one another's homes, and the luxury of two cars in every driveway. What had impressed, amused, and mystified him then was no longer impressive, amusing, or mystifying, of course. Childhood wonder and innocence were almost embarrassing in retrospect; but what kind of adult would you be without once having seen things through wide eyes?

The street was as quiet as he'd expected on a summer afternoon. A few kids rode by on bicycles, a woman pushed a baby carriage, a delivery van was stopped up the road and the driver was chatting with a woman at her door. It was a street of big front porches, a uniquely

American phenomenon, as he'd discovered in his travels, though houses in America were not built that way any longer. Small children played on some of the porches, old people rocked. He was glad Annie lived on this street.

As he approached her house, something odd happened: His heart began thumping and his mouth went dry. The house was to his right, and before he realized it, he was passing it, and he pulled over. He noticed a beat-up station wagon parked in the driveway, and an older man was carrying a stepladder to the rear of the house. And there she was, just a glimpse of her as she turned away and disappeared around the back of the house with the old man. It was only a second or two, from fifty yards away, but he had no doubt it was her, and this instant recognition of her features, her stride, her bearing, astonished him.

He backed up and opened the car door, then stopped. How could he just show up at her door? But why not? What was wrong with the direct approach? Phoning her or dropping her a note was not what he'd pictured in his mind. He thought it was important that he should just ring her doorbell and say, "Hello, Annie," and let whatever happened happen, spontaneously and without rehearsal.

But what if she had company? What if her kids were home, or her husband? Why hadn't he thought of that likely possibility even once when he replayed this scene over and over again through the years? Obviously, the imagined moment had become so real that he'd excluded anything that would have ruined it.

He closed the door and drove off. He headed toward the farm, his mind racing faster than the car. *What is wrong with you, Landry? Get a grip, pal.*

He took a deep breath and slowed down to the

speed limit. No use getting off on the wrong foot with the local gendarmes. Which reminded him of Annie's husband. Surely, he thought, if she weren't married he'd have had the nerve to stop and say hello. But you couldn't compromise a married woman that way. Not around here. And in Spencerville you didn't do lunch or have drinks after work.

So maybe he should drop a note to her sister. Maybe he'd phone her. Maybe a guy who'd handled combat and a shoot-out in East Berlin could handle a phone call to a woman he once loved. "Sure." *In a few weeks, when I'm settled in. Make a note of that.*

He went back to the farmhouse and spent the afternoon on the front porch with his two six-packs, watching each car that passed by.

Bob Arles filled the chief's car. Self-service didn't mean Cliff Baxter had to pump his own gas. They chatted. Arles said, "Hey, Chief, had an interesting guy in here this morning."

"You got any of them beef jerkies?"

"Sure do. Help yourself."

Cliff Baxter went into the convenience store and touched his hat to Mrs. Arles behind the counter. She watched him as he gathered up beef jerky, peanut butter crackers, salted nuts, and a few Hershey bars. About twelve dollars' worth all together, she figured.

He took an Orange Crush out of the refrigerator case, sauntered over to the register, and dumped it all on the counter. "What we got here, Mary?"

"I guess about two dollars should cover it," which was what she said every time.

He flipped a few singles on the counter as she bagged his items.

Bob Arles came in with a municipal charge form,

and Cliff scribbled his name without looking at the gas total.

Arles said, "Appreciate the patronage, Chief."

Mary wasn't so sure of that. Men, she thought, had to make every business transaction into something like a bonding experience, with a little scamming thrown in. Bob overcharged the town for the gas, and Cliff Baxter fed his fat face for nearly free.

Cliff took his bag, and Bob Arles walked out with him. "Like I was saying, this guy comes in with his foreign car, Washington plates and all, and—"

"Look suspicious?"

"No, I'm sayin' he was from around here. Used to live here, now he's back looking for work, livin' out on his folks' farm. Don't get many who come back."

"Sure don't. Good riddance to 'em." Cliff got into his cruiser.

"Drivin' a Saab. What do they go for?"

"Well...let's see...maybe twenty, thirty, new."

"The guy did okay for himself."

"Nothin' okay about foreign cars, Bob." Cliff started to roll the window up, then stopped and asked, "You get his name?"

"Landry. Keith Landry."

Cliff Baxter looked at Arles. "What?"

Arles continued, "Folks had a farm down by Overton. You know them?"

Cliff sat silent a moment, then said, "Yeah... *Keith* Landry?"

"Yup."

"Moved back?"

"He said."

"Family?"

"Nope."

"What'd he look like?"

Bob shrugged. "I don't know. Regular guy."

"You'd make a hell of a cop. Fat? Thin? Bald? Dick growin' out of his head?"

"Thin. Tall guy, all his hair. Not bad-lookin', I guess. Why?"

"Oh, I thought maybe I'd keep an eye out for him. Welcome him home."

"Can't miss that car. He's out at his folks' place. Check him out if you want."

"I might do just that." Cliff pulled away and headed south toward Overton.

CHAPTER SIX

Cliff Baxter brooded over the events of that morning. "Don't know what got into her." Of course he knew exactly what had gotten into her. She hated him. He sort of accepted that, but he was still convinced that she also loved him. He loved her, so she had to love him. What really bothered him was that she'd gotten feisty, went and actually took one of his guns. She'd always had a smart mouth, but she'd never so much as thrown a dish at him. Now she was pumping buckshot over his head. "Got to be that time of the month. That's it. PMS. Pigheaded Monthly Shit."

He was sure he'd gotten the better of the argument, but that was true only if he discounted his bladder letting loose. He hadn't really evened the score on that one, so he tried to forget it happened. But he couldn't forget it. "That bitch."

He would have dwelled on this more, but he had a whole new problem to think about—Mr. Keith Landry, ex-boyfriend of Miss Annie Oakley.

He drove past the Landry farm and noted the black Saab in the gravel driveway. He noted, too, that there was a man on the porch, and he was certain that the man noticed the police car driving by.

Cliff used his mobile phone and called his desk sergeant. "Blake, it's me. Call Washington, D.C., Motor Vehicles, and get me whatever you can on a Keith Landry." He spelled it out and added, "Drives a black Saab 900. Can't tell the year and can't see the plate number. Get back to me ASAP." Cliff then dialed information. "Yeah, need a number for Landry, Keith Landry, County Road 28, new listing."

The information operator replied, "No listing for that name, sir."

Cliff hung up and called the post office. "This is Chief Baxter, put me through to the postmaster." A few seconds later, the postmaster, Tim Hodge, came on the line and said, "Help you, Chief?"

"Yeah, Tim. Check and see if you got a new customer, name of Landry, RFD, from Washington. Yeah, D.C."

"Sure, hold on." A few minutes later, Hodge came back and said, "Yeah, one of the sorters saw a couple of bills or something with a forwarding sticker from D.C. Keith Landry."

"How about a missus on that sticker?"

"No, just him."

"This a temporary?"

"Looks like a permanent address change. Problem?"

"Nope. Used to be a vacant farmhouse, and somebody noticed activity there."

"Yeah, I remember the old folks, George and Alma. Moved to Florida. Who's this guy?"

"Son, I guess." Cliff thought a moment, then asked, "Did he take a P.O. box?"

"No, I'd have seen the money if he did."

"Yeah. Okay...hey, I'd like to take a look at what comes in for him."

There was a long pause, during which the

postmaster figured out this wasn't a routine inquiry. Tim Hodge said, "Sorry, Chief. We been through this before. I need to see some kind of court order."

"Hell, Tim, I'm just talkin' about lookin' at envelopes, not openin' mail."

"Yeah...but...hey, if this is a bad guy, go to court—"

"I'm just askin' for a small favor, Tim, and when you need a favor, you know where to come. Fact is, you owe me one for your son-in-law's drivin' while totally fucked-up."

"Yeah...okay...you just want to see the envelopes when they're sortin'—?"

"Can't always do that. You make photocopies of his stuff, front and back, and I'll stop in now and then."

"Well..."

"And you keep this to yourself, and I'll do the same. And you give my regards to your daughter and her husband." Cliff hung up and continued to drive down the straight county road, oblivious to his surroundings, contemplating this turn of events. "Guy comes back, no phone yet, but wants his mail delivered. Why's he back?"

He put the cruiser on speed control and chewed on a beef jerky. Cliff Baxter remembered Keith Landry from high school, and what he remembered, he didn't like. He didn't know Landry well, at least not personally, but everyone knew Keith Landry. He was one of those most-likely-to-succeed guys, hotshot athlete, a bookworm, and popular enough so that guys like Cliff Baxter hated his guts.

Cliff remembered with some satisfaction that he'd jostled Landry in the halls a few times, and Landry never did a thing, except to say, "Excuse me," like it was his fault. Cliff thought Landry was a pussy, but a few of Cliff's friends had advised him to be careful with Landry. Without admitting it, Cliff knew they were right.

Cliff had been a year behind Landry in school, and he would have ignored the guy completely, except that Keith Landry was going out with Annie Prentis.

Cliff thought about this, about people like Landry in general who seemed to have all the right moves, who went out with the right girls, who made things look easy. And what was worse, Cliff thought, was that Landry was just a farmer's son, a guy who shoveled barnyard shit on weekends, a guy whose folks would come to Baxter Motors and trade in one shit car for a newer piece of shit and finance the difference. This was a guy who didn't have a pot to piss in, or a window to throw it out of, and who was supposed to shovel shit and bust sod all his life, but who went on to college on a bunch of scholarships from the church, the Rotary, the VFW, and some state money that the taxpayers, like the Baxters, got hit for. And then the son-of-a-bitch turned his nose up at the people he left behind. "Fuckhead."

Cliff would have been glad to see the bastard leave, except that he left for college with Annie Prentis, and from what Cliff heard, they fucked up a storm at Bowling Green for four years before she dumped him.

Cliff suddenly slapped the dashboard hard. "Asshole!"

The thought of this prick who'd once fucked his wife being back in town was more than he could handle. "Cocksucker!"

Cliff drove aimlessly for a while, trying to figure out his next move. For sure, he thought, this guy had to go—one way or the other. This was Cliff Baxter's town, and nobody, but nobody, in it gave him any shit—especially a guy who fucked his wife. "You're history, mister."

Even if Landry kept to himself, Cliff was enraged

at the mere thought of him being so close to his wife, close enough so that they could run into each other in town or at some social thing. "How about *that*? How about being at some wedding or something, and in walks this asshole who fucked my wife, and he comes over to say hello to her with a smile on his fucking face?" Cliff shook his head as if to get the image out of his mind. "No way. No fucking way."

He took a deep breath. "Goddamnit, he fucked my wife for four years, maybe five or six years, and the son-of-a-bitch shows up just like that, without a goddamn wife, sittin' on his fuckin' porch, not doin' shit—" He slammed the dashboard again. "Damn it!"

Cliff felt his heart beating rapidly, and his mouth was sticky. He took a deep breath and opened the Orange Crush, took a swig, and felt the acid rise in his stomach. He flung the can out the window. "Goddamnit! God damned—"

The radio crackled, and Sergeant Blake came over the speaker. "Chief, about that license plate info—"

"You want the whole fuckin' county to hear? Call on the damned phone."

"Yes, sir."

The phone rang, and Cliff said, "Shoot."

Sergeant Blake reported, "I faxed the Bureau of Motor Vehicles with the name Keith Landry, car make and model, and they got back to us with a negative."

"What the hell do you mean?"

"Well, they said no such person."

"Damn it, Blake, get the license plate number off the fuckin' car and get back to them with that."

"Where's the car?"

"Old Landry farm, County Road 28. I want all the shit on his driver's license, too, then I want you to call the local banks and see if he's opened an account, and get his Social Security number and credit crap, then go from there—Army records, arrest records, the whole fuckin' nine yards."

"Yes, sir."

Cliff hung up. After nearly thirty years of police work, he'd learned how to build a file from the ground up. The two detectives on his force kept the criminal files, which did not interest Cliff much. Cliff had his own files on nearly everyone in Spencer County who was important, or who interested him in some way.

Cliff was vaguely aware that keeping secret files on private citizens was somehow illegal, but he was from the old school, and what he learned in that school was that promotions and job security were best accomplished through intimidation and blackmail.

Actually, he'd learned that long before he joined the force; his father and his father's family were all successful bullies. And, to be truthful, the system hadn't corrupted him; he had almost single-handedly corrupted the system. But he couldn't have done it without the help of men who conveniently screwed up their personal and business lives—married men who had affairs, fathers whose sons got into trouble with the law, businessmen who needed a zoning variance or a tax abatement, politicians who needed to know something about their opponents, and so on. Cliff was always right there, sensing the signs of moral weakness, the little character flaws, the signals of financial and legal distress. Cliff was always there to help.

What the system lacked when he entered it was a broker, a central clearinghouse where a citizen could come to offer a favor for a favor, where a man could come to sell his soul.

From these humble beginnings, Cliff Baxter started keeping notes, which became files, which became gold.

Lately, however, a lot of people he didn't like were getting too involved in the system. Schoolteachers, preachers, housewives, even farmers. Already there was one woman on the city council, Gail Porter, a retired college professor, a nosy bitch, and an ex-commie. She got elected by a fluke, the guy running against her, Bobby Cole, getting himself caught in the men's room of the Toledo bus station. Cliff hadn't paid any attention to her until it was too late, but now he had a file on her thick as a lamb chop, and she'd be out on her ass in November. Women like that didn't appreciate the system, and Cliff knew if she stayed, there'd be more like her to follow.

The mayor was his cousin, the city council and county commissioners were men he knew, and every one of them had to run for election. But Cliff Baxter was appointed, and as far as he was concerned, he'd been appointed for life. The fact was, if he ever lost his job, he could think of about a hundred men and some women who'd go for his throat, so he had to hold on tight.

Cliff Baxter was not unaware that the world had changed and that the changes were coming across the borders of Spencer County and that they were dangerous to him. But he was pretty sure he could keep it all under control, especially since the county sheriff, Don Finney, was his mother's cousin. Don had only two deputies to patrol the whole county, so he and Cliff had an understanding that the Spencerville police could leave the city limits whenever they wanted, just as Cliff was doing now. It gave Cliff a lot more latitude in dealing with people who lived outside of town, like the Porter woman and her husband, and like Mr. Keith Landry.

So he'd keep a lid on things for a few more years, then, with thirty years in and his kids out of college, he could skip across the border into Michigan, where he had a hunting lodge. Meantime, he had to eat his enemies even when he wasn't hungry.

The part of him that was shark could smell blood in the water a mile away, but he smelled no blood on any of these new people, including Gail Porter. He'd shown her his file on her once, thinking he could get her in line, showed her all he knew about her left-wing activities at Antioch College, and some stuff about boyfriends that her husband wouldn't appreciate. But she told him to roll up the file, put a coat of grease on it, and shove it up his ass. Cliff had been more than pissed off, he'd been almost homicidal. If people weren't afraid, how was he going to keep them in line? This was a little scary.

The part of him that was wolf sensed danger before any other animal in his woods had an inkling of it. In the last few years, he'd noticed these new people sort of circling around, sizing him up like he was fair game instead of the other way around.

Then there was Annie. Little lady perfect who usually wouldn't say shit if she had a mouth full of it. Then all of a sudden, she gets the idea of checking up on him, then comes that close to blowing his head off. "What the hell's goin' on around here?"

He'd been working on these problems when this new thing came along. "Goddamnit! People after my ass, people after my job, and now my own wife tries to kill me, and some guy who used to fuck her shows up. Hey, God, what'd I do to deserve this shit?"

He wondered if Annie knew yet that her old boyfriend was back in town. Maybe that's why she tried to kill him. But that didn't make sense. She'd go to jail before she could fuck him. No, she didn't know yet, but she would, and he'd watch for it. It did occur to him that maybe she had no interest in Keith Landry, and he had no interest in her. Still, he didn't want this stiff cock around town.

He realized he couldn't watch both of them forever, but he'd watch for a while, and maybe catch them. If not, Landry was still going to get fucked, but not by Mrs. Baxter.

Cliff was a pro at lovers' lane busts, and in the old days, before kids started screwing in the houses of working parents or in motels out of the county, he'd grabbed a few every weekend in cars or abandoned barns. He had a sixth sense for knowing where they were and catching them naked or at least half-naked. This was the part of his tough job that he enjoyed, and if he thought about it, a night like that always ended with him going to one of his ladies' houses with big Johnson trying to bust out of his zipper. Sometimes he took Johnson home, and a couple of times Annie would comment that he must have been cruising lovers' lane. "Yeah, she's got a smart mouth." Too damned smart for her own good.

All this thinking about sex was getting him cranked up.

Cliff Baxter turned back toward town and drove into the south end, the part of town that was literally on the wrong side of the tracks. He called headquarters and said to Blake, "Takin' an hour. Beep if you need me. In fact, beep in an hour so I can get onta where I'm gonna be."

"Right, Chief."

Baxter pulled into the cracked concrete driveway of a wooden bungalow and used an electronic opener to raise the garage door. He parked the police cruiser inside the garage, got out, and hit the button to close the door.

He went to the back door and opened it with a key.

The kitchen was small, dirty, and always smelled like bad plumbing. Annie, at least, for all her other faults, knew how to keep a house.

He took a look into the untidy living room, then walked into the first of two bedrooms. A woman in her mid-thirties lay sleeping on her side on top of the bed sheets, wearing only a T-shirt. The room was warm, and a window fan stirred the hot air. Her white waitress uniform and underwear were thrown on the floor.

Baxter walked up to the bed. The T-shirt had ridden up to her hips, and Cliff stared at her pubic hair, then regarded her big breasts and the nipples pointing through the pink T-shirt. The shirt said, "Park 'n' Eat—Softball Team."

She had a good body, good muscle tone, and good skin if you overlooked a few zits and mosquito bites. The short hair falling over her face was blond, but the hair on her crotch was black.

The woman stirred and turned on her stomach. Cliff looked at her rounded rump and felt himself getting hard. He reached out and squeezed a handful of cheek. She mumbled something, then rolled over and opened her eyes.

Cliff Baxter smiled. "Hey, good-lookin'."

"Oh..." She cleared her throat and forced a smile. "It's you."

"Who'd you think it was?"

"Nobody..." She sat up, trying to clear her head, then pulled the T-shirt down to cover herself. "Didn't know you were coming."

"I ain't come yet, sweetheart. That's why I'm here." She forced a smile.

He sat on the bed beside her and put his hand between her legs, his fingers entering her. "You havin' a wet dream?"

"Yeah . . . about you."

"Better be." He found her clitoris and massaged it.

She squirmed a little, clearly not enjoying going from a sound sleep to having a man's fingers in her within sixty seconds.

"What's the matter with you?"

"Nothing. Got to go to the bathroom." She slid off the opposite side of the bed and went out into the hallway.

Cliff wiped his fingers on the sheets, lay on the bed fully clothed, and waited. He heard the toilet flush, water running, gargling.

Sherry Kolarik was the latest in a long line of women that had begun before his marriage, continued during his courtship of Annie and through his engagement and all through his marriage. They never lasted too long, and he never had a real heartthrob, a girlfriend, or a full-fledged mistress—they were all just sport fucks of short duration. In fact, somewhere in the back of his mind, he knew he was incapable of any real relationship with a woman, and his ladies were simply targets of opportunity—the town sluts, women who ran afoul of the law, desperately lonely divorcees, and barmaids and waitresses who needed a little extra cash—the lower elements of small-town American society; they were all easy marks for Police Chief Baxter.

Now and then, he picked on a married woman with a no-account husband such as Janie Wilson, the wife of the station house janitor, or Beth Marlon, wife of the town drunk. Sometimes he got the wife of a man who needed a favor real bad, like a prisoner. He enjoyed these conquests more than the others because fucking a man's wife meant you were fucking the man, too.

He was careful not to try his act on wives who had husbands who could become a problem. He did ogle female attorneys, schoolteachers, doctors, and other professional women, married and unmarried, who turned him on; but he knew without admitting it to himself that he didn't have a chance with these women. He knew, too, or rather had a dim awareness, that even if he scored with one of them, they'd reject him after they got to know him better. His only major conquest on that level had been Annie Prentis. But at that time, Cliff Baxter was better-looking, a little more charming, and also gave it everything he had. And, in truth, there had been a war on then, and the pickings in Spencerville were slim, so that a draft-deferred cop looked good to a lot of young ladies. He knew all of this without actually acknowledging any of it to himself. Thus, Cliff Baxter's ego was intact, while his predatory senses were always alert, a lone wolf who knew what prey was weak and vulnerable and what was dangerous.

Still, he had rape fantasies about the snippy female attorney in the county prosecutor's office, about the two female doctors at the hospital, and the uppity bitch bank president, and college girls home on vacation, and so forth. He knew that to fuck one of these women would be to fuck the whole class of people who looked down on him. Someday, he thought, he'd go for it. He'd cut one of the snobby ladies loose from the herd and lay the wood to her and dare her to make anything of it. Maybe she'd enjoy it. But for now, he'd settle for Sherry Kolarik and women like her.

She came back into the bedroom, and Cliff looked at his watch. "Now, I ain't got much time."

"I wanted to clean up for you."

"You don't got to clean up for what you got to do." He hopped out of bed and walked to the living room and left through the front door. He rang the bell and she came to the door and opened it, wearing a robe now.

"You Miss Kolarik?"

"Yes."

"Chief Baxter. I'd like to speak to you." He backed her up and closed the door. "Miss, you got a hundred dollars in parking tickets downtown. I'm here to collect the money or take you in."

If Sherry Kolarik thought it was romantic of Chief Baxter to re-create how they'd met, she didn't say so, didn't laugh and put her arms around Cliff. Instead, she said, "I'm sorry, I don't have the money."

He replied, "Then I got to take you in. Get dressed."

"No, please, I have to go to work. I can pay you Friday when I get paid."

"You had three months to make good on these here tickets. So now you're under arrest. You come peacefully, or I cuff you and take you in just like you are."

In fact, she'd been wearing her waitress uniform when this scene took place a month before. But she'd felt just as helpless and exposed then as now. Only now she didn't owe the bastard a hundred dollars. But there was still the matter of her car that had to pass the state inspection, and Baxter Motors could overlook some defects. She said, "Look, I work at the Park 'n' Eat, you know, you've seen me in there, and if you come around Friday, about noon, we can go over to the bank with my check. Can't you wait?"

"No, ma'am. I dragged my butt over here, and I'm goin' back to the station with a hundred bucks or with you. Don't mess with me." He jiggled the handcuffs on his belt.

"I'm sorry...I don't have the money, and I can't miss a day of work...look, I've got about twenty dollars..."

Cliff shook his head.

"A postdated check—"

"Nope."

"I've got some jewelry, a watch—"

"I ain't a goddamn repo man. I'm a cop."

"I'm sorry. I don't know what to..."

He took the cuffs off his belt. They looked at each other a long time, and both of them remembered the moment when she'd figured it out. She asked, "Can you loan me the money?"

"What's in it for me?"

"Whatever you want."

"Had lunch."

"Look, all I've got is me. You want me?"

"You tryin' to bribe me with sex?"

She nodded.

"Well, let's see what you got for collateral before I decide. Take 'em off."

She unfastened her robe and let it fall, then pulled the T-shirt over her head and dropped it on an armchair. She stood in the middle of the living room, naked, while Chief Baxter circled around her. Out of the corner of her eye, she saw the bulge in his pants.

"Okay, Miss Kolarik, you got real good collateral for a loan. Kneel right there. Park 'n' Eat, sweetheart."

She knelt on the rug.

He unbuckled his gun belt and put it on the armchair, then undid his belt and zipper and lowered his pants and undershorts. "Go for it, darlin'."

She took a deep breath, closed her eyes, and with one finger lowered his erect penis to her lips.

When it was over, Cliff said, "Swallow it." He pulled up his clothes, buckled on his holster, and threw a twenty on the armchair. "I'll take care of the tickets, but you owe me four payments."

Sherry nodded and mumbled, "Thank you." He'd said that the first time, and, for the last ten times, it had always been four more.

Cliff, not particularly sensitive, nevertheless saw she was a little upset and patted her cheek. "Hey, I'll see you later for coffee. Got to go."

He left through the back door.

She stood, went into the kitchen, spit in the sink and washed out her mouth, then ran into the shower.

Cliff Baxter drove around Spencerville, feeling very good. He had, at the moment, two women, which was enough for one time: Sherry, mostly for oral sex, and a separated woman with kids, named Jackie, trying to live on what her husband sent her from Toledo. Jackie had a nice bedroom and a good bed, and she was a good lay. Cliff always brought groceries, compliments of the local supermarket. He had a third woman, he realized, his wife. He laughed. "You are all *man*, Cliff Baxter."

The mobile phone rang, and he picked it up. Sergeant Blake said, "Chief, I had Ward drive by Landry's place with binoculars, and he got the license number."

"Okay."

"So I called these clowns back in D.C., and I gave it to them."

"Good. What we got?"

"Well...they said this plate was some kind of special thing, and if we needed to know more, we got to fill out a form, tellin' why and what it's about—"

"What the hell are you talkin' about?"

"They faxed me this form—two pages."

"What kinda shit is that? You call those sons-of-bitches and tell them we need a make on this plate now. Tell 'em the guy was DUI or somethin', can't produce a registration or nothin'—"

"Chief, I'm tellin' ya, I tried everything. They're tellin' me it's somethin' to do with national security."

"National... *what*?"

"You know, like secret stuff."

Cliff Baxter drove in silence. One minute he's on top of the world, pipes cleaned, feeling good, and in charge. Now this guy Landry shows up from outside, from Washington, D.C., after how many years...? Twenty-five maybe, and Cliff doesn't know a thing about him, and just finds out he can't even get a make on his car registration or driver's license. "Who the fuck is this guy?"

"Chief?"

"Okay, I want this bastard watched. I want somebody to swing by his place a couple times a day, and I want to know every time he comes to town."

"Okay... what are we lookin' for? I mean, why—?"

"Just do what the hell I tell you."

"Yes, sir."

Cliff hung up. "The man fucked my wife, that's why." And people in town knew, or they'd remember, or they'd hear about it soon enough. "I can't have that. No, siree, I cannot have that."

Several plans of action began to form in his mind, and he remembered something old Judge Thornsby once said to him—"Sometimes a problem is an opportunity in disguise."

"That's it. This stupid bastard came right onto my turf. And what I couldn't do twenty-five years ago, I can do now. I'm gonna kill him...no, I'm gonna cut off his balls. That's it. Gonna cut off his balls and put 'em in a jar on the mantel, and Annie can dust it once a week." He laughed.

CHAPTER SEVEN

A hot, dry wind blew in from the southwest, originating within some ancient weather pattern that once swept prairie fires across the grassy plains and stampeded endless herds of buffalo, blind with panic, into the Great Black Swamp where their bones were still turned up by plows. But now the wind blew through a million rows of corn and a million acres of undulating wheat, through the small towns and lonely farmhouses, and across pastures and meadows where cattle grazed. It swept across Indiana and into Ohio, and over the Great Lakes, where it met the arctic mass moving south.

By mid-September, when the west winds died, Keith Landry recalled, you could sometimes catch a whiff of the north, the smell of pines and lake air, and the sky was filled with Canada geese. One September day, George Landry said to his wife, Alma, "It's time we got smart like the geese." And they left.

The history of most human migration, however, was more complex, Keith thought. Humans had adapted to every climate on earth, and in ancient times had populated the world by their wanderings. Unlike salmon, they didn't have to return to their birthplace to spawn, though Keith thought that wouldn't be a bad idea.

Keith was acclimating himself to the almost suffocating dryness, the fine dust, the constant desiccating wind, and, like most northern Ohioans, he was thinking about the winter long before it arrived. But acclimating to the weather was easy; acclimating to the social environment was going to be a little more difficult.

It had been a week since his return, and Keith decided it was time to go downtown. He drove in at midday and headed directly for Baxter Motors, a Ford dealership on the eastern end of Main Street. His family had done business there for years, and Keith vaguely recalled that his father did not really care for those people. But the old man was perverse and felt that he could strike a better bargain with people he disliked, and he got a thrill from it.

He was not unaware that Baxter Motors was owned by the family of Annie's husband, and perhaps that influenced his decision, too, though he couldn't get a handle on that reasoning.

He got out of the Saab and looked around. The dealership was strictly Ford, with no foreign car franchise attached, as was common back east.

A salesman beelined across the parking lot and inquired, "How're you today?"

"Very fine. Thank you for asking."

The salesman seemed momentarily confused, then stuck out his hand. "Phil Baxter."

"Keith Landry." He looked at Mr. Baxter, a baby-fat man in his early forties with more chins than a Chinese phone book. Phil Baxter seemed pleasant enough, but that came with the job. Keith asked, "This your place?"

Phil laughed. "Not yet. Waitin' for Pop to retire."

Keith tried to picture Annie married to one of these genetic fumbles, then decided he was being uncharitable and petty. He got to the point, perhaps too quickly for local tastes, and said, "I want to trade this customized Ford in for a new one."

Phil Baxter glanced at the Saab and laughed again. "That ain't no Ford, buddy." He got serious and said, "We try not to take foreign cars. I guess you know that."

"Why's that?"

"Hard to move 'em. Local folk drive American." He squinted at the license plate. "Where you from?"

"Washington."

"Passin' through, or what?"

"I'm from around here. Just moved back."

"Yeah, name sounds familiar. We done business before?"

"Sure have. You want to sell me a new car?"

"Sure do . . . but . . . I got to talk to the boss."

"Pop?"

"Yup. But he ain't here now. What kind of Ford you lookin' for, Keith?"

"Maybe a Mustang GT."

Phil's eyes widened. "Hey, good choice. We got two, a black and a red. But I can get you any color."

"Good. What's the book on mine? It's last year's, eight thousand miles."

"I'll check it out for you."

"Are you going to take the Saab?"

"I'll get back to you on that, Keith. Meantime, here's my card. Give a call when you're ready."

Keith smiled at the small-town, low-key approach to sales. In Washington, any car salesman could be an arms negotiator or Capitol Hill lobbyist. Here, nobody pushed. Keith said, "Thanks, Phil." He turned to leave, then the imp of the perverse turned him around and he said, "I remember a guy named Cliff Baxter."

"Yeah, my brother. He's police chief now."

"You don't say? He did okay for himself."

"Sure did. Fine wife, two great kids, one in college, one about to go."

"God bless him."

"Amen."

"See you later, Phil."

Keith pulled onto Main Street and stopped at a traffic light. "That was a stupid move, Landry."

He certainly didn't need to go to Baxter Motors; he knew they wouldn't want the Saab, he didn't even know if he wanted a Ford, and surely he didn't have to mention Cliff Baxter's name. For an ex-intelligence officer, he was acting pretty stupid—driving past her house, going to her father-in-law's place of business. What next? Pulling her pigtails? "Grow up, Landry."

The light changed and he drove west, up Main Street. The downtown area consisted of rows of dark brick buildings, three and four stories high, with retail space at ground level and mostly empty apartments above. Almost everything had been built between the end of the Civil War and the start of the Great Depression. The old brickwork and wooden ornamentation were interesting, but most of the ground-floor storefronts had been modernized in the 1950s and '60s and looked tacky.

Street and sidewalk traffic was light, he noticed, and half the stores were vacant. The ones that remained open were discount clothing places, church thrift shops, video arcades, and other low-end enterprises. He recalled that Annie, in a few of her letters, mentioned that she managed the County Hospital Thrift Store located downtown, but he didn't see the shop.

The three big buildings in town were also closed— the movie house, the old hotel, and Carter's, the local department store. Missing, also, were the two hardware stores, the half dozen or so grocery stores, and three sweetshops with soda fountains, and Bob's Sporting Goods, where Keith had spent half his time and most of his money.

A few of the old places remained—Grove's Pharmacy, Miller's Restaurant, and two taverns called John's Place and the historic Posthouse. The courthouse crowd no doubt kept these places afloat.

Downtown Spencerville was surely not as Keith remembered it as a boy. It had been the center of his world, and without romanticizing it, it seemed to him that it had been the center of life and commerce in Spencer County, bursting with 1950s prosperity and baby-boomer families. Certainly, the movie theatre, the sweetshops, and the sports store made it a good place for kids to hang out.

Even then, however, the social and economic conditions that were to change Main Street, USA, were at work. But he didn't know that then, and, to him, downtown Spencerville was the best and greatest place in the world, teeming with friends and things to do. He thought to himself, "The America that sent us to war no longer exists to welcome us home."

You didn't have to be born in a small town, Keith thought, to have a soft spot in your heart for America's small towns. It was, and to some extent it remained, the ideal, if only in an abstract and sentimental way. But beyond nostalgia, the small town dominated much of the history of the American experience; in thousands of Spencervilles across the nation, surrounded by endless farms, American ideas and culture formed, took hold, flourished, and nourished a nation. But now, he thought, the roots were dying, and no one noticed because the tree still looked so stately.

He approached the center of town and saw one building that had not changed: Across from Courthouse Square stood the impressive police headquarters, and, outside, among the parked police cars, a group of police officers stood, talking to a man who Keith instinctively knew was Police Chief Baxter. He also noticed now, a few buildings away from police headquarters, the County Hospital Thrift Store.

Keith drove around the massive courthouse, which was set on a few acres of public park. The administration of justice, civil and criminal, and the proliferation of bureaucratic agencies were still a growth business at the close of the American Century, even in Spencer County. The courthouse was once thought of as a boondoggle and a giant folly, but the visionaries who built it must have anticipated the kind of society that was to inherit the nation.

Aside from the courts, the building housed the prosecutor's office, the Welfare Department, a public law library, the county surveyor, the state agricultural office, the Board of Elections, and a dozen other acronymic government agencies; the Ministry of Everything, its sixteen-story clock tower rising in Orwellian fashion above the decaying city around it.

There were a number of people in the park surrounding the courthouse, kids on bikes, women with baby carriages and strollers, old people on benches, government workers on break, and the unemployed. For a moment, Keith could imagine that it was the summer of 1963 again, the summer he'd met Annie Prentis, and that the past three decades had not happened, or better yet, had happened differently.

He came full circle around the courthouse, turned back onto Main Street, and continued toward its western end, where grand old houses stood. This was once a prime residential street, but it was run-down now, the big places given over to boardinghouses, informal day-care centers, a few low-rent offices, and the occasional craft shop that hopefully paid the mortgage and taxes.

Main Street widened into four lanes at the sign that said, "City Limits," and became the highway that led to the Indiana border. But it was no longer rural, Keith saw, and had become a commercial strip of chain supermarkets, convenience stores, discount stores, and gas stations. Huge plastic signs stood atop tall stanchions as far as the eye could see: Wendy's, McDonald's, Burger King, Kentucky Fried Chicken, Roy Rogers, Domino's Pizza, Friendly's, and other fine and fast-dining spots, one after the other, all the way out to Indiana, for all he knew, maybe all the way to California—the real Main Street, USA.

At any rate, this was what had killed downtown, or perhaps downtown had killed itself because of a lack of vision, as well as a profound break with, and misunder-standing of, the past. In a perfect little hometown such as the ones he'd seen in New England, the past and the present were one, and the future was built carefully on the existing foundations of time.

But Keith supposed that if he'd stayed here and seen the changes evolve, rather than experiencing them in five-year gulps, he'd be less nostalgic and not as startled by the physical transformation.

There being not a single grocery store left in down-town Spencerville, Keith had to forgo that experience, and he pulled into the lot of a big supermarket.

He took a cart and went inside. The aisles were wide, the place was air-conditioned and clean, and the goods were mostly the same as in Washington. Despite his longing for Mr. Erhart's chaotic grocery store, the mod-ern supermarket was truly America's finest contribution to Western civilization.

Ironically, Keith's urban shopping street in Georgetown was more like rural Spencerville than Spencerville. There, Keith, on his rare shopping trips, went from one small specialty store to another. The supermarket concept was alien to him but instantly understandable. He pushed his cart up and down the aisles, took what he needed, met the glances of housewives and old-timers, smiled, said "Excuse me," and didn't compare prices.

He was surprised at the number of people he didn't know and recalled a time when he'd wave to half the people downtown. However, there was a familiar face now and then, and some people seemed to recognize him but probably couldn't place his face or recall his name. He saw at least ten women of his own age that he'd once known and saw a man he'd once played football with. But dropping out of the sky as he had, he wasn't prepared to stop and identify himself.

He didn't see any of his former best friends and, if he had, he'd have been a little embarrassed because he hadn't kept in touch with any of them and hadn't attended a single class reunion. Aside from his family, his only contact with Spencerville had been Annie.

He saw her turning a corner and pushed his cart faster, then abandoned it and caught up with her. But it wasn't her, and in fact didn't look at all like her, and he realized he was having a tiny midafternoon hallucination.

He went back to his shopping cart, and, without finishing his shopping, he checked out and took his bags to his car.

A Spencerville police car with two officers inside was blocking him. He loaded his groceries and got into his Saab and started it up, but they didn't move. He got out of his car and went to the driver. "Excuse me, I'm getting out."

The cop stared at him a long time, then turned and said to his partner, "I thought all the migrant workers left by now." They both laughed.

This was one of those moments, Keith thought, when the average American citizen, God bless him, would tell the police to fuck off. But Keith was not an average American, and he'd lived in enough police states to recognize that what was happening here was a deliberate provocation. In Somalia or Haiti, or a dozen other places he'd been, the next thing to happen would be the death of a stupid citizen. In the old Soviet empire, they rarely shot you on the street, but they arrested you, which was where this incident was headed unless Keith backed off. He said, "Whenever you're ready."

He got back into his car, put it in reverse so that the backup lights were on, and waited. After about five minutes, a good number of shoppers had passed by and noticed, and a few of them had mentioned to the two cops that they were blocking the gentleman. In fact, the scene was attracting attention, and the cops decided it was time to move off.

Keith backed out and pulled onto the highway. He could have taken rural roads all the way home, but instead headed back into town, in case the gestapo had more on their minds. He kept an eye on his rearview mirror the whole way.

This was not a random incident of fascistic behavior toward a man with out-of-state license plates and a funny car. And Spencerville was not some southern backwater town where the cops sometimes got nasty with strangers. This was a nice, civilized, and friendly midwestern town where strangers were usually treated with some courtesy. Therefore, this was planned, and you didn't have to be a former intelligence officer to figure out who planned it.

So at least one of the questions in Keith's mind was answered: Police Chief Baxter knew he was in Spencerville. But did Mrs. Baxter know?

He'd thought about Cliff Baxter's reaction upon hearing that his wife's former lover was back in town. Big cities were full of ex-lovers, and it was usually no problem. Even here in Spencerville, there were undoubtedly many married men and women who'd done it with other people, pre-marriage, and still lived in town. The problem in this case was Cliff Baxter, who, if Keith guessed correctly, probably lacked a certain sophistication and savoir faire.

Annie had never written a word against him in any of her letters, not on the lines or between the lines. But it was more what wasn't said, coupled with what Keith remembered about Cliff Baxter and what he'd heard over the years from his family.

Keith had never solicited anything about Cliff Baxter, but his mother—God bless her—always dropped a word or two about the Baxters. These were not overly subtle remarks, but more in the category of, "I just don't know what that woman sees in him." Or more to the point, "I saw Annie Baxter on the street the other day, and she asked about you. She still looks like a young girl."

His mother had always liked Annie and wanted her stupid son to marry the girl. In his mother's day, a courtship was prelude to marriage, and a reticent beau could actually get sued for breach of promise if he ruined a girl's reputation by taking her on picnics unchaperoned, and then not doing the decent thing and marrying her. Keith smiled. How the world had changed.

His father, a man of few words, had nevertheless spoken badly of the current police chief, but he'd confined his remarks to areas of public concern. Neither sex, love, marriage, nor the name Annie ever came out of his mouth. But basically he felt as his wife did—the kid blew it.

But they could not comprehend the world of the late 1960s, the stresses and social dislocations felt more by the young than by the old. Truly, the country had gone mad, and somewhere during that madness, Keith and Annie had lost their way, then lost each other.

In the last five years since his parents had moved away, he'd had no other news of Spencerville, of Chief Baxter, or of how pretty Annie looked in a flowery sundress, walking through the courthouse park.

And that was just as well, because his mother, though she meant well, had caused him a lot of pain.

Keith drove slowly through town, then turned south on Chestnut Street, crossed the tracks, and continued through the poor part of town, past the warehouses and industrial park, and out into the open country.

He looked in his rearview mirror again but did not see a police car.

He had no idea what Chief of Police Baxter's game plan was, but it really didn't matter, as long as both of them stayed within the law. Keith didn't mind petty harassment and, in fact, thrived on it. In the old Soviet Union and the former Eastern Bloc, harassment was the highest form of compliment; it meant you were doing your job, and they took the time to express their displeasure.

Cliff Baxter, however, could have shown a little more cleverness if he'd lain low for a while.

But Keith suspected that Baxter was not patient or subtle. He was no doubt cunning and dangerous, but, like the police in a police state, he was too used to getting instant gratification.

Keith tried to put himself in Baxter's place. On the

one hand, the man wanted to run Keith Landry out of town very quickly. But the cunning side of him wanted to provoke an incident that would lead to anything from arrest to a bullet.

In the final analysis, Keith understood, there wasn't room in this town for Keith Landry and Cliff Baxter, and if Keith stayed, someone was probably going to be hurt.

CHAPTER EIGHT

The next week passed uneventfully, and Keith used the time to work around the farmyard and the house. He cleared the bush and weeds from the kitchen garden, turned over the ground, and threw straw in the garden to keep the weeds down and the topsoil from blowing away. He harvested a few grapes from the overgrown arbor and cut back the vines.

Keith gathered deadfall from around the trees, sawed and split it into firewood, and stacked the wood near the back door. He spent two days mending fences and began the process of cleaning out the toolshed and barn. He was in good shape, but there was something uniquely exhausting about farm work, and he remembered days as a boy when he barely had the energy to meet his friends after dinner. His father had done this for fifty years, and the old man deserved to sit on his patio in Florida and stare at his orange tree. He didn't fault his brother for not wanting to continue the hundred-and-fifty-year tradition of backbreaking labor for very little money, and certainly he didn't fault himself or his sister. Yet, it would have been nice if an Uncle Ned type had continued on. At least his father had not sold the land and had kept the farmhouse in the family. Most farmers these days sold out, lock, stock, and barrel, and if they had any regrets, you never heard about it. No one he knew ever returned from Florida, or wherever they went.

In the toolshed, he saw the old anvil sitting on the workbench. Stamped into the anvil was the word Erfurt, and a date, 1817. He recalled that this was the anvil that his great-great-grandfather had brought with him from Germany, had loaded onto a sailing ship, then probably a series of riverboats, and finally a horse-drawn wagon until it came to rest here in the New World. Two hundred pounds of steel, dragged halfway around the globe to a new frontier inhabited by hostile Indians and strange flora and fauna. Surely his ancestors must have had second thoughts about leaving their homes and families, their civilized, settled environment, for a lonely and unforgiving land. But they stayed and built a civilization. Now, however, what Indians and swamp diseases couldn't do, civilization itself had done, and this farm, and others, were abandoned.

As he worked, he was aware that chopping firewood for the winter was a commitment of sorts, though he could give away the firewood, come to his senses, and leave. But for now, he felt good taking care of his parents' farm, his ancestors' bequeathal. His muscles ached in a pleasant way; he was fit, tan, and too tired to indulge himself in urban-type anxieties, or to think about sex. Well, he thought about it but tried not to.

He'd gotten the phone connected and called his parents, brother, and sister to tell them he was home. In Washington, not only was his number unlisted, but the phone company had no record of his name. Here in Spencerville, he'd decided to put his name and number in the book, but he hadn't gotten any calls so far, which was fine.

His mail was forwarded from Washington, but there wasn't anything important, except a few final bills that he could pay now that he'd opened a checking account at the old Farmers and Merchants Bank in town. UPS had delivered his odds and ends, and the boxes sat in the cellar, unopened.

It was interesting, he thought, how fast a complicated life could wind down. No more home fax or telex, no car phone, no office, no secretary, no airplane tickets on his desk, no pile of pink message slips, no monthly status meetings, no briefings to deliver at the White House, no communiqués to read, and nothing to decipher except life.

In fact, though he'd finally informed the National Security Council of his whereabouts, he hadn't heard a word from them officially, and hadn't even heard from his Washington friends and colleagues. This reinforced his opinion that his former life was all nonsense anyway, and that the game was for the players only, not the former stars.

As he worked, he reflected on his years with the Defense Department and then the National Security Council, and it occurred to him that Spencerville, as well as the rest of the country, was filled with monuments to the men and women of the armed forces who served and who gave their lives, and there was the monument in Arlington to the unknown soldier who represented all the unidentified dead, and there were parades and special days set aside for the armed forces. But for the dead, disabled, and discharged veterans of the secret war, there were only private memorials in the lobbies or gardens of a few nonpublic buildings. Keith thought it was time to erect a public monument in the Mall, a tribute to the Cold Warriors who served, who got burned-out, whose marriages went to hell, who got shafted in bureaucratic shuffling, and who died, physically, mentally, and sometimes spiritually. The exact nature of this monument escaped him, but sometimes he pictured a huge hole in the middle of the Mall, sort of a vortex, with a perpetual fog rising from the bottom, and if there was any inscription at all, it should read: *Dedicated to the Cold Warriors, 1945–1989? Thanks.*

But this war ended, he thought, not with a bang, but a whimper, and the transition from war to peace was mostly quiet and unremarked. There was no cohesiveness among the Cold Warriors, no sense of victory, no pomp and ceremony as divisions were deactivated, ships decommissioned, bomber squadrons put out into the desert. There was just a fading away, a piece of paper, a pension check in the mail. In fact, Keith thought, no one in Washington, nor anywhere, even said thank you.

But he was not bitter, and, in fact, he was very happy to see these events transpire in his lifetime. He thought, however, the government and the people should have made more of it, but he understood his own country, and understood the innate tendency of the American people to treat war and history as something that usually happened somewhere else to someone else, and was, at best, a nuisance. Back to normalcy.

Time to chop wood. He pruned the old oaks around the house, gathered up the branches in a pull cart, and took them to the sawhorses. He cut, split, and stacked.

Aunt Betty had stopped by, and so had some of his distant relatives. The Mullers from the next farm to the south came by, and so had Martin and Sue Jenkins from the farm across the road. Everyone brought something in the way of food, everyone seemed a little awkward, and everyone asked the same questions—"So, you stayin' awhile? Miss the big city yet? Been downtown? Seen anybody?" And so forth. No one had asked what was on their minds, which was, "Are you nuts?"

Keith got a cold beer and took a break on the front porch. He stared at the lonely farm road and watched the fields and trees moving in the wind. Butterflies, bumblebees, and birds. Then a blue and white police cruiser came by. They came by once or twice a day, he figured, maybe more. It occurred to him that, if by some miracle Annie drove up, there could be a problem. He thought about getting word to her through her sister, but he felt foolish doing that and didn't know quite what to say. *Hi, I'm back and being watched by your husband. Stay away.*

Obviously, her husband would also be watching *her*. But, most likely, she had no intention of stopping by, so why worry about it? Whatever was going to happen would happen. He'd spent too many years manipulating events, then worrying about his manipulations, then trying to discover if his manipulations were working, then doing damage control when things blew up, and so forth and so on. "Be alert, be on guard, be prepared. Do nothing." Sounded like good advice. But he was getting itchy.

The following morning, Keith drove to Toledo and exchanged the Saab for a Chevy Blazer. The Blazer was dark green, like half the ones he'd seen around, and it blended well. The dealer secured Ohio plates for him, and Keith put his Washington plates under the seat. He had to send them back to where they came from, which was not the Bureau of Motor Vehicles.

Late in the afternoon, he started for home. By the time he reached the outskirts of Spencerville, it was dusk, and by the time he reached the farm, long purple shadows lay over the farmyard. He passed the mailbox and turned into the drive, then stopped. He backed up and saw that the red flag was up, which was odd because he'd gotten his mail that morning. He opened the mail-box and took out an unstamped envelope addressed simply "Keith." There was no mistaking the handwriting.

He drove the Blazer around to the back of the house, so it couldn't be seen, got out, and went inside. He put the envelope on the kitchen table, got a beer, put it back, and made himself a stiff Scotch and soda instead.

He sat at the table and sipped his drink, poured a little more Scotch into it, and did this a few times until he looked at the envelope again. "Well."

He thought about things, about her: *They'd had a monogamous and intense relationship for two years in high school, then four years of college, and they'd graduated Bowling Green State University together. Annie, a bright and enthusiastic student, chose to accept a fellowship at Ohio State. He, bored with school, restless, and in any case not in a financial position to do graduate work, chose not to apply to Ohio State. He did follow her to Columbus, but before the summer was over, he was swept up in the draft as soon as the Spencerville draft board learned of his status.*

Keith opened the envelope and read the first line. "Dear Keith, I heard you were back and living at your folks' place."

He looked out into the dark yard and listened to the locusts.

They had that summer together, a magic two months in Columbus, living in her new apartment, exploring the city and the university. In September, he had to go. He said he would return; she said she'd wait. But neither of those things happened, nor were they likely to happen in America in 1968.

Keith took a deep breath and focused again on the letter. He read, "The local gossip is that you're staying awhile. True?"

Maybe. He poured a little more Scotch and thought back.

He'd gone to Fort Dix, New Jersey, for his basic and advanced training, then to Officer Candidate School at Fort Benning, Georgia, and within a year was commissioned a second lieutenant. Not bad for a farm kid. They wrote, often at first, then less frequently, of course, and the letters were not good. She found her monogamy hard to defend or justify and let him know she was seeing other men. He understood. He didn't understand. He spent his pre-embarkation leave in Spencerville, not Columbus. They spoke on the phone. She was very busy with difficult classes. He was very anxious about going into a combat zone and really didn't care about her classes. He asked her if she was seeing anyone at the moment. She was, but it was not serious. After about ten minutes of this, he looked forward to combat. He said to her, "You've changed." She replied, "We've all changed, Keith. Look around you."

He said, "Well, I've got to go. Good luck in school."

"Thanks. Take care, Keith. Home safe."

"Yup."

"Bye."

"Bye."

But they couldn't hang up, and she said, "You understand, I'm making this easy for both of us."

"I understand. Thanks." He hung up.

They continued to write, neither of them able to comprehend that it was over.

Keith pushed the Scotch aside. The alcohol wasn't working, his hands were trembling, and his mind was not getting pleasantly numb. He read, "Well, welcome home, Keith, and good luck."

"Thank you, Annie."

He'd served as an infantry platoon leader, saw too many dead people lying on the ground, fresh blood running, or bloating in the hot sun. He had no frame of reference for this, except the stockyards in Maumee. Very nice villages and farms were blown to hell, and sandbags and barbed wire were all over the place, and he'd wept for the farmers and their families. He'd completed his tour and returned to Spencerville on leave.

Keith wiped the sweat off his lip and focused on the letter, read it from the beginning, then read, "I'm leaving tomorrow to drive Wendy to school. She's starting as a freshman at our old alma mater. Can't wait to see it again. Be gone a week or so."

He nodded and took a deep breath.

He'd spent his thirty-day post-combat leave in Spencerville, and did mostly nothing but eat, drink, and take long rides. His mother suggested he drive to Columbus. Instead, he'd called. She was working on her doctorate by then. It was a very strained conversation, he recalled. He hadn't asked her about other men, because he'd come to accept that. He'd had other women. It didn't matter. But she'd changed in a more profound way in the last year. She'd become more politically active, and she had ambivalent feelings about a man in uniform and had given him a lecture on the war.

He was angry, she was cool; he barely controlled his anger, and she kept her tone frigid. He was about to hang up on her when she said, "I have to go," and he realized she was crying, or close to it. He offered to come see her, she said that would be all right. But he did not go to Columbus, and she did not come to Spencerville, nor did they meet halfway.

Keith read the final lines of her letter. "My Aunt Louise still lives out by you, and next time I'm that way, I'll stop and say hello. Take care. Annie."

He put the letter in his pocket, stood, and went out the back door. The hot wind had died down, and it was cooler now. There was some sun left on the western horizon, but in the east he could see stars.

Keith went out to where the corn began and walked between the tall rows, a few hundred yards to a small hill that was thought to be an Indian burial mound. The rise was gentle and tillable, but no one in his family had ever planted there, and the Mullers were asked to do the same. Rye grass grew tall on the hill, and a single birch had been planted or had taken root on its own near the top of the hill.

Keith stood beside the birch and looked out over the corn. He'd played here as a boy and come here to think as a young man.

Nor did they meet halfway. It was his pride, his ego, or whatever. He simply could not accept the fact that she'd been sexually involved with other men when they were supposed to be going together. But then again, he hadn't proposed marriage, perhaps because he didn't want to make her a young widow. It was the classic dilemma of wartime: to marry or not to marry? He couldn't recall exactly what had transpired between them regarding this subject, but he was certain she'd remember.

He sat at the base of the birch tree and looked out at the stars. In Washington, he could barely see the stars, but here in the country, the night sky was breathtaking, mind-boggling. He stared up at the universe, picking out the constellations he knew, and remembered doing this with her.

After his post-Vietnam leave, he had less than a year of service remaining, but he'd decided to stay in a while longer, and requested and was accepted to Army Intelligence School in Fort Holabird, Maryland. This was an interesting field, and he actually enjoyed the work. He received orders for a second tour in the never-ending war, but this time as an intelligence analyst. He'd been promoted to captain, the pay was all right, the duty not bad. Better than combat, better than Spencerville, better than returning to a nation going crazy.

They stopped corresponding, but he heard she'd dropped out of the doctorate program and traveled to Europe, then returned to Spencerville for a cousin's wedding. It was then, at the wedding, according to a friend who had been there, that she'd met Cliff Baxter. Apparently, they had a good time at or after the wedding, because they married a few months later. This was what he'd heard, anyway, but by that time, it was a subject he no longer wanted to be informed about.

Keith took the letter out of his pocket but couldn't read it in the fading light. Nevertheless, he stared at it and recalled most of it. The sentences, the words, were innocuous, but as a product of everything that had come before, it was everything he wanted to hear. He knew what it took for her to write that letter, he knew there was an element of danger for her to put it in his mailbox and to say that she'd stop by. And the danger was not only physical in the form of Cliff Baxter but emotional as well. Neither of them needed another disappointment or a broken heart. But she'd decided to take a chance, to in fact take the lead, and he liked that.

Keith put the letter in his pocket and plucked at the grass around him.

After he heard she was married, he put her out of his mind. That lasted about a week, and against his better judgment, he wrote her a short note of congratulations, care of her parents. She wrote a shorter note thanking him for his good wishes and asked him not to write again, ever.

He had always thought, and perhaps she thought, that they'd somehow get together again. In truth, neither of them could have forgotten the other. For six years, they'd been friends, soulmates, and lovers, and had formed each other's lives and personalities, shared the pains and happiness of growing up, and never imagined a life apart. But the world had finally intruded, and her letter made it clear that, indeed, it was now over between them, forever. But he never believed that.

After he was stationed in Europe, some months after her wedding, she wrote again, apologizing for the tone of her last letter, and suggested that writing was okay, but to please write care of her sister Terry in the next county.

He waited until he returned to the States, then wrote from Washington, saying little, except that he was back and would be at the Pentagon for a year or so. Thus began a two-decade-long correspondence, a few letters a year, updates, the births of her children, changes of address, his transfer to the Defense Department, her local news from Spencerville, his postings all over the world.

They had never exchanged photographs; neither had asked for a picture and neither had offered one. It was, Keith thought, as though they each wanted to hold on to the moving, living memory of the other, uncomplicated by a succession of rigid snapshots.

There had never been the hint of anything but an old and maturing friendship—well, perhaps once in a while, a letter written late at night with a line or two that could be taken as more than "Hello, how are you?" He wrote once from Italy, "I saw the Colosseum at night for the first time and wished you could have seen it, too."

She wrote back, "I did see it, Keith, when I was in Europe, and funny, I had the same thought about you."

But these types of letters were rare, and neither of them went too far out of bounds.

Whenever his address changed to some new, exotic locale, she wrote, "How I envy you all your traveling and excitement. I always thought I'd be the one leading the adventurous life, and you'd wind up in Spencerville."

He usually replied with words like, "How I envy you your stability, children, community."

He'd never married, Annie never divorced, and Cliff Baxter did not conveniently die. Life went on, the world moved forward.

He was in Saigon on his third tour when the North Vietnamese arrived in 1975, and he took one of the last helicopters out. He wrote to Annie from Tokyo, "I knew this war was lost five years ago. What fools we've all been. Some of my staff have resigned. I'm considering the same."

She replied, "When we played Highland, we were down 36–0 at the half. You went out there for the second half and played the best game I ever saw you play. We lost, but what do you remember best, the score or the game?"

Keith listened to a nightingale in the far-off tree line, then looked out at the Mullers' farmhouse. The kitchen was lit, and dinner was probably being served. He supposed that he'd played a more interesting game than the Mullers, but at the end of the day, they gathered together for dinner. He honestly missed having children, but in some odd way, he was happy that Annie did. He closed his eyes and listened to the night.

He'd almost married, twice in fact, during the next five or six years; once to a colleague he served with in Moscow, once to a neighbor in Georgetown. Each time, he broke it off, knowing he wasn't ready. In fact, he was never going to be ready, and he knew it.

He decided that the letters had to stop, but he couldn't make the break completely. Instead, he let months go by before answering her, and his letters were always short and remote.

She never commented on the change in tone, or the infrequency of his letters, but went on writing her two or three pages of news, and once in a while, reminisced. Eventually, though, she followed his lead, and they wrote less frequently, and by the mid-eighties, it seemed as though the letter relationship had ended, except for Christmas cards and birthday cards.

He had returned to Spencerville now and then, of course, but he never told her in advance, intending each time to see her when he was there, but he never did.

Sometime around 1985, she'd written to him after one of his visits, "I heard you were in town for your aunt's funeral, but by then you'd left. I would have liked to have a cup of coffee with you, but maybe not. Before I found out for sure you'd left, I was a nervous wreck thinking you were in town. After I was sure you'd gone, I felt relieved. What a coward I am."

He had replied, "I am afraid I'm the coward. I'd rather go into combat again than run into you on the street. I did drive past your house. I remember when old Mrs. Wallace lived there. You've done a nice job restoring it. The flowers are very nice. I felt very happy for you." He'd added, "Our lives took different paths in 1968, and those paths cannot cross again. For us to meet again would mean leaving our paths and traveling into dangerous territory. When I'm in Spencerville, I'm just passing through, and I intend to do no harm while I'm there. If, on the other hand, you ever find yourself in Washington, I'd be happy to have that cup of coffee with you. I'm leaving in two months for London."

She did not reply immediately, but wrote him in London, and never mentioned the last exchange of letters, but he remembered her reply. She'd written, "My son, Tom, played his first football game on Saturday, and I thought of the first time I sat in the stadium and saw you come onto the field in uniform. You don't have all these familiar places and things around you, but I do, and sometimes something like a football game makes me remember, and I get teary. Sorry."

He'd replied immediately, and without any pretense at being cool, wrote, "No, I don't have those familiar places and things around to remind me of you, but whenever I'm very lonely or frightened, I think of you."

After that, their correspondence increased, but more to the point, it had taken on a more intimate tone. They were not kids anymore, but were approaching middle age, with all that implied. She wrote to him, "I can't imagine not seeing you one more time."

He'd replied, "I promise you, God willing, we'll meet again."

Apparently, God was willing.

Yet the last six years or so had passed without that promised meeting, and perhaps he was waiting for something to happen, something like a divorce, or her falling ill. But nothing of the sort happened. His parents moved from Spencerville, and he had no reason to return.

The Berlin Wall fell in 1989, and he was there to see it, then he was posted again to Moscow and witnessed the attempted coup of August 1991. He was at the very top of his career and was helping to make policy in Washington. His name was mentioned in the newspapers now and then, and he felt somewhat fulfilled professionally; but personally, he knew very well there was something missing.

The euphoria of the late 1980s became the letdown of the early '90s. There was a Churchill paraphrase that had been making the rounds among his colleagues—The war of the giants is over, the wars of the pygmies have begun. Needing fewer people for the wars of the pygmies, his colleagues were being told to go home, and finally he, too, was asked to leave, and here he was.

Keith opened his eyes and stood. "Here I am."

He looked around at the burial mound and, for the first time, made the connection between this mound and the similar burial mounds he'd seen in Vietnam.

The burial mounds being the only high terrain in otherwise flat wet rice paddies, his platoon would often dig into them for night defensive positions. This was desecration, of course, but good tactics. Once, an old Buddhist monk had come up to him while his platoon was digging and said to him, "May you live in interesting times." Young Lieutenant Landry had taken it as a blessing of some sort, and only afterward learned that it was an ancient curse. And much afterward, he came to understand it.

The sun had set, but the moon illuminated the fields as far as he could see. It was quiet here, and the air smelled of good earth and crops. It was one of those beautiful evenings that would stick in your mind for years afterward.

He came down from the mound and walked between the rows of corn. He remembered the first time his father had planted forty acres of corn as a test crop, and, as the corn started to get higher, Keith had been fascinated with it. It formed an incredible maze, acres of high green walls, an enchanted world for him and his friends. They played hide-and-seek, they made up new games, they spent hours getting lost and pretending that there was some danger lurking in the maze. The fields were deliciously scary at night, and they often slept out under the stars, between the rows, armed with BB guns, posting guards through the night, getting themselves worked up into a state of pure terror.

We were all little infantrymen in training, he thought. He didn't know if that was biological or perhaps a cultural memory from the days when this place had been the western frontier. *Lacking any real danger, we had to create one, we resurrected long-dead Indians, transported wild beasts to the cornfields, and imagined bogeymen. Then, when the real thing came along—the war—most of us were ready.* That was what had really happened to him and Annie in 1968. He knew he could have gone to graduate school with her, they could have married and had kids and roughed it together like so many of their college friends. But he was already pro-grammed for something else, and she understood that. She let him go because she knew he needed to go slay dragons for a while. What happened afterward was a series of missed opportunities, male ego, female reserve, failures to communicate, and just plain bad luck and bad timing. *Truly, we were star-crossed lovers.*

CHAPTER NINE

It rained all day, and it was not one of those summer storms from the west or southwest that came and went. It was a cold, steady rain from over Lake Erie, a taste of autumn. The rain was welcome because the corn was not ready and wouldn't be until sometime between Halloween and Thanksgiving. Keith thought if he was still around then, he'd offer the Mullers and the Jenkinses a hand with their harvests. The machinery did most of the work these days, but an able-bodied man who sat around during the harvest was still thought of as a slothful sinner, predestined for hell. People who pitched in, on the other hand, were quite obviously among the saved. Keith had a little trouble with Protestant predestination and suspected that most of his neighbors, except for the Amish, weren't too sure about it themselves anymore. But to play it safe, most people acted like they were among the saved, and, in any case, Keith wanted to bring in a harvest again.

There was some work to do in the house, so he didn't mind the rain. He had a list of handyman chores—plumbing, electric, ripped screens, things that were too loose and things that were too tight. His father had left the entire workshop in the cellar, complete with tools and hardware.

Keith found he enjoyed the small chores, which gave him a sense of accomplishment that he hadn't felt in some time.

He began the task of changing all the rubber washers in all the faucets in the house. This may not have been what other former senior intelligence officers were doing at the moment, but it was just mindless enough to give him time to think.

The week had passed without incident, and Keith noticed that the police cars had stopped cruising past his house. This coincided with Annie's absence, and for all he knew, Cliff Baxter had gone to Bowling Green as well, though he doubted it. He doubted it because he understood a man like Baxter. Not only would Cliff Baxter be an anti-intellectual in the worst tradition of small-town America, but on a personal level Baxter would not go to a place where his wife had spent four happy years, premarriage.

Another type of man might be secure in the knowledge that his wife had only one lover in four years of college and hadn't screwed the entire football team. But Cliff Baxter probably considered his wife's premarital sex as something he should be pissed off about. Surely, the woman had no life before Mr. Wonderful.

Keith had given some thought to driving to Bowling Green. What better place to run into each other? But she said she'd stop by when she returned. And there was still the possibility that Cliff Baxter had gone with her, to keep an eye on her and to be certain she was miserable while showing their daughter around the town and university. Keith could only imagine what kind of discussions had taken place in the Baxter house when Wendy Baxter announced she'd applied to and been accepted by her mother's alma mater.

Keith understood, too, that now with both son and

daughter away at school, Annie Baxter had to do some thinking. Annie had hinted as much in one of her recent letters, but referred only to "making some decisions about finishing my doctorate, or getting a full-time paying job, or doing things I've been putting off too long."

Maybe, Keith thought, there was some preordained destiny at work, as Pastor Wilkes had preached, and life was not the chaos it seemed. After all, hadn't Keith Landry's arrival in Spencerville coincided with Annie Baxter's newly empty nest? But this confluence of events was not totally serendipitous; Keith knew from Annie's letters that Wendy was going away to college, which may have subconsciously influenced his decision to return. On the other hand, his forced retirement could have occurred two or three years ago, or two or three years from now. But more important, he was ready to change his life, and, by the tone of her recent letters, she was long overdue. So coincidence, subconscious planning, or miracle? No doubt a little of each.

He was torn between action and inaction, between waiting and doing. His Army training had taught him to act, his intelligence training had taught him patience. "There is a time to sow and a time to reap," said his Sunday school teacher. One of his intelligence school instructors had added, "Miss either of those times and you're fucked."

"Amen."

Keith finished the last faucet and paused to wash his hands in the kitchen sink.

He'd accepted an invitation to attend a Labor Day barbecue at his Aunt Betty's house a few miles away. The weather had been good, the steaks were terrific, the salads were all homemade, and the sweet corn, which ripened long before the field corn, was fresh off the stalk.

About twenty people had shown up, and Keith knew most of them or knew of them. Men his own age, not yet fifty, looked old, and this gave him a scare. There were a good number of kids there, too, and the teenage boys seemed interested in his having lived in Washington, and they all wanted to know if he'd ever been to New York. His years of living in Paris, London, Rome, Moscow, and elsewhere in the world were so far removed from their frame of reference that no one seemed curious about those places. Regarding his job, most everyone had heard his parents say that Keith was in the diplomatic corps. Not everyone understood precisely what this meant, but neither would they have understood his last job with the National Security Council; in truth, after over twenty years with Army Intelligence, the Defense Intelligence Agency, and the NSC, Keith himself understood less of his job description with each transfer and promotion. When he'd been an operative, a spy, it was all crystal-clear. Further up the ladder, it got foggy. He'd sat at White House conferences with people from the Foreign Intelligence Advisory Board, the Central Intelligence Agency, the Bureau of Intelligence and Research, the Net Assessments Group, the National Security Agency—not to be confused with the National Security Council—and ten other intelligence groups, including his former employers, the Defense Intelligence Agency. In the world of intelligence, overlap equaled maximum security. How could fifteen or twenty different agencies and subagencies completely miss something important? Easy.

The waters may have been muddy in the 1970s and '80s, but at least they were all running in the same direction. After about 1990, things got not only muddier but stagnant. Keith supposed that he'd been saved about five years of confused embarrassment. His last assignment had been on a committee that was seriously considering implementing a secret pension plan for former high-ranking KGB officials. One of his colleagues described it as "a sort of Marshall Plan for our former enemies." Only in America.

Anyway, the Labor Day barbecue ended with a twilight baseball game on a jerry-built diamond in Aunt Betty's yard. Keith had a better time than he thought he would.

The only real awkwardness was as a result of the presence of three unattached women: a third cousin, Sally, unmarried at thirty years old and a hundred and seventy pounds or so, but sweet, and two divorced women, Jenny, with two children, and the unfortunately named Anne, no children, both in their late thirties, both nice-looking. He had the distinct impression they weren't there for the homemade salads.

In truth, Jenny was cute, tomboyish, played a good game of baseball, and was terrific with the kids. Kids and dogs were often better judges of character than peers were, as Keith had learned.

Jenny had informed him that she did light housecleaning to make extra money and to call her if he needed help. He told her he would. In fact, around these parts, a man in his forties who'd never been married was cause for some concern, as well as the subject of speculation regarding his adequacy or orientation. Keith had no idea of what Jenny thought in this regard, but he gave her credit for wanting to find out.

In some odd way, however, since he'd returned, Keith felt he was supposed to be faithful to Annie Baxter. He had no problem with this and wouldn't have had it any other way. On the other hand, he felt it was prudent to show some interest in other women lest people start thinking about Keith Landry and Annie Baxter. So he'd taken Jenny's phone number, thanked his aunt, said his good-byes, and left them to their speculations. He'd had a nice Labor Day.

Keith was about to go up to the attic when the front doorbell rang. He looked out the window and saw an unfamiliar car, a gray compact of some sort. He went to the door and opened it. A middle-aged man with a drooping mustache stood on the porch, a folded umbrella in his hand. He was slightly built, wore wire-rim glasses, and had a fringe of long brown hair around a bald pate. The man said, "The war *was* obscene and immoral, but I'm sorry I called you a baby killer."

Keith smiled in recognition of the voice. "Hello, Jeffrey."

"Heard you were back. Never too late to apologize." He put out his hand, and Keith took it.

Keith said, "Come on in."

Jeffrey Porter took off his raincoat and hung it on the peg in the big foyer. He said, "Where do we start after all these years?"

"We start by me saying you're bald."

"But not fat."

"No, not fat. Left-wing, Bolshevik, bed-wetting comsymps are always skinny."

Jeffrey laughed. "I haven't heard those sweet words in two decades."

"Well, you came to the right place, pinko."

They both laughed and belatedly embraced. Jeffrey said, "You look good, Keith."

"Thanks. Let's get a few beers."

They went into the kitchen and filled a cooler with beer, then carried it out to the front porch and sat in rockers, watching the rain, drinking, each thinking his own thoughts. Finally, Jeffrey said, "Where have the years gone, Keith? Is that a trite thing to say?"

"Well, it is and isn't. It's a good question, and we both know too well where they went."

"Yes. Hey, I really was a little rough on you back there."

"We were all a little rough on one another back there," Keith replied. "We were young, we had passion and convictions. We had all the answers."

"We didn't know shit," said Jeffrey, and popped open another beer. He said, "You were the only guy in high school and at Bowling Green who I thought was nearly as smart as me."

"Smart as I. Actually smarter."

"Anyway, that's why I was so pissed that you were such an idiot."

"And I never understood how a smart guy like you bought the whole line of radical bullshit without thinking for yourself."

"I never bought it all, Keith, but I mouthed it."

"Scary. I've seen whole countries like that."

"Yeah. But you bought the whole line of patriotic flag-waving shit without much thought."

"I've learned better since then. How about you?"

Jeffrey nodded. "I learned a lot. Hey, enough politics. We'll wind up having another fistfight. What's the story? Why are you here?"

"Well, I got sacked."

"From where? You still with the Army?"

"No."

"Then who sacked you?"

"The government."

Jeffrey glanced at him, and they fell into silence.

Keith watched the rain falling in the fields. There was something very special about watching the rain from a big open porch, and he'd missed this.

Jeffrey asked, "You married?"

"Nope. You ever marry that girl . . . ? The hippie with hair down to her ass that you met in our senior year?"

"Gail. Yes, we got married. Still married."

"Good for you. Kids?"

"No, too many people in the world. We're doing our part."

"Me, too. Where're you living?"

"Here. Moved back about two years ago as a matter of fact. We stayed at Bowling Green for a few years."

"I heard. Then what?"

"Well, we both got fellowships at Antioch, and we both got tenured and taught there until we retired."

"I think if I'd spent one more year on or around a campus I'd have blown my brains out."

"It's not for everyone," Jeffrey conceded. "Neither is the government."

"Right."

"Hey, have you seen Annie since you've been back?"

"No." Keith opened another beer.

Jeffrey watched his old friend and classmate, and Keith was aware of the eyes on him. Finally, Jeffrey said. "You can't still be messed up about that, can you?"

"No."

"I've run into her a few times. I keep asking if she's heard from you, and she says she never had. Funny how we were all so close...those were the days, my friend we thought they'd never end..."

"We knew they would."

Jeffrey nodded. He said, "I've asked her to stop by and have a drink with Gail and me, but she keeps putting me off. I was hurt at first, but then I got to know a little about her husband. He's the fuzz-führer—you know that? Anyway, I saw them at some hospital charity thing at the Elks Lodge once, and Annie was charming, like Annie can be, and this Nazi of a husband was watching her like he was about to make a drug bust— you know what I mean? This Neanderthal was getting

himself worked up because she was talking to men—
married guys, for Christ sake, doctors, lawyers, and
such. She wasn't doing anything really, and he should
have been thrilled that his better half was working the
room—God knows, he needs all the good public rela-
tions he can get. Anyway, he takes her by the arm, and
they leave. Just like that. Hey, I may be a socialist and
an egalitarian, but I'm also a fucking snob, and when
I see a well-bred, college-educated woman putting up
with that shit from—where you going?"

"Bathroom."

Keith went into the bathroom and washed his face.
He looked in the mirror. Truly, he'd been blessed with
the right genes and didn't look much different than his
pictures from college. Jeffrey, on the other hand, was
barely recognizable. He wondered how Annie looked.
Jeffrey would know, but Keith wasn't about to ask him.
Anyway, it made no difference what she looked like. He
returned to the porch and sat. "How'd you know I was
back?"

"Oh . . . Gail heard it from somebody. Can't remember who." Jeffrey went back to the other subject. "She
looks good."

"Gail?"

"Annie." Jeffrey chuckled and said, "I'd encour-
age you to give it a go, Keith, but that bastard will kill
you." He added, "He knows he got lucky, and he's not
about to lose her."

"So, Antioch, home of the politically correct crowd.
You fit right in there."

"Well . . . I guess I did. Gail and I had some good
years there. We organized protests, strikes, trashed the
Army recruiting station in town. Beautiful."

Keith laughed. "Terrific. I'm getting my ass shot
off, and you're scaring away my replacement."

Jeffrey laughed, too. "It was a moment in time. I wish you could have been with us. Christ, we smoked enough pot to stone a herd of elephants, we screwed with half the graduate students and faculty, we—"

"You mean you screwed other people?"

"Sure. You missed the whole thing fucking around in the jungle."

"But...hey, I'm just a farm boy...were you guys married?"

"Yeah, sort of. Well, yeah, we had to for a lot of reasons—housing, benefits, that kind of thing. It was a real cop-out—remember that expression? But we believed in free love. Gail still claims she coined the expression 'Make love, not war.' Nineteen sixty-four, she says. It came to her in a dream. Probably drug-induced."

"Get a copyright attorney."

"Yeah. Anyway, we rejected all middle-class bourgeois values and sentiments, we turned our backs on religion, patriotism, parents, and all that." He leaned toward Keith and said, "Basically, we were fucked-up but happy, and we *believed*. Not all of it, but enough of it. We really hated the war. Really."

"Yeah. I didn't think much of it either."

"Come on, Keith. Don't lie to yourself."

"It wasn't political for me. Just a Huckleberry Finn thing with guns and artillery."

"People died."

"Indeed they did, Jeffrey. I still weep for them. Do you?"

"No, but I never wanted them to die in the first place." He punched Keith in the arm. "Hey, let's forget it. No one gives a shit anymore."

"I guess not."

They each had another beer and rocked. Keith thought that in twenty years they'd have lap blankets, drink apple juice, and talk about their health and their childhood. The years in between the beginning and the end, the years of sex, passion, women, politics, and struggle, would be fuzzy and nearly forgotten. But he hoped not.

Keith said, "How many of us from Spencerville were at Bowling Green? Me, you, Annie, that weird kid who was older than us...Jake, right?"

"Right. He went out to California. Never heard from him again. There was that girl, Barbara Evans, quite a looker. Went to New York and married some guy with money. I saw her at the twentieth class reunion."

"Spencerville High or Bowling Green?"

"Bowling Green. I never went to a high school reunion. Did you?"

"No."

"We just missed one this summer. Hey, I'll go next year if you do."

"You're on."

Jeffrey continued, "There was another guy from our high school at Bowling Green. Jed Powell, two years younger than us. Remember him?"

"Sure. His folks owned that little dime store in town. How's he doing?"

"He got a head wound in Vietnam. Came back here, had a few bad years, and died. My parents and his were close. Gail and I went to the funeral and handed out antiwar literature. Shitty thing to do."

"Maybe."

"You getting mellow or drunk?"

"Both."

"Me, too," said Jeffrey.

They sat awhile and caught up on family, then reminisced a little about Spencerville and Bowling Green. They told stories and recollected old friends, dragged up from the basement of time.

It was getting dark now, and the rain still fell. Keith said, "Nearly everyone I knew sat on this porch at one time or another."

"You know, Keith, we're not even old, and I feel like we're surrounded by ghosts."

"I know what you mean. Maybe we shouldn't have come back here, Jeffrey. Why'd you come back?"

"I don't know. It's cheaper than Antioch. We're not financially comfortable. We forgot about money in our zeal to produce little radicals." He laughed. "I should have bought defense stocks."

"Not a good investment at the moment. You working?"

"Tutoring high school kids. So's Gail. She's also on the city council for a dollar a year."

"No kidding? Who the hell voted for a pinko?"

"Her opponent was caught in a men's room."

Keith smiled. "What a choice for Spencerville."

"Yeah. She'll be out of office in November. Baxter's got it in for her."

"I don't wonder."

"Hey, watch that guy, Keith. He's dangerous."

"I obey the law."

"Don't matter, my friend. The guy's sick."

"Then do something about it."

"We're trying."

"Trying? Aren't you the guy who tried to topple the United States government once?"

"That was easier." He laughed. "That was then."

Moths beat against the screened windows of the house, and the rockers creaked. Keith popped open the last two beers and handed one to Jeffrey. "I don't understand why you both left cushy teaching jobs."

"Well . . . it got weird."

"What got weird?"

"Everything. Gail taught sociology, and I taught Marx, Engels, and other dead white European males who are now dead for sure. I sat there in my ivory tower, you know, and I couldn't see what was going on in the real world. The collapse of communism sort of caught me by surprise."

"Me, too. And I got paid to avoid surprises."

"Did you? You some kind of spy?"

"Go on. Your heroes had feet of clay. Then what?"

He smiled. "Yeah, so I didn't know if I should rewrite my lectures or rethink my life."

"I hear you."

"Anyway, my classes were not well attended, and whereas I was once in the vanguard of social thought, I found myself bringing up the rear. Christ, I couldn't even get laid anymore. I mean, maybe I'm getting too old for the undergraduate women, but...it's more a head thing than physical. You know? Also, they've got these rules now, whole pages of rules on sexual conduct...Jesus Christ, they tell you you've got to get a verbal go each step of the way—Can I unbutton your blouse? Can I undo your bra? Can I feel your breast?" He laughed. "No joke. Can you imagine that when we were undergrads. Christ, we just got high and fucked. Well, *you* didn't, but...anyway, Gail got a little behind the times, too. Her potential students all signed up for Feminist Studies, Afro-American History, Amerindian Philosophy, New Age Capitalism, and stuff like that. No one takes straight sociology anymore. She felt... sort of establishment. Jesus Christ, has the country changed, or what?"

"Antioch might not be representative of the country, Jeffrey."

"I guess not. But, jeez, there's nothing as pathetic as an old revolutionary who doesn't get it anymore.

The revolution always eats its own. I knew that thirty years ago. I just didn't expect to be on the take-out menu so soon."

"They sack you?"

"No. They don't do that. Gail and I just woke up one morning and made a decision. We quit on principle. Stupid."

"No. Smart. Good. I can't say the same for myself. I wish I would have done what you did. But I got axed."

"Why? Cutbacks?"

"Yup. The price of victory is unemployment. Ironic."

"Yeah, well, but you won. Now I can't look forward to a socialist paradise on earth." He finished his beer and crushed the can. "Politics suck. They divide people."

"I told you that." Keith sat silent for a while and thought about what Jeffrey had said. He and his childhood friend had lived different lives and believed in different things, and apparently had nothing in common by their senior year in college. In reality, they had more in common than they knew.

They'd been little boys together, they'd played in the same schoolyard, and left for the same college the same day. Each considered himself an honest man and perhaps an idealist, and each probably believed he was doing the best he could for humanity. They'd served in different armies while others stood aside. But, in the end, they'd each been misled, used, and abused by different systems. Yet here they were, old Spencerville boys, sharing too many beers on the front porch. Keith said to Jeffrey, "We've both been left in the scrap heap of history, my friend. We're useless relics who both lost the war."

Jeffrey nodded. "Yeah. Can we get the next thirty years right?"

"Probably not. But we're not going to make the same mistakes."

"No, but the past clings to us, Keith. Word got out that Gail and I are Reds, which isn't really true, but it hasn't helped the tutoring business. I mean, what are we supposed to do? Join a church? Go to Fourth of July picnics dressed in red, white, and blue? Register as Republicans?"

"God forbid."

"Right. We're still radicals. Can't help it."

"No, and you love it. That's why you're here. Your act was yesterday's news in Antioch. Here, you're weird and dangerous."

Jeffrey slapped his knee. "Right! This place is in a time warp. I love it." He looked at Keith. "And you? Do you know why you're here?"

"I think so."

"Why?"

"Well . . . I'm a burned-out cynic. I don't think they even understand cynicism here, so I'm here to get well again."

"Yeah. Cynicism is humor in ill-health. H. G. Wells. I hope you get better."

"Me, too."

"Maybe I can get cured of my idealism. You know what an idealist is? That's a man who notices that a rose smells better than a cabbage, so he thinks the rose will make a better soup. That's my problem. That's why I'm broke, out of work, and a social outcast. But I'm not cynical. There's hope."

"God bless you. Can I say that to an atheist?"

"Anytime. You join a church yet?"

"No."

"You should."

"Is that you, Jeffrey?"

"Yeah...I saw the power of religion in Poland, in Russia...I don't agree with any of it, but I've seen what it can do for troubled minds. You need a dose."

"Maybe."

Jeffrey stood unsteadily. "Hey, I've got to go, buddy. Dinner's on. Come over tomorrow and have dinner with us. Gail wants to see you. We're still vegetarians, but you can bring your own pig or something. We have wine and beer. We do drink."

"I see that." Keith stood, also unsteadily. "What time?"

"Who cares? Six, seven. Also, I've got a stash." Jeffrey moved to the steps and steadied himself on the porch column. He said, "Hey, you want to bring a friend? Lady type?"

"No."

"What're you doing for sex? Don't choke the chicken. This town's full of divorced women. They'd love a piece of you."

"Can you drive?"

"Sure. It's a straight run. We're renting a farmhouse and a few acres for organic vegetables. Two miles up the road. The old Bauer place."

"Let me drive you."

"No...if I get stopped, I can put the fix in through Gail. If you get stopped, they'll nail your ass."

"Why do you say that?"

Jeffrey moved back toward Keith and put his arm on Keith's shoulder. He said softly, "That's what I came to tell you...even if we didn't get along, I was going to tell you. Gail has a source close to the police...actually in police headquarters, but forget that. And the word is that Baxter is after your ass, and I guess we both know why. You be damned careful, buddy."

"Thanks."

Jeffrey hesitated, then said, "I don't know if you and

she have been in contact, but I have this feeling that you two...what am I trying to say? I could never picture you two separate...whenever I see Annie, I think of Keith, and when I saw you here, I thought of Annie, like you should have come to the door together like you always did in Bowling Green...Christ, I'm babbling." He turned and walked down the porch steps and through the rain without his umbrella, got into the car, and left.

Keith watched the taillights disappear on the dark, rainy road.

CHAPTER TEN

The following morning dawned clear, and Keith wanted to work around the farm, but everything was wet from the rain, so he put on clean jeans and a new short-sleeve shirt and went into town to take care of some business.

He was tempted to drive past the Baxter house, but the police might have discovered his new car by now. In any case, there was no reason to see if she was back or not; in her own time, she'd drive out to her Aunt Louise and stop by to see him.

He drove into the center of town and found a parking place near the state liquor store. He went inside and looked over the selection of wines, which ran toward domestic brands whose labels didn't ring a bell. He recalled that Jeffrey and Gail, like everyone else they knew at Bowling Green, drank cheap, sweet wine that today they'd deny ever having heard of. Nevertheless, as a joke, Keith found a bottle of apple wine and a bottle of something called grape wine, which was actually grape juice and alcohol, manufactured locally. He also found a decent bottle of real Italian Chianti, which would also bring back memories.

He paid for the wine, went back to the Blazer, and

put the bottles in the rear compartment. He took his Washington license plates, which were in an addressed manila envelope, and walked toward the post office on the west side of Courthouse Square.

The post office was one of those old Federalist buildings with classical columns, and, as a boy, Keith had always been awed by the place. He'd once asked his father if the Romans had built it, and he'd been assured that they had. His sense of history was a little better now, and he smiled at the memory, then understood what Annie meant when she'd written about memories. He recalled accompanying her several times to the post office to buy stamps and to mail letters.

There was no line at one of the windows, and he took the envelope to the clerk, where it was weighed and stamped. Keith requested return receipt and was filling out the tag when he heard the clerk a few windows away say, "You have a good day, Mrs. Baxter."

He turned to his right and saw a woman with shoulder-length auburn hair, wearing a simple pink and white cotton summer dress, walking toward the door. She left.

He stood motionless a moment, and the clerk said to him, "Finished?"

"Yes. No...forget it." He crumpled the form and left quickly.

On the steps, he looked up and down the sidewalk but didn't see her, then spotted her with three other women walking toward the corner. He hesitated, then bounded down the steps and followed.

His mental image of Annie was of how she looked twenty-five years before, the last time he'd seen her on the day he left to report for induction. They'd made love in her apartment in Columbus, and at dawn he'd kissed her and left. Now, in her mid-forties, her figure was still youthful, and she walked with the same girl-ish jaunt he remembered. She was laughing and joking with her friends, and he couldn't get a good look at her face, except in brief profile as she turned to talk.

Keith found that his heart was beating rapidly, and he stopped and watched the four women. They paused at the corner and waited for the light to change. Keith took a step forward, hesitated, took another step, then stopped again. *Go, you idiot. Go.*

The light turned, and the four women stepped off the curb into the crosswalk. Keith stood watching them. Then Annie said something to her friends, and the three of them continued without her toward the courthouse park. Annie stood motionless a moment, then turned and walked directly toward him.

She smiled and put out her hand. "Hello, Keith. Long time."

He took her hand. "Hello, Annie."

"I'm flustered," she said.

"You look fine. I'm about to faint."

She smiled. "I doubt it." She took a step back. "Let's look at you. You haven't aged a day."

"I've aged twenty-five years. You look very good."

"Thank you, sir."

They made eye contact and held it. Her eyes were as big and sparkly as ever, he noticed, and she still wore the same pale pink lipstick he remembered. Her skin had a healthy glow, but he was surprised she wasn't tan, because she used to love the sun. There were a few wrinkles, of course, but they gave her otherwise girlish face a little maturity. She had been pretty then; she was beautiful now.

He fished around for some words, then said, "So... I got your letter. In my mailbox."

"Good."

"How was Bowling Green?"

"It was...nice. Sad."

"I was going to...I didn't know if you went alone, or..."

"Yes, I did. My daughter and I." She added, "I looked for you there. Well, not physically, but, you know..."

He nodded, then looked at her. "Do you believe this?"

"No. I'm dreaming."

"I'm...I can't find the words..."

She looked around. "Another minute or so, then I have to go."

"I understand."

"I sent you a letter. It was returned. I thought you were dead."

"No...I mean, I didn't leave a forwarding address at the office..."

"Well, I was upset for days." She cleared her throat and said, "Lost my pen pal."

He was surprised when he noticed that her eyes were moist, and he wanted to offer her a handkerchief, but knew he shouldn't. She took a tissue from her purse and pretended to pat her face but wiped her eyes. "So..." She took a deep breath. "So, how long are you here for?"

"I don't know."

"Why did you come back?"

He considered several evasive replies, then said, "To see you."

He saw she was biting her lower lip, and she was looking at the ground, clearly about to cry.

Keith didn't feel in complete control either, so he didn't speak.

Finally, she looked up at him and said, "You could have seen me anytime you were here."

"No, I couldn't, Annie. But now I can."

"God...I don't know what to say...I mean...do you...are you still...?"

"Yes."

She dabbed at her eyes again, then glanced across at the park where her friends were at the ice cream vendor's truck, looking at her and Keith. She said to him, "I have about thirty seconds before I'm doing something wrong."

He forced a smile. "It's still a small town, isn't it?"

"Real small."

He said, "I want you to know that your letters got me through some rough times."

"Same here. I have to go."

"When can we have that cup of coffee?"

She smiled. "I'll drive out to your place. When I go to see my aunt. But I don't know when I can do that."

"I'm usually home."

"I know that."

He said, "Your husband—"

"I know that, too. I know when to come."

"Okay."

She extended her hand, and he took it. Keith said with a smile, "In Europe, Washington, or New York, we'd kiss goodbye."

"In Spencerville, we just say, 'You have a real nice day now, Mr. Landry. Real good seeing you again.'" She squeezed his hand and turned away.

Keith watched her cross the street and noticed the three women taking it all in.

He stood a moment, not remembering where he was, where his car was, or what he was supposed to do next.

He found he had a lump in his throat and kept glancing at the park across the street, but they were gone now. He wanted to go find her and take her arm and tell her friends, "Excuse me, we're in love, and we're leaving."

But maybe she needed some time to think about it. Maybe she didn't like what she saw. He thought about the conversation, replayed it so he wouldn't forget it, and tried to remember the look on her face and thought about what he'd seen in her eyes.

From what he'd gathered, she'd had a bad time of things, but you couldn't tell by her eyes, or her face, or her walk. Some people showed every scar, every disappointment, every sorrow. Annie Prentis was the eternal optimist, happy, perky, and unbowed by life.

He, on the other hand, had done well in life, and perhaps he didn't look burned-out, but he carried in his heart every sorrow, disappointment, and human tragedy he'd ever seen or experienced.

It didn't do any good to wonder about how life might have been if they'd married and had children. It would have been fine. They always said that they were made exclusively for each other. It was more important now to see if it was really possible to pick up where they'd left off. The cynic in him said no. The young Keith Landry, the one who had loved completely and unconditionally, said yes.

He found his car, got inside, and started it. He was vaguely aware that he had a list of errands to do, but he started for home.

As he drove, he remembered that day, twenty-five years ago, in her bedroom in Columbus. Dawn was breaking, and he'd been awake and dressed for hours. He'd sat looking at her sleeping naked on her back in the warm room, the unforgettable profile of her face and body, her long hair tumbling onto the pillow.

Certainly, he'd known that it would be a long time

before they would see each other again. But it never occurred to him that a quarter century would pass and that the world they knew would have vanished so completely. Sitting in her bedroom, he'd thought briefly about the war in Asia, about the possibility that he would die, but it all seemed too remote then. They were small-town kids who'd had four idyllic years of college, and this two-year Army hitch was just a bump on the road. His only concern was that, after being inseparable in high school and college, she'd be lonely without him.

He'd finished his training at Fort Dix, but, instead of getting leave time, his training battalion had been given a crash course in riot control and sent to Philadelphia because of antiwar protests that had turned ugly. Again the world had intruded, as it did in time of war, but it was a new experience for him.

He'd managed to call her from a pay phone, but she wasn't in her apartment, and there were no answering machines in those days. He'd had a second brief opportunity to call, late at night, but her line was busy. He'd finally written her, but it took a few weeks before her reply found him back at Fort Dix. Communication was not easy in those days, and it became more difficult in a larger sense in the following months.

Keith found himself at the farm and turned into the drive that led to the house. He pulled the Blazer around the back near the garden and sat at the wheel.

He wanted to tell himself that everything would be all right now, that love conquers all. He thought he knew how he felt about her, but, aside from the memories and the letters and now seeing her, he didn't know her. And how did she feel about him? And what were they going to do about it? And what was her husband going to do about it?

CHAPTER ELEVEN

I t was seven P.M. when Keith Landry pulled up to Gail and Jeffrey Porter's place, the old Bauer farm. The evenings were getting shorter and cooler, and the sky was that deep purple and magenta that Keith associated with the end of summer.

The farmhouse, a white clapboard building in need of paint, sat near the road.

Gail came out the front door and across the crabgrass lawn and met him as he climbed out of the Blazer with the wine bottles and Jeffrey's umbrella. She hugged and kissed him and said, "Keith Landry, you look terrific."

He replied, "I'm the delivery boy, ma'am. But you look pretty good yourself, and you kiss good."

She laughed. "Still the same."

"We wish." Actually, he'd only known her in their senior year when Jeffrey started seeing her, and he barely remembered what she looked like, because she had looked like a lot of thin-faced, lithe-bodied, granny-glassed, long-haired, no-makeup, peasant-dressed, barefoot girls of the time. In fact, she was still wearing a peasant dress, probably an original, her hair was still long, and she was indeed barefoot. Keith wondered if he was supposed to dress sixties for the occasion. She was still thin, too, and still braless, as he saw by the low-cut dress. She wasn't pretty then and wasn't pretty now, but she had been, and still was, sexy. He handed her the umbrella. "Jeffrey left this."

"It's a wonder he remembered where he lived. You guys had a good time, I gather."

"We did."

She took his arm and walked him toward the house. She said, "Jeffrey tells me you were a spy."

"I have laid down my cloak and dagger."

"Good. No politics tonight. Just old times."

"Hard to separate the two."

"True."

They entered the house through a battered wooden screen door, and Keith found himself in a barely furnished living room, lit only by the setting sun. From what he could make out, the furniture was sort of minimalist European modern, and it probably came in boxes with instructions badly translated from Swedish.

Gail threw the umbrella in a corner, and they passed through the dining room, which had the same sort of furniture, and into the big kitchen, a blend of original country kitchen and 1950s updates. Keith put the wine on the counter, and Gail took the bottles out of the bag. "Oh, apple wine and spiked grape juice! I love it!"

"Kind of a joke. But there's a good Chianti, too. Remember Julio's, the little Italian place near campus?"

"How could I forget? Bad spaghetti before it was called pasta, checkered tablecloths, and melted candles stuck in straw-covered Chianti bottles—what happened to the straw?"

"Good question."

She put the apple and grape wine in the refrigerator and gave Keith a corkscrew to open the Chianti. She found two wineglasses, and he poured. They touched glasses, and she toasted, "To Bowling Green."

"Cheers."

She said, "Jeffrey is out back, gathering herbs."

Keith saw a big pot simmering on the stove, and the kitchen table was set for three, with a loaf of dark bread in a basket.

Gail asked, "Did you bring meat for yourself?"

"No, but I looked for roadkill on the way here."

She laughed. "Disgusting."

He asked her, "Do you like it here?"

She shrugged. "It's all right. Quiet. Plenty of empty farmhouses at rents we can afford. And Jeffrey's people are still here, and he's been doing his memory-lane thing for the last two years. I come from Fort Recovery, so it's not much different. How about you? You okay here?"

"So far."

"Nostalgic? Sad? Bored? Happy?"

"All of the above. I have to sort it out."

Gail filled their glasses again and poured one for Jeffrey. "Come on outside. I want to show you our gardens."

They walked out the back door, and Gail called out, "Company!"

About fifty yards away in a garden, Keith saw Jeffrey stand up and wave. He came toward them wearing baggy shorts and a T-shirt, carrying a wicker basket piled with vegetation that Keith hoped was weeds destined for the garbage can and not something he was supposed to eat.

Jeffrey wiped his hand on his shorts and extended it to Keith. "Good to see you."

Keith asked, "You made it home all right?"

"Sure." He took his glass of wine from Gail and said, "I'm becoming a juicehead in my old age. We only do grass on special occasions."

Gail added, "We put on oldies, turn out the lights, get naked, get high, and fuck."

Keith didn't comment but looked around the yard. "Good gardens."

Jeffrey replied, "Yeah, we've got use of four acres and all the corn we can steal from the fields. Thank God this guy grows sweet corn, or we'd be eating cattle feed."

Keith looked out over the acres of gardens. This was more kitchen garden than the average farmer kept, and he figured that the Porters depended on this for much of their food. He stopped feeling sorry for himself with his adequate government pension and his family-owned acres.

Jeffrey said, "Come on, we'll show you around."

They toured the garden plots. There was a plot devoted entirely to root vegetables, another with vine vegetables such as tomatoes and squash, and another garden was planted with more varieties of beans than Keith knew existed. The most interesting thing was the herb gardens, the likes of which were rarely seen in Spencer County. There was a culinary herb garden with over forty different varieties, and also what Jeffrey called "a garden of historical and medicinal herbs," plus a garden of herbs used for dyes and miscellaneous household needs such as soap and cologne. And beyond the gardens, stretching out to where the cornfield began, was a profusion of wildflowers that had no use at all except to please the eye and ease the mind. "Very nice," Keith said.

Gail said, "I make perfume, potpourri, tea, hand lotion, bath scents, that sort of thing."

"Anything to smoke?"

Jeffrey laughed. "God, I wish we could. Can't risk it here."

Gail said, "I think we could, but Jeffrey is chicken."

Jeffrey defended himself. "The county sheriff is a little brighter than the Spencerville police chief, and he's keeping an eye on us. He thinks all this stuff is psychedelic."

Gail said, "Oh, Jeffrey, you have to treat the fuzz the way you grow mushrooms—keep them in the dark and feed them shit."

They all laughed.

Jeffrey said, apropos of the subject, "I have a source in Antioch. I make a run about once a month." He added, "I just made a run." He winked at Keith.

It was almost dark now, and they went inside. Gail put the herbs in a colander and washed them while Jeffrey stirred the contents of the pot, which looked like stew sans meat. Gail poured some of the Chianti into the pot and added the herbs. "Let that simmer awhile."

Keith had a strange feeling of déjà vu, then recalled his first dinner with Jeffrey and Gail in their little apartment off campus. Not much had changed.

Gail poured the remainder of the Chianti into their glasses and said to Keith, "You probably think we're stuck in the sixties."

"No." *Yes.*

"Actually, we're selectively sixties people. There's good and bad in each era, each decade. We've totally rejected the new feminism, for instance, in favor of the old feminism. Yet we've adopted the new radical ecology."

Keith remarked dryly, "That's very astute."

Jeffrey laughed. "Same old wiseass."

Gail smiled. "We're weird."

Keith felt compelled to say something nice to his hosts, and offered, "I think we can be as weird as we want to be. We've earned it."

"You said it," Jeffrey agreed.

Keith continued, "And you've put your money where your mouth is by resigning as a matter of principle."

Gail nodded. "Partly principle. Partly, we felt uncomfortable there. Two old radicals who got laughed at behind our backs." She added, "These kids have no heroes, and we were heroes. Heroes of the revolution. But the kids think the history of the world began on their birthdays."

Jeffrey said, "Well, it wasn't that bad. But professionally we felt unfulfilled."

Keith pointed out, "That's not exactly what you said last night."

"Yeah, well, I was drunk last night." He thought a moment, then confessed, "But maybe I was closer to the truth last night. Anyway, here we are, tutoring high school dull normals."

Gail said to Keith, "Jeffrey tells me you were sacked."

"Yes, and none too soon."

"Were they laughing at you?"

"No, I don't think so. Old warriors are still honored within the imperialist military-intelligence community."

"Then why were you sacked?" Gail asked.

"Budget cuts, end of the Cold War...no, that's not the whole truth. I was sacked because I was tottering between burnout and epiphany. They can smell that a mile away, and they don't like either." He thought a moment and said, "I was starting to ask questions."

"Such as?"

"Well...I was at a White House briefing once... I was there to give answers, not ask questions"— Keith smiled at the memory of what he was about to relate—"and I asked the secretary of state, 'Sir, could you explain to me this country's foreign policy, if any, so that I can figure out what you want?'" Keith added,

"Well, you could have heard a pink slip drop in the room."

Jeffrey inquired, "Did he explain it to you?"

"Actually, he was polite enough to do so. I still didn't get it. Six months later, I got a letter on my desk explaining budget cuts and the joys of early retirement. There was a place for my signature. I signed."

They sipped their wine, Jeffrey turned his attention to the stew, which he stirred, and Gail took a platter of raw vegetables and bean dip out of the refrigerator and put it on the counter. They all nibbled on the vegetables.

Jeffrey said finally, "Sounds as if you resigned on principle, too."

"No, I was asked to accept an early retirement for budget reasons. That's what the press release and the internal memo said. So that's the way it was." Keith added, "My job was to discover objective truths, but the truth needs two people to make it work—the speaker and the listener. The listeners weren't listening. In fact, in the last two decades, they rarely did, but it took me a while to figure it out." He thought a moment, then said, "I'm happy to be out of there."

Gail nodded. "We can relate to that. So here we all are, back on the farm where the bullshit is good for the garden." She opened the refrigerator and took out the apple and the grape wine that Keith brought, saying to Jeffrey, "Remember this? Eighty-nine cents a bottle. What did you pay for these, Keith?"

"Oh, about four bucks each."

"Robbery," said Jeffrey. He unscrewed the cap of the apple wine and sniffed it. "It's ready." He emptied the bottle into three water tumblers, Gail added sprigs of peppermint, and they touched glasses. Jeffrey said, "To days past, to absent friends of our youth, to ideals and humanity."

Keith added, "And to a bright future without the nightmare of nuclear extinction."

They drained off the wine, put down their glasses, and made exaggerated smacking sounds of pleasure, then laughed. Jeffrey said to Keith, "Actually, not bad. You have any more?"

"No, but I have a source."

Gail said, "I'm getting a buzz." She went to the kitchen table, carrying the grape wine, and sat. Jeffrey brought over the vegetable platter and turned off the lights, then lit two candles on the table.

Keith sat and poured wine for them. They ate the raw vegetables and dip, and Keith praised their gardening abilities, which they took as a high compliment from a farmer's son.

They made small talk for a while, Jeffrey and Keith reminisced about high school, Gail told them they were boring her, and they switched to their senior year at Bowling Green. Gail found a jug of wine and put it on the table. Jeffrey was apparently in charge of stirring and got up now and then to perform this task while Gail kept the glasses filled.

Keith was having a good enough time despite the fact that he had little in common with his hosts, except a shared experience in school. Even then, he hadn't had much in common with skinny little Jeffrey Porter, though they always got along well in high school, probably because they were intellectual peers, and as teenagers, neither had any opinions about politics, war, or life.

In college, they'd been drawn together at first because they were from the same hometown and had the same problems adjusting to a new environment. In fact, Keith thought, though he wouldn't admit it afterward, they'd become friends.

But as the war radicalized and polarized the campus,

they'd found they were on different sides of too many issues. Like the Civil War, the Vietnam War and its attendant upheavals pitted brother against brother, neighbor against neighbor, and friend against friend. In retrospect, intelligent people of goodwill should have found common ground. But Keith, like many others, lost old friends that he'd cared for and made new ones that he didn't particularly want. He and Jeffrey had wound up exchanging punches in the middle of the student union building. In truth, Jeffrey wasn't much of a fighter, and Keith had knocked him down only as often as Jeffrey insisted on getting up. Finally, Keith had walked away, and Jeffrey was carried away.

About a year and a half later, Jeffrey had written to Keith in Vietnam, getting his address from Keith's mother, who was happy to give it to one of her son's old friends. Keith had expected the letter to be conciliatory and concerned about Keith's frontline duty, and Keith was preparing a congenial reply in his mind as he opened the letter. Then he read, *"Dear Keith, Kill any babies today? Keep score of the women and children you murder. The Army will give you a medal."* And so on.

Keith recalled that he hadn't been hurt so much as enraged, and, had Jeffrey been there, Keith would have killed him. Now, looking back, he realized how far along the road to insanity they'd all traveled.

But a quarter century had passed, Jeffrey had apologized and Keith had accepted, and they were both different people, hopefully.

On that thought, Keith couldn't help but think about himself and Annie. She'd gone to graduate school, Europe, married, had children, lived with another man for about two decades, had twenty Christmases, birthdays, anniversaries, and thousands of breakfasts and dinners with him. Keith Landry and

Annie Baxter surely had no more in common now than he and Jeffrey had. On the other hand, he hadn't slept with Jeffrey Porter for six years. Keith mulled this over.

Gail said to him, "Yo, Keith! Did you check out?"

"No...I..."

Jeffrey got up and went to the stove. "Ready." He ladled the stew into three bowls and managed to carry them to the table without incident. Gail sliced the bread and said, "Home-baked."

They ate. The bread smelled like things that Keith used to feed to the livestock and horses, but the stew was good.

Dessert was a homemade strawberry pie, which was also good, but the smell of the herbal tea reminded Keith of places in Asia he'd just as soon forget.

Gail said to Keith, "Did Jeffrey tell you I'm on the city council?"

"He did. Congratulations."

"Sure. My opponent got busted blowing somebody in a men's room."

Keith smiled. "Did that become an issue?"

Gail added, "I've blown lots of guys myself, but that's different."

Clearly, everyone was drunk, but, nevertheless, Keith was a little uncomfortable with that remark.

Gail said, "I never got caught in a men's room. Anyway, come November, I'll be facing some prissy country club Republican lady with shit for brains. The worst thing she ever did was wear white after Labor Day."

Jeffrey said, "There are a lot of us who've gotten together to try to turn this town and county around. We've got a plan to restore downtown to its historic look, to attract tourism, attract new business, to stop the spread of the commercial strip through zoning, to get Amtrak to reinstate passenger service, to get a

Spencerville exit put on the interstate." Jeffrey went on, outlining the plans to revive Spencerville and Spencer County.

Keith listened, then commented, "So you've scaled back on your plans to overthrow the United States government?"

Jeffrey smiled and replied, "Think globally, act locally. That's the nineties."

"Well," Keith observed, "it sounds like good old-fashioned midwestern boosterism. You remember that word?"

"Sure," Jeffrey said. "But this goes beyond that. We're also interested in ecology, clean government, health care, and other quality-of-life issues that go beyond business and commerce."

"Good. Me, too. In fact, I see what you see here, and I had the same thoughts. But don't assume everyone shares your vision." Keith added, "I've been all over the world, guys, and if I learned one thing, it's that people get the kind of government and society they deserve."

Jeffrey said, "Don't be cynical. This is still a country where good people can make a difference."

"I hope so."

Gail said, "Will you two stop the philosophical debate? Here's the problem we face. The city and county governments have become lethargic, partly corrupt, and mostly stupid." She looked at Keith. "In fact, your ex-girlfriend's husband, Cliff Baxter, is at the core of most of these problems."

Keith did not reply.

Gail continued, "This son-of-a-bitch blackmails people. He's a fucking J. Edgar Hoover clone. The bastard has illegal files on people, including me. He showed me my file, the stupid shit, and I'm going to subpoena all his records now."

Keith looked at her and said, "Be careful with this guy."

They all sat in silence a moment, then Jeffrey said, "He's a bully, and, like all bullies, he's basically a coward."

Keith replied, "Even cowards can be dangerous when they're armed."

Jeffrey nodded. "Yes, but we're not frightened. I've faced armed soldiers with fixed bayonets, Keith."

"Maybe you faced me, Jeffrey. Were you in Philadelphia in the autumn of 1968?"

"No, and we weren't at Kent State when the soldiers fired, but we had friends who were there, and I'll tell you, I would have been there if I'd known what was going to happen."

Keith nodded. "Yeah, you probably would have. But that was a different time and maybe a better cause. Don't get killed over zoning ordinances."

Again, no one spoke for a while, and they drank the jug wine. The candles flickered in a soft breeze coming through the window, and Keith could smell the wildflowers and honeysuckle, an incredible medley of scents.

Gail asked Keith, "Do you know anything about him?"

"Who?"

"J. Edgar Baxter."

"No. I think I remember him from high school. But that's not what we call current intelligence."

"Well," said Jeffrey, "I remember him quite well. He hasn't changed much. Same asshole. The family has some money, but they're all short on brains and social skills. The Baxter kids were always in trouble—remember? The boys were bullies, and the girls were pregnant at the altar. In the jargon of small towns, 'There's bad blood in that family.'"

Keith didn't reply. Clearly, Jeffrey and Gail were not simply gossiping or complaining to him. They wanted to recruit him. He recognized the method.

Gail said, "He's a very jealous and possessive man. I'm talking about his marriage now. Annie, by the way, is still very attractive, which makes Mr. Baxter watch her like a hawk. From what I hear, she's the paragon of virtue, but he doesn't believe it. People on their street whom we know say he keeps their house under constant surveillance when he's away. A few weeks ago, there was some kind of firearm incident there at about five in the morning. He was home. The neighbors were told that it was an accident."

Keith said nothing, and his face revealed nothing except perhaps his well-practiced mixture of mild interest and a touch of skepticism whenever the monologue got into areas of hearsay. He had a feeling he was sitting in some European café again, getting a pitch about something or another.

Gail continued, "He's not a nice guy, but people in town have to deal with him. Even some of the men who work for him find him brutish and offensive. Yet, in some perverse way, he can be charming. He's from the old school and tips his hat to the ladies, calls women 'ma'am,' and he's outwardly respectful to the town fathers, clergymen, and so forth. He's even been known to pinch babies and help old ladies across the street." Gail smiled, then added, "But he also pinches waitresses' butts and helps damsels in distress out of their clothes. This guy's got a wild weasel." Gail poured the last of the jug wine into their glasses.

Keith listened to the night birds and locusts. Somehow none of this was news to him, though actually hearing it made a difference. Somewhere in the back of his mind, the place where the old-learned morality resided, was the thought that he should not be contemplating breaking up a marriage, a home, a family. He'd been involved in a lot of situations over the years that might be considered somewhat indelicate, maybe even gross and shameless, but that was then and there. This was here and now. This was home. Yet, if he believed Gail and Jeffrey, the Baxters were not entirely happy, and Mr. Baxter was a sociopath, and Mrs. Baxter needed help. Maybe.

Jeffrey said to him, "Professionally, the guy is a Neanderthal. He has a serious problem with the kids in town. Yeah, a lot of the kids dress weird, wear their hair down to their shoulders, or shave their heads, and they blast their boom boxes in the park, and hang out and all that. We did some weird shit, too. But Baxter hassles them instead of helping them. His police force has no youth officer, no school outreach program. It only has patrol cars, cops, and a jail. The town's dying, but Baxter doesn't see it. He's into law and order and not much else."

Keith commented, "Law and order is his job."

"Yeah," agreed Jeffrey, "but I'll tell you something else—he's not real good at that either. We still have low crime here, but it's starting to get worse. There are drugs now—not good grass, but hard stuff—and Baxter doesn't have a clue about where it's coming from, who's selling it, or who's buying. The nature of crimes and criminals has changed, and Baxter hasn't. We have more domestic violence, we had a few car-jackings, we had two rapes so far this year, and we had a gang who came from Toledo by car and pulled off an armed robbery at the Merchants Bank. The state police caught them, not Baxter. Anyway, the state has offered the Spencerville force advanced training, but it's not mandated, so Baxter blew them off. He doesn't want anyone knowing how inept or corrupt he and his gestapo are."

Keith didn't respond. In fact, he'd been charitable enough to think that maybe Cliff Baxter was a tough but effective cop. A lousy human being but a good chief, dedicated to public safety. On the other hand, the incident in the supermarket parking lot and the police car drive-bys had already told him he was dealing with a corrupt police force.

Jeffrey went on, "Baxter blames drugs for this mini crime wave, and he's partly right. But he also blames the schools, parents, television, MTV, movies, music, video arcades, smut magazines, and all that. Okay, maybe some of this is true, but he doesn't see the relationship between crime and unemployment, and teenage boredom, and lack of opportunities, and lack of stimulation."

Keith commented, "Jeffrey, when has small-town America been any different? Maybe a tough police force is just what's needed. Look, maybe progressive solutions could work in the cities, but this is not Columbus or Cleveland, my friend. Here we need small-town solutions to small-town problems, and you guys need a reality check."

Gail said, "Okay, we're open to reality. We're not the wild-eyed idealogues we used to be. But the problem remains the same." She asked him, "Do you care?"

Keith thought a moment, then replied, "Yes, it's my hometown. I thought maybe things hadn't changed much, and I could find some peace and quiet here, but I see you two aren't going to let me go fishing."

Gail smiled and said. "Old revolutionaries don't fade away like old soldiers, Keith. They just find a new cause."

"So I see."

Gail continued, "We think Baxter is vulnerable, that he's developed some career problems which we want to exploit."

"Maybe he just needs counseling and sensitivity training. That's what progressives like yourselves offer criminals. Why not cops?"

Gail said to Keith, "I know you're baiting us, and you're good at it, but I also know you're an intelligent man. You know, or you're soon going to find out, that Cliff Baxter is beyond salvation, professionally, spiritually, or otherwise. Christ, *he* knows that. And he's getting nervous, like a trapped rat, and that makes him more dangerous."

Keith nodded and thought, *And certainly not a better husband.*

Gail said, "We think it's time to get him fired. We need a moral victory, something to galvanize public opinion." She added, "Keith, with your background—"

He interrupted, "You don't know my background. Whatever I told you doesn't leave this house."

Gail nodded. "All right. With your intelligence, wit, and charm, you can help us. We'd like you to join us."

"Who is us?"

"Just a group of reformers."

"Do I have to become a Democrat?"

Jeffrey laughed. "God, no. We have no party affiliation. We have people from all parties and all classes. We have ministers, businesspeople, schoolteachers, farmers, housewives—hell, we've got most of Annie's family with us."

"Is that a fact? I wonder what Thanksgiving dinner is like at the Baxters'?"

Jeffrey said, "Like a lot of our supporters, they haven't gone public yet." Jeffrey asked, "Can we count on you?"

"Well..." In truth, Keith had his own grudge against Cliff Baxter, which was that he was married to Annie Baxter. Keith said, "Well...I'm not sure I'm staying around."

Jeffrey observed, "I had the impression you were."

"I'm not sure."

Gail said, "We're not asking you to meet him on Main Street at high noon for a duel. Just say you're in favor of getting rid of him."

"Okay. In principle, I'm in favor of getting rid of any corrupt public official."

"Good. That's Cliff Baxter. There's a meeting next week, Thursday night, at St. James Church. You know it?"

"Yes, it's my old church. Why are you meeting outside of town?"

"People don't want to be seen at this meeting, Keith. You understand that."

"Indeed I do. But you may be overdoing the revolutionary melodrama. This is America. Use the damned town hall. That's your right."

"Can't. Not yet."

Keith wondered how much of this was the Porters trying to recapture the romance of revolution and how much was real anxiety and fear. Keith said, "I'll think about being there."

"Good. More pie? Tea?"

"No, thanks. Time to hit the road."

"It's early," Gail said. "None of us has shit to do tomorrow." She stood, and Keith thought she was going to clear the table, so he stood, too, and picked up his plate and glass.

Gail said, "Leave that. We're still pigs." She took his arm and led him into the living room.

Jeffrey followed, carrying a potpourri jar. He said, "The dinner was superb, the conversation stimulating, and now we retire into the drawing room for a post-prandial smoke."

Gail lit two incense lamps and two scented candles

in the dark room. Jeffrey sat cross-legged on the floor in front of the coffee table, and, by the light of one of the candles, he transferred the contents of the potpourri jar into rolling papers that he'd spread out on the low table.

Keith watched him in the candlelight, quick fingers and a flicking tongue, producing five nicely packed joints faster than an old farmer could roll a single cigarette.

Gail put a tape in the deck, *Sergeant Pepper's Lonely Hearts Club Band*, then sat on the floor with her back to an armchair.

Jeffrey lit a joint, took a toke, and passed it to Keith. Keith hesitated a moment, took a drag, then passed it across the coffee table to Gail.

The Beatles played, the candles flickered, the smell of incense and pot filled the air. It was 1968, sort of.

The first joint was now held with a pair of tweezers, then snuffed out, and the roach was put carefully in an ashtray for future use in the pipe that Keith noticed on the table. The second joint was lit and passed.

Keith recalled the protocols and rituals as if it were yesterday. No one said much, and what was said didn't make a whole lot of sense.

Gail, however, did say in the low, hushed tone associated with cannabis and candlelight, "She needs help."

Keith ignored this.

Gail added, as if to herself, "I understand how and why a woman stays in that kind of situation...I don't think he abuses her physically...but he's fucking with her head..."

Keith passed the joint to her. "Enough."

"Enough what?" She took a toke and said, "You, Mr. Landry, could solve your problem and our problem at the same time..." She exhaled. "...right?"

Keith had trouble forming his thoughts, but after

a few seconds, or a few minutes, he heard his voice say, "Gail Porter...I've butted heads with the best in the world...I've had enough experience with women to write the book on the subject...don't try to fuck with *my* head..." He thought this was what he wanted to say. It was close enough.

Gail seemed to ignore him and said, "I always liked her...I mean, we weren't big buddies, but I...she was kind of like...always had a smile, always doing some good deed...I mean, I could puke, you know...but deep down inside, I envied her...completely at peace with her man and her...like, uninvolvement with anything..."

"She became an antiwar something or other at Columbus."

"Really? Wow. That piss you off?"

Keith didn't reply, or thought he didn't. He couldn't tell any longer if he was thinking or speaking things.

The room seemed to be silent for a long time, then Gail said, "I mean, if you do nothing else here, Keith, if you do nothing else with your life after conquering the fucking world...get that woman away from him."

Keith tried to stand. "I think I'm leaving."

Jeffrey said, "No way, buddy. You're sleeping here. You can't even find the front door."

"No, I have to—"

Gail said, "Subject closed. All subjects closed. No more heavy shit. Get mellow, folks." She handed the joint to Jeffrey, then stood and changed the tape and began dancing to "Honky Tonk Woman."

Keith watched her in the flickering light. She was graceful, he thought, her thin body moving in good time to the music. The dance was not particularly erotic in and of itself, but it had been a long time since he'd been with a woman, and he felt a familiar stirring in his pants.

Jeffrey seemed indifferent to his wife's fugue and concentrated on the candle flame.

Keith turned away from Gail and helped Jeffrey look at the flame.

He didn't know how much time passed, but he was aware that the tape had changed again and was now playing "Sounds of Silence," and Jeffrey was declaring that this was the ultimate musical accompaniment to pot, then Keith was aware that Gail was sitting opposite him again, drawing on a joint.

She spoke, as if to herself, and said, "Hey, remember no bras, and see-through blouses, and nude swimming, and group sex, and no killer diseases, and no hang-ups, no Antioch rules of sexual conduct, and men and women who actually liked one another? Remember? I do." She added, "God, what has happened to us?"

No one seemed to know, so no one replied.

Keith's mind was not working very well, but he did remember better days, though perhaps his idea of better was different from Gail's or Jeffrey's. The point was, things were once better, and his heart suddenly ached with a sense of loss, a nostalgia and sentimentality partly induced by the cannabis, partly by the evening, and partly because it was true.

Gail did not offer herself to him, which was a relief, because he didn't know what he would have said or done if she had. The evening ended with him sleeping on the couch in his underwear with a quilt thrown over him, and the Porters upstairs, in their bed.

The incense burned out, the candles guttered and died, a Simon and Garfunkel album ended, and Keith lay in the quiet dark.

At dawn, he rose, dressed, and left before the Porters awakened.

CHAPTER TWELVE

It was a few days after dinner with the Porters, a Friday night, and Keith Landry, reacting to some remembered behavior of farm life, decided to go into town.

He put on slacks and a sport shirt, got into his Blazer, and headed for Spencerville.

He'd seen no sign of Annie during the past few days, but that was not for lack of vigilance on his part. He'd been home, he'd stayed within earshot of the phone, he'd checked his mailbox a few times a day, and he watched the cars that went by. In short, he'd reverted to a lovesick adolescent, and the feeling was not entirely unpleasant.

The day before, he'd seen a blue and white patrol car from Spencerville pass about noon, and that morning he'd seen a green and white county sheriff's car go by. The sheriff's car might have been a random thing, but the town police car was a long way from home.

In any case, he kept his Blazer out of sight, and he didn't know if they'd discovered his new automobile, unless, of course, they'd run his name through the Bureau of Motor Vehicles.

It was sort of a low-key cat-and-mouse game at

this point, but Keith knew it had the potential for confrontation.

He drove up Main Street, which was quieter than he'd remembered it on Friday nights. In those days, Friday was called market day, and there had been a huge farmer's market on the blocked-off street north of Courthouse Square. Now, everyone, including the farmers, bought most of their food in supermarkets, prepackaged.

The commercial strip outside of town probably got the majority of Friday night shoppers, Keith thought, but there were a few shops open downtown, and the bank was open late. Also open, with cars parked nearby, were Miller's Restaurant and the two taverns—John's Place and the Posthouse.

Keith pulled into a space near John's Place and got out of the Blazer. It was a warm Indian summer evening, and there were a few people on the sidewalk. He walked into the tavern.

If you want to know a town, Keith had learned, go to the best and the worst bar, preferably on a Friday or Saturday night. John's was obviously the latter.

The tavern was dark, noisy, smoky, smelled of stale beer, and was inhabited mostly by men dressed in jeans and T-shirts. The T-shirts, Keith noticed, advertised brand-name beers, John Deere tractors, and locally sponsored sports teams. A few T-shirts had interesting sayings such as, "Well-diggers do it deeper."

There were a few video games, a pinball machine, and in the center of the tavern was a billiards table. A jukebox played sad country-western songs. The bar had a few vacant stools, and Keith took one.

The bartender eyed him for a moment, making a professional evaluation that the newcomer posed no potential threat to the peace of John's Place, and asked Keith, "What can I get you?"

"Bud."

The bartender put a bottle in front of Keith and opened it. "Two bucks."

Keith put a ten on the bar. He got his change, but no glass, and drank from the bottle.

He looked around. There were a few young women, all of them escorted by men, but mostly this was a male domain. The TV above the bar broadcast the Yankees vs. Blue Jays in a tight pennant race, and the sportscaster competed with some country singer sobbing about his wife's infidelities.

The men ranged in age from early twenties to late fifties, mostly good-old-boys as likely to buy you a beer as split your head with a barstool, and meaning nothing personal by either. The women were dressed like the men—jeans, running shoes, and T-shirts—and they smoked and drank beer from bottles like the men. All in all, it was a happy and peaceful enough crowd at this hour, though Keith knew from experience it could get a little rough later.

He swiveled his stool and watched the billiards game awhile. He'd had little opportunity to hang out in any of the few taverns in town because he'd been drafted and was being shot at about the time he could legally vote or drink. Now you could be shot at and vote, but still had to wait until you were twenty-one before you could order a beer. In any case, he'd hit John's Place and the Posthouse once in a while when he was home on leave, and he recalled that a good number of the men at the bars were recent veterans with some stories to tell, and some, like him, were in uniform and never had to buy a drink. Now, he suspected, most of the men in John's Place hadn't been far from home, and there seemed to him a sort of restless boredom among them, and he thought they had the look of men who had never experienced any significant rite of passage into manhood.

He didn't recognize any of the men his own age, but one of them at the end of the bar kept looking at him, and Keith watched the guy out of the corner of his eye.

The man got off his stool and ambled down the bar, stopping directly in front of Keith. "I know you."

Keith looked at the man. He was tall, scrawny, had blond hair down to his shoulders, bad teeth, sallow skin, and sunken eyes. The long hair, the jeans and T-shirt, and the man's mannerisms and voice suggested a man in his twenties, but the face was much older.

He said in a loud, slurred voice, "I know who you are."

"Who am I?"

"Keith Landry."

A few of the men around them glanced their way, but otherwise seemed disinterested.

Keith looked at the man again, and realized that he did know him. He said, "Right, you're..."

"Come on, Keith. You know me."

Keith searched his memory, and a profusion of high school faces raced through his mind. Finally, he said, "Billy Marlon."

"Yeah! Hell, man, we was buddies." Marlon slapped Keith on the shoulder, then pumped his hand. "How the hell are ya?"

Keith thought perhaps he should have gone to the Posthouse instead. "Fine. How are you, Billy?"

"Just great! All fucked-up!"

"Buy you a beer?"

"Sure can."

Keith ordered two more Budweisers.

Billy sidled up next to him at the bar and leaned

close enough for Keith to smell the beer on him, and other odors. Billy said, "Hey, man, this is great."

"Sure is."

"Hey, you look great, man."

"Thanks."

"What the hell you doin' here?"

"Just visiting."

"Yeah? That's great, man. How long you been back?"

"A few weeks."

"No shit? Great to see you."

Obviously, Billy Marlon was happy to see him. Keith tried to recall what he knew of Billy, what they'd had in common, so he could carry his end of what promised to be a stupid conversation. Finally, it all came back to Keith as Billy jabbered away. Marlon had been on the football team with him, had played halfback, but not very well, and mostly sat on the bench cheering on the starting lineup. Marlon had been the sort of kid who wanted to be liked, and there was little not to like about him, objectively, but most people found him annoying. In fact, Keith still found him likable and annoying.

Marlon asked, "You get fucked-up in Vietnam?"

"Probably."

"Me, too. You was with the First Cav. Right?"

"Right."

"Yeah, I remember that. Your mom was worried sick. I told her you'd be okay. Hell, if a fuckup like me could survive, a guy like you would be okay."

"Thanks." Keith recalled that Billy had been drafted right out of high school. Keith had availed himself of the college draft deferment, which in retrospect was a monumental government blunder. The rich, the bright, the privileged, and anyone else who could get into college had four good years of protesting the war or ignoring it, while the poor and stupid got killed and maimed. But instead of the war ending in a reasonably acceptable time frame, it went on, and the college graduates, like himself, started getting called. By the time he got to Vietnam, Billy Marlon and most of his high school class were already out of the Army or dead.

Billy said, "I was with the Twenty-fifth Division—Tropical Lightning. We kicked some gook ass over there."

"Good." But not enough gook ass to end the damned thing.

"You saw some shit, too."

"Yes, I did." Apparently, Billy had been following Keith's Army career while probably regaling Spencerville with his own exploits.

"You kill anybody?" Billy asked. "I mean up close."

"I think so."

"It's a kick."

"No, it's not."

Billy thought a minute, then nodded. "No, it's... but it's hard to forget it."

"Try."

"I can't, man. You know? I still can't."

Keith looked at his former classmate. Clearly, Billy Marlon had degenerated. Keith asked, "What have you been up to?"

"Oh, shit, not too much. Married twice, divorced twice. Got kids from the first marriage. They's all growed now and live in Fort Wayne. They went there when they was young with their mother. She married some, like, asshole, you know, and I never really seen the kids. Second wife...she moved away." He went on, relating a predictably barren life to Keith, who was not surprised by any of it, except when Billy said, "Shit, I wish I could do it over again."

"Yeah, well, everybody feels a little of that. But maybe it's time to go on."

"Yeah. I keep meaning to go on."

"Where you working?"

"No place. I do odd jobs. Do some hunting and fishing. I live a mile outside of town, west of here, got a whole farmhouse to myself. All I got to do is look after the place. Retired people living with one of their kids in California. Cowley. You know them?"

"Sounds familiar."

"They got the place sold now, so I got to find something else by November."

"Why don't you check yourself into a veterans' hospital?"

"Why? I ain't sick."

"You don't look well."

"Ah, I've been pounding the suds too much since I learned I got to move. I get real nervous when I don't have no place to live. I'll be okay."

"Good."

"Where you stayin'?"

"My folks' place."

"Yeah? Hey, if you need company, I can pay a little rent, do the chores, put some game on the table."

"I'll be gone by November. But I'll see what I can do for you before I leave."

"Hey, thanks. But I'll be okay."

Keith ordered two more beers.

Billy inquired, "What're you doin' for a living?"

"Retired."

"Yeah? From what?"

"Government."

"No shit. Hey, you seen anybody since you been back?"

"No. Well, I saw Jeffrey Porter. Remember him?"

"Hell, yeah. I seen him a few times. He don't have much to say."

They spoke a while longer, and it was obvious to Keith that Billy was too drunk. Keith looked at his watch and said, "Hey, I've got to run." He put a twenty on the bar and said to the bartender, "Give my friend one more, then maybe he should head home."

The bartender pushed the twenty back to Keith and said, "He's cut off right now."

Billy made a whining sound. "Aw, come on, Al. Man wants to buy me a drink."

"Finish what you got and be off."

Keith left the twenty on the bar and said to Billy, "Take that and go home. I'll stop by one day before I leave."

"Hey, great, man. See ya." Billy watched him as he left, and waved. "Great to see ya, Keith."

Keith went out into the fresh air. The Posthouse was on the other side of Courthouse Square, and Keith crossed the street and began walking through the park.

There were a few people on the benches, sitting under the ornate lampposts, a few couples strolling. Keith saw an empty bench and sat a moment. In front of him was the Civil War monument, a huge bronze statue of a Union soldier with musket, and on the granite base of the statue were the names of Spencer County's Civil War dead, hundreds of them.

From where he sat, by the light of the lampposts, he could make out the other war memorials, which he knew well, beginning with an historical marker relating to the Indian Wars, proceeding to the Mexican War, and on and on, war by war, to the Vietnam War, which was only a simple bronze plaque inscribed with the names of the dead. It was good, he thought, that small towns remembered, but it did not escape him that the monuments seemed to diminish in size and grandeur after the Civil War, as if the townspeople were getting frustrated with the whole business.

It was a pleasant night, and he sat awhile. The choices of things to do in a small town on a Friday night were somewhat limited, and he smiled to himself, recalling evenings in London, Rome, Paris, Washington, and elsewhere. He wondered if he could really live here again. He could, he thought. He could get back into a simple life if he had company.

He looked around and saw the lighted truck of the ice cream vendor and a group of people standing around. It had occurred to him that if he came into town on a Friday night, he might see Annie. Did the Baxters go out to dinner? Did they shop together on a Friday night? He had no idea.

He remembered the summer nights when he and Annie Prentis sat in this park and talked for hours. He recalled especially the summer before college, before the war, before the Kennedy assassination, before drugs, before there was a world outside of Spencer County, when he and his country were still young and full of hope, and a guy married the girl next door and went to the in-laws for Sunday dinner.

This park, he remembered, had been filled with his friends; the girls wore dresses, the boys wore short hair. Newly invented transistor radios played Peter, Paul and Mary, Joan Baez, Dion, and Elvis, and the volume was low.

The preferred smoke was Newport menthols, not grass, and Coke was drunk, not snorted. The couples held hands, but if you got caught necking behind the bushes, you got a quick trip to the police station across the street and a tongue-lashing from the old police magistrate on duty.

The world was about to explode, and there were inklings of it, but no one could have predicted what finally happened. The summer of '63, Keith reflected,

had been called the last summer of American innocence, and certainly it had been *his* last summer of
innocence, when he lost his virginity in Annie Prentis's
bedroom.

He had never seen a naked woman before Annie,
not even in pictures or in the movies. *Playboy* existed
in 1963, but not in Spencer County, and risqué movies
were censored before they got to Spencerville. Thus,
he had no idea what a naked woman, let alone a vagina,
looked like. He smiled to himself and recalled their first
fumbled attempt to consummate the act. She had been
as inexperienced as he, but her instincts were better. He
had gotten the condom, which he'd carried in his wallet for no good reason, from an older boy who had gotten a box of them in Toledo, and it had cost Keith two
dollars for one, a fortune in those days. He thought, *If
we had known what lay ahead, we would have tried to
keep that summer going forever.*

Keith stood and began walking. A boom box blasted
somewhere, rap music, a few teenage boys sat in a circle
on the grass playing handheld electronic games, and a
few old men sat on the benches. A young couple lay side
by side on the lawn, grappling in fully clothed frustration.

Keith thought back to that summer, then to the
autumn of that year. He and Annie had become per-
fectly matched lovers, reveling in their experimenta-
tions, their discoveries, their adolescent enthusiasm
and stamina. There were no books on the subject, no
X-rated videotapes, no guide to the mysteries of sex,
but in some incredible instinctual way, they'd discovered oral sex, the sixty-nine position, the erogenous
zones, erotic undressing, a dozen different positions,
dirty talk, and playacting. He had no idea where all that
came from, and they would sometimes jokingly accuse
the other of having long sexual histories, or watching

illegal blue movies made in Europe in those days, or of getting information from their friends. In reality, they were both virgins, both clueless, but they were inquisitive and surprisingly uninhibited.

They had made love every chance they had, every place they could, and kept it secret, as lovers had to do in those days.

Away at college, they could be more open, but the dorms were segregated by sex and tightly policed. The motels refused that sort of trade, so, for two years, they made love in an apartment off campus that belonged to married friends. Eventually, Annie rented a single room above a hardware store, though they still lived in their dorms.

Keith wondered again why they hadn't married then. Perhaps, he thought, they hadn't wanted to destroy the romance, the mystique, the taste of the forbidden fruit. And there seemed to be no rush, no need, no insecurities, while they were in the cloistered world of college.

But then came graduation and the draft notice. Half the men he'd known then regarded the draft notice not as a call to arms, but as a call to the altar. It didn't get you out of the Army, but it made life easier if you were a married soldier. You got to live off post after training, got extra pay, and being married reduced your chances of being sent into the meat grinder.

Yet they never really discussed marriage. *Ultimately,* he thought, *we had different dreams. She liked campus life. I was itching for adventure.*

They had been soulmates, friends, and lovers. They'd shared thoughts, feelings, and emotions. They'd shared their money, their cars, and their lives for over six years. But for all their openness with each other, neither could broach the subject of the future, neither wanted to hurt the other, so in the end, he'd leaned over her bed, kissed her, and left.

Keith was nearly at the other side of the park, and he could see the Posthouse across the street.

He heard loud voices to his left and turned. About thirty feet up an intersecting path stood two uniformed policemen. They were shouting at a man lying on a park bench, and one of them was tapping the man on the soles of his shoes with his nightstick. "Get up! Stand! Stand!"

The man stood unsteadily, and, in the illumination of a postlight, Keith saw that it was Billy Marlon.

One of the cops said, "I told you not to sleep here."

The other cop shouted, "You're a goddamned drunk! I'm sick of seeing you here! You're a bum!"

Keith wanted to tell the young men that Billy Marlon was an ex-combat vet, a onetime football player for Spencerville, a father, a man. But he stood there and waited to see if the incident was finished.

But it wasn't. Both cops had Billy backed up against a tree now, and they were face-to-face with him, hurling verbal abuse at the man. "We told you to stay out of town! Nobody wants to see you here! You don't listen real good! Do you?" and so on.

Billy stood with his back to the tree, then suddenly shouted, "Leave me alone! I'm not bothering nobody! Leave me alone!"

One of the cops raised his nightstick, and Billy covered his face and head with his hands. Keith stepped forward, but the cop only hit the tree above Billy's head. Both cops laughed. One of them said to him, "Tell us again what you're going to do to Chief Baxter. Come on, Rambo, tell us." They laughed again.

Billy seemed less frightened now and looked at both of them. He said, "I'm going to kill him. I'm a combat vet, and I'm going to kill him. You tell him I'm going to kill him someday. Tell him!"

"Why? Tell us why."

"Because...because..."

"Come on. Because he fucked your wife. Right? Chief Baxter fucked your wife."

Billy suddenly sank to his knees and put his hands over his face. He began sobbing. "Tell him to stay away from my wife. Tell him to stop. Stay away from my wife. Stop, stop..."

The men laughed. One of them said, "Get up. We're taking you in again."

But Billy had curled up into a ball on the ground and was crying.

One of the cops grabbed him by his long hair. "Get up."

Keith walked up to them and said, "Leave him alone."

They turned and faced him. One of them said, very coolly and professionally, "Please move away, sir. We have the situation under control."

"No, you don't. You're harassing this man. Leave him alone."

"Sir, I'll have to ask you—"

The other cop poked his partner and said, "Hey, that's..." He whispered in his partner's ear, and they both looked at Keith. The first cop stepped up to Keith and said, "If you don't leave, I'm going to arrest you for obstructing justice."

"I haven't seen any justice here. If you arrest me or him, I'll tell the district attorney exactly what I saw and heard here, and I'll press charges against both of you."

The two policemen and Keith stared at one another for a long minute. Finally, one of them said to him, "Who's gonna believe you?"

"We'll find out."

The other cop said, "Are you threatening us?"

Keith ignored them and went over to Billy. He helped the man to his feet, got Billy's arm around his shoulder, and began walking him toward the street.

One of the cops yelled to Keith, "You're gonna pay for tonight, Mister. You are definitely going to pay."

Keith got Billy on the sidewalk and walked him around the park toward the car.

Billy was staggering, but Keith kept him moving.

Finally, Billy said, "Hey, what's happening? Where we going?"

"Home."

"Yeah, okay, not so fast." He broke free of Keith and navigated the sidewalk on his own. Keith walked behind him, ready to catch him if he fell. Billy was mumbling to himself, "Goddamn cops always bustin' my balls. Hell, I never did no harm to nobody...they got it in for me...he fucks my wife, then—"

"Quiet down."

A few people on the sidewalk looked and gave them a wide berth.

"That son-of-a-bitch...then he laughed at me...he said she was a lousy lay, and he was finished with her..."

Keith said, "Shut up! Damn it, shut up!" He grabbed Billy by the arm and propelled him up the street and pushed him into the Blazer.

Keith drove out of town and headed west. "Where is this place? Where do you live?"

Billy was slumped in the front seat, his head lolling from side to side. "Route 8...oh. I'm sick."

Keith rolled down the passenger-side window and pushed Billy's head out. "Get sick outside."

Billy made a gagging sound but couldn't get it out. "Oh...stop the car..."

Keith found the old Cowley farm, which had the

family name painted on the barn. He pulled up to the dark farmhouse and parked behind an old blue pickup truck, then wrestled Billy out of the car and onto the front porch. The front door was unlocked, as Keith suspected it would be, and he half carried Billy inside, found the living room in the dark, and threw Billy on the couch. He walked away, then came back, arranged him a little more comfortably and pulled off his shoes, then turned to leave again.

Billy called out, "Keith. Hey, Keith."

Keith turned. "Yeah?"

"Great to see you, man. Hey, it's great…"

Keith put his face in front of Billy's and said in a slow, distinct tone, "Get your act together, soldier."

Billy's eyes opened wide, and, in a moment of forced clarity, responded, "Yes, sir."

Keith walked to the front door, and, as he left, he heard Billy call out, "Hey, man, I owe you one."

Keith got in his Blazer and pulled onto the county road. Parked on the shoulder was a Spencerville police car. Keith kept going, waiting for the headlights to start following him, but they didn't, and he wondered if the police were going to finish their business with Billy. He considered turning around, but figured he'd pushed his luck enough for one night.

About halfway back to his house, Keith picked up another Spencerville police car that followed him with its bright lights on.

Keith approached the turnoff for his house and stopped. The police car stopped a few feet behind him. Keith sat. The cops sat. They all sat for five minutes, then Keith pulled into his driveway, and the cop car continued down the road.

Obviously, the game was heating up. He didn't bother to put the Blazer behind the house, but parked it near the porch and went inside through the front door.

He went directly upstairs and took his 9mm Glock from the cabinet, loaded it, and put it on his night table.

He got undressed and went to bed. The adrenaline was still flowing, and he had trouble getting to sleep, but finally entered a state of half-sleep that he'd learned in Vietnam and perfected in other places; his body was at rest, but all his senses were placed on a moment's notice.

His mind took off in directions that he wouldn't have allowed if he'd been in full control of his thought processes. What his mind was telling him now was that home had become the last battlefield, as he always knew it would be if he ever returned. That was the great subconscious secret he had been keeping from himself all these years. His memories of Cliff Baxter were not as dim as he'd indicated to the Porters, nor as fleeting as he'd told himself. In fact, he remembered the bullying bastard very well, remembered that Cliff Baxter had jostled him more than once, recalled Baxter's heckling from the stands during football games, and very clearly remembered Cliff Baxter eyeing Annie Prentis in the halls, at school dances, at the swimming pool, and he recalled the incident at an autumn hayride when Baxter put his hand on Annie's butt to help her up into the hay wagon.

He should have done something about it then, but Annie seemed almost unaware of Cliff Baxter, and Keith knew that the best way to enrage a person like Baxter was to pretend he didn't exist. And, in fact, Baxter's rage grew month by month, and Keith could see it. But Cliff Baxter was smart enough not to step over the line. Eventually, he would have, of course, but June came, Keith and Annie graduated, and they were off to college.

Keith never knew if Baxter's interest in Annie was genuine or just another way to annoy Keith, whom Cliff Baxter seemed to hate for no reason at all. And when Keith had heard that Cliff Baxter and Annie Prentis had married, he was not so much angry at Annie or Cliff Baxter as he was shocked by the news. It had seemed to him that heaven and hell had changed places, that everything he believed about human nature had been wrong. But as the years passed, he came to understand the dynamics between men and women a little better, and he thought he understood the processes that had brought Cliff Baxter and Annie Prentis together.

And yet, Keith wondered if things would have been different if he'd called Baxter out, if he'd simply beaten the hell out of the class bully, which he was physically capable of doing. He thought about doing now what he'd failed to do in high school. But if he chose a confrontation, then a fistfight in the schoolyard wasn't going to settle it this time.

At about midnight, the phone rang, but there was no one there. A little while later, someone was leaning on his car horn out on the road. The phone rang a few more times, and Keith took it off the hook.

The rest of the night was quiet, and he got a few hours of sleep.

At dawn, he called the Spencerville police, identified himself, and asked to speak to Cliff Baxter.

The desk officer seemed a little taken aback, then replied, "He's not here."

"Then take a message. Tell him that Keith Landry would like to meet with him."

"Yeah? Where and when?"

"Tonight, eight P.M., behind the high school."

"Where?"

"You heard me. Tell him to come alone."

"I'll tell him."

Keith hung up. "Better late than never."

CHAPTER THIRTEEN

Keith Landry shut off his headlights and pulled the Blazer into the parking lot behind the high school on the outskirts of town. The blacktop lot ran up to the back of the old brick school where bike racks, basketball courts, and equipment sheds stood. Keith saw that mercury vapor lights illuminated the area, but otherwise nothing much had changed since he and his friends used to meet behind the school on summer nights.

He stopped near one of the basketball nets, shut off the ignition, then climbed out of the Blazer. He put his Glock semiautomatic on the hood, took off his shirt, and threw it over the pistol.

Keith took a basketball out of the rear compartment, and, by the light of the mercury vapor lamps, he began shooting baskets, layups and jump shots, and the sound of the basketball echoed off the building in the quiet night air.

He dribbled up to the net, faked a pass, then jumped and put the ball through the hoop.

As he worked up a sweat, he reflected on the other game he'd come here to play, and it occurred to him that this was not a particularly smart move. He'd lost his temper and had thrown out a childish challenge. "Meet me behind the high school, punk." Sounded good. But given the circumstances, this could turn out to be a fatal mistake. He knew he could handle the class bully with no problem, but Baxter might not come alone as instructed.

Keith hadn't brought his M-16 rifle or his bullet-proof vest, wanting to be evenly matched with Baxter. But there was no way of knowing what Baxter would show up with. In truth, it was possible that a half dozen police cars with a dozen men would surround him, and if Baxter gave the order to fire, it wouldn't matter what Keith was wearing or carrying. And Keith had no doubt that Chief Baxter would have a plausible legal scenario worked out for the death of Keith Landry.

Keith took a short break and looked at his watch. It was seven forty-five P.M. He tried to make an informed guess as to Baxter's response to the challenge. If it was true that the boy is father to the man, then Baxter would come, but not alone. However, the picture painted by the Porters was of an egotistical and conceited personality who might very well underestimate his enemy; the type of man who'd like to saunter into the station house with the news, "I just killed a bad guy out at the high school. Send a meat wagon."

He continued playing his solo game as the sky got darker. He decided that if Baxter did come alone, Baxter might never return to the station house. Keith had had a few homicidal rages in his professional career, and he was surprised at how badly he wanted to kill Cliff Baxter. No doubt this had been building in him a long time and had festered inside his soul.

Keith glanced at his watch. It was eight P.M. He looked toward the school, then at the open playing fields and adjoining streets, but didn't see any head-lights or movement. He did a series of layup shots.

It occurred to Keith that Baxter's men knew, more or less, what the problem was between the chief and this guy Landry, and knew that Landry had said for Baxter to come alone. So what was Baxter going to tell his men? That Landry was bothering Mrs. Baxter, but he didn't want to meet Landry alone? In the world of male macho, this was about as sissy a thing as a guy could do. Keith realized that consciously or unconsciously, he'd put Baxter in a situation where he couldn't ask for help without looking like a total wimp, so he had to come alone, or not come at all and live with the consequences of his cowardice.

At five after eight, Landry knew that, by the unwrit-ten rules of this game, he could leave. But he stayed, shooting baskets, dribbling across the court, but never getting too far from where the Glock sat on the hood of the Blazer. At ten after eight, he was satisfied that he'd lived up to his end of the dare.

As he walked toward his car, headlight beams appeared from around the side of the school, then a vehicle came around slowly and turned toward him, catching him in the beams.

Keith bounced the basketball casually and contin-ued toward the Blazer.

The car, which he could now see was a police vehi-cle, stopped about fifty feet from him, the headlights still aimed directly at him.

The passenger door of the car opened, and a fig-ure stepped out. Keith couldn't make him out in the glare, but he looked taller and leaner than Cliff Bax-ter. Keith put the basketball down, then took his shirt off the hood of the Blazer, and with it, the pis-tol. He wiped his sweaty face with his shirt and got his hand around the pistol grip and his finger on the trigger.

The man took a few steps toward him, then called out, "Keith Landry?"

Although Keith hadn't heard Cliff Baxter's voice in nearly three decades, he knew this was not him. He replied, "Who's asking?"

"Officer Schenley, Spencerville police." The man continued on toward Keith.

"Who else is in the car?"

"My partner."

"Where's Baxter?"

"He couldn't come." Schenley was about ten feet away now, and Keith saw he was holding something in his hand, but it wasn't a pistol.

Schenley stopped about five feet from him and asked, "You alone?"

"Maybe. Where's your boss? Looking for his balls?"

Schenley laughed, then said, "Hey, he wanted to come, but he couldn't."

"Why not?"

Schenley held out the thing that was in his right hand, which turned out to be a folded newspaper.

Keith said, "Why do I want that?"

"There's a story in here you should read."

"Read it to me."

Schenley shrugged. "Okay." He unhooked his flashlight from his belt and trained it on the newspaper. He said, "This here is the social column...here it is..." He read, "'At the Elks Lodge this Saturday evening, Chief of Police Cliff Baxter will be honored by the mayor and city council in recognition of his fifteen years as police chief of Spencerville. Mrs. Baxter, the former Annie Prentis, will join Chief Baxter's friends and coworkers in relating interesting as well as amusing incidents of the chief's career.'" Schenley snapped off the flashlight. "Okay? He would have been here if he could."

Keith replied, "He knew about his party long ago. He could have rescheduled our meeting."

"Hey, don't push it, fella. The man's got obligations. Don't you got nothing better to do on a Saturday night?"

"I can't think of anything better than clocking your boss."

The patrolman laughed. "Yeah? Now, why would you want to do something stupid like that?"

"You tell me. Man-to-man, Schenley."

Schenley grinned. "Well...word is that you and Mrs. Baxter used to be an item."

"Maybe. Do you think that would make the chief angry?"

"Probably."

"Do you think he'll get over it?"

The patrolman laughed again, then said, "Hey, you know how guys are."

"I sure do. Do me a favor, Schenley. Tell the chief that the next time I make an appointment with him, he should notify me in advance when he knows he can't make it."

"I guess he wanted to see if you'd come."

"I already figured that out. He doesn't have to wonder about that. I'm here, and I'll be here, or anyplace he wants to meet me, anytime. His turn to ask."

"You're a cool customer. I'll give you some advice. Don't mess with this guy."

"I'll give you, Baxter, and the rest of you guys some advice—back off. I'm tired of your bullshit."

"I'll pass it on."

Keith looked at Schenley. He seemed a little less belligerent than the two guys in the park. In fact, Schenley seemed almost embarrassed by this whole thing. Keith said, "Don't get involved in the boss's personal squabbles." Keith put his left hand over his shirt, which still covered the Glock, pulled back on the slide and released it, cocking the automatic with a loud metallic noise that was unmistakable. He said, "It's not worth it."

Schenley's eyes focused on the shirt draped over Keith's right hand, and he seemed to stare at it a long time, then looked up at Keith. "Take it easy."

"Take a walk."

Schenley turned slowly and walked back to the car. Keith picked up the basketball and got into the Blazer. He kept an eye on the police car as it turned and went back around the school.

Keith drove across the playing fields and came out onto a road that bordered the school property. He turned toward town and drove past the Elks Lodge, noting that the parking lot was filled, then turned out into the country and headed for home.

"So, Mrs. Baxter will tell amusing stories about her husband. Maybe she can tell them about his wild weasel."

He got a little better control of his emotions and said, "Well, what do you expect in a social column?" He couldn't believe he felt a tinge of jealousy. "Of course she has an official life as the wife of a leading citizen." He remembered again how she'd looked at him on the street when they spoke. "Right. The wives of important men and politicians stand by their man and smile even when the guy is an adulterer, coward, and totally corrupt. Comes with the territory."

He discarded this subject and thought about what had just happened. Obviously, Cliff Baxter felt it important that he show Keith Landry why he hadn't come. Baxter cared what Landry thought of him. This

was nothing new; the class bully was uniquely inse-
cure, which was why he persecuted and belittled people
around him while puffing himself up.

And then there were Baxter's own men, such as
Officer Schenley. They knew something, and they
wanted to see how the boss was going to deal with it.
Keith suspected that unless they were corrupt to the
core, they secretly hated their chief. But they also feared
him, and, unless and until somebody bigger and bad-
der came along to deal with the chief, they were going
to follow orders. Loyalty toward a bad leader was con-
ditional, but you couldn't count on the troops mutiny-
ing or running away. Men were profoundly stupid and
sheeplike in the face of rank and authority, especially
soldiers, cops, and men in government service. That's
what had almost happened to him in Washington.

Keith saw the porch lights of his house ahead and
turned into the dark driveway. Well, he thought,
tonight was a draw. But somewhere down the road, one
of them was going to score a point, and as far as Keith
was concerned, the game was already in sudden-death
overtime.

CHAPTER FOURTEEN

The next several days passed uneventfully, despite the schoolyard incident. No police cars passed by, the phone didn't ring in the middle of the night, Baxter did not call to reschedule their showdown, and all was quiet. This was meant to be unnerving, the calm before the storm. But Keith was not unnerved.

At seven o'clock one morning, Keith walked across the road to the Jenkins house and found the family at breakfast, where he knew they'd be at that hour. Seated at the kitchen table were Martin and Sue Jenkins, a couple in their late thirties, and a teenage boy and girl, Martin Jr. and Sandra, both in high school.

Sue invited Keith to have breakfast, but he said coffee would be fine. They talked about the weather, which was definitely cool now, the coming harvest, the possibility of rain, and the *Farmer's Almanac* prediction of a harsh winter. Sue thought the almanac was idiotic, but Martin put great faith in it.

The two kids excused themselves to do their chores before school and left.

Keith said to the Jenkinses, "I know you've got chores, too, so I won't be long."

"What can we do for you?" Martin asked.

"Well, I just wanted to let you know about that horn honking a few nights back."

"Heard it. Saw it."

"I got into a little scrape with the Spencerville police, and they were doing some payback."

Martin nodded.

Sue said, "They have no business out here. I called them that night, but the desk sergeant said he didn't know anything about it, so I called Don Finney, the sheriff, and he said he'd check it out. He didn't call back, so I called him again, and he said nobody at police headquarters knew anything about it."

Martin added, "We were going to call you and see if you knew anything, but I figured you didn't."

"Well, as I said, they got themselves riled up about something."

The Jenkinses didn't ask what, nor would they ever ask, but Sue added, "Don is some sort of kin to Cliff Baxter, and they're two peas in a pod, as far as I'm concerned."

Keith said, "I'll try to see that it doesn't happen again."

"Not your fault," Sue said. She added, "Those people are getting out of control. Citizens ought to do something about it."

"Probably. Hey, the corn looks good."

"Real good," Martin agreed. "Good all over the damned state. Gonna be a glut again. Lucky to get two dollars a bushel."

And that, in a nutshell, Keith thought, was the problem with farming. Supply always outstripped demand and prices fell. When he was a boy, about ten percent of the American population were farmers. Now it was about two percent, and farmers were a rare species. Yet production kept rising. It was sort of a miracle, but if you had four hundred acres, like the Jenkinses and most family farms did, your overhead ate up your sales. In a bumper year when the prices were down, you broke even, and in a bad crop year when the prices were up, the yield was down, and you broke even. It was the kind of job you had to save up for. Keith said, "Sometimes I think I'd like to give farming a try."

Sue laughed, and nothing more had to be said.

Keith asked, "Do you want to sell or rent one of your horses?"

Martin replied, "Never thought about it. You need a horse?"

I think I'd like to ride. Pass the time."

"Hell, you don't want to own one of them things. They're more trouble than a hay baler. You just take one out and ride it when you want. The kids only ride on weekends and holidays."

"Thanks, but I'd like to pay you."

"Hell, no, they need the exercise. Do 'em good. Just water 'em and wipe 'em off after you ride them, maybe give them some feed. The gray gelding is gentle, but the young mare's a bitch." He laughed. "Same around here."

She commented, "If I see you looking at that postwoman again, you *will* be a gelding."

On that note, Keith stood and said, "Thanks for the coffee. Mind if I take one of them now?"

"Go right ahead. Gelding's name is Willy, mare is Hilly. Hilly and Willy. Kids named 'em."

Keith went out to the barn and found the stable door. Inside, the two horses stood in their stalls, feeding. He opened both stalls, and the horses wandered out. Keith slapped them both on the flanks, and they ran out into the paddock.

He went out and watched them awhile. The gelding

was sort of listless, but the young mare had a lot of spirit.

He found a bridle in the tack room and approached the mare, getting the bridle on her, then tied her to the fence post while he got a blanket and saddle. He saddled her up and walked her out the gate. Keith mounted and rode toward his farm, across the road, and out toward a wooded area that ran along a creek between his farm and the one to the west.

He got into the trees and rode down to the creek, which was nearly dry. He headed south through the creek bed, following it downstream toward Reeves Pond.

It was quiet except for the flowing water and a few birds. This was nice. His father never kept horses, and most farmers didn't, because they cost money and had no practical use. Now what extra money a farmer had for fun went into snowmobiles and road bikes, noisy things that went too fast for thinking and looking. Keith liked the feel of the animal beneath him, its warmth and living movement, and its occasional snort and whinny, and they smelled better than exhaust smoke.

He and Annie had borrowed horses now and then and ridden to secluded spots where they could make love. They'd joked that the only place they hadn't done it was on horseback, and Keith wondered if that was possible.

He gave the horse its lead, and it seemed content to follow the creek with a good gait.

Any thought he'd had about spending the rest of his life here, he realized, wasn't possible as long as Baxter was around. He'd let Baxter bait him, and he'd risen to the bait. This was bad strategy.

He reflected on his objective, which was not to engage Cliff Baxter in a contest, but to engage Mrs. Baxter in conversation. If nothing else, he'd like to speak to her one more time, for an hour or two, and resolve whatever issues remained between them. They'd never done that in their letters, and Keith felt he couldn't get on with his life until he understood clearly how and why they'd parted.

The next item on that agenda, of course, would be to see if they wanted to get back together. He thought she did, he thought he did.

Cliff Baxter obviously was an impediment to that, but it might be better for all concerned if Keith simply went around him rather than take him on. This was what he'd advise a young intelligence man on assignment in a dangerous environment.

The creek widened, and the trees thinned out, and within a few minutes Keith came to the big pond. No one was swimming or fishing, and it looked deserted. He used to come here a lot in the summer with his friends, to sail toy boats, to fish and swim, and in the winter people would build bonfires on the shore and skate or go ice fishing.

He reined the horse to the left and began riding along the muddy shoreline.

If this were actually a mission in a foreign country, he thought, it would be relatively easy to run off with the enemy's prize possession. But this was not exactly the same as escaping a foreign country with a codebook or a defector. No, there was another dimension to this problem.

Annie. This was not an intelligence operation, it was old-fashioned wife-stealing, not much different from what tribes and clans did in the past. But in this society, you first made sure the wife wanted to go with you.

It occurred to him that neither he nor Annie, separate or apart, could have Cliff Baxter on their trail for the rest of their lives.

Another option, of course, was to pack up, get in his car, and get as far away from here as he could. But he kept thinking of Annie standing there on the sidewalk, tears in her eyes, and all those letters over the years and the ache he still felt in his heart. "Can't leave, can't stay..." And he couldn't even declare a truce, because Cliff Baxter would just take that as a sign of weakness and step up the pressure.

Keith came around the far end of the lake and started back along the opposite shore.

Maybe, he thought, Cliff Baxter *could* be reasoned with. The three of them should sit down, have a beer, and talk it out in a civilized manner. "*That* is the answer to the problem. Right." No ugly scenes, no bloodshed, no rescues or abductions. "Mr. Baxter, your wife and I love each other and always have. She doesn't care for you. So be a good fellow and wish us well. The divorce papers are in the mail. Thank you, Cliff. Shake?"

Cliff Baxter, of course, would go for his gun. But if Cliff Baxter had the power of articulate speech, if he were in fact a civilized and clever man, he'd reply, "Mr. Landry, you *think* you love my wife, but more likely you're obsessed with a long-ago memory that has no reality now. Also, you're a little bored since being forcibly retired, and you're looking for adventure. Add to that the fact that you don't like me because of some childhood conflicts, and taking my wife is your way of getting back at me. This is not healthy, Mr. Landry, nor is it fair to Annie, who is going through a rough time now, what with empty-nest syndrome, the pressures of my job, and the realization that middle age has arrived. Annie and I are happy in our own way, and we look forward to my retirement and growing old together. Right, Annie?"

Keith didn't like what Baxter said at all, because it had a grain of truth in it.

In reality, there would be no such meeting, and Keith Landry, Cliff Baxter, and Annie Prentis Baxter would just stumble and fumble their ways through this, the way most people did, causing maximum damage and hurt along the way. And when it was all finished, there'd be remorse and deep scarring, and no happily-ever-after.

On that note, Keith entered the tree line and found the creek. He headed back to the farm, resolved now to pack his bags and leave home again, as he'd done twenty-five years before, but this time with less expectation of ever coming back.

CHAPTER FIFTEEN

Early that evening, Keith sat at the kitchen table, trying to draft a final letter to Annie, but he was having trouble with it. Should he suggest a last meeting before he left? Should he be brief, with no long explanations, or did he owe her a full baring of his mind and soul? No, that would just open the possibility of more misery. No long good-byes, no last meeting. Be noble, be strong, be brave, and be brief.

He wrote, "Dear Annie, We can't undo the past, we can't go back to our Spencerville, or to Bowling Green. We've lived and made separate lives, and, as I wrote to you once, I'm just passing through and intend to do no damage while I'm here. Take care and please understand. Love, Keith."

There. That was it. He put the letter in an envelope and addressed it care of her sister.

He stood and looked around the kitchen. He'd packed a few things, but his heart wasn't in it.

He knew he should mail the letter after he'd left, and he knew he should leave very soon, before something else happened to affect his decision. Every day he stayed here opened the possibility of a confrontation with Baxter, or the possibility of seeing Annie.

You arrived in life, he reflected, at a time not of your own choosing, then you stayed for a time, also not of your own choosing, and finally, you left, and the only choice you had then was to leave early, but not one moment later than the time you were allotted. Between your arrival and your departure, however, you had some real choices, but choices came in four varieties— good and bad, hard and easy. The good ones were usually the hard ones.

"Choice. Pack up or have dinner?" He chose dinner and opened the refrigerator. "What should I have for dinner?" Not much choice. "Coors or Budweiser?" He chose a Bud.

The phone rang, and he chose not to answer it, but it kept ringing, so he changed his mind and picked it up. "Landry."

"Hello, Landry. This is Porter. Can you tell which one?"

Keith smiled and said, "Gail."

"No, Jeffrey. My shorts are tight."

"What's up?"

"Reminding you of the meeting at St. James tonight. Eight P.M."

"Can't make it, buddy."

"Sure you can."

"Sure I can, but I don't want to."

"Sure you do."

"No, I don't."

"Do you want the revolution to start without you?"

"That would be fine. Send me the minutes. I'm about to have dinner."

"Don't fuck with me, Keith. I have fifty calls to make."

"Look, Jeffrey, I'm ... I've decided—"

"Hold on—" He covered the phone, but Keith could hear his muffled voice, then Jeffrey came back on and said, "Gail says she'll do whatever you want if you come, and anyway, you owe her for the great weed."

"Look...oh, all right—"

"Good. Do you want to say a few words?"

"Yes. Good-bye."

"At the meeting. Do you want to talk about your impressions of Spencerville after a twenty-year absence? Your hopes for the future?"

"Perhaps some other time. See you later." He hung up and said, "I'm still working on the past."

That night, Thursday evening, Keith drove out to St. James Church. The grass parking areas were filled with about fifty cars and pickup trucks, far more than he'd ever seen at St. James, except for Christmas and Easter.

He parked near the cemetery and walked toward the church. At the door, a few young men and women were handing out pamphlets. In the narthex, a group of people were welcoming the arrivals. Keith saw Gail and Jeffrey and tried to slip past them, but they spotted him and hurried over. Gail said, "So what do I owe you?"

"A kiss will do."

She kissed him and said, "You're easy to please. I was willing to give more."

Jeffrey said, "Please, Gail, we're in church. I'm surprised the ceiling hasn't fallen in on us already."

"Surely," Keith remarked, "you don't believe in divine retribution."

"You just never know," Jeffrey answered.

Gail said, "There are over a hundred people here already. The pews are full, and so is the choir loft. I told you, people are fed up. They want a change."

Keith informed her, "No, Gail, they're here *because* things have changed. They want to turn back the clock, and that can't be done. You should make them understand that."

She nodded. "You're right. The three of us have rural roots, but we've forgotten how people here think. We have to change that thinking and change old attitudes."

Keith rolled his eyes. No wonder revolutionaries scared the hell out of everybody. He said, "No, they don't want their thinking or attitudes changed. They want their values and beliefs endorsed, and they want government and society to reflect *their* values and beliefs, not yours."

"Then they want to turn back the clock, and that can't be done."

"No, not literally, but you should paint a picture of the future that looks like the past, with brighter colors. Sort of like a Currier & Ives lithograph that's been cleaned up."

Gail smiled. "You're as manipulative as we are. Did you do this for a living?"

"Sort of...yeah. I worked in propaganda once... but I didn't like it."

"It sounds fascinating. You could use that stuff in your personal life and really make out."

"I wish." Keith changed the subject. "By the way, who's the pastor here who was crazy enough to let you use this place for seditious activities?"

Jeffrey replied, "Pastor Wilkes."

"Really? I thought he'd be retired or dead by now."

"Well," said Jeffrey, "he could be both. He's really old. But he was amenable to this. In fact, I had the impression he didn't particularly care for Chief Baxter."

"Is that so? I wouldn't think he'd know Cliff Baxter personally. The Baxters always went to St. John's in town where the important people go. This is just a farmers' church."

"Well, apparently he knows Baxter by reputation, and apparently he talks to the other clergy in town. I wish we had that kind of intelligence network. Anyway, what you're going to hear tonight is that Chief Baxter is a sinner and an adulterer."

"Doesn't make him a bad guy."

Gail laughed. "You're impossible. Go stand in the corner."

"Yes, ma'am." Keith went into the small church and found standing room behind the last pew. He saw that the church was indeed filled to capacity and also that screens had been set up to block the altar, so that the simple interior, which had no stained-glass windows, now more resembled a Quaker or Amish meeting hall than a Lutheran church.

The people around him and in the pews seemed to represent a cross section of Spencer County. There were men and women who, no matter how they dressed, Keith could identify as farm folk. In fact, he saw Martin and Sue Jenkins. There were also people from town, working people and professional people, and there were all age groups, from high school kids to the very elderly.

Keith remembered a time, before television and other electronic diversions had taken a firm hold, when meetings of one sort or another were deeply ingrained into rural life. His parents were always going to a club meeting, a church meeting, a civic meeting, or something of the sort. And there were sewing bees and quilting groups for the women, and political meetings and grange meetings for the men. Keith even had some early memories of gathering in people's parlors for piano playing, punch, and parlor games. But this way of life had passed, and, in truth, a good movie or football game and a six-pack was preferable to bad piano playing, parlor games, and punch. Yet there had been a time when rural people depended on themselves for entertainment. But more important, many of the great social movements in the nation, such as abolition and populism, had begun in small country churches. As he'd already noted, however, this was no longer an agrarian nation, and there were neither the numbers nor the will to affect national policy. So the hinterland turned in on itself, and feeling perhaps abandoned by and isolated from the urban centers of power, they were beginning to act and think for themselves—maybe with a little help from urban and academic refugees such as himself and the Porters.

He looked at the people still filing in and spotted Jenny, whom he hadn't seen or spoken to since Labor Day. She saw him, smiled, and gave him a big wave, but she was with a man, and they squeezed into a pew together.

Keith watched the crowd settling in. Undoubtedly, there were at least two spies—people who would report to Chief Baxter after the meeting. This was a given, and he was certain that Jeffrey and Gail, old revolutionaries, knew this even if the simple citizens of Spencerville had no inkling of it. Keith hoped that the Porters understood what they were involving these people in. The professional revolutionary, Keith reflected, came in two basic varieties—the romantic and the pragmatic. The romantic got themselves and people around them arrested and killed. The pragmatic, like the early Nazis and Bolsheviks, were total whores who did and said anything to stay alive and win. The Porters, despite their obvious longevity, had a romantic bent and had survived over the years only because American culture was still hospitable to revolutionaries, and because the government knew better than to create martyrs out of people who posed no threat of stirring a nation that was perpetually ready for bed.

Yet, on the local level, people could be awakened and could be called to action. Obviously, the entrenched establishment of the town and county had violated paragraph one of the social contract, which was and would always be, "Keep the citizens happy, or confused, or both."

The meeting began with the pledge of allegiance to the flag, which Keith thought must have given the Porters heartburn. The pledge was followed by a prayer for guidance, given by a young pastor whom Keith didn't know. Keith glanced at the Porters, who were standing at the dais, and saw they were bowing their heads. Maybe, he thought, they'd learned a little pragmatism over the years.

Everyone except the standees sat, and Gail Porter went to the center of the dais and tested the microphone by saying, "Keith Landry—can you hear me back there?"

Nearly everyone turned in his direction and Keith had the urge to strangle Gail. Instead, he nodded, and Gail smiled, then began. "Welcome to what I hope will be the first of many meetings like this. The purpose and objective of this meeting is simple—to explore ways that will lead to a city and county government that is clean, responsive, and competent." She glanced at Keith, then added, "Just like it was years ago. A government that reflects our values and beliefs."

Keith and Gail made brief eye contact, and she went on, without being specific about values and beliefs.

As Gail spoke, it occurred to Keith that, whether or not Cliff Baxter was in or out of power, Cliff Baxter was still Cliff Baxter. And knowing how small towns worked, Keith was sure that the county sheriff, kin to Cliff Baxter, would just deputize the stupid bastard for a dollar a year, and he'd still have his gun and badge.

Gail continued, "As a member of the city council, and, I think, the only elected official here, I want you to know that I extended invitations to all the other elected officials in the town and county, but their response was to call a joint meeting of the city council and the county commissioners at the courthouse. So I don't think any of them are here." She looked around and said, "If any of you are here, please stand and come up to the dais. We have room."

No one stood, and Keith was impressed with Gail's showmanship.

Gail said, "I've asked the Spencerville Gazette to send a reporter tonight. Is he or she here?" Gail looked around the church. "No? Could that be because the newspaper is owned by the mayor's family, or because Baxter Motors is the biggest advertiser?"

Several people laughed and there was some applause.

Keith saw that Gail was enjoying tweaking some prominent noses, and he was sure she understood she was going to make more enemies than she had friends in her adopted community. Gail might spark the revolution, but neither she nor Jeffrey would lead it or have a place in any new regime. In fact, they'd remain outcasts, poor and friendless, cut off from their original hometown roots, alienated from the larger world they helped bring about, and now strangers in a strange land. They sort of reminded Keith of himself.

Gail went on for a minute, speaking in generalities, then got down to cases, beginning with Chief of Police Cliff Baxter.

She said, "In my dealings with Chief Baxter, I've found him to be, in my opinion, incompetent, ineffective, and dictatorial. But don't take my word for it. We have several people here tonight who have volunteered to come forward with their own stories about Chief

Baxter. Some of these stories will shock you, and it takes a lot of courage for these people, your neighbors, to tell you their stories. Most of what you're going to hear brings no credit on the people who will speak, but they have decided to do something positive for themselves and their community. They will tell you about corruption, bribery, bid fixing, voting irregularities, and yes, as you already know, sexual misconduct."

Gail knew when to pause and listen to the murmurs and startled sounds coming from the good citizens of Spencerville. Despite the fact that everything Gail said and was going to say was probably true, and likewise for the people who were about to speak, Keith had the sense that he was attending a seventeenth-century witch trial where witness after witness got up and told stories about one of their neighbors. The only thing missing was the defendant.

Gail made a few more remarks, then related her own story about Cliff Baxter regarding his illegal file on her and ended with, "I'm bringing a civil suit against him and will subpoena that file and make it a public record. I have nothing to hide or be ashamed of. My past is known to many of you, and I'll let you be the judge. I cannot and will not be blackmailed. Furthermore, I'm considering pressing criminal charges against Mr. Baxter, and I've spoken to the county prosecutor about it. If I can't get justice in Spencer County, I'll go to Columbus and speak to the state attorney general. I do this, not for myself, but for everyone in the county who has been the subject of illegal investigations and file-gathering by the police chief."

She looked out over the audience and said, "Some of Baxter's victims are here tonight, some wish not to be identified, and I'll respect that decision. Some have volunteered to come forward. So without having to listen to me any longer, I'll introduce our first volunteer, and she can speak for herself." Gail looked into the first row and nodded.

Hesitantly, looking as though she wanted to be anywhere else on earth, an attractive young woman stood and made her way to the dais. Gail greeted her with a warm embrace and said something to her as she steered the woman to the microphones.

The woman stood silently a few seconds, and Keith thought she looked pale and frightened. She cleared her throat several times, then said, "My name is Sherry Kolarik, and I'm a waitress at the Park 'n' Eat in town."

Sherry Kolarik took a sip of water, then glanced at Gail, who was sitting beside her, then continued, "I first met Chief Baxter when he came to my house six months ago to collect on some overdue parking tickets. I knew I owed the money, but I didn't have it, and I told him that. I thought it was kind of strange that the police chief himself would come out to my house...I mean, I never met him before, but I knew what he looked like because he came to the Park 'n' Eat for breakfast a lot. I never waited on him because he always sat at the table that another girl had—I won't mention her name, but he sat there because he was dating her."

This brought some murmurs from the crowd who knew that Chief Baxter was a married man. But Keith knew this was going to get even better—or worse.

Sherry continued, "One time, though, this girl was out, and he sat at my table. He didn't say much, except he pointed to my name tag...you know, on my left breast, and said, 'Sherry. That's a nice name for it. What's the other one called?'"

There were a few involuntary laughs from the crowd, and Sherry smiled in embarrassment, then everyone settled down, and she continued. "Anyway, about a few weeks later, he came to my door looking for the parking fines. I let him in and we talked. I tried to tell him I didn't have the money, but I'd have it on payday. But he said he wanted it then or he'd take me in. He said if he arrested me, it would be the next day before I could see the judge, and I'd have to spend the night in jail. He said every prisoner had to be searched, had to take a shower, and had to put on prison clothes. I found out later this wasn't true with something like parking tickets, but I was real scared."

Keith had seen the misuse of power all over the world, and he particularly didn't like men who used their authority, or their guns, to intimidate defenseless women for the purpose of sex, which was where this story was heading.

Sherry continued her story, and within a minute had gotten to the point of it. She said, "So I...I offered...I offered to have sex with him..."

The crowd was absolutely silent now.

"I mean...I'm not claiming he brought it up... but I sort of had the feeling that he was...well, kind of leading me there, and like I said, I was scared, and I was broke. I mean, I don't claim to be pure or anything. I've had a few boyfriends, but they were people I liked, and I never did it for money or with anyone I didn't like...but I didn't see any other way out of this. So...I offered, and he accepted." She added, "He said he'd give me the money, but it was a loan, and told me to take off my clothes so he could see what kind of collateral I had."

This remark caused a collective gasp from the audience, and Sherry hung her head, then looked up, took a deep breath, and made brave eye contact with the crowd. Keith sensed that none of this was an act—the

woman was truly humiliated, frightened, and coura-
geous. He could only guess at her motives for exposing
herself like this in public, but he guessed it had less to
do with civic duty than with revenge. But what difference did it make?

Keith had heard enough, and he made his way
through the crowd as Sherry began a somewhat graphic
description of what followed.

He passed through the narthex where the crowd
was straining to hear, and out the doors and down the
steps into the cool air.

He noticed that there were men moving among
the vehicles, shining flashlights, and, as he got closer,
he saw they were policemen. They were taking down
the license plate numbers of the parked vehicles. This
didn't surprise him on one level, yet he found it hard
to believe it was happening. He approached one of the
policemen, who happened to be a deputy sheriff rather
than a Spencerville city cop. Keith said to him, "What
the hell do you think you're doing?"

The man seemed embarrassed, which was a hopeful
sign. He replied, "Just following orders."

"Whose orders?"

"Can't say."

"Who's in charge here?"

The man looked around. "Nobody, really. No
bosses here."

Keith spotted a policeman wearing the uniform of
a Spencerville cop and went over to him and saw it was
the cop who'd been at the high school. Keith said to
him, "Officer Schenley, do you realize you're breaking
the law?"

Schenley looked around and called out to two other
cops. "Hey, Kevin. Pete. Over here."

The two cops approached, and Keith saw they were

the same ones who had been harassing Billy Marlon in the park. There were only about fifteen cops on the Spencerville force, and Keith had the feeling he'd know them all if he stayed around. The name tags on these two read Ward and Krug. Ward, the one who'd been hitting Billy on the soles of his shoes, said, "Well, well, look who's here. You're like cow shit, aren't you? Always getting underfoot. Take a hike while you can."

Keith addressed them by name and said, "Officer Ward, Officer Krug, and Officer Schenley, this is a lawful assembly, protected by the First Amendment to the United States Constitution, in case you didn't know. If you don't leave now, I'm calling the state police, and I'll have you all arrested."

The three cops looked at one another, then back at Keith. Ward asked him, "You crazy or what?"

"I'm pissed off. You get the hell out of here now."

"Whoa! Whoa! You take it easy, fella."

"You've got sixty seconds to clear out, or I'm going back inside that church, and I'll get everybody out here."

There was a long moment of silence, during which all the other cops, seven of them, joined the other three. Ward said to them, "This guy says he's going to call the cops on us."

There were a few tentative laughs, but none of them seemed happy.

Keith added, "And I'll assemble that meeting out here."

Clearly, none of the police wanted to confront their friends and neighbors under these circumstances, but neither did they want to be run off by a single irate citizen. It was sort of a standoff, and Keith wondered if he should give them a graceful way out, then decided they didn't deserve it. He said, "You have about ten seconds to get out of here."

Officer Ward retorted, "You got less than that before I cuff you."

"Five seconds."

No one moved.

Keith turned to go into the church but realized he was surrounded, and, to get through the cordon, he'd have to push or jostle one of the cops, which is what they wanted. He said, "Get out of my way."

They didn't.

Keith approached the policemen blocking his way to the church. They drew their nightsticks and extended their arms and legs.

Keith considered bucking through the line, full-back style, but the defensive line in this case had clubs and guns. Obviously, he was in as difficult a situation as they were, and no one wanted to make the first move.

Ward, behind him, said, "You're an asshole. You're also stupid."

Keith turned and stepped up to Ward. "Where's Baxter tonight? Getting another honor at the Elks Lodge?"

Ward said, "None of your business."

"I'll bet he's at the city council meeting covering his ass while you're out here putting your jobs on the line. And where are your sergeants? What a bunch of ball-less wonders you've got commanding you. Tell Baxter I said that."

Clearly, Keith had hit a nerve, because no one said anything, but then Ward felt obligated to reply and said, "You can tell him yourself, smart guy, when we bring you in."

"Then bring me in. Arrest me, or get out of my way."

But they seemed inclined to do neither. Keith wondered how long that meeting was going to last.

After a few minutes of standoff, Keith decided to

go for it. He turned toward the church and was about to buck the blue line when a voice called out, "What's going on here?"

From the direction of the small parsonage, a man approached, walking with a cane. As he got closer, Keith saw he was very old and finally recognized him as Pastor Wilkes.

The pastor, dressed in slacks, sport shirt, and tweed jacket, said again, "What's going on?"

Officer Ward replied, "It's under control, sir."

"That's not what I asked. What's going on?"

Ward didn't have a specific answer and didn't reply.

Pastor Wilkes walked through the cordon and stopped in front of Keith. "Who are you?"

"Keith Landry."

"Name sounds familiar. You with the group inside?"

"Yes, sir."

"Why are these policemen here?"

"You should ask them."

Pastor Wilkes turned to Officer Ward. "Did anyone call you here?"

"No, sir."

"Then why are you here?"

"To . . . provide protection and security."

"Sounds like hogwash to me, son. Please get off my property."

Ward looked at the other men and cocked his head toward the police cars. They walked off, but Ward stepped up to Keith and he said, "If I were you, I'd get my butt back to Washington. Fast."

"Don't forget to tell Baxter what I said."

"You can count on that, smart guy." Ward turned and left.

So, Keith thought, they knew he'd come from Washington, which was no surprise. He wondered what else they knew about him. But it didn't really matter, if he was leaving, though Cliff Baxter was inadvertently going out of his way to keep Keith Landry from doing that.

Pastor Wilkes said, "Do you have a minute?"

Keith considered, then said, "Yes."

Wilkes motioned Keith to follow him, and they walked toward the parsonage. Keith recalled that the last time he'd been in the parsonage, when he was eighteen, he'd gotten a lecture from Pastor Wilkes on the temptations of the world outside Spencer County, specifically the temptations of alcohol and sex at college. A lot of good it did him.

CHAPTER SIXTEEN

The parsonage was an old white clapboard structure built at the same time, and in the same style, as the hundred-year-old church.

Inside, Wilkes led Keith to the small sitting room and indicated a sagging armchair. Keith sat, and Wilkes sat opposite him in a rocker. Wilkes said, "I've got some sherry."

"No, thank you." Keith looked at Wilkes in the dim light. Keith had seen him a few times at weddings and funerals over the years, but it had been at least seven years since the last time. The man seemed to have shrunk and shriveled a little more each time.

Wilkes asked, "Why were the police here?"

"Writing down license numbers."

Wilkes nodded. He didn't say anything for a while, then looked at Keith. "You're George and Alma's boy."

"Yes, sir."

"Did I baptize you?"

"That's what they tell me."

Wilkes smiled and said, "Did I marry you?"

"No. sir. I've never married."

"That's right. You went off to the Army, then worked for the government."

"I went to college first. Bowling Green. You warned me about loose college women."

"Did it do any good?"

"Not a bit."

Wilkes again smiled, then asked, "Are you back to stay?"

"I don't think so."

"Why'd you come back at all?"

"To look after the house."

"Is that all?"

Keith considered, then replied, "I'd rather not lie, so I'd rather not say."

"Well, I heard a rumor about why you're back, but I don't spread gossip, so I won't tell you what I heard."

Keith didn't reply.

Wilkes asked, "How're your folks?"

Keith filled him in on the family and added, "How is Mrs. Wilkes?"

"The Lord saw fit to call her home."

Keith realized that the standard response of "I'm sorry" wasn't appropriate to that statement, so he said, "She was a fine woman."

"Indeed she was."

Keith asked, "Why didn't you attend the meeting?"

"I don't mix religion and politics. Too many young preachers do that today, and they make half the congregation mad."

"Yes, but there *is* social injustice in the world, and the churches can help."

"We do. I preach love and charity, grace and good deeds. If people listened, there wouldn't be any social injustice."

"But they can't listen if they don't come, and even when they come, they don't listen."

"Some come, some don't. Some listen, some don't. I can do no more."

"You know, Pastor, I saw Lutheran ministers in Dresden organize those marches you saw on TV. They helped bring down the communist government. Same with the Catholic priests in Poland."

"God bless them. They followed their conscience." He added, "If it will make you feel better, I can tell you I'd die for my faith with no hesitation."

"Hopefully, that's not required."

"You never know."

"But you did let those people use your church. And you did run the police off."

"Yes, I did."

"Do you know what that meeting is about?" Keith asked.

"I do."

"Do you approve?"

"To the extent that nothing illegal or violent is discussed, I do." He added, "You know, it's an old rural tradition to use churches as meeting places. Goes back to a time when the church was the only rural building big enough to hold a lot of people, and town was too far away by horse and buggy. St. James has seen all types of political and patriotic rallies going back to the Spanish-American War. I don't own the place, I'm just God's steward."

"Yes, but you'd keep the local Klan out, I'm sure."

"God's steward is not a bigot or an idiot, Mr. Landry." He added, "I didn't invite you in here to question me. I want to ask *you* some questions. If I may."

"All right."

"Thank you. Do *you* approve of that meeting?"

"In principle."

"Have you discovered that all is not well in Spencerville?"

"Yes, I have."

"Do you happen to know Chief Baxter?"

"We went to high school together."

"But I sense by the words and actions of those policemen that you've come to his attention more recently than high school."

"No . . . well, perhaps I have. But I think it has more to do with the fact that there was some bad blood between us in school."

"Is that a fact? Were you rivals?"

"Well, I never considered that we were. But apparently he thought so." Keith wasn't sure where this was going, and there weren't many people he'd sit still for with this type of questioning, but Pastor Wilkes was one of them.

The old man seemed to be thinking, then said, "My memory is not as good as it once was, but I seem to recall that you were courting his present wife."

Keith didn't reply.

"In fact, I think your mother told me that."

"She probably did."

"Perhaps, then, Mr. Baxter is upset that his wife's former beau has decided to return to Spencerville."

"I was her lover, sir. In college." No reason to mention high school and get the man upset.

Wilkes replied, "Call it what you will. I understand. Do you suppose that upsets Mr. Baxter?"

"That would be very immature of him."

"God will forgive me for saying so, but none of the Baxters have shown a great deal of maturity over the years."

Keith smiled.

"Her maiden name . . . ? Prentis, correct?"

"Yes. Annie."

"Yes, Annie Prentis. Good family. Pastor Schenk at St. John's speaks highly of them. We all talk, you know. Even the priests at Immaculate Conception. The ecumenical council meets monthly, and, after the business is done, we gossip terribly. We never use names unless it's absolutely necessary, and nothing leaves that room. But one hears things."

"I can well imagine." Keith realized that Pastor Wilkes sat on a joint board similar to the one Keith had recently left. In fact, as Jeffrey suggested, Pastor Wilkes was privy to great quantities of intelligence information that would rival anything that Police Chief Baxter had in his files.

Wilkes added, "Our purpose is not idle gossip. We want to help, to try to head off divorces, to counsel young people who've gone astray, to keep temptation from men and women, and vice versa. In short, to save souls."

"That's very admirable."

"That's my job. Oh, I know what you're thinking. You think Spencerville has become the village of the damned. Well, most people here are good, God-fearing Christians. But many people have strayed. It's no different in other communities. I'd like you to come to church this Sunday, then join us afterward for tea and fellowship."

"Perhaps I will. But you know you're preaching to the converted. You should reach out to the others."

"They know where we are."

Keith wanted to be gone before the meeting broke up, so he said, "Well, thank you for rescuing me from the law."

But Pastor Wilkes took no notice of Keith's wanting to leave, and he said, "Mr. and Mrs. Baxter are having some difficulties, as you may know. Pastor Schenk is counseling Mrs. Baxter."

"What is that to me?"

"Someone saw you speaking to her downtown."

"Pastor, this may be a small town, but an unmarried gentleman may speak to a married woman in public."

"Don't lecture me, young man. I'm trying to help you."

"I appreciate—"

"Let me be blunt. Thou shalt not covet thy neighbor's wife."

This did not completely take Keith by surprise. He replied, "And I would advise you, Pastor, to tell Pastor Schenk to remind Mr. Baxter of the adultery commandment."

"We all know about Mr. Baxter. What I'm telling you...I shouldn't reveal this confidence, but perhaps you already know that Mrs. Baxter is very taken with you."

This was the best news that Keith had heard in weeks, and he considered several replies, including not replying, but said, "We've corresponded over the years, and she's never indicated that to me. She's done nothing wrong."

"That depends on how you view a married woman writing her former...boyfriend."

"She's done nothing wrong. If there were any improprieties, they came from me."

"That's very noble of you, Mr. Landry. I know you think I'm being very old-fashioned, and I thank you for humoring me."

"I'm not humoring you, I'm listening to you, and I understand your position and your concern. I assure you my relationship with Mrs. Baxter has been strictly platonic."

"Well, see if you can be the strong one and keep it that way."

Keith looked at Pastor Wilkes and, against his better

judgment, or perhaps because he had to tell someone, he said, "To be honest with you, Pastor, the spirit is indeed willing, but the flesh is weak."

Pastor Wilkes seemed momentarily speechless, then said, "I appreciate your honesty." He added, "And am pleased you remember scripture."

Keith stood and said, "I should be going."

Pastor Wilkes took his cane and stood also. He walked Keith to the door, they went out onto the porch, and Keith saw that the meeting was still in progress. He wondered how many witnesses Gail and Jeffrey had assembled to confess to their dealings and intercourse with the devil. Keith turned back to Pastor Wilkes and said, "Apparently you knew more about me than you indicated when I sat down."

"Yes, but I didn't know if you were the type of man I could talk to. I saw that you were, and I gave you unsolicited advice and information. I hope you're not offended by the advice and that you keep the information to yourself."

"I'm not offended, and I'll keep this conversation to myself. But I am concerned that people are talking about me."

"Mr. Landry, you came home to a small town that is very troubled, and ironically, one of our problems, the problem of Mr. Baxter as public official and as husband, has become your problem. But don't let it be."

"Why not? Why should I do less than the people in that church?"

"You know very well why. Examine your motives, and consider the consequences of your actions."

"Pastor, since I left Spencerville, I've served as a military officer in various capacities, and all of those capacities had life-and-death consequences, for me, my colleagues, and, between us, for this nation."

"Then you don't need a sermon from a country preacher."

"But I appreciate your concern."

Pastor Wilkes put his hand on Keith's shoulder and looked him in the eye. "I like you. I don't want to see anything happen to you."

"Me, neither. But if something does happen, will you see to the arrangements here at St. James?"

"Yes...of course." Pastor Wilkes took Keith's arm and said, "Let me walk you to your car. Help me down the steps." As they walked, Wilkes said, "Keith...may I call you Keith?"

"Of course."

"I know that something is going on between you and Annie Baxter, and, to be quite honest, I'm not totally opposed to it. But you must go about it the right way, or it will never be right for either of you."

Keith replied, "I'm still not admitting to coveting my neighbor's wife, Pastor. But I'm listening."

"Good. Listen, and forget where you heard this." He said, "She, the woman in question, is in an unhappy and unhealthy marriage, according to her pastoral counselor. Her husband is an adulterer and a verbally abusive man. I may be from the old school, but I listen to the young pastors, and I'm convinced that she has to leave that marriage before it becomes dangerous. He's become enraged at the suggestion of counseling, and neither the pastoral counselor nor the wife in question sees any hope for a change."

Keith did not reply. He found his car and stood beside it.

Pastor Wilkes continued, "Divorce is acceptable under these circumstances. After her divorce, she is free to do whatever she wishes. You, Mr. Landry, must be patient and must not become part of the problem. This is a good woman, and I don't want to see her hurt."

Both men stood in the dark, a faint light coming from the church windows casting shadows over the gravestones. Keith said, "Neither do I."

"Mr. Landry, I'm sure your intentions are honorable, but the only honorable thing you can do now is to break off any contact with her. Things will work themselves out with God's help."

"And without my help."

"Precisely." He asked, "Do you or do you not intend to stay here to live?"

"I did, but I'm not certain now."

"I think your presence here is fuel to the fire. Can you go somewhere for a while? No doubt, your parents would like to see you."

Keith smiled. "Are you running me out of town?"

"I'm suggesting that if you leave, I can see a happy ending for both of you. If you stay, I see only disaster."

Apparently, he and Pastor Wilkes had reached the same conclusion independently of each other. Keith said, "I didn't think you were going to advise me on how to win another man's wife. I thought I was going to get hellfire and brimstone."

"That's the fundamentalist church down the road. Here we do love and compassion. Will I see you Sunday?"

"Perhaps. Good night."

CHAPTER SEVENTEEN

Keith pulled away from the church. Obviously, he thought, there was nothing simple about a simple rural community. In fact, life was simpler in the big city. Here, they cared about your soul and made you think about it, too, and that really got complicated.

Keith drove along the dark country road. He knew that the police could stop him anytime, anyplace, on any pretext, and he'd resigned himself to that. He'd been in the hands of the police in other countries, and he knew the drill, knew when they just wanted to scare you and when they intended to knock you around. He'd never had the experience of being really tortured and obviously hadn't faced a firing squad, though there was one time in Burma, years ago, when he knew they were talking about it.

Being a veteran of a few arrests, he couldn't imagine that the Spencerville police station could hold many terrors for him, but you never knew what they had on their minds until you got there and saw how they were acting. A more unsettling scenario than the unlikely possibility of dying in police custody was the more likely possibility of dying trying to escape arrest, which was far more common in the civilized countries. Keith didn't imagine that there'd be much of an inquiry if he was shot on a country road, especially if the police put a weapon in his hands after he was dead. But they'd have to supply their own weapon to plant, because he didn't have his with him, though he wished he did.

But was this police force that far down the road toward criminality and viciousness? He thought not, but Cliff Baxter certainly was, especially after being baited by Keith Landry.

He glanced in his rearview mirror but didn't see any headlights. He turned onto a series of farm roads and took an indirect way back to his house. The bottom line, though, was that there was only one road that passed his farm and one way in. If they were at all bright, they'd simply wait for him at either end of that road.

As he drove, he thought about what he'd heard in the church and in the parsonage, not to mention what happened outside. It all came down to Cliff Baxter, this sort of evil fog that covered the once sunny and happy countryside.

Enter the hero, the savior. "No. Exit the hero. Everyone here will get what they deserve, for better or worse." Wilkes was right. Leave it to God, or to Annie, or to the Porters, whoever acted first. "Do not get ego-involved in this."

"Here's the question, Landry—if Annie were not the wife of Cliff Baxter, would you take on this fight in the interest of justice?"

Well, he thought, he'd done that often enough, though he'd gotten paid for it. But there wasn't enough money involved for the risks he'd taken. Obviously, he'd been motivated by patriotism and a sense of justice. But when that waned, he'd been motivated by a selfish desire for adventure and career advancement, and that wasn't enough. Here, in Spencerville, he found he could accomplish several objectives with one act: By killing Baxter, he could do the town and himself a favor, free Annie, and then perhaps have Annie. But that didn't seem like the right thing for the right reasons, no matter how he dissected it.

He found himself on the road that led to Route 28, his road. Rather than get onto 28, he swung the Blazer off the road and followed a dirt tractor path that crossed the Muller farm through the cornfields. He put the Blazer into four-wheel drive and navigated by the dashboard compass, eventually making his way onto his property, which was planted with the Mullers' corn, and within ten minutes, he came out into the clearing of his own farmyard near the barn.

He shut off his headlights, turned toward the house, and parked near the back door.

Keith got out, unlocked the door, and went into the dark kitchen. Feeling both foolish and angry, he left the lights off and listened. He knew he wouldn't be doing much night driving anymore, and if he did, he'd take the Glock or the M-16 with him.

He considered going upstairs and getting his pistol, but his instincts told him it was safe, or if it wasn't, he'd be better off here in the kitchen, near the door. He opened the refrigerator and got a beer.

"So, should I turn the other cheek and leave, as Wilkes suggested?" But this was not what his life had been about.

He opened the beer and, still standing, took a long drink. "Or do I stalk Baxter instead of the other way around? I catch him coming out of one of his girlfriends' houses and cut his throat. A little wet stuff, one more time. Yeah, people think I did it, but there're a thousand other suspects, and no one's going to look too closely at it."

Sounded good, but that left a widow and two fatherless children, and maybe you didn't kill a man for being a bad husband, a corrupt cop, and a bully. "But why not? I've killed better men for less reason."

He finished the beer and got himself another one. "No, I can't murder the son-of-a-bitch. I just can't do it. So I have to leave." He went to the kitchen table and, by the faint light from the back door and window, he looked for the letter he'd left on the table, but didn't see it. He turned on the light hanging over the table and searched the chairs and the floor, but the letter was gone.

Alert now, he shut off the light and put the beer can down. He listened, but there was no sound. It occurred to him that Aunt Betty or any of that crowd may have come by to clean or deliver food. They'd seen the letter, taken it, and mailed it. But that didn't seem likely.

If there was anyone still in the house, they knew he was there. He could forget about the guns upstairs, because even if he made it that far, the guns wouldn't be there any longer.

He moved quietly toward the back door and put his hand on the knob.

He heard a familiar squeak from the direction of the living room, then heard it again. He turned from the back door, went into the hallway, which was empty, and entered the living room, where the constant squeak came from. He turned on the floor lamp and said, "How long have you been here?"

"About an hour."

"How did you get in?"

"The key was in the toolshed, under the workbench, where it's been for a hundred years."

He looked at her, sitting in the rocker, wearing jeans and a pullover. The letter was in her lap.

She said, "I thought you'd be home, but you weren't, and I almost left, then I remembered the key, and I decided to surprise you."

"I'm surprised." But somehow he'd known it was her in the living room.

"Do you mind that I came into the house?"

"No."

"It still feels like my second home."

Keith had the distinct feeling this was not real, that it was a dream, and he tried to remember when he'd gone to sleep.

She asked, "Are you alone?"

"Yes."

"I thought I heard you talking in the kitchen, so I just sat here, quiet as a mouse."

"I'm alone. I talk to myself. Where's your car?"

"In the barn."

"Good thinking. Where is Mr. Baxter?"

"At a city council meeting."

"And where are you?"

"At Aunt Louise's."

"I see . . . did you hear what I was saying?"

"I could only hear the tone. Are you angry about something?"

"No, I just argue with myself."

"Who won?"

"The good angel."

"But you looked troubled."

"That's because the good angel won."

She smiled. "Well, I argued with myself about coming here. This is not a chance meeting on the street."

"No, it's not."

She held up the letter. "It was addressed to me, so . . ."

"Yes, that's all right. Saved me a stamp."

She stood and came toward him. "And, yes, I *do*

understand. You're right. We can't...you remember that poem we both liked? 'Though nothing can bring back the hour of splendor in the grass, of glory in the flower, we will grieve not, rather find strength in what remains behind.'" She added, "I think we liked it because we knew we were going to be star-crossed lovers, and that poem was our comfort..." She hesitated, then leaned toward him and kissed him on the cheek, saying, "Good-bye, darling." She walked past him and into the hallway.

He heard her go into the kitchen and heard the back door open and close. Be strong, be noble, be brave. But don't be a complete idiot. He turned and moved quickly into the kitchen as the screen door shut. "Wait!"

She turned as he came out the door and she said, "No, Keith. Please. You're right. This won't work. We can't...it's too complicated...we've been fooling ourselves—"

"No, listen...we have to...we need to understand...I have to know what happened...I mean..." He couldn't find any of the words he wanted or needed, then said, "Annie, we're not going to just walk away again."

She took a deep breath and said, "I can't stay here. I mean outside."

"Come in. Please."

She thought a moment, then came back into the kitchen.

He said, "Can you stay awhile?"

"Yes, all right...we'll finally have that cup of coffee. Where's the pot?"

"I don't want coffee. I need a drink." He turned on the small light over the sink, went to the cupboard, and took his bottle of Scotch down. "Want one?"

"No, and neither do you."

"Right." He put the bottle back. "You make me nervous."

"*You're* nervous? I can hear my heart beating, and my knees are shaking."

"Me, too. Do you want to sit?"

"No."

"Well...look, I know the risk you took coming here—"

"I took two risks, Keith. One, that I wasn't followed, the other, that I wouldn't get my heart broken. No, I'm sorry, I can't put that on you."

"Don't be sorry. I'm glad you came. I'm more than glad. Look, I wrote that letter—"

"Don't explain. I understand. Really."

They stood looking at each other across the kitchen, then Keith said, "This is not the way I pictured this."

"How did you picture it?"

He hesitated, then walked to her and took her in his arms. "Like this."

They embraced and kissed, and he remembered exactly how she felt in his arms, how she smelled, how she tasted, and how her mouth and body moved against his.

She pulled away, then buried her face in his shoulder. She was crying, he realized, her body trembled, then shook convulsively. She couldn't stop crying, and he didn't know what to do, but he held her close against him.

Finally, she backed away and pulled a tissue out of her jeans, wiped her eyes and blew her nose, then laughed. "Oh, God...look at me...I knew this would happen...don't laugh at me."

"I'm not laughing." He took a handkerchief out of his pocket and wiped her cheeks. "My God, you're beautiful."

"Sure. My nose is running." She wiped her nose, then looked up at him. "Well..." She cleared her throat. "Well, Mr. Landry, I enjoyed seeing you again. Will you walk me to my car?"

"Don't leave."

"I have to."

"Will he call your aunt's house after the meeting?"

"Yes."

"What will she say?"

"That I'm on my way home. I told Cliff my car phone wasn't working, so he can't call me. My aunt will call here."

"She knows where you are?"

"Yes. Please answer it and tell her I'm on the way home."

"Why don't we just wait for her phone call?"

"Because I want to leave now."

"Why?"

"Because...I mean, we can talk another time... we have to talk, but I don't want anything to happen tonight."

He smiled. "That's exactly what you said to me when you were sixteen, the night we lost our virginity."

"Well, this time I mean it." She laughed. "God help me, I can't keep my hands off you."

They embraced again and kissed. She put her cheek on his chest and said, "Just hold me."

He held her and ran his fingers through her hair.

Her face still against his chest, she said, "I was going to go up into your bedroom and really surprise you."

He didn't reply.

"Then I thought to myself, what if he brings someone home? What if he has someone up there?"

"No. No one up there, and no one since I came back."

"Not for lack of admirers, from what I hear."

"Well, I don't hear anything, and I'm minding my own business."

"Good." She added, "You don't have to...I mean, it's all right if you...this is silly, you know, because it's none of my business—"

"Annie, there's only you."

She hugged him tighter, then stood on her toes and began kissing him on the cheeks, on the lips, on his forehead and neck. She said, "I guess I'm not good at hiding my feelings. I should be a little less obvious. How should I play this, Keith?"

"Let's try honesty this time."

"Okay. I love you. I've always loved you."

"I love you and always have. That's why I came back. I can't get you out of my mind."

"I curse the day I let you go."

"You didn't. I left. I should have asked you to marry me." He looked at her. "What would you have said?"

"I'd have said no."

"Why?"

"Because you wanted to go. You were bored, Keith. You watched your friends go off to war, you were obsessed with the war news on TV. I saw that. And you wanted other women."

"No."

"Keith."

"Well...wanting and doing are two different things."

"I know, and you would never have cheated on me, and you'd resent a life without some sexual adventure. God, Keith, everyone else was doing it with everyone else, except us."

He tried to make a joke and said, "I'm not too sure about you."

She smiled, then said, "Can I be honest? I wanted

to try other men. We both wanted to experiment, but we couldn't because we had an understanding, a commitment. We were two country kids, crazy in love, having sex and feeling guilty about it, but wanting other people and feeling even more guilty about that. I mean, in some ways, we were more than married."

"I think you're right." He smiled. "So you wanted other men?"

"Sometimes. Am I blushing?"

"A little." He thought a moment, then asked, "What should we have done?"

"We didn't have to do anything. The world did it for us. To us."

"I suppose. But why didn't we get together again?"

"You couldn't accept the other men."

"No, I couldn't. And you?"

"Women are different. I just wanted you to get it out of your system."

"Well, I have."

"Me, too." She added, "I've never had an affair."

"I don't care if you have. You deserved one."

"No, listen to me. I'm hopelessly old-fashioned. But in your case, Mr. Landry, I'll make an exception."

"Well . . . I'd like nothing more right now. But . . . we have to understand the consequences if we—"

"Keith, I don't give a damn about the consequences. We've cleared up the past, and that's all we had to do. Make love to me now, and the hell with the future."

He took her arm and led her toward the stairs, his heart pounding, afraid the phone would ring, afraid it wouldn't.

He didn't even remember how he got into the bedroom, but there they were with the lamp on. She looked nervous, he thought, and he said, "Do you want a drink?"

"No, I want to do this with a clear head." She

looked around the room. "We did it here once when your family was out visiting."

"Right. I pretended I was sick and stayed home."

She didn't seem to hear him and kept looking around, then looked into one of the wardrobes, which he noticed was open. He could see, and she could see, the hanging holster, the bulletproof vest, the sword, the uniforms, and the M-16 rifle. She turned to him but made no remark, except, "I see you know how to keep a room tidy."

"I'm a tidy bachelor."

They stood awkwardly, facing each other, and they seemed to have run out of small talk. She pulled her turtleneck out of her jeans and said, "Well, I'll break the ice." She pulled the sweater over her head and threw it aside, then unhooked her bra, slipped it off, and let it drop to the floor. "Okay?" She held out her hands, and he took them. She put his hands on her breasts, and he caressed them, feeling her nipples harden.

She reached out and unbuttoned his shirt, then ran her hands over his chest. "You feel the same, Keith."

"You, too."

She pressed her breasts against his chest, and they kissed while she slipped his shirt off. Still kissing, she undid her jeans and pulled them with her panties down to her thighs. She directed his hand between her legs, and he felt her pubic hair, then her vagina, which was moist.

She moved back and sat on the bed, pulling off her shoes, socks, jeans, and panties. Completely naked now, she looked at him and smiled. "Is this really happening?"

"My God, Annie, you are beautiful."

She suddenly stood and threw her arms around him. "I love you."

He picked her up and carried her back to the bed, laying her on the quilt with her legs over the foot of the bed, then he bent over her and kissed her breasts, her stomach, then he knelt and ran his tongue down to the soft inside of her thigh, and she spread her legs so he could kiss her between her legs. She arched her back, and he put his hands under her buttocks and pushed his face deeper between her legs.

He stood slowly, and undid his belt and trousers.

She lay on the bed, breathing hard, then slid back and put her head on the pillow, watching him undress. She watched every move he made as he came toward her, and when he was in reaching distance, she took his hands in hers.

He straddled her and kissed her on the cheek. He said, "Okay?"

She nodded.

He lowered himself, and she put him inside her.

They kissed softly and held each other gently, caressing, moving slowly as if they had all the time in the world.

They lay on the bed, on their sides, she behind him with her arms around him and her legs entwined in his like nesting spoons. She kissed his neck. "Sleeping?"

"No. Dreaming."

"Me, too." She hugged him tighter and ran her feet over his calves.

"I like that."

"I know."

He turned toward her and, still on their sides, they wrapped their arms and legs around each other. She said, "If you knew how often I fantasized about this..."

"Not more than I did."

"Really?"

"Yes."

She said, "I told you I never had an affair. Not even a fling."

"It doesn't matter either way."

"It does to me. This is very special to me."

"I understand."

"I'm not telling you that so you think you have to marry me. I'm already married. I'm just saying it was very special to me. And if this turns out to be the end of it, I'll understand. This is all I ever wanted. This one more time."

"Do you mean that?"

"No."

He laughed.

She tousled his hair, then sat up. "Tell me...there were other women, I know, but was there any *one* woman?"

"Nothing to write home about." He thought a moment, then said, "I honestly couldn't get you out of my mind. So I couldn't...I mean, there was no reason to marry."

She didn't reply for a long time, then said, "Maybe if I hadn't had children, I'd have shown up at your doorstep one day."

"There were times and places when I didn't even have a doorstep. It wouldn't have been much of a life for us."

"We'll never know. There were times I envied you, times I thought you were dead..."

"And times you wished I was dead."

She thought a moment, then replied, "No. I was angry, but I prayed for your safety." She added, "There were times, though, I wished *I* was dead."

"I'm sorry."

"It's okay now." She added, "I've been sleeping with a man I don't love for twenty years. That's a sin. But I will sin no more."

He didn't want to ask, but felt he had to and said, "Annie, why did you stay with him?"

"I ask myself that every day. I guess because of the children . . . family ties, community . . ."

"You mean if you filed for a divorce—?"

"I'd have to leave. He would get . . ."

"Violent?"

"I don't know. Anyway, I used to hope that he'd die. That someone would kill him. That's terrible. I hate myself for that."

"That's all right. You don't have to wait for someone to kill him now."

She didn't reply, and he thought she was considering the double meaning of what he said, so he added, "You can just leave him."

"I will." She didn't ask for his help or any assurances from him but said, "Maybe I was sort of waiting for you. I always knew you'd come back. But I don't want anything from you, no promises to take care of me, and no offers to take care of him. I want to do this myself. Now that my daughter is in college, I can leave."

"Well, you know I'm going to help, so—"

"Keith, he's dangerous."

"He's bush-league."

She picked herself up on one elbow and looked down at him. "If anything happened to you, I swear I'd kill him myself. Promise me you won't confront him."

The phone rang, and Annie said, "That's my aunt."

Keith picked it up. "Hello."

"Well, I thought I saw lights in your house. How'd you get home?"

"Who is this?"

"Officer Ward. Just checking on you. You tucked in?"

"Sure. Had enough fun for one night."

"I didn't. I'm not a happy man tonight."

"I'm not here to make you happy."

Annie leaned over and put her ear near the phone. Keith turned away from her and said into the mouthpiece, "Don't call here again." He hung up.

She asked, "Who was that?"

"Car salesman."

She looked at him and was about to say something when the phone rang again. Keith picked it up. "Yes?"

A female voice with an old-fashioned midwestern twang said, "Mr. Landry?"

"Speaking."

"This is Mrs. Sinclair, Annie Baxter's aunt."

"Yes, ma'am."

"Annie said she might stop by your place for a minute on her way home."

Keith smiled at the strain in Aunt Louise's voice. He said, "She stopped by for less than a minute, Mrs. Sinclair. Never got out of the car. We chatted about farm prices through the screen door for about fifteen seconds—"

Keith felt a punch on his arm and heard Annie laugh and whisper, "Stop that."

Keith continued, "Then she left for home, licketysplit."

"I figured she'd be on her way home, and that's just what I told Mr. Baxter when he called here looking for her. She should be home shortly, I said."

"I'm sure she will be, Mrs. Sinclair."

"It was real nice talking to you, Mr. Landry. You take care."

"Thank you, Mrs. Sinclair. I appreciate the call." He hung up.

Annie rolled on top of him and pressed her nose against his. "You're funny."

"So's your aunt. Is she up to this?"

"Barely. I had to bring a bottle of dandelion wine when I stopped by." She laughed and kissed him, then rolled off and onto the floor. "Have to go." She walked naked out of the room, and Keith heard the water in the bathroom running.

He got out of bed and began to dress, sticking the Glock under his shirt.

She came back and said, "I can see myself out." She gathered her clothes and threw them on the bed. "I don't want to get dressed. I want to be naked for you all night, all week."

"Sounds good to me."

She put her bra on, then pulled her sweater over, sat on the bed, and slid her panties and socks on.

He observed, "You still dress from the top down."

"Doesn't everyone?" She pulled her jeans on, then her shoes. She stood. "Okay. You're walking me down?"

"That's what a gentleman does."

They walked down the stairs together, hand in hand, and she kept glancing at him, then said, "Can you believe this?"

"Hardly."

"I feel like a kid again. I haven't had a rush like this since...well, since you."

"That's very nice of you."

"I mean it. My heart is still pounding, and my legs are rubbery."

"And your face is flushed, and your eyes are on fire. Be careful when you get home."

"Oh..." She put her hand to her face. "Yes, I will. God, do you think—?"

"Just re-create in your mind a night with Aunt Louise. By the time you get home, you'll be fine."

"Okay..." She laughed and said, "But what if I still have semen running down my leg?"

Keith smiled. He remembered that one of the things he liked about her was the totally unexpected raunchiness that sometimes came out of that prim and proper mouth.

They walked to the kitchen door, and she opened it. "Keith, what are we going to do?"

"You name it, I'll do it."

"You love me?"

"You know it."

She smiled. "Was I a good lay? I can't believe I said that. Bye. I'll call you."

He held her arm. "No."

"I have to go."

"I know. But...your husband's men sometimes watch this house."

"Oh..."

"They didn't see you come in because they weren't watching earlier, or if they were, they saw me leave and followed. I'm going to leave first, and if they're watching, they'll follow me. You wait ten minutes, then leave."

She stayed quiet a moment, then said, "This is awful..." She looked at him. "Keith, I'm sorry. I can't put you through this—"

"This is *not* your fault. It's his fault. I can handle this. But can *you* handle this?"

She nodded. "For you, yes."

"All right. Now, remember—you were at Aunt Louise's all night. Stick to that story no matter what."

She nodded.

He asked, "What are you driving?"

"A Lincoln Continental. White."

"Ten minutes."

"Be careful, Keith."

He went out the door, got into his Blazer, waved to her, and went down the long drive to the road. He turned toward town and continued on a few miles until he got to an intersection and stopped.

There were no headlights behind him, and he continued on. He spotted a half-collapsed barn, shut off his headlights, and turned off the road onto the dirt track that led to the barn and nudged the Blazer into the collapsed timbers.

He got out and watched the road. After about five minutes, he saw headlights approaching at a high speed from the direction of his farm. He knelt behind some brush and waited.

The car tore past him, but he could make out the shape of a light-colored Lincoln Continental.

He waited ten more minutes, then went back to his Blazer and drove toward home.

He couldn't be sure she was safe, but if Baxter questioned her and she stuck to her story, she'd be okay.

He had the unsettling feeling that he was enjoying this, that this was an adrenaline rush. But so what? Fun was whatever you did best.

And he had no doubt that Annie enjoyed the intrigue to a point. She'd always been like that when they were trying to find times and places to make love. She got a kick out of the danger, the romance, the stolen fruit which always tasted better.

Yet, tonight, he had seen real fright in her eyes. She was brave, spunky, and willing to take a risk. But when getting caught was not just a matter of getting expelled from school or getting grounded forever, but of getting beaten or killed, then this took the fun right out of it. He realized he had to resolve this quickly.

He thought about her, about their lovemaking and pillow talk, and knew that they were together again.

They'd traveled the miles and the years and, against all
odds and all obstacles, they'd wound up in his old bedroom, naked in each other's arms. Body and soul were
satisfied, the flesh trembled, the spirit soared, the heart
sang. For the first time in weeks, months, Keith Landry
found himself happy and smiling.

CHAPTER EIGHTEEN

Cliff Baxter got to work early and called Kevin Ward into his office. He asked Ward, "Okay, what happened at St. James last night?"

Officer Ward cleared his throat and replied, "Well... they had a full house."

"Yeah? You get plate numbers?"

"Well... got some."

"*Some?* What the fuck do you mean *some?*"

"Chief... uh... that guy Landry..."

"Yeah?"

"Well... he was there..."

"Yeah? I ain't surprised."

"Yeah... he kind of gave us a hard time."

"What the hell does that mean?"

Ward cleared his throat again and related what happened, trying to put the best spin on it, but clearly Chief Baxter was not happy.

Baxter listed as Ward spoke, saying nothing. Finally, when Officer Ward finished reporting, Baxter said, "You mean to tell me, Ward, that one guy and one old preacher ran you off?"

"Well... they... I mean, it was the preacher's property and all, and if it was just Landry, hell, we would've run his ass in, and—"

"Shut the hell up. Okay, get me a make on the plates you *did* manage to get before you got evicted from the premises."

"Right, Chief."

"And get your balls put back where they belong. We're goin' out to Landry's place later."

"Yes, sir." Ward stood and went to the door.

Baxter said, "Next time I give you a job to do and it don't get done, maybe you want to think about goin' back into the fertilizer business with your daddy."

Ward hesitated, then said, "Chief, it might've helped if you were there with us. I mean, it wasn't legal what we were doing—"

"Get the hell out of here."

Ward left.

Cliff Baxter sat at his desk and stared at the wall awhile. He understood that things were starting to come apart. He looked at the framed photo of Annie on his desk and said, "Bitch."

He kept looking at her photograph and recalled last evening. She'd gotten home after him, and he'd waited for her in the kitchen. They hadn't said much to each other, and she went right to bed, saying she had a head-ache. He'd gone out to her car and tried the mobile phone. She hadn't answered any of his calls, but the phone worked fine. Still, you never knew with these car phones. On the other hand, she'd seemed weird last night, and he would have pushed her a little, but he had some checking to do first, and he knew not to ask questions until he already had answers.

Somewhere in the back of Cliff Baxter's mind was the important fact that his wife was smarter than he was. But smart people, he'd discovered, sometimes were too smart, too cocky, too sure of themselves, and they thought their bullshit didn't stink. He nodded to himself and said, "Aunt Louise. I ain't seen Aunt Louise in a while."

Cliff Baxter glanced at his watch and saw it was seven A.M. He picked up the phone and dialed.

Tim Hodge, the postmaster of Spencerville, answered in a sleepy voice, "Hello…"

"Hey, Tim, I wake you?"

"Yeah…who's this?"

"Let go of your cock and grab your socks, the mail must go through."

"Oh…hey, Chief, how you doing?"

"You tell me."

"Oh…" Tim Hodge cleared his throat. "Well… yeah, I went out to St. James last night…"

"You better have. What happened?"

"Well…let's see…they…uh…they had a crowd—"

"I know that. My name come up?"

"Yeah…yeah, it did. Matter of fact, it came up a bunch of times."

Baxter nodded. "Come on, Tim, I'm a busy man. Give me the who, what, where, when, and how."

"Yeah, okay. Well, the city council lady, Gail Porter, kind of led the meeting. Her husband was there, too, and they had…like a lot of witnesses."

"Witnesses? Was this a fucking meeting or a trial?"

Tim Hodge didn't reply immediately, then said, "Well…they had some people there who had a few… kind of complaints against you."

"Like *who?*"

"Like Bob Arles's wife, Mary, and some woman named Sherry…some weird last name."

"Kolarik?"

"Yeah."

Shit. "What did she say?"

"Which one?"

"*Both* of them. What did those lyin' bitches say?"

"Well…Mary went on about you taking things from the store, you know, and signing off on more gas than was pumped—"

"Fuck her. What did the other bitch say?"

"Well…something about…she sort of said that you… like you and her…like you had something going…"

Jesus Christ. "You mean this bitch got up there in front of all those people in church…and lied about… what'd she say?"

"She says you fucked her. Been fucking her for some time. That you paid her parking fines or something, and that, to pay you back, she had to fuck for you." Hodge added, "She got real detailed."

"Lying bitch."

"Yeah."

"People believin' that?"

"Well…I don't."

"Hey, why don't you stop by this afternoon for some coffee and tell me what you seen and heard last night. About three. Meantime, don't spread no gossip yourself, and keep your ears open."

"Right, Chief."

Baxter hung up and stared out the window onto Main Street. "Goddamnit!" He slammed his fist on the desk. "Goddamned bitches, can't trust any of them to keep their damned mouths shut."

He thought about how this development was going to affect him and decided he could keep it under control. Sherry Kolarik was a whore, the worst kind of witness. Mary Arles was another problem, but he'd get her husband to put a zipper on her big mouth real quick. Baxter wondered what else had come up at that meeting. He pulled a piece of paper toward him and began a list, writing the name Keith Landry, followed by Sherry Kolarik, then Mary Arles, then Gail Porter, then the other Porter whose first name he didn't remember, then hesitantly, he wrote "Pastor Wilkes," then thought a moment and added Bob Arles's name for good measure. He'd have written Annie's name, too, except that she always had the honorary first position on his weekly list of people who pissed him off.

He poured himself a cup of coffee from a thermos jug and sipped on it. Things were definitely getting out of control. This wasn't just a bad week, it was the start of a bad life unless he started to kick some ass.

He stood and went out into the office where Ward was entering the list of license plate numbers into the motor vehicle computer and getting names and addresses printed out. Baxter said, "Turn that fucking thing off."

Ward exited the file, and Baxter asked him, "You got a report on Landry's movements last night?"

"Sure do." Ward handed Baxter a typed sheet of paper, and Baxter glanced at it.

Baxter said, "Krug saw him leave his house at seven-thirty P.M., then you and Krug and the other guys saw him in the parking lot at St. James at eight thirty-five."

"Right. The meeting was still going on, but I guess he left early."

"Then what?"

"Well, then Landry went into the parsonage with Pastor Wilkes. I drove out to Landry's place and waited on 28 a couple hundred yards from his driveway, but I never saw anybody pull in. But then I noticed lights on upstairs, and I called him on the mobile phone, and he answered. Don't know how he got there unless he came in from the south, using the tractor roads. He must've been scared, you know, figuring we were laying for him." Ward added, "It's all there in the report."

Baxter glanced at the paper again and said, "You called him at ten thirty-eight and he answered?"

"Yup."

"He could have been home about an hour already."

"Could have. Depends on how long he stayed with Wilkes, and where he went after that. Like I said, I think he took the long way home. He was scared."

"Yeah. You really scared him. You see any other car goin' in or comin' out of his farm?"

"Nope."

"You stick around after you called him?"

"No, because it looked like he was in for the night. But about an hour later, I drove by again, and his light was still on upstairs. What are you thinking, Chief?"

"Nothin'. I'll be at the Park 'n' Eat for breakfast."

"Okay."

Cliff Baxter left police headquarters and walked the half mile down Main Street to the east end of town and entered the Park 'n' Eat at seven-thirty A.M.

He took his customary table, and an older waitress named Lanie came over and said, "How're you this morning, Chief?"

"Just fine."

"Coffee?"

"Sure thing."

She poured him a cup of coffee from a carafe and asked him, "Need to look at the menu?"

"Nope. Ham, two eggs over easy, home fries, biscuits, no toast, and no juice."

"You got it." She started to walk away, but Baxter said, "Hey, where's Sherry this morning?"

Lanie replied, "Called in sick."

"Yeah? Friend of mine saw her last night."

Lanie smiled. "Maybe too much partying."

"Nah. This guy saw her at church. St. James, out by Overton." Baxter studied the waitress's face, but clearly she didn't know anything.

"I'll get those eggs going for you."

"Yeah. Hey, if she comes in or calls, tell her I'm lookin' for her. We got to talk about some parking fines."

Lanie's smile dropped, and she nodded and moved off.

Breakfast came, and Cliff ate. Nearly everyone who came in greeted him, and he tried to guess who knew what at this early hour.

One of the city councilmen, Chet Coleman, who was also a pharmacist, came in and saw him. Coleman sat down opposite Baxter and, without any preliminaries, said, "Hey, Chief, you know about that meeting at St. James?"

"Heard about it."

"Yeah, while we were having our council meeting, those folks were bad-mouthing us."

"No shit?"

"I didn't like what I heard."

"How'd you hear?"

"Well...had a friend there."

"Yeah? A friend who stayed up late to call you, or a friend who got up early to call you?"

"Uh...this morning..."

"Yeah? Friend couldn't be named Mrs. Coleman, could it?"

Chet Coleman didn't respond to that, but he didn't have to.

Baxter said, "You know, Chet, this whole god-damned country is getting out of control. You know why? Pussies. When the men can't control the pussies, you might as well kiss the whole country good-bye."

"Yeah...well, there were a lot of men there, too, and from what I hear—"

"Let me give you some advice, Mr. Councilman. If your wife winds up on the wrong side of this thing, it ain't gonna look good for you in November, and it ain't gonna look good for your business ever." Baxter stood, threw a few dollars on the table, and left.

It was eight forty-five A.M. now, and there were cars and people on Main Street, not as many as there'd been twenty years ago at this hour, but enough so that Cliff Baxter felt like he was walking through his domain, greeting his subjects like a prince who'd stepped out of the palace to check out the mood of the populace. Most people seemed their usual selves, but now and then someone seemed to be avoiding him or looking at him funny.

Cliff Baxter stopped and spoke to a few citizens, shook a lot of hands, chatted with shopkeepers opening for business, tipped his hat to women, and even walked old Mrs. Graham across the street.

He lingered in front of police headquarters awhile and greeted everyone who walked by, calling most of them by name, joking with Oliver Grebbs, the bank president, about Oliver embezzling money to keep a mistress and both of them knowing the embezzlement was a joke, but the mistress wasn't.

He looked across the street at the courthouse where the city employees were walking through the park to go to work. At some point today or tomorrow, he knew, he'd have to go see the mayor.

Cliff Baxter couldn't get a sense of how the wind was blowing this morning, but he had the feeling that it was like an early north wind, gentle at first, almost imperceptible, so that it took a while to realize the warm west wind wasn't blowing anymore. In fact, it was calm, quiet, and only a few people noticed that the wind had changed direction.

Police Chief Baxter turned and went into police headquarters, where Sergeant Blake, at the front desk, greeted him with forced nonchalance.

Baxter walked into the inner office and said to Ward, "We ride at ten."

Baxter went into his office and closed the door. He went to the window and looked out at Main Street, the park, the courthouse, his world. A lesser man, he told himself, would be worried. But he felt he had his hands around enough prominent balls to hang on. But if he couldn't hang on, he'd take a whole lot of people down with him, starting with the short list on his desk and moving on to the longer list in his files.

In a way, he associated all this bad shit with the arrival of Keith Landry, though he knew this had been brewing a long time. Still, if he could get rid of Landry, at least one of his problems would be out of the way. Then he'd go for Gail Porter, not to mention Sherry Kolarik, the bitch, and Mary Arles, and any other women who thought they had more balls than Cliff Baxter. Then he'd go for the men if he had to. Basically, people frightened easily, he knew; there were no heroes left, only cowards who sometimes got together and thought they were heroes. He didn't think he had to kill anybody, only frighten them half to death—and if you frightened somebody half to death twice, they were a hundred percent frightened to death.

Keith woke at seven A.M., and the first thing on his mind was Annie.

Things were a little more clear now: They had made love, they were *in* love. He wasn't leaving. He wanted to stay, to make a life here with her, sit on the front porch with her and watch the sun go down.

But he knew she wouldn't stay if Cliff Baxter was still here, and she really didn't want her husband dead now that she had another option. But that option was to run off together, and Keith didn't want to run.

He lay, staring at the ceiling. It took him a while to realize he smelled her scent on the sheets.

It was a warm day, and he worked in the barn bare-chested. He wondered when and how they'd meet again, when they could make love again. He realized that he could take her away with probably no more than a few days' notice, and all this worry and fear would be behind them. They could be in Paris in less than a week. He wondered if she had a passport. No problem. He could get one for her within twenty-four hours. There were people who owed him favors.

Then, after a year or so, he would come back to Spencerville on his own and, if Baxter was still around, they should be able to settle matters at that point without bloodshed. Then Annie and he could return as husband and wife. "Good solution. Done."

At about quarter past ten, he heard a vehicle crunching over the gravel and went out through the barn doors.

Sitting in his driveway was a blue and white police car, and on its door was painted the gold shield of the chief of police.

The car was between him and the house, and Keith had no weapon with him. The driver of the car spotted him, and the car turned across the farmyard and came toward him. It stopped about thirty feet away, and he could see two men in the front seat. The passenger door opened, and a beefy man in tans, wearing mirrored sunglasses and a Smokey Bear hat, got out and came toward him.

Keith walked toward the man, who he saw was indeed Cliff Baxter. They stopped a few feet from each other and stared.

Keith's eyes went to the car, and he saw that the driver had gotten out. It was Officer Ward, but Ward didn't move, just stood near the car, watching.

Keith looked back at Baxter. He recognized him after nearly thirty years and saw that, despite the pot-belly, the man was still good-looking and still had the same sneer.

Keith studied the man's face, but, with the sunglasses and the wide-brimmed hat casting a shadow on his features, Keith couldn't determine the man's exact mood or intentions, or if Baxter knew anything about last night. Keith found he was worrying about Annie and not himself. Keith said, "I was starting to think you wouldn't come."

Baxter's mouth twitched, and he didn't respond, but kept staring through his glasses. Finally, he said, "I don't like you."

"That's good."

"Never did."

"I know that." He looked over Baxter's shoulder at Ward, who was now sitting on the hood of the car, smiling.

Baxter said, "Never will."

Keith said to him, "It's very rude to wear sunglasses when you're speaking to someone."

"Fuck you."

"Hey, Chief, you're what they call trespassing unless you have an official reason to be here."

Cliff Baxter glanced over his shoulder at Ward, then stepped closer to Keith and said, "You're a fucking asshole."

"Get off my property."

"Why're you here?"

"This is my home."

"Like hell it is. You don't belong here."

"Chief, I've got six generations of my people buried in this county. Don't tell me I don't belong here."

"*You're* gonna get buried in this county, sooner than you think."

Keith took a step forward so that they were face-to-face. He said, "Are you threatening me?"

"Back off or I'll kill you." He put his hand on his pistol, and Keith could see Ward slide off the hood of the car and reach for his gun.

Keith took a deep breath, then took a step back.

Baxter smiled. "You're not as stupid as you look."

Keith got himself under control and said, "Say your piece, Cliff, and leave."

Baxter obviously didn't like the use of his first name and all that it implied. He took his glasses off and stared at Keith a long time. Finally, he said, "You're fucking with my boys."

Keith didn't reply.

"And you're fucking with me."

Again, Keith said nothing.

"Behind the school. Meet me behind the school. That what you said?"

"Yup. I was there."

"You're lucky I wasn't. You'd be laid out right now at Gibbs, stiff as a board, with that pink shit they use in your veins. And I'd spit on your face if you had a face left after I got through with you."

Keith didn't reply.

"My boys told me you was hidin' behind that preacher's skirt at St. James."

"You can leave Pastor Wilkes out of this."

"Yeah? Why? Anybody who fucks with me or my boys is automatically in it—up to his ears—and that includes God Almighty himself."

Again, Keith didn't reply but just shook his head.

Baxter continued, "And what the fuck were you doing at Baxter Motors?"

"Speaking to your brother about a car."

"Yeah? And about my wife. If you keep asking around about me and my family, you're gonna die. Understand?"

Keith noticed that Baxter's eyes were set close together, the sign of a predator in the animal kingdom, and his head swiveled from side to side as he spoke, as though looking for prey or peril.

Keith tried to picture Annie with this guy for twenty years but knew that there was another Cliff Baxter, the home model. Cliff Baxter probably loved her, though she'd never tell Keith that, and Cliff Baxter thought he was a protective and caring husband, though most people would say possessive and abusive.

Baxter asked, "Cat got your tongue?"

"Nope."

"I'll bet you got to take a piss right now."

"Nope."

"Nope, yup, nope, yup. You got nothing else to say?"

"Yeah, I do. How did you get out of the draft? Mental or physical?"

"Hey, fuckhead, I was a cop. I did my duty here."

"Right. So did the women and schoolchildren who sent letters and packages."

"You motherfucker—"

"Hey, Chief, don't talk the talk if you haven't walked the walk. You want to prove you have balls? I'll go inside and get my piece, or you take off yours. You call it. Guns, knives, axes, fists. It doesn't matter to me how I kill you."

Baxter took a breath, and Keith saw by his body language that he wanted to take a step back. All said and done, Baxter still had the only gun between them, and there wasn't much keeping him from drawing it. Except, Keith thought, Baxter probably had other plans for Keith Landry, something he'd been thinking about for the last few weeks. Baxter hadn't come out here to kill him, so there was no reason to give him a reason. Yet, Keith couldn't resist the opportunity to mess with his mind and maybe draw him into a fair fight. Keith said, "Okay? You want to have it out? I was about to take a break anyway."

Baxter smiled. "Yeah, we're gonna have it out. But you ain't gonna see it coming."

"Still the class bully."

"Yeah, and you're still the class asshole. Hey, remember I used to bump you in the hall? You'd like to forget that, wouldn't you? I used to eye-fuck your girlfriend, and you didn't do shit. I'd feel her up every chance I got, and you saw me and just stood there. You know what? She loved it. She wanted a man, not a fucking pussy. And, hey, by the way, if I ever see you talking to her, I'll cut your balls off and feed 'em to my dogs. I kid you not."

Keith stood absolutely still. There was nothing to say after that, nothing to do now except let the man dig his own grave with his mouth.

Baxter, on a roll now, continued, "Hey, what do you do out here for pussy? If I catch you fuckin' the livestock, I'll run you in. You farm boys're always fuckin' the livestock, that's why they're so skittish. Your brother used to fuck the geese down by the lake and damn near killed half of them. He was the goose fucker. I remember him. And your sister—"

"Stop it. Please stop."

"Say again?"

"Please stop. Look...I'm leaving in a week. I just came back to see to the farm. I'm not staying. I'll be gone in about a week."

Baxter looked closely at him, then said, "Oh, yeah? Maybe I don't want you around that long."

"I just need a week."

"Tell you what—I'll give you six days. If you fuck up or piss me off, I'll kick the shit out of you and throw you on a fucking pig truck to Toledo. You understand?"

"Yes."

"Go back to your barnyard shit." He turned to leave, then spun around and buried his fist in Keith's stomach.

Keith doubled over and dropped to his knees.

Baxter put the toe of his boot under Keith's chin and flipped his head up. Baxter said, "Stay outa town."

He walked back to the car, and Keith saw him and Ward giving each other high fives.

They got into the car, turned and ran over a row of raspberry bushes, then peeled out on the gravel drive.

Keith got to his feet and watched the car turn onto the road. He smiled and said, "Thank you."

CHAPTER NINETEEN

Cliff Baxter sat at his kitchen table and sliced a hunk of meat off his pork chop. He said, "These damn things are burnt."

"Sorry."

"Potatoes're cold."

"Sorry."

"You forget how to cook?"

"No."

"No wonder you ain't eatin'."

"I don't have an appetite."

"Appetite or no, this stuff ain't edible."

"Sorry."

"And thanks for offering to make me something else."

"What would you like?"

"I'll go out and get something."

"All right."

He put down his knife and fork and looked at her. "Something bothering you?"

"No."

"You ain't sayin' much."

"I have a headache."

"That's too bad, 'cause I have a woody."

Annie stiffened but said nothing.

"You finished with your period?"

"No...not completely."

"Well, your gums ain't bleedin', are they?" He took a drink from his beer can but kept looking at her. He said, "I stopped by your Aunt Louise's today."

She felt her stomach tighten.

Cliff put down his beer can. "Now, there's a woman who knows how to cook. What'd she make you for dinner last night?"

"I...I didn't have dinner there."

"You didn't?"

"No."

"That ain't what she said, sweetheart."

Annie looked him in the eye and replied, "Aunt Louise is becoming very absentminded. I was there last week for dinner. Last night I was just visiting."

"Is that a fact? Absentminded must run in the family. You been walkin' around with your head up your ass since you got home last night."

"I'm not feeling well."

"How so?"

"I don't know...maybe I just miss the kids. I thought maybe I'd go visit them next week."

"They don't need you motherin' the hell out of them. If they want to see us, they can come home for the weekend."

"I wanted to make sure Wendy is settled in. It's her first time away from home, and—"

"You know, I don't like that place. I don't like Bowling Green, and I think I'm gonna pull her outa there."

"No!"

He seemed almost startled by her tone. He leaned toward her. "Say what?"

"She likes it there."

"Oh, yeah? What she likes is that fucking coed dorm. They have that when you were there?"

"No."

"What the fuck are they tryin' to do there? Promote fucking?"

"Cliff...the world has changed—"

"Not around here. This is a Christian house and a Christian community, and men and women don't live under the same roof if they're not married."

"I trust her to practice what she's been taught in church...and to follow our example." *God help her*, Annie thought.

Cliff regarded her a long time, then observed. "Yeah, there's somethin' on your mind."

"I just told you what was bothering me. Are you working tonight?"

"Maybe. Hey, speaking of college, an old friend of yours is back in town."

She got up and took her glass to the refrigerator, opened it, and poured iced tea. Her hands were shaking.

"You know who?"

"No."

Cliff stood and put his hand on the refrigerator door before she could shut it. "I need a beer." He took a can out, and she closed the door.

He stood looking at her a few seconds, then asked again, "You don't know who?"

She made a decision and said, "Oh, you mean Keith Landry."

"You know who the hell I mean."

"I heard he was back."

"I'm sure you did. I am sure you did. What else did you hear?"

"Nothing. Do you want dessert?"

"I ain't had dinner. Why do I want dessert?"

"Are you going out for dinner?"

"Don't fuck with me, lady. I'm talkin' to you."

"I'm listening, Cliff. Keith Landry is back in town. So what? Is there anything more?"

"Well, now, that's the question."

"What do you mean?"

"Jesus Christ, you fuckin' women know how to jerk a guy off, don't you?"

"What do you want me to say, Cliff? He's back in town. I heard it, you heard it. Why are you so angry at me?"

They looked at each other, and of course they both knew exactly why Cliff Baxter was angry. He asked her, "Why didn't you tell me he was back?"

"It never crossed my mind."

"You're full of shit."

"Don't speak to me that way." She felt a real anger rise up in her which overcame her fear. She raised her voice and said, "You may *not* speak to me that way. I'm leaving." She threw her glass in the sink and turned toward the door.

He grabbed her shoulder, spun her around, and held her arms. "You're not goin' nowhere."

"Stop it! Stop this! Let me go!"

He took his hands off her and backed away. "Okay...I'm sorry. Okay, just calm down. Here, sit down. I just want to talk to you."

She didn't trust him at all, but, reluctantly, she sat.

He sat across from her and played with his beer can. Finally he said, "Well...you know how I am. I just get real jealous sometimes. And I got to thinking about your old boyfriend back in town, and I find out he's single, and I guess I just got myself worked up. Now, you should be happy that I care so much about you. Right?"

She thought of several sarcastic replies, any one of which would send him off the deep end. She said, "I understand. But I really don't want to talk about this. There's nothing to talk about."

"Well, but you can see how this is going to bother me."

"It shouldn't."

"Why not? You mean a man who was fucking my wife is now livin' down the road, and that shouldn't bother me?"

"Cliff...look, whatever I say is going to get you angry. If I say I don't care if he's down the road, you'll take it wrong, if I say it bothers me that he's here, you'll take it—"

Baxter slammed the table and the dishes, and Annie jumped. He said, "You fucked the guy for six fucking years. And all you got to say is I shouldn't be fucking pissed off that he's down the road. What if one of my old girlfriends was down the road? How'd you like that?"

She wanted to remind him that he'd sometimes point out his old girlfriends to her and that all she felt was pity for them. Instead, she said, "I guess that would really bother me."

"You're fucking right it would!"

"Please don't shout. I know you're angry, but—"

"Hey, you remember Cindy North? I fucked her for a year right before I started seeing you. What if she moved in next door and was single? Would that piss you off?"

"Of course."

"Yeah. So I'm not supposed to be pissed off?"

"I didn't say that. Just don't be angry at me. I didn't do anything."

"But maybe you'd like to."

"Cliff, don't say that."

"You remember the good times with him, don't you?"

"I don't remember any of it. It was over twenty years ago."

He seemed almost surprised, she thought, that it was that many years. He said, "But when you heard he was back, you got to thinkin' about those rolls in the hay. Where'd you fuck him? In the barn? You go down on him in your car?"

She stood, and he reached across the table, grabbed her belt, and pulled her down in the seat.

Annie was frightened, but not for herself. She could handle him, but she had to warn Keith that Cliff was getting himself worked up. She took a deep breath and said, "Cliff, sweetheart, I know you're angry, but there's no one in the world for me except you."

He seemed to calm down, but clearly he was still seething. "There damn well better not be."

"There isn't. I know you love me, and that's why you're angry. I'm very flattered." She knew she should quit while she was ahead, but she hated him so much, she couldn't resist lighting his short fuse again. She said, "I don't want you thinking about what Keith and I did for six years."

He looked at her but said nothing.

She added, "We were just young high school and college kids, and we just did what everyone was doing then. You should be happy I only did it with him and not—"

"Shut up!"

"Sorry."

"Shut up."

She hung her head and stared at her plate, trying to suppress a smile.

A minute went by, then Cliff said, "I don't want you talking to him or about him."

"I won't."

"Has he called you?"

She shook her head. "Why would he—?"

"You tried to call him?"

"Not in a million years."

"Yeah? So you two ain't spoken since he's been back?"

Again, she made a decision, got up, and stood behind his chair. She said, "Cliff, I can't lie to you...I ran into him on the street."

He didn't say anything.

She continued, "I was with Charlene Helms, old Mrs. Whitney, and Pastor Schenk's wife, Marge. I just left the post office and ran into him. I didn't even recognize him, and when he started talking, I didn't even know who it was. You know, when people think you know who they are, and they start jabbering. It happens to you all the time. Then I realized who it was, and I just said, 'You have a nice day, Mr. Landry.' Then I walked off with the girls."

She kept her hands on his shoulders and, though she couldn't see his face, she could feel his muscles tense up. She added, "It really slipped my mind, Cliff, and when I remembered to mention it to you, you weren't around. I knew you might get angry, but I thought you should know I ran into him. But I guess I was a little scared to mention it, so maybe I buried it in my mind. I figured he was just visiting, and that was the end of it." She said, "I'm sorry I didn't tell you. I'll never speak to him again. I swear."

He sat motionless for a full minute, then said, "You won't be able to."

She felt her heart skip a beat and couldn't speak. Finally, she knew she had to say something, but she couldn't ask the obvious question. She said, "I won't."

"You can't, you won't. I ran the son-of-a-bitch out of town."

"Oh…"

He stood and faced her, and he smiled. "I stopped by his place this morning. That surprise you?"

"No."

"I told him to get the fuck out of town. He said he'd be gone in a week."

"A week…?"

"Yeah. He's a fucking pussy, if you care to know."

"I don't care."

"He fucking begged me to let him stay a few more days. I gave him six days. I also gave him a shot in the gut, and he folded like a leaf. You shoulda seen that. He just went down like a log and laid there while I poured shit all over him. He wouldn't even defend himself. Hell, I offered to take off my gun and badge if he wanted to duke it out, but he was so scared he nearly pissed his pants. I can't believe you went out with this pussy."

Annie bit her lip to keep it from trembling, but a tear ran down her cheek.

"Hey, you crying?"

"No…" She wiped her face. "I'm just upset…that you had to do that."

"Upset? What the fuck is upset? You pissed at me?"

"No."

"Jesus Christ, I don't get you. You cryin' because I decked him?"

"No. Women get upset when their husbands do something dangerous."

"Dangerous? That fucking guy is not dangerous… well, I suppose he could have been. I didn't know when I went out there what to expect. But I knew I had to settle this thing, man-to-man."

"Please promise me you won't go out there again."

"I'm goin' out there to make sure he listened."

"Don't. Send someone else."

He pinched her cheek. "Don't worry about it. The guy must've lost his balls in 'Nam. Lucky you didn't marry him."

"He never asked."

"What the fuck do I care?"

She reached out a took a plate from the table. "I'll clean up here."

"Later. You go on upstairs." He added. "I'll be right up. You be ready."

"Cliff…"

"Yeah?"

She wanted to say to him, "I fucked Keith last night, and I don't want you near me." She wanted to say that more than she wanted to plunge the carving knife in his heart. "Cliff…I…"

"Yeah? Got a headache? *Upset?* Havin' your period? What's your problem?"

"Nothing."

She walked out of the kitchen and into the hallway. She wanted to run out the front door, but she wouldn't get far. She wanted to scream, to go upstairs and cut her wrists, to drop a lamp on his head when he came up, to set the house on fire, to do anything except have sex with Cliff Baxter.

She steadied herself on the banister and tried to think clearly. The only thing she could do was to pretend that everything was all right. She did that easily enough when she spoke to him, but in bed she could never pretend. He didn't seem to care or notice as long as she submitted. But this time she couldn't do even that. She came back into the kitchen.

He was at the table, finishing his beer and looking at the newspaper. He glanced up at her. "Yeah?"

"I'd like a drink."

He laughed. "Yeah? Why? You can't fuck me sober?"

"Sometimes a drink helps get me in the mood."

"Then have a bunch of drinks. God knows you ain't been in the mood for some time now."

She went to the cupboard, took down a bottle of peach brandy, got a glass, and walked over toward the hallway.

Cliff glanced at her over his newspaper and said, "Get yourself in the mood for some things you ain't done in a while, darlin'."

She went into the hallway, up the stairs, and into their bedroom. She poured a tumbler full of brandy, closed her eyes, and drank it. Tears streamed down her cheeks. She poured another, drank half of it, and sat on the bed and cried.

She barely remembered taking off her clothes, but remembered when he came into the room. After that, she remembered nothing.

CHAPTER TWENTY

The phone rang at the Landry farm at twenty minutes past eight on Saturday morning. Keith was in the kitchen making coffee, and he answered it. "Hello."

"Keith, I have to speak to you."

He shut off the coffeepot. "Are you all right?"

"Yes. I'm at a pay phone in town. Can you meet me someplace?"

"Of course. Where?"

"I thought maybe the fairgrounds. There'll be no one there today."

"Then we don't belong there. Listen, you remember Reeves Pond, south of my place?"

"Where we used to skate?"

"Yes. Get some bread or something and go feed the ducks. I'll be there in twenty minutes. Is everything okay?"

"Yes. No." She said, "You have a rifle. I saw it—"

"Yes, okay. Are you safe now?"

"Yes, I'm all right. I'm sorry. I'm just worried about you. He's suspicious—"

"Twenty minutes." He added, "If you've been followed, go feed the ducks anyway, but leave your car door open as a signal. Understand?"

"Yes."

"Take it easy." He hung up, went upstairs, and opened the wardrobe. He found his binoculars, then took two full magazines and put one in his pocket. The other he slammed into his M-16 rifle, pulled back on the charging handle, and chambered a round.

He slung the rifle and the binoculars, went downstairs and out the front door. He crossed the road and ran to the Jenkins barn.

Within five minutes, he'd saddled and mounted the mare, gave her a slap, and rode her out through the open paddock gate, across the road, and into the woods.

He ducked as the mare picked her way through the trees and down the slope toward the shallow streambed. He reined her around, and they headed south downstream, toward the pond.

A hundred yards from where the stream came out of the trees, he reined her in, dismounted, and tied her to a sapling.

Keith continued on along the bank and stopped in the shadows of the last trees, a few yards from the sunlit shore of the big pond. There was no car parked on the grassy slope that descended to the pond on the far shore, and, in fact, there was no one in sight.

The only road was a few hundred yards farther to the south, and he couldn't see it because it lay on the opposite side of the rise, but now and then he saw the top of a big rig go by.

He looked at his watch. It was a quarter to nine. He wondered what had happened between the time he'd seen her two nights ago and now.

At a few minutes to nine, he saw the nose of a car crest the rise, then descend through the high grass toward the pond. But it wasn't a Lincoln, it was a Ford

Fairlane, which was what the Spencerville police used for their marked and unmarked vehicles, purchased no doubt from Baxter Motors.

The car, which bore no police markings, stopped at the edge of the grass where the muddy shore began, and Keith raised his binoculars. The driver's-side door opened, and Annie got out, wearing a red skirt and white blouse. She stood beside the open door a moment, looked around, then closed the door.

She walked down to the water's edge, carrying a loaf of bread. Keith watched her as she absently ripped open the wrapper and threw whole slices into the water. A few dozen ducks and geese swam toward the floating bread. Every few seconds, she looked over her shoulder.

Keith let a few minutes pass, then walked out of the tree line and waved to her.

She saw him, threw the loaf down, and hurried along the shore toward him as he came around to meet her.

As they drew closer, he saw by her expression that she was anxious but not terrified. She smiled and sprinted the last ten yards and literally jumped into his arms, wrapping her arms and legs around him. "Hello, Mr. Landry."

They kissed, then she slid down and took his hands. She said, "It's good to see you." She glanced at the barrel of the rifle rising above his shoulder and said, "Maybe you didn't need that."

"I'm just out varmint shooting. Let's walk into the woods."

They walked side by side along the shore, and she glanced back a few times. She said, "I don't think I was followed. I brought my Lincoln in to Baxter Motors this morning and said I had a knock in the engine. They gave me a loaner. The damned Lincoln sticks out like a sore thumb around here. I think that's why Cliff's father gave it to me."

He smiled and said, "Sounds to me like you *have* had a few affairs."

"No, sir, but I've given some serious thought to how I would go about it. How about you, wise guy? Leave the car door open if you've been followed."

"That was my vocation. My avocation was tennis." He asked her, "Did Aunt Louise blow it?"

"Sort of. But it wasn't her fault. Cliff made it his business to stop by and see her and, for some reason, she told him I had dinner with her, and he asked me what I had for dinner."

"The devil is in the details."

"You can say that again. I'm just not good at this, Keith. Anyway, he's suspicious. He's always suspicious. This time, he's right."

They reached the trees and walked along the bank of the stream. It was cooler out of the sunlight, and the trees, mostly birch and willow, were just starting to turn. Keith had always liked autumn in the country, the trees ablaze with color, pumpkins and cider, the hunting season, and the harvest. He hadn't seen anything like it anywhere else in the world, and perhaps more than summer, it was the autumn that he thought of when he thought of home.

Annie tapped him on the shoulder and pointed up ahead. "Is that your horse?"

"It's a loaner horse. The Jenkinses' across the road."

"So that's how you got here. Are they still following you?"

"Maybe. I didn't want to find out today."

"Can't you get a court order or something."

"I sort of enjoy the attention."

"I don't." Annie walked up to the mare and

patted her neck. "This is a nice animal. We used to ride. Remember?"

"I do. You still ride?"

"No. But I'd like to." She took off her shoes and slipped off her panty hose, then untied the reins and led the horse around to drink from the stream. "She's thirsty."

Keith unslung his rifle and binoculars and laid them on a tree stump. He sat on a fallen trunk and watched her.

Annie asked, "Has she been fed?"

"I fed her about seven. No one's fed me yet."

She laughed. "Bachelors are so dumb. If you move their plates six inches to the left, they'd starve to death." Without looking at him, she asked, "Who took care of you all these years?"

"Uncle and Amex."

She glanced at him as she led the horse up the bank and tied the reins. "Did you have a good life, Keith?"

"I did."

"I did, too, despite my marriage. I learned how to enjoy other things."

"You always found something good in any situation. I was always looking for the dark lining in the silver cloud."

"Not always. You acted more cynical than you were."

"You read me too well."

"Well enough." Still barefoot, she walked to where he was sitting and lay down along the length of the trunk, her feet in his lap. "They're cold."

He dried her feet with his handkerchief and rubbed them.

"Feels good."

"How are we doing for time?"

"Who cares?"

"We do."

"Oh, we're all right. I'm doing Saturday errands around town. He's fishing up at Grey Lake in Michigan with his cronies. We have a hunting lodge there. He won't be home until late afternoon."

"You're sure?"

"The only thing he enjoys more than bothering me is fishing and hunting with his friends." She thought a moment and said, "God, I hate that place, but I'm glad he likes it. Keeps him away...we can be together when he's there."

"Do you go with him?"

"Sometimes." She added, "The few times we went up there alone, without the kids or without company, he was another person. Not necessarily better, and not actually worse...just another person...quiet, distant, as if he's...I don't know...thinking of something. I don't like to go up there with him alone, and I can usually get out of it."

"Okay, so what happened?"

She closed her eyes and, as he massaged her feet and calves, she said, "Well, we had a little scene at dinner last night. First, about the dinner being burned." She laughed. "I did it on purpose."

"You sound like fun to live with."

"No comment. Anyway, then he tried to trap me about dinner at Aunt Louise's, then we got onto the subject of Wendy in a coed dorm, then we got to Keith Landry, the guy who fucked me for six years—quote, unquote—and who's now living down the fucking road, then he tried to trap me again by asking if I'd seen you. I figured he already knew, so I told him I bumped into you at the post office."

Keith nodded and said, "Good thinking."

"Well, it didn't improve his mood much. He's still

very angry and suspicious. That's what I wanted to tell you. But I guess you know that." She said, "He told me he came out to your place yesterday."

Keith didn't reply.

She took her feet out of his lap, sat up, and slid over beside him on the trunk. She took his hand. "I'm sorry. You don't need this."

"Annie, when I got in my car in Washington and drove here, I knew where this was headed. And I also knew what I wanted here."

She squeezed his hand. "But you didn't know the whole situation."

"The only thing I had to find out was how *you* felt."

"Keith, you knew. You had to know how I felt."

He smiled. "Your letters could have been read by your aunt and my aunt without a blush."

"*My* letters? You signed yours 'Sincerely.'"

"I did not." He added, "I meant 'Love.'"

They sat for a while listening to the stream, the horse snorting, the rustle of the leaves and the birds. Finally, she said, "You understood, didn't you, that I still loved you, and I was waiting for you?"

"I understood. But I may never have come."

"I always knew you would." She picked up a twig and scratched it around on the ground. She said, "But if you didn't, then there was no one else." She wiped her eyes, and, still looking at the ground, she took a deep breath and said, "Oh God…I thought you'd get killed, I thought you'd get married, I thought you'd stopped loving me."

"No."

"But why did you wait? Why?"

"I don't know…I mean, right after I left, we were both angry at something…then, before I went overseas, it occurred to me that I might get killed, or lose a leg or arm, or something…"

"If I was your wife, I would have taken care of you. If I was your widow, I'd have honored your memory."

"Well, you didn't need any of that. Then, when I got home...I don't know...we couldn't connect. Then you got married, and I hated you, then I hated myself, then the years just went by...the letters came, they didn't come...you had children, you had a life... I could picture you here with friends and family...you never wrote much about your marriage..."

"You never wrote a word about how you felt."

"I did."

"You never wrote a word about *us*."

"Neither did you."

"I tried...I was afraid. Afraid the letters would stop."

"Me, too."

She wiped her eyes again and tried to smile. "We're idiots. We used to talk about everything, then, for over twenty years, we couldn't even say 'I love you' and 'I miss you.'"

"I know." He thought a moment, then said, "You know, it's twenty-five years this month since we said good-bye in your apartment in Columbus."

"I know. Hard to believe." She put her hand on his leg. "After you left, I cried for weeks. Then I got myself together and buried myself in schoolwork. I didn't date—"

"It's all right. Really."

"Let me speak. So, anyway, I started to realize that...I started getting angry at you...and when women get angry, they get spiteful."

"I didn't know that."

She punched his leg. "Listen. So I went to see this campus shrink, and he was helpful. He said that I was manufacturing an anger toward you because it was the only way I could deal with the possibility of losing you to another woman, or of your getting killed. He said I really loved you, and I should tell you."

"I don't remember that happening."

"Because you never got that letter. I ripped it up. Then I wrote it again, and I ripped it up. I did that about a dozen times. Then I realized I was still angry, I was hurt, I felt betrayed. I remembered a line I read somewhere—men who are happy at home do not go to war."

"But even happy men get restless."

"Well, but you weren't there to tell me that. And when you called, you sounded distant."

"You, too."

"I know. I hate telephones. So I got myself all worked up, and I decided to see other men. I want you to know, Keith, I never loved any of them. Not the way I still loved you. In fact, not at all." She laughed and said, "I got dumped by all of them. They all had the same complaints. Annie, you're cold, stuck-up, selfish, self-centered, and so on. I was none of those things. I was in love with another man."

"You don't have to tell me any of this."

"Sure I do. So I went to Europe, to get away, and I was stunned by the beauty—I mean, where had I been? Spencerville, Bowling Green, and Columbus. And every time I saw something that moved me, I'd say, 'Keith, look at that. Keith, isn't that beautiful?'" She put her elbows on her knees and buried her face in her hands. "I'm sorry...I haven't cried in years, and I've been crying for weeks now."

"It's okay."

She found a tissue in her pocket and blew her nose. "Okay...so then I came home, and my cousin was getting married and I was her maid of honor, and at the reception I met Cliff Baxter."

"I heard that from someone who was there. I also

heard from my mother that you got engaged to him, and that I was a fool."

"Your mother was right. So was my mother. She told me not to marry him. Funny thing is that my father liked him at first. Most guys seemed to like him, and a lot of women did, too. The women liked him because he had a new car every year, he had some charm, and he was good-looking. He still has a new car."

"Annie—"

"Quiet. So I was still sort of inexperienced with men, and I couldn't judge...I thought, well, there'll never be another Keith, but Cliff is the boy next door, Cliff has a responsible job, Cliff is draft-exempt, and the other guys are married, or in the Army, and Cliff always liked me. Can you imagine such narrow, immature, small-town thinking?"

"Sure. This is who we were, Annie."

"Yes, it was. So...he asked me to marry him... down on one knee, if you can believe that...I was flattered, I was feeling low about myself, I was stupid."

Keith asked her, "Annie, why did you marry him? Really. You have to know it, and you have to say it."

She glanced at him, then stood and replied, "To get back at you."

He stood also, and they looked at each other.

She said, "You bastard. Do you know what you did to me? Do you know? I hate you. I hate what you did to me, what you made me into, what I did because of you."

"I know. Feel better?"

She nodded.

He took her hand, and they sat on the edge of the stream and watched the water. She said, "Thank you. I do feel better."

"Me, too."

She said, "I don't hate you anymore."

"Maybe just a little."

"No, I don't. I'm angry at myself."

"So am I. But I think we can forgive ourselves if we do it right this time."

She asked him, "And you're sure you aren't still angry with me? I mean for the way I treated you when you went off to the Army and for marrying Cliff?"

"Well, I was. You know that. But I came to understand it a little. I mean, we never wrote about it, but just the act of writing and keeping in touch was sort of our way of saying we both made mistakes, we both regretted what had happened, and we were sort of apologizing, forgiving, and still loving—without saying 'I'm sorry, forgive me, I love you.'" He added, "I'm glad you decided to bring it up. I'm glad you feel you can talk to me."

"I do. You're the first man I've called a bastard since . . . well, since you—that time you had lunch in the student union with that little bitch, whatever her name was."

"Karen Rider."

"Bastard." She laughed.

They watched the rippling water for a long time, thinking their own thoughts, then Annie said, "It's peaceful here. I used to take the kids fishing at the pond. I taught them to skate there. I think you'd like them. They take after me."

"That's good."

"They're not actually kids anymore, are they? They're very mature."

"Then they're doing better than us. We don't want to grow up."

"We grew up. I want to be a kid again."

"Why not? Pick an age you like and stick with it. That's my new motto."

She laughed. "Okay, twenty-one."

"Well, darling, you have the body for it."

"You noticed. I'm the same size as I was in college. I'm very vain about my looks. Very shallow."

"Good. Me, too. By the way, you looked good in jeans the other night. What are you dressed for today?"

"Well . . . he wants me to dress when I go into town. I can't even go to the public pool and be seen in a bathing suit. One time he came by the high school where I was taking an aerobics class, and he got one look at what I was wearing in a coed class and he freaked out, so now I work out at home . . . sorry. You don't want to hear this."

"Are you allowed to have sex with a horseman you just met in the woods?"

"That happens to be one of my recurring sexual fantasies."

"Good." He stood and looked around. "A little rough here."

"Oh, be inventive, Keith. Here—we'll do it on that log." She took his hand and led him back to the big fallen trunk they'd sat on. She took off his shirt and laid it on the log. "Sit. No, first you have to take your pants off."

He pulled off his shoes and then his jeans as she undid her blouse and bra. She slipped her panties off under her skirt and said, "We shouldn't get completely naked in case someone comes by. I can say I'm picking mushrooms, and I don't know who you are."

"Good thinking. Well . . ." He sat on the trunk, still wearing his shorts, and Annie, still wearing her blouse, bra, and skirt, held his shoulders and threw one leg at a time over the log, then lowered herself into his lap. She put her hand under her skirt, found him, and slid it in. "Oooh . . . that's nice . . ."

She wrapped her arms around him, and he steadied himself with his hands on the log. He said, "We're going to fall backwards."

"So what?" She rested her head on his shoulder as she moved up and down on him. "Oh...that feels... different...how are you doing?"

"Just fine."

"Are we going to fall?"

"No, I've got it."

She pressed her breasts against his bare chest as she moved slowly up and down on him, then quickened her movements and began breathing harder. She suddenly stiffened and climaxed, and he ejaculated.

Her body went limp in his arms, and she held him loosely as she caught her breath. After a minute, she said, "I feel like such a whore. It feels great. How do we get out of this position?"

"Wait for a forest ranger." He put his arms around her, stood, and stepped away from the log. She slid down from him, and they embraced and kissed. He said, "That was very nice."

"*I* had fun." She put her hand on his groin and said, "We have to clean you up."

"I like to wear it."

"Is that so?" She picked her panties up, wet them in the stream, then cleaned him off and cleaned herself. "There. Can't go around sticking to things."

"You're funny."

"I feel funny. Giddy." She threw her panties in a bush. "I feel like a kid. I haven't done this outdoors since high school. Next, we'll do it in your barn, then the backseat of my car."

"Maybe we'll get a motel room."

"That, too."

He picked up his pants, but she said, "No. Take off

your shorts. I've never seen a naked man in the woods. I wish I had a camera. Your socks, too."

He slid off his shorts and socks. "You're embarrassing me."

"Turn around." She came up behind him and ran her hands over his back and buttocks, squeezing his cheeks. "You're all muscle."

"You been in jail, or what? Can I get dressed?"

"No, turn around."

He turned around, and she moved her hands over his chest and down to his stomach. "I told you, I can't keep my hands off—" She looked at his stomach. "What's that?"

"A bruise."

"Oh..." She hooked her bra and buttoned her blouse. He got dressed.

She went back to the streambank and sat in a patch of sunlight near the water, her back to a willow tree.

Keith came and sat beside her.

Annie threw twigs in the water and watched them run downstream, cascading over the stones. She asked, "What happened when he came out to your place?"

"About what you'd expect."

"Tell me."

"Well, he was a lot crazier than the situation required, so I had the thought that he'd found out about your visit to me, and I was...I was really worried for a minute there. About you."

"Thank you."

"But he sort of had the drop on me, and I was a little worried about me, too. Then I realized he didn't know anything, but that he was just nuts."

"Was he alone?"

"No. He had one of his men with him. A guy named Ward. You know him?"

"Yes, he's my keeper." She added, "Cliff led me to believe he was alone."

Against his better judgment, Keith replied, "If he was alone, he'd be dead."

She didn't speak for a while, then said, "He's a coward and a liar."

"He's also dangerous, Annie. You have to be careful."

"He's never hit me. I know how to handle him."

"Your kids are gone, his job is in trouble, I'm in town, and he's ready to blow. Believe me."

She asked him, "How do you know his job is in trouble?"

"I went to that meeting at St. James. You know about that?"

"Yes. As a matter of fact, my parents were there. They've been acting weird since then. I guess the subject of Cliff Baxter came up, but no one will tell me about it. Will you tell me about it?"

"No."

She thought a moment, then said, "I'm not completely naive. I know he fools around, but I can't believe that came up at a public meeting."

"Tell you what—there's a transcript available. You remember Jeffrey Porter?"

"Yes. I run into him once in a while. And his wife, Gail. That was the girl he was seeing at school."

"Right. I've caught up on old times with them. In fact, I trust them, and if you ever need anything and you can't contact me, go to them. I'll speak to them and set it up."

"Keith...no. I don't want anyone else knowing about us. It's too dangerous."

"Listen to me, I know when to bet my life on someone. These are trustworthy people. But go and speak to them first, and let me know what you think."

"Okay...and they have a transcript of the meeting?"

"They do. He called me yesterday. They're selling it all over town for five bucks, and they can't keep up with the demand. But for you, it's free."

"Keith, what's in the transcript? Will I be embarrassed, humiliated, or both?"

"I'm sorry, Annie. They got a little carried away with witnesses against your husband. But you shouldn't feel embarrassed or humiliated. You may, however, be angry."

"Actually, I don't care anymore."

"Go see the Porters. We may need their help."

"With what?"

"Rendezvous. Cover stories."

"And how long will we need cover stories?"

He took her hand. "That's up to you, Annie. Are you ready to leave?"

She looked at him. "Are you proposing, Mr. Landry?"

"Yes, I am, Miss Prentis."

"I accept."

He put his arm around her, and they rolled over, with her on top of him. She kissed him, then said, "It took you a while to get around to it."

"I'm shy."

"You are, you know. You may be a man of the world, but you're still shy."

"Don't tell anyone."

She said, "You've changed, Keith. Of course you have—but I still know you."

"You haven't changed much. I still like you."

She snuggled on top of him, and they lay together on the sloping bank. He thought she drifted off, but then she said, "When?"

"When what?"

"When can we elope?"

"Oh...well, what do you think about just moving into my place?"

She rolled off and knelt beside him, looking down at him. "We can't, Keith. This is not Washington. People don't just change partners here. They run off. They always run. They have to. You know that."

"I know. But I don't like to run, Annie."

"There is no other way." She added, "I'll go with you anywhere you want. But not here."

"Okay...but I'm going to speak to him first."

"No. He'll get violent."

Which was exactly what Keith wanted. He said to her, "He and I should talk, man-to-man and all that."

She stared down at him a long time, then said, "Keith, look at me."

He sat up and looked at her. "Yes?"

"Promise me you won't hurt him."

Keith didn't reply.

She put her hands on his shoulders. "I know he hit you, and I know you're not the kind of man who's going to forgive or forget that. But you don't have to settle the score. Let it go. For me."

Again, Keith didn't reply.

She said, "Please. Let God or Spencerville deal with him. We don't need that as part of our history." She added, "He's Tom and Wendy's father."

"I promise I won't kill him."

She looked at him and said, "No violence of any sort, Keith. Please. Not even the beating he deserves." She took his head in her hands and said, "There's nothing worse you or I can do to him than what we're about to do. Leave it at that."

"All right. I promise."

"I love you." She leaned forward and kissed him.

He stood and said, "Let me walk you back."

"Let's walk in the stream."

"Okay." He pulled off his shoes and socks and left them on the bank, rolled up his jeans, and slung his rifle over his shoulder while she gathered up her panty hose and shoes.

They walked down the stream toward the pond, hand in hand. She said, "I need a week to get my affairs in order. Is that too long?"

"Not after twenty-five years."

She squeezed his hand. "Where will we go?"

"Do you have a passport?"

"No. But I can apply for one."

"Not at this post office, you can't."

"No, I can't. I'll go up to Toledo."

"We'll go to Washington first. Bring all your personal papers."

"Okay. I've never been to Washington."

"What city did you like best in Europe?"

"Rome."

"Rome it is."

"Are you serious?"

"If you are, I am."

She thought a moment, then said, "I am."

He glanced at her and asked, "Do you understand what it means to leave home?"

"No, but if I'm with you, I'm home. How's that for lovesick?"

"I know the feeling. But have you thought about what it's like to miss your children, your family, and community?"

"Yes. I've thought about that. But it's time I did something that Annie Prentis wants to do."

"And your job? Do you still manage the hospital thrift store?"

"Yes, and I like it, but it's hardly challenging." She added, "It's a husband-approved job. No men, no money, no weekends, flexible hours, and down the street from his office."

Keith nodded. "I saw it when I was downtown."

"Would you mind if I worked?"

"You can do whatever you want."

"Can I work long hours in an office, bring work home on weekends, and go on business trips with men?"

"Don't push it, Prentis."

She smiled and squeezed his hand.

They continued through the ankle-deep stream, picking their way around the stones, and Keith liked the feel of the silt on his bare feet and her hand in his.

Annie said, "Maybe someday we can return to visit."

"Maybe."

"And how about you, Keith? This is your home, too. Did you want to stay?"

"I did, but I knew I couldn't. But maybe someday."

She thought awhile, then said, "If...he wasn't here..."

"What would he do if he got sacked?"

She replied, "He wouldn't stay. He couldn't. He'd be humiliated. And too many people secretly hate him." She thought a moment, then said, "You know, if Mrs. Baxter runs off with another man, he may actually be embarrassed enough to resign and leave town. Then we can return if we want to."

Keith nodded, then asked her, "Where would he go?"

"Grey Lake. In fact, that's where he said we were going if and when he retires." She smiled. "That may be sooner than he thinks. Only, he'll be going alone. He knows he can't stay in Spencerville as the ex-chief of police."

"You mean there'd be no more testimonial dinners at the Elks Lodge?"

She glanced at him, then said, "I guess you read about that in the papers. God, that was one of the worst nights of my life." When he didn't respond, she said, "Did that make you jealous?"

"I had some unhealthy emotion or another. Couldn't figure out what it was."

"Well, sweetheart, I thought about you all that night and wondered what you were doing on a Saturday night. Do you know how many Saturday nights I wondered where you were after we first separated?"

"I was having fun in basic infantry training." He added, "I stood in long pay phone lines on Saturday nights to call you. You weren't in."

"I sure was. But I wasn't going to answer it." She added, "Pride and stubbornness are sins, and we paid for them."

"We did."

"Jealousy is also a sin. I'm not jealous, but...you know I called you from the Elks Lodge. I just wanted to hear your voice that night. But *you* weren't in."

"I went to the high school and shot some baskets, then got home around nine, took a very cold shower, and went to bed."

"Good. Did you dream about me?"

"Probably. I know that the first thing on my mind every morning is you."

"Me, too."

They got to the edge of the trees where the stream widened and flowed into the big pond. They climbed the bank and looked out over the grassland and water. There were other cars parked near Annie's now, and a few bicycles lay in the tall grass.

Keith watched a few kids floating on a big rubber raft and saw two older men fishing. Two mothers with toddlers were playing with toy boats at the water's edge.

It was a placid pond with a mirrored surface, but now and then a small fish broke the water, sending out concentric ripples. Dragonflies hovered over the water and cattails swayed in the breeze. There was a clump of pond lilies near the shore whose sweet roots could be cooked and eaten, and Keith wondered if kids knew about that anymore.

Reeves Pond didn't look much different than Keith remembered it on any warm Saturday thirty years before, except that there used to be a lot more kids; the organized-activity generation, maybe the last of the Huckleberry Finn-type kids who cooked lily root and chewed smartweed, and fished with bamboo poles and used old inner tubes for floats, and annoyed small animals and adults with slingshots, and got around on iron bikes that weighed more than they did.

Annie asked, "What are you smiling about?"

"I was just remembering that the guys used to skinny-dip here on hot summer nights. We smoked cigarettes, drank beer, and talked about girls."

"I know. We used to lie in the high grass up there and watch."

"You did not."

She laughed. "We did. Twice. We couldn't see too much, but we all said we did."

"Why didn't you join us?"

"We probably should have. One night we were going to steal your clothes, but we got chicken."

"Well, I'll tell you what—some summer night you and I will come back here and go skinny-dipping."

"It's a date."

They stood quietly awhile, not wanting this time to end. She said, "This is probably the last weekend of warm weather."

"Yes, I can smell a touch of autumn."

"Me, too."

They watched the people around the pond, then Keith said, "You know Pastor Wilkes at St. James, don't you?"

"Yes."

"I spoke to him the night of the meeting at St. James."

"How is he?"

"Old. But still in there pitching."

"What's he pitching?"

"Sliders and curves."

"Meaning?"

"He advised me not to covet my neighbor's wife."

"Did he? Well, if he means Mrs. Jenkins or Mrs. Muller, that's very good advice. But I guess he was referring to me. How embarrassing."

"He likes you. He didn't seem to be judgmental toward me, but he advised me to wait until you get a divorce. Then I can covet."

"He really said that?"

"He did. He's an old romantic underneath it all."

She thought about this, then said, "I didn't think you'd go to anyone, not even a pastor, for advice."

"As a matter of fact, I didn't. He broached the subject."

"You mean he knew about…how would he know…?"

"From your pastor, the Reverend Schenk. I'm only telling you this in case you thought about going to Pastor Schenk for advice or absolution, or something."

"I…I have discussed my marriage with him." She hesitated, then said, "To be honest, I spoke to him about you."

"Did you? Did you tell him you had sexual fantasies about me?"

"Certainly not." She laughed. "Not in so many words."

"Well, if you speak to him again, he'll tell you what Wilkes told me—get a divorce and, meantime, do not commit adultery."

"A little late for that."

"Also, these things do get around."

She nodded. "I'm friends with Pastor Schenk's wife, Marge...what else did Pastor Wilkes tell you?"

"I can't say, but with all good intentions, they know too much."

"I'll be careful." She looked at him and said, "One week from today, Keith."

"One week from today."

She sat down on the ground and untangled her panty hose. "Can you dry me off?"

He knelt beside her and dried her feet with his shirt-tail and helped her put her panty hose and shoes on. He said, "Where're your underwear?"

"Lost 'em." She put out her hand, and he pulled her up. She said, "Good Lord, look at me...I'm covered with leaves, my clothes are dirty..." She laughed. "Looks like I just had sex in the woods." She brushed herself off and smiled. "Do you think I should go home before I go grocery shopping? Hello, Mrs. Smith, yes I *did* have sex in the woods, as a matter of fact. A tall stranger on horseback. How are the carrots today?"

Keith smiled. "You're having fun, aren't you?"

"Yes. And I know what you're thinking—what's it going to be like when there's no more danger and excitement of illicit sex. Well, this *is* fun, but I'm frightened, truly frightened. I just want to be safe, with you, and twenty years from now, when you walk into the room, my heart will still skip a beat."

"I believe that."

"You should, or you're doing the wrong thing. I'm leaving here no matter what, Keith, and I'd like your help. But you don't have to make any promises. Get me out of here, then you can do what you want. I mean that."

"No, you don't..." He looked at her. "Well... maybe you do. But that's not the program. This is real simple—I came back to be with you."

"What if I was three hundred pounds?"

"I would have walked past you on the sidewalk, if I could get around you. Stop giving me a hard time."

"Did anyone write to you about me?"

"Yes, a few people. My mother especially. She kept track of your weight."

"She's been gone five years."

"Is this a test?"

"No, just things I promised myself I'd say to you."

"Is that it?"

"That's it. You're hooked. Do you have a plan?"

"No, but the simpler, the better. What's he usually do on Saturdays?"

"Saturday is good. He always spends Saturdays with his friends, either at the lodge on Grey Lake, or Lake Michigan, or Lake Erie. They boat, they fish, they shoot in season. Bird season just started."

"What if it rains?"

"They go anyway. They usually play cards someplace—most of them have places in Michigan."

"Okay. Just pack the bare essentials, and we'll meet someplace. I'll drive us to Toledo Airport, and we're gone."

"All right...I'll go to my sister Terry's house. Any Spencerville police cars in Chatham County don't belong there, and they'll be easy to spot."

"Good plan."

"Do you mind meeting me at my sister's house?"

"No. We used to get along. I'd like to see her again

and thank her for forwarding twenty years of mail to you. I sent her a card every Christmas."

"I know. You're sweet, and she likes you. She used to cover for me in high school when you and I were where we weren't supposed to be."

"I remember." He thought a moment, then asked, "Will she be all right with this?"

"She hates Cliff. No, she *despises* Cliff. So does her husband." Annie added, "Obviously, she knows we weren't sending recipes for twenty years."

"You two never discussed this strange correspondence?"

"Of course not. Well, maybe once in a while." Annie smiled. "God, every time a letter came from you, she'd get excited and phone me right away. We had a code, just in case. She'd say, 'I just got a mail-order catalog I'd like you to see.' Then we'd arrange to meet at her place, or in Spencerville, or halfway at Louise's. I'd give her a letter to mail to you from her post office—I never trusted the people at the Spencerville post office. They gossip."

"I noticed all your letters were postmarked outside of Spencerville." He smiled. "It sounds like you two enjoyed yourselves."

"We were like schoolgirls. Anyway, there's not much excitement out in Chatham County, and this was almost as good as the soaps."

"Yes, but...letters are one thing—helping you run off with a man is another."

"She'll wish us well."

"Will she be safe from Chief Baxter?"

"Her husband, Larry, is pretty tough. Nice guy, but he hates Cliff, and Cliff is afraid of him. Larry is also an honorary deputy sheriff in Chatham, and he'd like nothing better than to tangle with Cliff Baxter."

"Okay, just so they both understand."

"I'll talk to them and tell them we'll be there Saturday at . . . what time?"

"There's a two-fifteen direct flight to Washington. If we leave your sister's at ten, we'll make the flight."

She nodded. "All right. Cliff will leave early with his friends. I'll pack and drive out to Terry's house—I'll put my things in shopping bags and cardboard boxes, so if my keeper sees me packing the car, he won't get suspicious."

"Do you watch spy movies?"

"I was Phi Beta Kappa. My brain still works."

"I see that. You know, I've been in police states where the cops weren't as much trouble as here."

"They're stupid. Anyway, I should get to Terry's about nine. You can get there earlier if you want. They'll be expecting you. We'll have a cup of coffee, I'll give them letters to mail to Tom and Wendy, we'll say good-bye, and Terry will go speak to Mom and Dad."

"Have you eloped before?"

"Keith, I've run away a thousand times in my mind. I wish I'd had the nerve to do it for real, but I'm glad I waited." She looked at him and said, "I never thought I'd run off *with* you, but I always fantasized that I was going to join you somewhere."

"I'm sort of overwhelmed."

"*You're* overwhelmed? I can't believe this is happening. My head is spinning, my heart is fluttering, and I'm so in love I can't see straight. I feel happier now than I've felt since the day before you got your draft notice. I knew nothing would be the same for me after that."

"I thought it would. You understood it better."

"Darling, we both understood, but we hoped for the best." She thought a moment, then said, "People make stupid mistakes in their twenties, but we can't judge ourselves two decades later. We had a great six years, Keith, and I thank God I had that time with you. God willing, we'll have the rest of our lives together."

Keith couldn't say anything, but he took her hand and kissed it.

She took a deep breath. "I should go. Do we meet again before next Saturday?"

"No, it's not safe, and don't call. I'm concerned about a phone tap."

She nodded. "I can almost guarantee my phone calls are recorded at police headquarters. That's why I called you from a pay phone. Do you think your phone—?"

"Maybe. And possibly the Porters'. Will you be all right at home?"

"I'll try. Yes, I will. I won't give him any cause for suspicion." She looked at him. "You understand?"

He nodded.

"Do you still have Terry's address?"

"I think, after twenty years of addressing envelopes, I might remember it."

"You still have a sarcastic streak in you. I'll work on that."

"No, darling, you'll learn to live with it."

"Okay, I get real bitchy that time of the month, and the rest of the month, I have a smart mouth."

"Looking forward to it."

They stood a moment, then she said, "I don't want to walk away."

"Then stay."

"I can't . . . I have errands that should be done before he gets home, or he'll wonder where I've been all day."

"He sure keeps a tight leash."

"He sure does. You never did."

"And I never will."

"You don't have to." She put out her hand, and he took it. She said, "You have a good day now, Mr. Landry. I'll see you next Saturday, and we'll run off together."

He smiled, then made eye contact with her and said, "Annie . . . if you change your mind . . ."

"No, and neither will you. Be there, Keith. Red brick Victorian. Off County Road 6." She kissed him, turned, and hurried away.

He watched her walk along the shore. She spoke to a few people as she passed by, then stopped and chatted with the two older men who were fishing. They laughed at something she said, and watched her as she walked away.

Annie got to her car, opened the door, and looked back at the trees. Although she couldn't see him in the shadows from that distance, she waved, and he waved back. She got into the car, backed up over the rise, and disappeared.

Keith stood awhile, then walked back upstream.

CHAPTER TWENTY-ONE

Keith Landry went to St. James for Sunday services, mostly because he'd been specifically invited by Pastor Wilkes, but partly out of curiosity and nostalgia.

The small church was almost full, and in the tradition of rural people, everyone was dressed in their Sunday best. Pastor Wilkes delivered a nicely pointed sermon on morality in government, specifically mentioning that public officials who break the Ten Commandments and ignore the laws of God are not fit to hold positions of trust in the nation or the community. Keith figured that Wilkes had read a transcript of Thursday's meeting and got right to work on the sermon. Pastor Wilkes didn't mention names, of course, but Keith was pretty sure everyone around him got it. He was also happy that Wilkes hadn't taken the opportunity to give a sermon on the coveting and adultery thing.

There was only one service at this small rural church, which put some peer pressure on the congregation, who couldn't play hooky and leave it to their neighbors to assume they'd gone to the other service. Keith had found this a problem when he was a teenager, but by his junior year of high school, he'd started going to St. John's in Spencerville and somehow always wound up near the Prentis family. His church attendance improved dramatically, and Mr. and Mrs. Prentis liked to see him there, but he felt guilty about his motives, not to mention the thoughts that ran through his mind during the service.

Keith looked around St. James and saw a number of people he knew, including his Aunt Betty, the Muller and Jenkins families, Jenny, without her friend of Thursday evening, but with two young children, and, interestingly, Police Officer Schenley from the high school and church parking lot incidents, with his family. Also there was Sherry Kolarik, of all people, who Keith imagined had returned to the scene of her public confession as a first step toward spiritual health. Like himself, Ms. Kolarik was undoubtedly relieved that Pastor Wilkes wasn't looking at her. However, the pastor did make an oblique reference to her predicament by reminding everyone that women were the weaker vessel, more sinned against than sinners themselves. Keith wondered how that would play in Washington, D.C.

Keith did not see the Porters and hadn't really expected to, but he had thought, or hoped, that Annie would surprise him by being there. But he guessed that this wasn't possible, that she'd be at St. John's with her sinning husband, and Keith wondered if he should drive into town for the eleven A.M. service there. He mulled this over, but decided it was not a very smart move at this juncture of events.

The service ended, and Keith walked down the church steps, where Pastor Wilkes shook the hands of everyone there and called them by name. Keith usually managed to avoid this familiarity after church, but this time he stood in line. When he got to Pastor Wilkes, they shook hands, and the old man seemed genuinely happy to see him, saying, "Welcome home, Mr. Landry. I'm delighted you could come."

"Thank you for inviting me, sir. I enjoyed your sermon."

"I hope you're able to come next week. Our discussion gave me an idea for a sermon."

"About the return of the prodigal son?"

"I had something else in mind, Mr. Landry."

"I may be out of town next Sunday."

Wilkes smiled mischievously. "Pity. I was going to discuss the role of the church in public affairs."

"Good topic. Perhaps you could send me a copy of it."

"I will."

They shook hands again, and Keith moved off. It was a cool, blustery morning, and a north wind blew through the cornfields and the trees, scattering the first leaves of autumn over the grass and through the tombstones of the churchyard. It was a starkly beautiful day, the white church and parsonage, the tall swaying elms, the picket fence of the cemetery, the clouds sailing across a pewter-colored sky. But there was something foreboding about it, Keith thought, something portentous about the autumn wind that blew the summer away and turned the land into hues of red and gold, which were deceptively pleasant harbingers of the dark season. As much as he wanted to stay, he was somehow glad he wouldn't be here much longer.

Keith ran into his aunt in the parking field, and she told him how pleased she was that he'd come to church, then invited him to Sunday dinner. Unable to think of a polite way to refuse—except to say that he'd rather watch the Redskins game and drink beer, which she wouldn't think was polite—he accepted.

*   *   *

At the appointed hour, around kickoff time, he arrived at Aunt Betty's with a bottle of French red Burgundy. Aunt Betty studied the label awhile, mouthing the French words, then put the bottle in the refrigerator. It didn't matter, because as it turned out, she didn't own a corkscrew anyway, and Keith sat in the living room with a glass of caffeine-free instant iced tea with too much sugar in it.

Also invited to dinner were some of the people he'd seen at the Labor Day barbecue—his mother's other cousin, Zack Hoffmann, and Zack's wife, Harriet, and their grown daughter, Lilly, and Lilly's husband, Fred. With Lilly and Fred were their three young boys, whose names Keith didn't catch and who were too young to demand that the Redskins-Cleveland game be turned on. The boys went outside and played in the yard.

Keith made small talk, aware that these people were related, and kept the conversation going by playing the family-tree game. Keith actually found it interesting in some essential, tribal way.

At dinner, which was traditional roast beef, gravy, mashed potatoes, peas, and biscuits—the sort of American food that had disappeared from the nation's capital two decades ago—Harriet, still on the family-tree subject, mentioned, "My sister, Dorothy, married Luke Prentis. I think you know the Prentis family, Keith."

He looked at her and remembered why she looked familiar.

"I believe you once went out with my niece, Annie."

"Yes."

"She married one of the Baxter boys. Cliff. He's chief of police."

Keith wondered if he could open the wine bottle with a screwdriver.

Zack looked up from his roast beef and said, "I heard they had a meeting about Cliff Baxter at St. James. That fella is a..." He glanced at the boys and said, "...is a wild one, if you want my opinion."

Lilly and Fred agreed. Aunt Betty was oblivious, and the boys asked permission to be excused, which was granted.

Zack watched them go, then leaned forward and said in a conspiratorial tone, "I heard he fooled around. They had some woman up there in the church, and brazen as can be she told everyone she and Cliff Baxter was up to somethin'."

Aunt Betty asked, "Does anyone want seconds?"

Harriet turned to Keith and asked him, "Have you seen Annie since college?"

"No."

Fred said, "I hear there was another woman up there, Mary Arles, and she and her husband, Bob, own that gas station on 22, and she told how Cliff Baxter would help himself to things in their convenience store, then make her put the charge on the town gas bill."

Harriet said, "My sister was at that meeting, and what she heard about her son-in-law's fooling around made her sick." She looked at Keith.

Keith listened to the conversation, noting that Fred and Zack were more concerned about the police chief's financial misdeeds than his marital transgressions, while Lilly and Harriet were fixated on the sanctity of marriage.

Lilly said, "If I heard that my husband was fooling around, I'd kick him out without another thought."

Fred didn't look like the type who would or could fool around, Keith thought, but having been forewarned, he looked almost chastised.

Aunt Betty said, "There's plenty more in the kitchen."

Harriet said to Keith, "I wouldn't be surprised if she walked out on him."

"Who?"

"Annie."

"Oh...right. The spouse is usually the last to know."

"My niece is a saint," Harriet said. "She raised two fine children and keeps that house like a showcase for him. She deserves better."

Lilly said to her mother, "Someone should let her know, in case she doesn't know. If it was my husband doing that, and no one told me, they wouldn't be my friend, I'll tell you that." She looked at Fred, whom Keith was beginning to suspect of adultery.

Harriet came to the defense of her son-in-law and said, "Fred wouldn't even *think* of fooling around."

People liked the topic of adultery, Keith had discovered, here or in Washington, Rome, Paris, Moscow, everywhere. But as interesting as it was in the abstract, or in specific cases at hand, it always got touchy and too close for comfort, and so, though everyone at that table was free of sin—except for himself—the topic was dropped. Harriet said to Keith, "I'll tell Annie I saw you. I'm sure she'd tell me to say hello to you."

"Thank you. Please send her my best regards."

"I certainly will. Maybe you'll run into her someday."

"You never know." Keith made a mental note to tell Annie to send Harriet a postcard from Rome.

Aunt Betty announced, "We have lime gelatin with marshmallows for dessert. Does anyone want coffee? I have instant, decaffeinated. I can boil water."

Keith stood. "I hate to eat and run, Aunt Betty, but I promised someone I'd meet them at five."

"It's only a quarter to. Have some dessert first."

Keith recalled that Aunt Betty always had some problems with chronological reasoning, so he said, "I like to drive slow. Thank you, it was a terrific meal." He kissed her and shook hands all around, saying to Fred, "Stay out of trouble," and to Harriet, "My best regards to your sister and to Mr. Prentis."

"They'll be thrilled."

"I hope so."

He left, said good-bye to the boys, who were throwing a football around, and got into his car.

On the way home, he replayed parts of the conversation. What interested him was not what was said about Cliff Baxter, or Annie Baxter, but that good old Harriet was playing Cupid. Keith laughed. There were people, he thought, who, no matter how old they were or how they were raised, had romance in their hearts. Poor Lilly and Fred had no spark of it and probably never did, and neither did Aunt Betty. But old Zack and Harriet still looked at each other with a gleam in their eyes. Lovers, Keith decided, *were* special people, and all lovers recognized other lovers, so he knew that Harriet heard his heart beat every time she mentioned Annie.

The next three days, Monday to Wednesday, Keith spent at home. He did not want to risk even one foray away from the farm, not one incident or confrontation with Baxter or his men. He was too close to the goal line, to use football analogy, the clock was ticking, and it was no time for anything fancy or risky. The last play would be a running play.

Although he was safely within the confines of his own home, and under the law he was king in his own castle, he had another concern. While he couldn't imagine that Baxter could present a judge with any reason to approve a phone tap, it had occurred to him that Baxter might put a tap on the line anyway. One of the standard gadgets in Keith's briefcase was a bug alert which he'd never thought he'd use again, but he had swept the house with it a few times, discovering nothing. He also checked the inside phone connection in the cellar every time he left the house and returned. There was a device to detect a telephone pole line tap, but he didn't have the device in his bag of tricks. Another possibility was a directional microphone aimed at his house, but he could see for a mile in any direction from his second-floor window, and he never saw a vehicle parked for a long time. He doubted if the Spencerville police had any high-tech eavesdropping devices anyway. But you never knew.

Keith knew, prior to Saturday, that Baxter had not had a tap, legal or illegal, on his phone, because if he had, then Cliff Baxter would have been at Reeves Pond on Saturday, and one of them would be laid out at Gibbs Funeral Home today. But even if there had been no tap on his phone Saturday, there could be one today, and he'd operate on that assumption. In any case, he didn't think he needed to use his phone to finalize or change any plans.

Some weeks ago, when Keith thought he was going to stay around, he had considered buying a cellular phone, and he was also going to call his former colleagues in Washington and do a complete electronic check as well as a search of court records to see if anyone had requested a tap. The National Security Council was as interested in his phone security as he was, though in this case for different reasons.

With that thought in mind, Keith wondered why he hadn't heard a word from anyone in Washington. He didn't care, except that the silence was getting ominous.

By Wednesday afternoon, his self-imposed seclusion was becoming tedious. He wondered about Annie, worried about her, but satisfied himself with the adage that no news was good news, which was not true regarding Washington, and was absolutely contrary to the lessons of the last twenty years of intelligence work.

Later in the afternoon, as he was pruning and splinting the raspberry bushes that had been run over, he threw down his pruning hook and kicked a bushel across the yard. "Damn it!" He didn't like to be confined, self-imposed or otherwise, and he worried about her. He jumped in the Blazer, where his M-16 rifle sat on the passenger seat, and, with his Glock tucked in his belt, he drove out to the road. He sat there, near the mailbox, and finally got himself under control. He drove back to the house.

Keith packed the bare essentials, mostly his personal papers, passport, and a few changes of clothes. He couldn't take the weapons on the aircraft, though he'd take his briefcase with the gadgets and gizmos such as a tear-gas pen, microfilm camera, a graphite knife, and, if you were having a bad day, a cyanide capsule, plus other weird things, none of which he'd ever used, but which he felt obligated not to leave in the house.

He went to the kitchen and realized he was completely out of food, including beer. No one in Spencer County delivered food, as far as he knew, and it was a long time until Saturday morning. He supposed he could impose on Mrs. Jenkins or Mrs. Muller to pick up a few things for him, but he had another idea that would solve three problems at once, and he picked up the phone and dialed the Porters.

Jeffrey answered, and Keith said, "This is the FBI. You're under arrest for advocating the violent overthrow of the United States government."

"I think you want my wife."

"How are you?"

"Fine. Meant to call you—"

"Are you guys free for dinner tonight?"

"Sure. Your place?"

"Right. About seven."

"Looking forward to it."

"Do me a favor, Jeffrey."

"Sure."

"I'm completely out of food, and my car won't start. Could you guys bring everything?"

"Sure."

"And wine."

"No problem."

"And I need some cash."

"Should we bring the dinnerware, too."

"No, I've got that. Also, can you cash a thousand-dollar check for me?"

"Sure. Hey, a friend of yours stopped by—"

"Tell me about it later."

"No, you want to hear this now—"

"Later. Thanks." He hung up. *Annie.* It had to be Annie by the tone in Jeffrey's voice. "Good. She's all right, everything is fine." Which solved the problem of finding out if she was all right, and the Porters would bring food and money, which solved the other problems of the moment. There was something uniquely satisfying about beating the bad guys at their own game, but if he didn't put himself in these situations in the first place, he wouldn't have to get out of them, and he might discover that he'd be just as happy mastering chess.

The Porters arrived twenty minutes late, which for ex-hippies was pretty good. Out on the porch, Keith took a canvas bag of herbs from Gail, and Jeffrey carried a cardboard box filled with plastic containers. Gail said, "I cooked everything. We wouldn't eat for hours otherwise. You only have to heat it."

"I think I have a stove."

Inside, Gail said, "What a charming house. You grew up here?"

"I was born and raised here. I haven't grown up yet."

She laughed, and Keith showed them into the kitchen. They put the food down, and Gail said, "Curry In A Hurry."

"Excuse me?"

Jeffrey explained, "In Antioch, they had this great little Indian carry-out place called Curry In A Hurry, and every time Gail doesn't want to cook now, she says, 'Call Curry In A Hurry.' But I don't think they deliver to Spencerville."

"Worth a try. Hey, I'm sorry to put you out like this."

Gail replied. "No problem. You owed us dinner, and we're glad to deliver it for you."

Jeffrey went back to the car for the wine. As Gail and Keith found pots and pans, she said, "We brought jumper cables. Didn't you buy that car new?"

"There's nothing wrong with the car."

"Oh. I thought—"

"I'll explain later."

"Maybe I can guess. The fuzz is harassing you."

Keith began setting the table. "You got it."

"That's disgusting. You have to fight back, Keith."

"It's a long story. If you brought enough wine, I'll tell you."

"Okay."

Jeffrey returned with three bottles of red wine, and Keith opened one. He emptied a bottle into three big water glasses. "The stemware is out being mono-grammed. Cheers."

They drank, then sat at the kitchen table, where Gail had set out crackers and some sort of multicolored spread. Keith asked, "What's this?"

"Vegetable pâté."

"Looks like Play-Doh. Tastes good."

They drank wine, ate, talked, but clearly there were some unanswered questions at the table. Gail related to Jeffrey what Keith said about the police, and Jeffrey remarked, "You can't stay here trapped like an animal."

Gail inquired, "When is the last time you've eaten?"

"Am I being a pig?"

"Keith, this is not like you," Jeffrey said. "You can't let the police intimidate you."

"It's a long story. Hey, how are the sales of True Confessions?"

"Incredible," Jeffrey replied. "Sold five hundred copies already. They're being passed around, so we can assume a few thousand people have read it. That's a lot of people for a small county. I think we have this guy on the run. In fact, that's what I was going to tell you on the phone. Who do you think shows up at our door and asks to buy a copy?"

Keith sipped his wine. "Who?"

"You have to guess."

"Cliff Baxter."

Gail laughed. "Close."

"Come on," Jeffrey said, "I told you it was an old friend of yours."

"Annie Baxter."

"Bingo! Can you believe that?"

"I can."

Gail said, "That took some courage." She smiled at Keith. "She looked good."

"Good."

"In fact, for a woman whose husband is being exposed as a blackmailer, graft-taker, and adulterer, she seemed pretty cooled-out. Almost cheerful."

"Maybe she's got a boyfriend."

Gail observed, "That could explain her mood."

Jeffrey said, "We gave her the transcript for free, of course, and we invited her in. I was surprised she accepted. She had a cup of tea. It was nice talking to her again. We caught up on old times." He added, "I told her you were back, and she said she'd run into you outside the post office."

"Right."

Gail inquired, "Did you feel a little thump-thump?"

"Sure."

"Well, I wouldn't be surprised if she's on the market soon," Gail said. She added, "You know, I felt a little bad. I mean, we never intended to cause problems for her at home, but I guess that was a natural result of what we had to do to get at him. But he brought it on himself."

"I suppose. If you play, you pay."

"Unless you have an understanding like Jeffrey and I do. No one can come between us with evidence of infidelity."

"That's an interesting observation. But what if one of you fell deeply in love with a lover?"

"Well…" Gail seemed actually uncomfortable, and obviously something like this had happened to one or the other or both, once, twice, or more times. Gail said, "People fall in love across a room. It's actually less likely to happen with casual sex partners." She added, "Love has less to do with sex than with missing a person when they're not around. Didn't you say your heart went thump when you saw Annie? I mean, after twenty-some years, there's still something there. How many women have you screwed since her?"

"Counting foreigners?"

She laughed, then said, "And why hasn't a good-looking man like you gotten married?"

"I should have called Curry In A Hurry."

Jeffrey smiled. "Leave him alone, Gail. This subject obviously bothers him."

"Right," Keith agreed. He asked, "Are the Spencerville cops giving you guys any trouble?"

Jeffrey shook his head. "Not yet. I mean, Gail is a city councilwoman. I think they're waiting until after the election. We'll see who's still standing then."

Keith looked at both of them. "You ought to be careful in the meantime. Baxter is unstable."

Gail and Jeffrey glanced at each other, and Jeffrey said to Keith, "We're watching ourselves."

"Do you have a gun?"

"No," said Jeffrey. "We're pacifists. We get shot *at*."

"I have a rifle. Let me give it to you."

"No," Jeffrey said. "We won't use it."

"You might if it was in the house, and someone—"

"No. Please respect that, Keith."

"All right. But if you ever need help, give a holler."

"Okay."

Jeffrey got up and stirred the two pots. "Soup's ready."

They had the soup, then a vegetable curry, and were working on the last bottle of wine.

Keith made coffee and Gail unveiled a carrot cake. Over cake and coffee, Jeffrey said, "Hey, I almost forgot." He put his hand in his pocket and came out with a bank envelope. "There's a thousand."

"Thanks." Keith took a check from his wallet and gave it to Jeffrey, who glanced at it and said, "This is for two thousand."

"That's a contribution to the cause. I never gave money to pinkos before."

Gail smiled. "We can't accept that, Keith."

"Yeah, you can. I don't need the money, and I want to do something."

"You can help us by joining us."

"I could, and I would. But I'm leaving."

Neither of them spoke.

Keith said, "Look, guys, I trust you, and I like you. Also, I may need your help. Ready for a long story?"

They nodded.

"Okay, I returned to Spencerville to go back to the starting line and see if I could run the race over again. Well, you can't do that. The race is over, but you can run a new race. Yeah, I'm beating around the bush. Okay, I'm in love with Annie, and—"

Gail slapped the table. "I knew it! See, Jeffrey, I *told* you."

"I told *you*."

"May I? This isn't easy. Anyway, we've been writing for twenty years—"

"I love this. Go on. Does she love you?"

Jeffrey said, "Gail, keep quiet."

"So, anyway, yes, she does, and we're running off. End of story."

"Like hell it is," said Gail. "Have you done it yet?"

"That's not relevant . . . No, we haven't—"

"Liar. I knew it. See? That's why she was floating on clouds. She asked if we'd spoken to you in the last few days. This is terrific. That pig deserves what he gets. Oh, Keith, I'm so happy for you." She stood and kissed him, which he figured was coming, and Jeffrey followed suit with a handshake.

Keith felt a little impatient and said, "Okay, so that answers a lot of questions for you, and I thought I owed you an explanation of why I couldn't commit to—"

"Hey," Jeffrey said, "you're doing your part by stealing his wife."

"I'm not actually stealing—"

"I always knew you two would get back together," Jeffrey said. "When are you leaving?"

"I can't say. But soon."

"How can we help?"

"Well, for starters, don't say a thing over the phone if we speak. I'm concerned that your phone or mine could be tapped."

"Yeah, they could be. What else?"

"Well, you brought the money, looks like enough food left for a few more days, and maybe Gail could keep her eyes and ears open around city hall."

"I always do. And I have a cop who's a source."

"Good. But don't trust him, either."

"When it comes to revolution, we don't trust too many people."

Keith nodded. "You know the game."

Jeffrey said, "So you're laying low until you...do you call it elopement if she's married?"

"For want of a better word, yes. I'll give you a key to the house, and I'd like you to look after it."

"No problem."

Gail asked, "Where did you do it? How many times? How did you get away with it?"

"We're old pros from high school days." Keith changed the subject and said, "Her husband is generally suspicious, and specifically pissed off at me for coming back here. He came out here last week, and we had some words. But he doesn't really know anything. He did give me a week to get out of town, and that time ends on Friday, but I won't be gone by then. He may come around again, and I'll ask for a few days' extension, because that's less complicated than killing him, which I promised not to do."

They seemed stunned by that remark, and Keith looked at them. "This is serious business. Not a game. He's borderline psychotic. You watch yourselves. The offer of the gun stands."

They stayed silent awhile, then Jeffrey said, "Hey, this is heavy stuff. Mind if I smoke?"

"Go right ahead."

Jeffrey took a pouch and papers out of his shirt pocket and rolled one. He lit it with a match and offered it to Keith, who declined, then to Gail, who also declined. He shrugged, sat back, and smoked.

Gail asked, "Do you think Annie is safe?"

"I think so. But I'm getting these vibrations, if I can use that old word, and these vibrations tell me that people have picked up on something, sort of like they're intercepting these signals that go between this farm and Williams Street," Keith smiled. "Blow that smoke away, Jeffrey. I'm sounding like you."

Gail said, "No, I understand. I mean, even we figured something was up. Who else, besides Baxter?"

"Oh, just people. Pastors, and somebody's sister, and nice elderly ladies. I'm probably paranoid, but I'm concerned that Baxter's going to get onto something concrete. I have to ask you guys not to say or do anything that could arouse suspicion. Lay low yourselves until the weekend. Okay?"

"Done."

"If the plan falls apart, I may need you."

"We're here."

"I appreciate it. Hey, Jeffrey, who would have thought we'd be having dinner together again?"

Jeffrey took a toke and looked at him. "Time has healed a lot of those wounds, Keith. I'm glad we lived long enough to get smart."

Gail said, "If this is a prelude to male bonding, I'll go out on the porch."

Jeffrey said to Keith, "She feels threatened. That's why you need a woman, Keith, to balance out the dynamics of our interlocking relationships, and ...

whatever. Hey, where are you two going to go? Can we join you for dinner someplace?"

"Sure. I'll let you know."

Gail said, "We're going to miss you, Keith. We don't have many friends here."

"Maybe you will after you get rid of Police Chief Baxter."

"I don't think so. But perhaps. Will you come back here someday?"

"I'd like to. Depends on what happens with Baxter."

"Yeah," Jeffrey agreed, "I wouldn't advise you to look for a house on Williams Street for a while." He laughed. "Hey, I'd love to see his fucking face when he comes home and finds a fuck-you note on the refrigerator." Jeffrey got the giggles and slapped the table a few times.

Keith stood. "Let's sit on the porch. The maid will clear."

They sat on the porch and watched the sun go down. No one spoke for a long time, then Gail said, "What an amazing thing, Keith."

"What?"

"Love, I mean, through college, and turmoil, and war, and decades, and distance, and everything that life throws at you. If I were sentimental, I'd cry."

CHAPTER TWENTY-TWO

On Thursday morning, Keith woke up not feeling particularly well and didn't know why. By stages, he remembered the Porters being over for dinner, then recalled breaking out the hard liquor and realized why he had a headache and recalled what they had been celebrating.

He got out of bed and opened the window, feeling the cool air rush in. It looked like another sunny day, a good day for the corn, but they could use one more good rain before the harvest.

He walked down the hall in his underwear toward the bathroom and bumped into Jeffrey, also in his underwear. Jeffrey said, "I'm not well."

"You slept here?"

"No, I came back in my underwear to get the Tupperware containers."

"Where's Gail?"

"She went to get us breakfast. You want to use the bathroom?"

"No, go ahead." Keith got his robe and went down the stairs into the kitchen. He washed his face in the sink, found aspirin in the cupboard and took two, then put on a pot of coffee.

A car pulled around to the back door, and Gail came in, carrying a grocery bag. "How are you feeling?"

"Okay." He sat at the kitchen table, and Gail unpacked a bottle of orange juice and three corn muffins.

She said, "A police car followed me from here all the way to town."

Keith nodded. He said, "Now they know there's a connection between us. You're on the list."

"Hey, I was on the list before you got here." She sat down and poured a glass of juice for each of them.

Keith sipped his juice. He asked, "Did they pull you over?"

"No, I pulled them over. I got out of my car, identified myself as a councilwoman, and told them to fuck off or I'd have their badges."

"You've become very establishment, Gail. You're supposed to scream about your civil rights."

"They wouldn't know what the hell I was talking about. The only thing that scares them is the thought of losing their guns and their badges."

"Yeah, these cops turned bad. They have a bad boss."

She stayed quiet a minute, then asked him, "Were you serious about killing Baxter?"

"No."

She looked at him awhile, then said, "I was scared out there on the highway."

"I know. I'd like to take care of the problem before I leave, but I promised I wouldn't."

"I understand. Can I ask you . . . have you ever done that? I mean, I guess in Vietnam . . ."

Keith didn't reply, but he thought about her question. Yes, he'd killed in Vietnam, but that was in combat. In his early years in intelligence work, he'd literally had a license to kill, but before they'd given him his gun and silencer, they'd given him the rules: There were only two absolute times for killing—in combat and in self-defense. But everyone in America had the same right. His license, however, extended into murkier areas, such as a preemptive kill, if you *felt* threatened. And it got even murkier than that, like the right to kill in order to remove a great evil, whatever that was. Keith thought that Cliff Baxter was a great evil, for instance, but Mr. Baxter's parents and children might not agree. It was sort of a case-by-case thing, and Keith never had to make the decision by himself, and neither did he have to be the gunman if he had a problem with the committee decision. Here in Spencerville, however, far removed from any restraints or advice, he was on his own.

She said, "Have you thought about the fact that you'll never be really safe as long as he's around?"

"I don't think Cliff Baxter's balls travel well. We'll stay away from his turf."

"Did you ever think he might take out his rage on . . . well, let's say Annie's family?"

"What are you suggesting, Gail? I thought you were a pacifist."

"Jeffrey is a pacifist. If someone threatened my life, or the lives of my family or friends, I'd kill them."

"With what? A carrot?"

"Be serious. Listen, I feel threatened, and I obviously can't go to the police. I'll take that rifle."

"Okay. I'll get it." He stood, but Jeffrey came down the stairs.

Gail said to Keith, "We'll put it in my trunk later."

Jeffrey came into the kitchen. "Put what in the trunk?"

Gail replied, "The Tupperware."

"Right." He sat down, and they had breakfast.

Jeffrey said, "Hell of a party last night. Glad we

could finally celebrate the Landry-Prentis engagement announcement."

Keith asked, "Did you ever wonder what our lives would have been like without the war and the turmoil?"

"Yeah, I thought about it. Dull, I think. Like now, I think we had a unique experience. Yeah, a lot of people got hurt and fucked-up, but most of us came through it okay. We're better people because of it." He added, "My students were totally boring, self-centered, selfish, irresolute, and without character. Christ, you'd think they were Republicans, but they thought they were rebels. Right. Rebels without a clue."

Gail said, "You got him started."

Keith said to Jeffrey, "You remember Billy Marlon?"

"Sure. Goofy kid. An obsessive pleaser, wanted to be everyone's best friend. In fact, I ran into him a few times. I wanted to be nice, for old time's sake, but he's a burnout."

"I ran into him at John's Place."

"Christ, Landry, I wouldn't take a piss in that place."

"I was feeling nostalgic one night."

"Go to the sock hop. Why'd you ask about him?"

"Well, sometimes when I see a guy like that, I say to myself, 'There but for the grace of God go I.'"

Gail commented, "If God's grace existed, there wouldn't be people like that for you to say, 'There but for the grace of God.'"

Jeffrey said, "You got *her* started. I understand what you're saying, Keith, but I think the Billy Marlons of the world would have gotten fucked-up in any decade. That's not us."

"I wonder."

"Yeah, we're fuckups, but we're functional." He thought a moment and said, "We pulled ourselves out of this place, Keith, you and I and a few others. We weren't born with money like the Baxters, or into a tradition of education like the Prentis family. Your old man was a farmer, mine was a railroad worker. The sixties didn't fuck us up, they broke us loose from convention and class structure." He added, "And we got laid a lot. You know, I once figured out that I probably got laid more than every male and female in my family put together, going back to maybe 1945. I think people got laid a lot during the Second World War, but not before or after."

Keith smiled. "Was that one of your prepared lectures?"

"It was, actually."

"Okay, we had some great times. But as you once said, we did some shitty things then. You sent me a shitty letter, for instance. It's okay. I got the same kind of letters from total strangers. But we all talked love, love, love, and we did a lot of hateful things. Me, too." He added, "When I got your letter, I wanted to literally kill you. I would have if you were there."

"What can I say? We were young. There were solar storms, and Jupiter and Mars were lined up or something, and the price of grass dropped, and we went totally fucking bonkers. If it hadn't happened, you and I would have been at John's Place last night, bitching about farm prices and railroad wages, and maybe Billy Marlon would have owned the place and been a city councilman if he hadn't gone to Vietnam. Christ, I don't know." He took a bite of muffin and said, "Some of who we are is in our genes, some of it is our culture, some of it is in our stars, and a lot of it is our personal history. You, me, Cliff Baxter, Annie Prentis, and Billy Marlon. We were born in the same hospital within a year of one another. I don't have any answers."

"Me, neither. I'd like you to do me another favor.

After I'm gone, go see if there's anything you can do for Marlon. He lives out at the Cowley farm on Route 8. See if you can get him into a VA hospital."

"Sure. You're a good guy."

"Don't let it get around."

Gail said, "You must have a lot of mixed feelings right now. You're about to leave home again, and you're embarking on a great and unknown journey into a new life with another person. Are you excited or scared shitless?"

"Yes."

They finished breakfast and Gail asked Keith if he had an extra toothbrush.

"Sure. I'll find it. Come on up."

They went upstairs and into Keith's room. He opened the wardrobe.

Gail looked at the uniforms, the saber, the bulletproof vest, and the odds and ends of a career that required many accessories. She asked, "What exactly did you do?"

"This and that." He took out the M-16 rifle. "Basically, I spent twenty-five years fighting commies. They got tired of it about the same time I did."

"Was it fulfilling?"

"Toward the end, it was about as fulfilling as your job. Here—this is called the fire control selector. It's on safety now. Move it here, and it's ready to fire. You just keep pulling the trigger. It chambers a new round and cocks itself automatically. This is the magazine. It holds twenty rounds. After you empty the magazine, you push this catch and the magazine pops out, then you push a fresh magazine in and make sure it clicks in place, then you pull this handle back and it will chamber the first round, then it's automatic again." He handed the rifle to her.

She said, "It's so light."

"And it doesn't have much kick."

She practiced loading a magazine, chambering a round, and aiming. She said, "It's pretty simple."

"Right. It was designed for people like Billy Marlon. It's simple, light, easy to aim, and very deadly. All you need is the will to pull the trigger."

"That I don't know."

"Then you shouldn't take it."

"I'll take it."

"Okay. Here's the carrying case. There are four fully loaded magazines in these side pouches, and in this pouch is a scope, but don't bother with that. It's for long-distance firing. I don't think you'll wind up in a firefight with the Spencerville police, but you'll feel better at night if this is under your bed. Okay?"

"Okay."

She said, "I'll go unlock the trunk, then take Jeffrey for a walk." She went downstairs, and a few minutes later, as Keith got dressed, he saw them through the window out by the barn. He went downstairs and out the back door and put the carrying case in their trunk beside the empty food containers. He closed the trunk and went inside and poured another cup of coffee.

A few minutes later, Gail and Jeffrey returned. Gail said, "Really nice place here." They made small talk for a few minutes, then Gail said, "Well...time to go." She put her arms around him and kissed him. "Good luck, Keith. Call or write."

"I'll write. Meanwhile, get a security company down from Toledo to check out your phones, and get a mobile phone."

"Good idea." Jeffrey took his hand. "Hey, if you need anything before you take off, don't call—stop by."

"I think it's all set. The house key's under the workbench in the toolshed."

"Okay. We'll keep an eye on things until you get back."

"Thanks for everything. Good luck with the revolution."

They all embraced again, then the Porters left, and Keith watched them drive off, reasonably certain he'd see them again in better times.

At about ten A.M., Keith was on a ladder, replacing the rusted hinges on the door of the haymow. Working outdoors had cleared his mind, and he felt better.

He heard the sound of tires on the gravel and turned to see a gray Ford Taurus coming up the long drive, a cloud of dust trailing it.

Keith couldn't imagine who it was, but it might be Annie. Then again, it might not be. He came down off the ladder in time to pick up his Glock 9mm from atop the toolbox, stick it in his waistband, and throw his shirt on over it. He walked toward the house as the driver's-side door of the car opened.

A man of about his own height and age, with sandy hair and wearing a blue suit, got out and looked around, then the man saw Keith and waved, "Howdy! This the Landry farm?"

Keith continued walking toward the man who came to meet him.

The man said, "Fine spread you got here, son. I'm fixin' to buy you out, or run you out. All you sodbusters got to clear out for my cattle."

Keith came up to the man. "This is Ohio, Charlie. We don't talk that way."

"I thought this was Kansas. How the hell are you?"

They shook hands, then embraced briefly and patted each other's backs.

Charlie Adair, of Washington, D.C., and the

National Security Council, had been Keith Landry's immediate civilian superior and Keith's sometimes good friend. Keith wondered what he was doing here and guessed it was some administrative thing, paperwork to be signed, or maybe just a physical check to see that Keith was where he said he was, how he lived, that sort of thing. But somehow, Keith knew this wasn't so.

Charlie Adair asked, "How have you been, Keith?"

"Fine until two minutes ago. What's up?"

"Oh, I just came by to say hello."

"Hi."

Charlie looked around. "You were born here?"

"Yup."

"Was it a good place to grow up?"

"It was."

"You get cyclones here?"

"At least once a week. You just missed one. There's a tornado later today if you're still around."

Adair smiled, then asked, "So, you settled in?"

"I am."

"What's a place like this worth?"

"I don't know...four hundred acres, house, building, a little equipment...maybe four hundred thousand."

"No kidding? That's pretty good. But outside of D.C., in Virginia, those gentlemen's farms go for a million."

Keith didn't think Charlie Adair came to Spencer County to talk about the price of land. Keith asked him, "You just fly in?"

"Yeah, took an early morning flight to Columbus and rented a car. Nice drive. I found you without too many problems. Police knew right where you were."

"This is a real small place."

"I see that." Adair observed, "You got some good tan. Lost some weight."

"Lot of outdoor work on a farm."

"I guess." Adair stretched. "Hey, can we take a walk? Long flight and long drive."

"Sure. I'll show you around."

They walked around the farmyard, and Charlie feigned an interest in everything, while Keith feigned an interest in showing it to him. Charlie asked, "This all yours?"

"No. It belongs to my parents."

"Will you inherit it?"

"I have a brother and sister, and we don't have primogeniture in this country, so we'll have to make a decision someday."

"In other words, if one of you wanted to farm the place, that person would buy out the other two."

"That's what sometimes happens. Used to happen. Now the heirs usually sell out to a big concern and take the money and run."

"Too bad. That's what's killing the family farms. Plus estate taxes."

"No estate taxes on farms if you keep it in the family."

"Really? Hey, that's something those assholes in Congress did right."

"Yeah, that's a short list."

They went into the cornfields and walked between the rows. Charlie said, "This is where my cornflakes come from."

"If you're a cow. This is called field corn. You feed it to cattle, they get fat, you kill them, and they become hamburgers."

"You mean I can't eat this?"

"People eat sweet corn. The farmers plant a little of that, but it's mostly harvested by hand around August."

"I'm really learning something. You planted all this?"

"No, Charlie, it was planted about May. I got here in August. You don't think corn would get this high in two months."

"I don't have a clue. So this isn't yours?"

"The land is mine. It's contracted. Rented."

"I got it. They pay you in corn or money?"

"Money." Keith made his way to the Indian burial mound, and they climbed atop it.

Charlie looked out over the fields. "This is the heartland, Keith. This is what we defended for all those years."

"From sea to shining sea."

"You miss the job?"

"No."

Charlie took a pack of cigarettes out of his jacket. "Can I smoke here?"

"Why not?"

He blew a stream of smoke into the air and pointed off in the distance. "What kind of corn is that?"

"That's soybean."

"Like in soy sauce?"

"Yup. There's a Japanese-owned processing plant not far from here."

"You mean to tell me there are Japanese *here?*"

"Why not? They can't ship a million acres of American farmland to Japan."

He thought a moment, then said, "That's...scary."

"Don't be xenophobic."

"Hey, comes with the job." He smoked for a while, then said, "Keith, they want you back."

Keith already knew that. He said, "Forget it."

"They sent me to bring you back."

"They told me to leave. So you go back and tell them I'm gone."

"Don't give me a hard time, Keith. I had a bumpy flight. They told me not to come back without you."

"Charlie, they can't just say you're out, then change their minds."

"They can say whatever they want. But they also want to extend an apology for any inconvenience this may have caused you. They acted hastily, without due consideration of the developing situation in the East. You remember where that is. Will you accept their apology?"

"Of course. Good-bye. When's your flight?"

"They offer a civilian contract for five years. You'll get your thirty in and full retirement pay."

"No."

"And a promotion. A military promotion. One-star general. How's that sound to you, Colonel?"

"Your timing's bad."

"This is a White House job, Keith. Very high visibility. You could be the next Alexander Haig. I mean, he thought he was president, but this job has such potential that you could actually run for president like people wanted Haig to do. The country is ready for a general as president again. I just read a secret poll about that. Think about it."

"Okay. Let me think a second. No."

"Everybody wants to be president."

"I want to be a farmer."

"That's the point. The public will love it. A tall, good-looking, honest man of the soil. You know the story of Cincinnatus?"

"I told *you* the story."

"Right. So your country needs you again. Time to step up to the plate and stop shoveling shit."

Keith wasn't sure about that mixed metaphor. He replied, "You know, if I were president, the first thing I'd do is fire you."

"That's very pretty, Keith. Not very statesmanlike."

"Charlie, stop jerking me around. You wear thin."

"I'm not jerking you around. Forget president.

After your White House job, you could come back here and run for Congress, then live in Washington. Best of both worlds. You could do something for your country *and* your community." Adair ground out his cigarette. "Come on, let's walk."

They walked between the rows of corn. Adair said, "Look, Keith, the president's got it in his mind that he'd like you to be on his staff. You owe him the courtesy of a personal reply. You got to do face time with this. So, even if you don't want the job, you have to tell him in person to fuck off."

"He told me to fuck off by letter."

"It wasn't him."

"Whoever it was, it doesn't matter. If someone screwed up, it's not my problem. You know I'm right."

"It's dangerous to be right when the government is wrong."

Keith stopped walking. "Is that a threat?"

"No. Just good advice, my friend."

They resumed their walk. Charlie said, "Will you like it here this time next year?"

"If I don't, I'll move on."

"Look, Keith, maybe you could rusticate out here and maybe be happy, and you could have stayed pissed off at those guys. But now that I brought you sincere apologies and an offer, you're not going to be at peace with yourself. So I fucked up your day and your retirement. Now you have to deal with the new situation."

"*This* is the new situation. Here. Back there is the old situation. You know, I *was* pissed off, but I'm not anymore. You guys did me a favor. You can't *make* me go back, so stop the bullshit."

"Well...you know, you're still in the military. You haven't worn a uniform in about fifteen years, but you're still a reserve colonel, and the president is commander in chief."

"Speak to my lawyer."

"The president may call on you from time to time to discharge the duties of your office, and so forth. The time has come, buddy."

"Don't try that with me."

"Okay, let me try this. Save my ass. Come to Washington with me and tell them Adair gave it his best shot, but you're there to tell them personally to fuck off. Okay? I know you want to do it that way. You don't owe them anything except a face-to-face fuck-off. But you owe me a few favors, and all I'm asking to square our account is that you come to D.C. with me. Then I'm off the hook, and you can say what's on your mind. Fair? You bet."

"I . . . I can't go with you . . ."

"You owe me, Keith. I'm here to collect, not to beg, threaten, or cajole. To collect."

"Charlie, look—"

"Bucharest. Not to mention the messiness in Damascus."

"Look, Charlie . . . there's a woman—"

"There's always a woman. That's how you almost got us beheaded in Damascus."

"There's a woman here—"

"*Here*? Christ, buddy, you haven't even been here two months."

"From long ago. You know, high school and college. I may have mentioned her in a maudlin moment."

"Oh . . . yes. Yes, you did. I see." He thought a moment and asked, "Husband?"

Keith nodded.

"Well, we can't help you with that." He winked. "But we can work something out."

"I've already worked it out, thank you."

They came back into the farmyard, and Charlie sat on the small garden tractor. "Can I smoke on this thing?"

"Yeah. It's just a tractor. It doesn't fly."

"Right." He lit another cigarette and seemed to be thinking. He said, "I don't see the complication."

"She's married. How would it look if a presidential aide was living with a married woman?"

"We'll get her a divorce."

"That could take years."

"We can pull a few strings."

"No, you can't. You can't do whatever you want to do. You *think* you can, but you can't. There are laws that govern this."

"Right. Well, did you intend to live with her anytime soon?"

"Yeah. Real soon."

"So we get her a separate apartment in Washington. Why are you making such a big deal of this?"

"Charlie, this is not what she and I had in mind. I am not that important to global peace. The world will do fine without my advice. The danger has passed. I did my duty. My life is important to me now."

"That's good. It never was, but I hear you. You know, you can have a life *and* a career. Done all the time."

"Not *that* career."

"It won't be as crazy this time. Sure, the hours are still long, and you might have to fly here or there now and then, but you don't have to go behind the Iron Curtain anymore. It blew away."

"Yeah, I was there."

"Right." He studied the controls on the tractor and asked, "You know how to run this?"

"That's how it got out of the barn."

"I thought these things were bigger."

"This is a garden tractor. Sort of a utility vehicle for around the yard."

"No kidding? Where's the big one?"

"My father sold it." Keith said, "So thanks for stopping by. Say hello to everyone. What time is your flight?"

Charlie looked at his watch. "Return from Toledo at two-fifteen. How long will it take me to get to the airport from here?"

"Maybe an hour or more with traffic. You may want to leave now to play it safe."

"No. I have time for a beer."

"Come on inside."

Charlie got off the tractor, and they went into the house through the kitchen door. Keith said, "I'm out of beer."

"It's a little early anyway. I'm just thirsty."

"I don't doubt it. You've been blowing steam for the last half hour." Keith opened the refrigerator and got a jug of water. He poured two glasses. "This is genuine spring water."

Charlie drained off half the glass. "It's good."

"There's mostly limestone under the soil. This was a prehistoric sea. You know, a billion years of little sea creatures compressed into layers of limestone."

Charlie looked at the glass suspiciously. "Is that a fact?"

"I'm going to bottle it. Sell it to the yuppie swine in D.C."

"Good idea. Let's sit a minute." They sat at the big table and Charlie stayed silent for a while, which Keith didn't like. Charlie said, "Did you intend to stay here with her?"

"No."

"Where were you planning to go?"

Keith didn't like the past tense of that sentence. He replied, "I don't know where we are going."

"You'd have to let us know. It's the law."

"I'll let you know so you can send my checks."

Charlie nodded absently. He said, "You know, something funny happened on my way here."

Keith didn't reply.

Charlie said, "When I stopped at the police station, this guy, the desk sergeant, named Blake, I think...I asked him if he knew where you lived, and he got sort of weird. Started questioning me. I mean, *I'm* asking the questions. Right? He wants to know what my business is with you. Can you believe that shit? I thought I was back in East Germany or something. Can I smoke in here?"

"Sure."

Charlie lit a cigarette and tapped the ash into his glass. "So I get to thinking. I mean, I'm a spy. Right? Used to be anyway. I'm thinking that maybe someone is bothering you here, and the police are being protective. Or maybe you contacted them when you got here, identified yourself as an ex-spook, and asked them to notify you if anyone was looking for you. Like someone named Igor with a Russian accent. But that didn't make sense, and when I got here, you looked surprised, so I know they didn't call to tip you off."

"Charlie, you've been in this business too long."

"I know. That's what I decided. But then I go outside, and this other cop follows me out to my car. Heavyset guy, said he was chief of police. Name's Baxter. He asks me what my business is out at the Landry farm. I'm too clever to tell him to fuck off because I want to draw him out. By this time, I'm thinking you're in trouble with the law. So I flash my official-looking ID and tell him it's official government business."

"You have to learn how to mind your own business, Charlie."

"No, I don't. Anyway, I'm concerned about you now. I mean, these guys were *weird*. Like in some grade B horror flick, you know, where that whole small town is taken over by aliens? You remember that one? Anyway, now this guy Baxter is a little less ballsy and asks me if he can be of any help. I say maybe. Mr. Landry has been pensioned off by the U.S. Fish and Wildlife Service." Both Charlie and Keith smiled at the old joke. "Anyway, Mr. Landry has applied for part-time work with the local office of the U.S. Fish and Wildlife Service, and I'm here to do a background check on him and see if he's of fine moral character and an accepted member of his community. That was pretty quick, wasn't it?"

"How the mighty have fallen. Is that what you've been reduced to?"

"Give me a break. I haven't done fieldwork in fifteen years and I miss it. Anyway, Chief of Police Baxter informs me that Mr. Landry has had several scrapes with the law—in the park right across the street—drunk and disorderly. Trespassing on school property. Interfering with police officers in the performance of their duty in some parking lot. Menacing, harassment...what else? I think that's it. He said he talked with you about your anti-social tendencies, but you gave him a lot of lip. He recommended you not be hired. He also said someone should see if you deserved a government pension at all. I don't think he likes you."

"We were high school rivals."

"Really? Something else. He said he tried to run your D.C. plates through the Bureau of Motor Vehicles, but you don't exist. At that point, I got interested in Mr. Baxter." He dropped his cigarette in the glass.

"What's happening, Keith? We did high school rivals already."

"Yeah. Well, then, *cherchez la femme,* wise guy."

"Ah."

"I'll take one of those cigarettes."

"Sure." Charlie handed him the pack and the lighter. Charlie asked, "You're not fucking the police chief's daughter, are you?"

Keith lit the cigarette and exhaled. "No. His wife."

"Right. *The* woman. I thought you came here to relax."

"I told you, this is a preexisting condition."

"Right. That's very romantic. Are you out of your fucking mind?"

"Probably."

"Well, we can integrate this situation into the equation."

"Speak English."

"Okay. Are you running off with her?"

"That's the plan."

"When?"

"Saturday morning."

"Can it wait?"

"No. It's getting hot here."

"I'll bet it is. That's why you have that piece stuck under your shirt."

Keith didn't reply.

Charlie asked, "Does the husband know?"

"No. If he did, this place would have been under fire when you drove up." Keith added, "He knows his wife and I were an item way back. He doesn't like that. He gave me until tomorrow to get out of town."

"Are you going to kill him?"

"No. I promised her I wouldn't. They have two kids. In college."

"Well, they had him around a long time. Good memories, life insurance, tuition taken care of."

"Charlie, don't joke about killing. I've had enough of that."

"Termination. You don't say kill, and you have to make a joke about it or it sounds ugly." He added, "Wouldn't life be easier for you if this guy committed suicide or had an accident? I didn't like him."

"He doesn't meet our requirements for termination."

"Did he threaten you with bodily harm?"

"Sort of."

"There you go. Paragraph five of the rules of termination."

"Commandment one. Old Testament."

"You got me. Hey, do what you have to do. Actually, if you come live in D.C., you'll be okay. She'll like the capital."

"Not to live there for five years. She's a country girl, Charlie."

"I'd like to meet her."

"Sure." Keith put out his cigarette.

Charlie said, "You're coming back with me on the two-fifteen. You know that, don't you?"

"First I've heard of it."

"There's no way out of this one, Keith. Believe me. But I'd rather you come as a favor to me. Not because you owe me a favor, but so I can owe you a favor."

"I'd like to keep the bullshit out in the farmyard."

"You're coming to Washington to save my ass. I can't go back there and report to the secretary of defense that I couldn't get you to see him and the president. Jesus, I'd be spending the next five years in Iceland counting radar blips. My wife would run off with somebody like you."

"Cut it out." Keith stayed quiet for a while, then

said, "They rely on our loyalty toward one another more than our loyalty toward the government, don't they?"

"That's all that works these days."

"Don't you feel used?"

"Sure. Used, underpaid, unappreciated, and unneeded. You're right, the danger has passed, and we're...how does that ditty go? 'The danger's passed, the wrong is righted; the veteran's ignored, the soldier's slighted.'"

"There you are."

"But so what? We'll play if they pay." He looked at Keith. "You know, buddy, I sometimes feel like I'm on a football team that just won the big game. The other team's gone home, the stands are empty, and we're running plays against nobody, in the dark." He sat quietly a moment, and Keith could see that Charlie Adair was having his own little crisis of conscience and confidence. But with Charlie, you never really knew.

Charlie looked up. "The meeting is tomorrow morning."

Keith said, "In fact, I had planned to fly to Washington on Saturday on the two-fifteen. Can we make the meeting for Monday?"

Charlie adopted his make-believe officious tone of voice, and replied, "My good man, you have an appointment with the secretary of defense at eleven-thirty A.M. tomorrow in the Cabinet Room, then you will go into the Oval Office at precisely eleven fifty-five where you will shake hands with and say hello to the president of the United States. As much as these two gentlemen would like to work their schedules around yours, they may possibly have other appointments on Monday."

"Perhaps a little advance notice would have been appreciated by a private citizen who has all sorts of constitutional rights not to be summoned by—"

"Keith. Cut it. You're no more a private citizen than I am. And you know how these things happen. It happened to Sir Patrick Spence."

"Who?"

"The guy in the Scottish ballad. My people are Scottish, and this place is named Spencerville. That's how I happened to think of it."

"Think of *what?*"

"The Scottish ballad." He recited, " 'The king sits in Dumferling Town, drinking his blood-red wine, oh, where will I get a good sailor, to sail this ship of mine?'—that's the president talking. Then, 'Up and spoke an elderly knight, who sat at the king's right knee'—that's the secretary of defense, who says, 'Sir Patrick Spence is the best sailor, that sails upon the sea.' That's you. Then, 'The king wrote an official letter, and signed it with his hand, and sent it to Sir Patrick Spence who was walking on the sand.' That's me coming here. Then, 'The first line that Sir Patrick read, a loud laugh laughed he; the next that Sir Patrick read, a tear blinded his eye'—that's you again."

"Thank you, Charlie."

" 'Oh, who is this that has done this deed, this ill deed to me, to send me out this time of year, to sail upon the sea? Make haste, make haste, my merry men all, our good ship sails at morn'—actually two-fifteen—'Oh say no more my master dear, for I fear a deadly storm.' " Charlie Adair said to Keith, "So that's how these things happen. That's how they've happened since the beginning of time. The king's sitting around, not doing shit, pounding down a few, and some harebrained idea pops into his head, and some asshole flunky tells him it's a great idea. Then they send me to pass it on." He looked at his watch. "So make haste, make haste, Mr. Landry."

"What happened to Sir Patrick Spence, if I may ask?"

"He drowned in the storm." Charlie stood. "Okay, you can travel as you are, minus gun, but please pack a suit. We don't want to overdo the Cincinnatus thing in the West Wing."

"I have to be back here tomorrow night, latest."

"You got it. Hey, if you're coming to D.C. with your lady on Saturday, Katherine and I will take you to dinner. It's on Uncle Sam. I'd like to meet her."

"I'm turning down the job."

"Wrong. You'll tell them you need the weekend to think it over. You have to speak to your fiancée. Okay?"

"Why mess around?"

"Maybe you owe it to—what's her name?"

"Annie."

"To Annie to be consulted. We'll take her around Washington, we'll have private tours of everything, and we'll talk it over. Katherine is good at that."

"Annie is a simple country girl. I told you, this is not the life—"

"Women love cities. Shopping, good restaurants, shopping. Where are you staying?"

"I don't know."

"I'll book the Four Seasons. She'll love Georgetown. Looks like downtown Spencerville. You can show her your old haunts. Stay away from Chadwick's. Linda still hangs out there, and we don't want a scene. I'm looking forward to this weekend. Let's roll."

"You're a shit."

"I know."

Keith left Charlie in the kitchen, went upstairs, and packed a garment bag.

On the way to the airport, Keith said, "When they asked me to leave, you didn't stand up for me, Charlie."

Charlie lit a cigarette as he drove. "I didn't want to. You were burned-out, buddy. You wanted to leave. You know that. Why would I want to prolong your unhappiness?"

"What makes you think I'm any less burned-out now?"

"I don't know. This was not my idea. They think there's some energy left. It's like carbon soot, you know? You run it through the afterburners and apply more heat, and you get a little more fire out of it."

"Interesting analogy. What happens to the burned soot?"

"It turns into vapor and blows away."

CHAPTER TWENTY-THREE

Keith directed Charlie to Toledo Airport, and they made the flight with a few minutes to spare.

They had first-class tickets, and Keith asked, "Do I get a twenty-one-gun salute at National?"

"Absolutely. And a red carpet."

"Brass band?"

"The whole works. The White House travel office does it right."

Keith put on the earphones and read during the flight, so he didn't have to listen to Charlie Adair.

The aircraft began its approach and descent into National Airport. Keith and Charlie were sitting on the left side, which had the best view. Government and military air restrictions prohibited aircraft from approaching National from the east because of security concerns involving the White House, and aircraft approaching from the north, south, and west had problems getting low enough because of all the high-rise buildings on the Virginia side of the Potomac and noise restrictions in the Maryland suburbs. For this reason, when airliners approached from the north, as they were doing, they flew directly over the Potomac River, which afforded a spectacular panorama.

Keith, in the window seat, looked out at the sun-lit city. The aircraft seemed to glide over the river, and Keith could see Georgetown, the Watergate, then the Mall, the Lincoln, Washington, and Jefferson monuments, and in the distance the Capitol. It was truly a beautiful experience, and he never tired of it, especially after he'd been away awhile.

It occurred to Keith that, as he landed, the city was exerting its own gravitational pull on him, drawing him into its grip. It had probably occurred to Charlie Adair, too, when he booked seats on the left side of the aircraft.

They landed on time at National Airport. There was no twenty-one-gun salute, nor a red carpet or a band, but there was a government Lincoln Town Car and a driver who took them to the Hay-Adams Hotel on Sixteenth Street, a block from the White House.

Adair offered to come in and have a drink, but Keith said, "You've been kind enough for one day."

"Don't take it out on me."

"What time tomorrow?"

"I'll come by and collect you at ten-thirty."

"Too early for an eleven-thirty."

"You know the drill at the White House. A half hour early is late. A minute late is a bad career move."

"See you at eleven."

"We could hit traffic. The car could break down—"

"We can *walk*. I can see it from here. See?"

"Ten forty-five."

"Okay. Bring my return ticket, or I'm not going anywhere with you."

"I'll have it with me."

"And reserve me a car at the other end. Toledo, Columbus, or Dayton."

"Will do. See you tomorrow."

Keith went into the restored landmark hotel and checked in. The reservations having been made by the White House travel office, everyone was deferential. This was a town, he knew, that lived and breathed power, not politics, as people thought. Power.

Up in his room, he looked out over Lafayette Square at the White House and the huge dome of the Capitol beyond it. He'd been gone less than two months, but the mad energy of the place grated on his nerves. Too many cars, too many horns honking, too many people, too hot, too humid, too everything.

He considered calling the Porters, but there was still a possibility that their phone was tapped, and in any case, there was no reason to call them and no reason to call Annie's sister since he intended to be back in Ohio on Friday evening, home before midnight, and at Terry's house before ten A.M. Saturday.

He also considered calling friends in Washington, but there was no point in that, either. In this town, among government workers, your friends and your business colleagues were almost always the same people. If you lived in the suburbs, you might have neighbors who were also friends, but if you lived in town, as he had done, your social life was an extension of your career. He'd gotten a few letters from former colleagues, but basically, if you were out of the business, you were out of the loop, even if you stayed around.

He made himself a drink from the room bar and stared out at the city, which someone had recently described as the last and only power capital left in the world. Could he live here again? Why would he want to? Even as a retired government employee, he never considered it.

In many ways he was typical of hundreds of thousands of men and women, military and civilian, whose careers had been suddenly cut short by the end of the Cold War. And in this respect, too, he was no different from millions of other warriors in the past, the winners as well as the losers, whose services were no longer required. But unlike the soldiers or veterans in Charlie Adair's little ditty, he never felt slighted, and would have welcomed being ignored.

He watched the rush hour traffic below, then looked over the city. Most of the people he knew who were in his situation had not gone literally home as he had, but had found that they were more comfortable close to the Beltway where they'd spent probably half their careers. He, on the other hand, wanted a complete break with the past, and he thought he'd accomplished that. In fact, he *had* accomplished that. "I can say no to the president. That's what I fought for. Mr. President, what part of no didn't you understand?" He smiled to himself.

He had an early dinner alone in his room and ordered a bottle of Banfi Brunello di Montalcino to go with his Chateaubriand and truffles. He told himself he did not miss this kind of food, then admitted that he did. But if he wound up in Spencerville, he'd get a couple of good cookbooks. The Porters could do the vegetables, he'd do the meat, and maybe Annie could learn continental pastry. Maybe not. What difference did it make? And, in any case, he had no idea where he was going to wind up. The point was, this brief sojourn in Washington had highlighted the differences between here and Spencerville—not that they needed to be highlighted; they were monumental enough.

In some strange and perverse way, however, he missed this place. He had to admit that. Charlie Adair knew that, which was why he'd brought him here. Keith kept telling himself he wouldn't live in Washington again, and he couldn't live in Spencerville. So he'd find a neutral corner of the world where he and Annie could be happy and at peace.

He finished dinner and left the room. Downstairs, he asked the doorman to get him a taxi. Keith told the driver, "Georgetown."

The taxi made its way through the tail end of rush hour traffic and crossed Rock Creek at the M Street bridge. On M Street, Georgetown's main commercial street, they passed a number of his old haunts, which conjured up memories of bright and beautiful young people at the bars or sitting in booths, discussing art, literature, and travel, and sometimes they'd discuss sports, too. But these were all hors d'oeuvres, the things you nibbled on before the main course, which was politics and power.

Keith directed the driver past his old apartment on Wisconsin Avenue, then down some side streets where friends lived, or had once lived, including streets on which lived women he'd known. He didn't see anyone he knew on the streets, which was just as well, he thought.

He tried to picture Annie here and realized that she would be perplexed and perhaps bewildered by this world. Even the simple act of telling a doorman you wanted a taxi would be alien to her. Of course she'd pick it up quickly, but that didn't mean she'd enjoy urban living, not even in the quaint streets of Georgetown. No, she'd feel dislocated and she'd become dependent on him, and that would lead to resentment, and when a woman was resentful—who knew where that would lead?

They could live in the suburbs, of course, or the exurbs, and he could commute, but he pictured phoning her out in Virginia or Maryland at eight P.M. and telling her he had a meeting that would last until midnight. Younger couples in Washington and elsewhere led this kind of existence, but they were in the striving mode of their lives, and both spouses usually had careers, and one of them hadn't spent most of their lives in a rural town of fifteen thousand people.

She'd adjust, of course, and probably not complain, because that was how she was. But it would be such an uneven relationship; it would be his world, and his job, and his friends, and he no longer cared for this world, that job, or those friends and colleagues. *He* would be miserable.

But maybe not. That was the thought that kept nagging at him. He knew he didn't want to impress her with the so-called glamour and excitement of Washington cocktail parties, formal dinners, important people, and power. *He* wasn't impressed, and he doubted she would be. On the other hand, maybe a year or two wouldn't be bad, as long as it was finite. During that time, maybe the situation in Spencerville would resolve itself. He played around with this thought, then said, "Could it work?"

The cabbie glanced back. "Yes, mister?"

"Nothing. Take a right here." Keith read the name on the cabbie's license—Vu Thuy Hoang. He asked the man, "Do you like Washington?"

The man, from long practice and with the inherent politeness of the Vietnamese, replied, "Yes. Very good city."

Like so many of his displaced compatriots who lived and worked in the capital of the country that had tried to help and succeeded in failing, this man, Keith thought, had suffered. He didn't know how or to what extent, but there was a story of suffering in Vu Thuy Hoang's history that would shame most Americans, like himself. Keith didn't want to know the story but asked the man, "What part of Vietnam are you from?"

Used to the question from one too many Vietnam veterans, he replied quickly, "Phu Bai. You know?"

"Yes. Big air base."

"Yes, yes. Many Americans."

"Do you go home?"

"No."

"Would you like to go home?"

The man didn't reply for a few seconds, then said, "Maybe. Maybe for visit."

"You have family in Phu Bai?"

"Oh, yes. Many family."

"You are welcome back? You may go to Vietnam?"

"No. Not now. Someday. Maybe."

The man appeared to be in his mid-forties, and Keith imagined that for some reason or another, he was persona non grata in his native land. Perhaps he'd been a government official under the old regime, or a military officer, or had worked too closely with the Americans, or done something more sinister, like been a member of the old, despised National Police. Who knew? They never told you. The point was that in Phu Bai there was a police chief, and the police chief had a list, and on that list was this man's name. That police chief was sort of the Phu Bai equivalent of Cliff Baxter, except that Keith's problem with Baxter wasn't political or philosophical—it was purely personal. But the bottom line was the same—some people could not go home again because other people didn't want them to.

Keith said to the man, "Back to the hotel."

"Yes? No stop?"

"No. No stop."

At the Hay-Adams, Keith gave Vu Thuy Hoang a ten-dollar tip and free advice. "As soon as you can, go home. Don't wait."

CHAPTER TWENTY-FOUR

The following morning, the phone rang in Keith's room, and he answered it.

Charlie Adair said, "I'm downstairs. Whenever you're ready."

Keith resisted several sarcastic replies. At some point in the middle of the night, he'd come to agree that none of this was Charlie's fault. He said, "Five minutes."

Keith straightened his tie in the mirror and brushed the jacket of his dark blue Italian silk suit. If he didn't count putting on a sport jacket and tie for Sunday service at St. James, this was the first suit he'd had on since his retirement party almost two months before, and he didn't like the way he looked in it. "You look like a city slicker, Landry." He left the room and took the elevator down.

Charlie greeted him with some wariness, trying to judge his mood, but Keith said to him, "You're right, it's not your fault."

"Good insight. Let's go."

"The ticket."

"Oh, right..." Charlie found the airline ticket in his jacket and gave it to Keith. "I booked you to Columbus on USAir, nonstop. There's a rental car reservation slip, too."

Keith examined the ticket and saw he was leaving National Airport at 7:35 and arriving at 9:05. He asked, "Couldn't you get something earlier?"

"That was the next available nonstop in first class."

"I don't care about nonstop or first class. Anything earlier to Toledo or Dayton?"

"Dayton? Where's that? Look, the White House travel office booked it. I don't think there are a lot of flights going out there, buddy. Just be happy it's Columbus, Ohio, and not Columbus, Georgia. See the travel office later if you want."

"This is okay. Let's roll."

They walked out the front door to where a Lincoln sat waiting. It was raining, and the driver walked them to the car, holding an umbrella over their heads.

In the backseat, Charlie said, "I spoke to the secretary's aide, Ted Stansfield, last night, and he was delighted you could come."

"What were my choices?"

"That's the way they talk. Mock humbleness. The secretary of defense will say to you, 'Keith, I'm delighted you could come. I hope we haven't inconvenienced you.'"

"Is that when I tell him to fuck off?"

"I don't think so. He's prepared to welcome you back on the team, so if he says, 'Good to have you back,' you say, 'Good to be back in Washington,' like you didn't quite catch his meaning. Then you go shake hands with the president. If they've briefed him that you're wavering, he'll say, 'Colonel, I hope you give this offer your full consideration and that you'll accept it.' Then you say, 'I will, sir,' meaning you'll give it your full consideration and not meaning you'll accept it. Get it?"

"Charlie, I was a master of the equivocal phrase, an expert at the meaningless sentence, a scholar of the ambiguous word. That's why I don't want to come back. I'm relearning plain English."

"That's very disturbing."

Keith added, "I assume you didn't tell Ted Stansfield that I didn't want the job."

"I didn't, because I wanted you to have some time to think about it. Have you thought about it?"

"I have."

"And?"

"Well, I took a taxi around town last night and did some deep thinking. I went to the Lincoln Memorial and stood in front of the statue of the great man, and I asked him, 'Abe, what should I do?' And Mr. Lincoln spoke to me, Charlie. He said, 'Keith, Washington sucks.'"

"What did you expect him to say? He got shot here. You should have asked someone else."

"Like who? The fifty thousand guys whose names are on the black wall? You don't want to hear what they have to say about Washington."

"No, I don't."

The government car went around Lafayette Square and approached the West Wing entrance from Seventeenth Street.

Charlie said, "Look, Keith, it's your decision. I did what I was asked to do. I got you here."

"They never asked you to sell the job to me?"

"No, they didn't. They thought you'd jump at it. But I knew differently."

"You were right."

"That's why this meeting could be a little awkward for me."

"I'll cover your ass."

"Thanks."

Keith glanced out the window. Directly across from The West Wing on Seventeenth Street was his former workplace, the Old Executive Office Building, a hundred-year-old pile of granite and cast iron, built in a style called French Second Empire. People either loved it or hated it. Keith was ambivalent. The recently restored interior was palatial enough to be embarrassing, especially if you had an upper-floor window that looked south toward the black ghettos.

The building was about four times the size of the White House itself and once housed the War Department, the State Department, and the Department of the Navy with room to spare. Now it couldn't even hold all the people who made up the White House staff and was limited to senior-level White House offices such as the National Security Council. The NSC was more or less an advisory group to the president, a clearinghouse for intelligence product that was produced by the CIA, the Defense Intelligence Agency, for whom Keith once worked, the National Security Agency, which dealt mostly with cryptography, State Department Intelligence, and the other spook outfits that abounded in and around the District of Columbia.

People who served on the actual Council included the director of the CIA, the secretary of defense, the secretary of state, the chairman of the Joint Chiefs of Staff, and such other highly placed people as the president might appoint. It was indeed an elite group, and in the days of the Cold War, the NSC was far more important than the Cabinet, though no one was supposed to know that.

Some years ago, Keith had been invited to leave his job with the Defense Intelligence Agency in the Pentagon and accept a staff position with the NSC, located in the Old Executive Office Building. There was less physical danger associated with the job compared to what he'd been doing around the world for the DIA, and the NSC office was closer to his Georgetown apartment, and he'd thought he might enjoy working with civilians. As it turned out, he missed the danger, and though it was a good career move to be working so close to the White House, it turned out to be not such a good move in other ways.

Among the people he'd met at the NSC was a Colonel Oliver North. Keith hadn't known the man well, but after Colonel North became famous, Colonel Landry became troubled. North, by all accounts, had been a good soldier, but working for the civilians had apparently been like working in a contagion ward for the young colonel, and he'd caught something bad. Keith could see that happening to himself, so he always wore a mask and washed his hands on the job.

And now they wanted him back, not in the old building, but apparently in the White House itself.

They drove up to the guard post on Seventeenth Street, and after a security check, they were waved through. The driver pulled up to the entrance, and they got out.

There were more security men at the entrance, but no check, just someone who opened the door for them. Inside the small lobby, there was a man at a sign-in desk who verified their names against an appointment list. Keith signed in, and under the heading "Organization and Title," he wrote, "Civilian, retired." The time was 11:05.

Keith had been in the West Wing of the White House a number of times, usually arriving via the little-known underground passage that ran beneath Seventeenth Street into the White House basement where the Situation Room was located, along with a few offices of the National Security Council. He'd been on the ground floor a few times whenever he'd had occasion to see the national security advisor in a previous administration.

After Charlie signed in, the appointments man at the desk said to them, "Gentlemen, if you'll take the elevator down, you can wait in the lounge. Someone will call you."

They took the small elevator to the basement, and another man met them and walked them to the lounge.

The lounge, a euphemism for the basement waiting room, was newly appointed with clubby-type furnishings and was pleasant enough. There was a television tuned to CNN, and a long buffet table against the wall where you could help yourself to anything from coffee to donuts, or fruit and yogurt for the health-conscious, or most any snack you wished, except alcohol and cyanide.

There were a dozen or so other people in the room, men and women, none of whom Keith recognized, but all of them throwing furtive glances toward the newcomers, trying to place their faces in the pantheon of Washington's gods and goddesses of the moment.

Charlie and Keith found two chairs at a coffee table and sat. Charlie asked, "You want coffee or anything?"

"No, thanks, boss."

Charlie smiled in acknowledgment of the changed situation. He said, "Hey, if you take this job, your immediate supervisor will be the president's national security advisor, not me."

"I thought I was going to *be* the national security advisor."

"No, you'll work directly *for* him."

"When can I be president?"

"Keith, I'm a little anxious about this meeting. Can you cut the shit?"

"Sure. Do some push-ups. Works for me."

"I'd like a cigarette, but I can't smoke here. What's this place coming to?"

Keith glanced around the room. Despite its nice

decor, it was still a windowless basement room, and the atmosphere was the atmosphere of waiting rooms all over the world. There was that electric hum originating somewhere in the bowels of this building that forced in cool air or hot air, depending on the season, and after being away from that big-city, big-building hum for two months, he noticed it and didn't like it.

More to the point, there was a heightened sense of the surreal in this room, a feeling of almost impending doom, as if each man and woman in the place were awaiting his or her fate in one of those less pleasant subterranean rooms in countries where they shot you if your name was on that day's list.

Keith had had the opportunity to visit the prison basement of the Lubyanka, the former KGB headquarters in Moscow, which had become sort of a tourist attraction for selected former enemies of the defunct Soviet state, such as himself. The cells were gone, replaced by clerical space, but Keith had imagined being in the old cells, hearing the screams of tortured men and women, the names being called out, the echoing gunshot at the end of the corridor, where his guide explained how prisoners were shot in the back of the head as they walked.

The waiting room of the West Wing of the White House was quite different, of course—yogurt and world news on TV—but the sense of waiting for the government to call your name was the same. It didn't matter what they were calling your name for, it only mattered that you had to wait for it to be called.

Keith decided then and there that he didn't ever again want to wait for the government to call his name. They'd called his name twenty-five years before, and he'd answered the call. They called his name yesterday, and he answered the call. They'd call his name today, but today was different: Today was the last time he'd answer.

The door opened, and an appointments man said, "Colonel Landry, Mr. Adair, will you come with me, please?"

They stood and followed the young man to the elevator. They rode up to the lobby and followed the man to the Cabinet Room at the east end of the wing. The man knocked on the door, then opened it, and they were shown in by the appointments man. Inside, another man, whom Keith recognized as Ted Stansfield, came forward to greet them. Charlie said, "Ted, you remember Keith."

"Indeed I do." They shook hands, and Stansfield said, "Delighted you could come."

"Delighted to be invited."

"Come, have a seat." He indicated two chairs at the long dark wooden table where the Cabinet met.

The Cabinet Room, Keith knew, was used for all types of meetings, large or small, when the Cabinet was not meeting. In fact, it was a tightly scheduled conference room, used by various people to impress and/or to intimidate. Colonel Keith Landry might have once been impressed, but never intimidated. Now he was slightly bored and restless.

He looked at Stansfield, a man of about forty, polished and smooth, a man who was truly delighted, mostly with himself.

Stansfield informed them, "The secretary is running a bit late." He said to Keith, "Your old boss, General Watkins, will also join us, as will Colonel Chandler, who is the current aide to the national security advisor."

"And will Mr. Yadzinski also join us?" Keith inquired, using the name of the national security advisor, though in official Washington, the very highest people were referred to by their title, such as "the president," "the secretary of defense," and so forth, as if these people had been transformed from mortals into deities, as in, "The God of War will join us shortly." Then again, the very lowest-ranking people were also referred to by their title, such as "the janitor."

Ted Stansfield replied, "The security advisor will try to join us if he can."

"They're all running a bit late?"

"Well, yes, I suppose they are. Can I get you anything?"

"No, thank you."

The three men waited, making small talk as was customary so as not to touch upon anything that would require someone saying something like, "Before you arrived, sir, Mr. Landry and I discussed that, and he informed me," and so forth.

Stansfield inquired, "So, did you enjoy your brief retirement?"

Rather than correct the man's use of the past tense and queer the whole charade for Charlie, Keith replied, "I did."

"How were you spending your time?"

"I went back to my hometown and looked up my old girlfriend."

Stansfield smiled. "Did you? And did you rekindle the old flame?"

"Yes, we did."

"Well, that's very interesting, Keith. Do you have any plans?"

"We do. In fact, I'm bringing her to Washington tomorrow."

"How delightful. Why didn't you bring her with you today?"

"Her husband won't be out of town until tomorrow."

Keith felt Charlie kick his foot at the same time Stansfield's idiotic smile dropped. Keith informed Ted Stansfield, "Charlie said it wouldn't be a problem."

"Well...I suppose it..."

Charlie interjected, "The lady in question is in the process of a divorce."

"Ah."

Keith let it go.

The door opened, and in walked General Watkins in mufti, and another man in mufti whom Keith recognized as Colonel Chandler, though they'd rarely had occasion to speak.

Charlie stood, as did Ted Stansfield, though as civilians, they didn't have to. Keith wasn't certain he had to either, but he did, and they shook hands. General Watkins said, "You look good, Keith. The rest did you good. Ready to get back in the saddle?"

"It was a nasty fall, General."

"All the more reason to climb on that horse again."

Keith knew that Watkins was going to say that, but it was his own fault for giving Watkins the opening for his inane reply. Keith didn't know how many more evasive and inane replies he could come up with before they got it.

Ted Stansfield said to Keith, "You probably remember Dick Chandler, whose job you're going to fill. Colonel Chandler is going on to bigger and better things at the Pentagon."

Colonels Landry and Chandler shook hands. The man looked relieved to see his replacement, Keith thought, or perhaps Keith was just imagining it.

Most soldiers didn't like a White House assignment, Keith knew, but it was difficult in peacetime to get yourself out of this place without causing career problems. In wartime, it was somewhat easier: You volunteered to go to the front and get shot at.

General Watkins, Colonel Chandler, Colonel Landry, Mr. Adair, and Mr. Stansfield remained standing, awaiting the imminent arrival of the secretary of defense.

Conversation was difficult, Keith noticed. Small talk in the West Wing was inappropriate if it went on too long, and big talk such as the deteriorating situation in the former Soviet Union was fraught with pitfalls, since anything you said could be construed as official and held against you later. Ted Stansfield saved the day by talking about a new executive directive he'd just read which clarified an earlier directive and had something to do with the worrisome problem of who reports to whom.

Keith switched channels, but the background static brought to mind the organizational chart of the intelligence community. The National Security Council, on which he had served, was headed by the president's assistant for National Security Affairs, known as the national security advisor, whose birth name was Edward Yadzinski. The job they were offering Colonel Landry was that of Mr. Yadzinski's assistant, or perhaps military aide or liaison, with some connection to the secretary of defense, upon whom they all now waited.

This organizational chart, Keith recalled, had these neat labeled boxes and rectangles, all somehow connected by tortuous lines that never crossed and resembled an electronic schematic for a nuclear submarine. Unlike an electronic schematic, however, which had to obey the laws of science to work, the intelligence community chart obeyed no known laws of science, God, or nature, only the laws of man, which were subject to executive whimsy and congressional debate.

That aside, Keith saw no real reason for his old boss, General Watkins, to be present, since Watkins was on the far right side of the chart, over on Seventeenth Street, while Keith was now in the center, a few guys away from the top dog himself. Keith suspected, though, that General Watkins was there to serve a sort of penance for letting Colonel Landry go, which of course was what he'd been ordered to do, but Watkins should have anticipated that, two months later, the president would ask for Colonel Landry by name. Poor General Watkins.

Watkins, of course, did not have to apologize for giving Colonel Landry the heave-ho, but he had to be present at Colonel Landry's rehiring, and he had to smile, or make what passed for a smile. Watkins was thoroughly pissed off, of course, as he had every right to be, but Watkins wouldn't utter a peep.

The center of power, Keith reflected, in any time or place, was by definition a haven for lunatics and lunatic behavior—the Kremlin, a Byzantine palace, the Forbidden City, a Roman emperor's villa, the Führerbunker—it didn't matter what it was called and what it looked like from the outside; inside was airless and dark, a breeding ground for progressive madness and increasingly dangerous flights from reality. Keith had a sudden impulse to charge for the door, shouting something about the inmates running the asylum.

General Watkins said, "Keith, you have that smile on your face that used to annoy me."

"I didn't know I was smiling, sir, and never knew it annoyed you."

"That smile was always a prelude to some smart remark. Can we expect one now?"

"General, I'd like to take this opportunity to—"

Charlie Adair interrupted. "Keith, perhaps you'd like to hold that thought for another time."

Keith thought the time was perfect to tell Watkins what he thought of him, but at that moment the door opened, and the secretary of defense ambled in. He was a slight, balding man with spectacles, not the type you'd guess would be head of the most powerful military machine on the face of the earth. And his meek appearance didn't mask a strong personality—there was no Mars, God of War, lurking in that frail body. He looked like a milksop, and he was a milksop.

Ted Stansfield presented the secretary of defense, who smiled, shook hands all around, and said to Keith, "Delighted you could come."

"Delighted to be here."

Stansfield pulled out a chair at the end of the long table, and the secretary sat. General Watkins and Colonel Chandler were directed by Stansfield to the secretary's right, and Keith and Charlie were directed across from them. Ted Stansfield, still standing, said, "Mr. Secretary, gentlemen, if you'll excuse me, I have another appointment." He left.

The secretary looked at Keith and said, "Well, Colonel Landry, you're probably wondering why you've been asked to come out of retirement, so I'll tell you. You made a favorable and lasting impression on the president during some of the intelligence briefing sessions, and a few days ago, he asked for you by name." The secretary chuckled and added, "When someone told him you'd retired, he said you looked too young to retire. So here you are." He smiled at Keith.

Keith considered several replies, including a recitation of Charlie's Scottish ballad. Instead, he took the occasion to set the record straight and said, "I was asked to retire, sir. It wasn't my idea." He didn't glance at General Watkins, because that would have been petty. Keith added, "But I've got twenty-five years of service, and I'm quite comfortable with my present situation."

The secretary didn't seem to follow all of that and replied, "Well, your name has been placed on the list for promotion to general officer. The president will review that list shortly."

Keith, still trying to get something on record, said,

"I'm no longer on active duty, sir, having retired from the Army at the same time I retired from government service. So I assume this promotion will be as a reserve officer on the inactive rolls."

The secretary had his own agenda and continued, "The position you are to fill is that of military aide and advisor to the president's national security advisor. Colonel Chandler will brief you on your duties later." The secretary added, "Your office will be here in the West Wing."

He said "West Wing," Keith thought, as if he were saying "at the right hand of God." And here they were, in the seat of power, where proximity to power was itself power, a short walk to the Oval Office—where you could literally bump into the president in the corridor—the very epicenter of national and international moving and shaking. It was not the sort of workplace, Keith thought, where your friends or family could drop in and have a cup of coffee or ask you to lunch. Keith asked, "Would my office be on the second floor or in the basement?"

Colonel Chandler answered, "In the basement."

"Can you see the sky? I mean, is there a little window?"

Chandler seemed a bit bemused. He replied, "It's interior. You get a secretary."

"Do you have plants?"

Charlie Adair forced a smile and explained to everyone, "Colonel Landry has spent the last two months on his family's farm and has become nature-sensitive."

"How delightful," said the secretary of defense. He asked Keith, "Do you have any questions for me, Colonel?"

The man was half out of his chair and staring at his wristwatch, so Keith replied, "No, sir."

The secretary stood, and so did everyone else. "Good.

If you will excuse me, gentlemen, I have another appointment." He looked at Keith and said, "General Watkins's loss is the White House's gain. Good luck." He left.

General Watkins seized on the defense secretary's departure as his opportunity to say to Keith, "I'm surprised you decided to return to Washington. I had the feeling you'd had enough."

"I had."

The general looked at him quizzically and added, "Maybe a new job will invigorate you."

Keith replied, "Perhaps when I'm wearing the same star that you have, sir, we can engage in some sort of athletic contest to see who has the most vigor."

General Watkins did not seem happy with that remark, but sensing a subtle shift in the power structure, he let it pass. He said, "Well, gentlemen, you don't need me any longer, and I, too, have an appointment. Good day." He looked at Keith and said, "Politics is not your strong suit, Colonel."

"Thank you."

Watkins departed, leaving Keith, Charlie Adair, and Colonel Chandler standing in the Cabinet Room. Since they were all peers, more or less, they sat without anyone inviting them to, and Keith took a seat several places away.

Chandler was speaking about the job, and Keith tuned out again. This entire so-called meeting was a staged performance, with a cameo appearance by the secretary of defense. It was also part protocol—the secretary was Colonel Landry's big boss, if Keith still considered himself a soldier—and the other players had their bit parts as well. Charlie Adair was Judas, General Watkins was the scapegoat, Colonel Chandler was Pilate washing his hands of the whole mess, and Ted Stansfield was the emcee. Keith knew his part but was not delivering his lines very well.

Keith's thoughts turned again to Annie, and he wondered what she'd make of all this if she were here. As he'd said to Charlie, she was a simple country girl, but she wasn't stupid, and in fact she'd done far better academically in high school and college than he had. She had also come from the same midwestern populist tradition that he had, and if she were here in this room, he had little doubt that she'd find all of this pomp, protocol, and pecking order slightly distasteful, and undoubtedly she'd see through this nonsense in a lot less time than it had taken him.

In the early days of his service, the world was more dangerous, but the government seemed to him a lot simpler and more benign. There had been men around in those days who'd helped defeat the Axis powers, men who were dedicated public servants and not pigs at the government trough, men with a sense of purpose and mission. Now even the Vietnam generation of men, such as himself, were retiring or were being asked to leave, and he didn't particularly care for the new crop.

During the next five minutes, Colonel Chandler described the duties and responsibilities of the job, putting it in the most favorable light, forgetting to mention twelve-hour days, homework, or crises in countries whose time zones, holidays, and Sabbaths didn't mesh well with those of Washington, D.C.

Keith interrupted Chandler and asked, "Did you enjoy it?"

"Enjoy?" He thought a moment, then said, "It's very stressful here in the White House, but very rewarding."

"How can anything stressful be rewarding?"

"Well...it *can* be. Maybe I should say I felt I was doing something for my country, not for myself."

"But were you doing the *right* thing for your country?"

"I thought I was. I *was.* It's not over, you know. There are still a lot of bad guys out there."

"Right. Maybe the new good guys can handle the new bad guys."

"We have the experience."

"We're experienced with the old bad guys. We may possibly understand the new realities, but we think in the old way." He looked at Colonel Chandler and asked him, "Do you suggest I take this job?"

Chandler cleared his throat and glanced at Adair, who made a motion with his hand as if to say, "Answer the man."

Colonel Chandler thought a moment, then replied, "I'm glad I have it in my résumé, but I wouldn't wish these last two years on my worst enemy."

"Thank you."

The door opened, and in strode Edward Yadzinski, the president's national security advisor. Everyone stood, and Yadzinski shook hands all around. He said to Keith, "I'm delighted you could come on such short notice."

"Thank you, sir. So am I."

"I have another appointment, but I wanted to chat a moment. I've read your file, and I'm quite impressed with the range of your experiences from rifle platoon leader to your last assignment. I'm looking for someone like you who will be forthright and honest with me. Colonel Chandler will vouch for that. I like military men because they have the attributes I want."

"Yes, sir." And Keith thought, because they usually had no political ambitions, they followed orders, and they could be transferred easily instead of having to be fired. Like priests or ministers, military officers had a calling that theoretically transcended their careers or personal lives. People in the executive branch found it useful to have a certain number of military people on staff: indentured servants in mufti.

Yadzinski continued, "Your former colleagues speak well of you, Colonel. Right, Charlie?"

Charlie Adair agreed. "Colonel Landry was an asset to my department and respected throughout the intelligence community."

Keith said to his potential boss, "I never got along with General Watkins, and I caused Mr. Adair a lot of anxiety."

Charlie winced, but Yadzinski smiled. "You're not much of a diplomat, are you? In fact, I was present that time in the Situation Room when you asked the secretary of state if we had a foreign policy." He chuckled. "I like that. And I'll back you up, Colonel. I work directly for the president, and you work directly for me."

Keith thought he might actually like Yadzinski and would have liked working for him five or six years ago. But it was too late. Keith said, "Despite my differences with Mr. Adair, I found him to be extremely knowledgeable, competent, and dedicated." Keith was glad he'd gotten that in, but clearly Yadzinski wasn't paying attention. Yadzinski said, "Colonel Chandler can answer any of your questions better than I can." He put out his hand, and Keith took it. Yadzinski said, "Welcome aboard, Colonel." As he shook hands with Keith, he looked at his watch. "I have another appointment." Still clasping Keith's hand, he asked, "When can you start?"

"Well, I'd like to take the weekend to consider—"

"Of course. Monday would be fine. Colonel Chandler will show you your office."

Charlie said, "Colonel Landry lives in Ohio, sir."

"Great state. Good day, gentlemen." He turned and left.

Keith looked at his watch and said, "I have another appointment. Good day, gentlemen."

Charlie forced a smile and said, "You have an appointment with the president."

Colonel Chandler added, "You're to wait in the waiting room until you're called." He grinned and said to Keith, "I don't have another appointment. I'm out of here." He went to the door, then turned and said, "If you wander around downstairs, you'll find my office. I've left my number if you have any questions. It's all yours." He left, and though Keith did not hear the word "sucker," it hung in the air.

Keith said to Charlie, "Charlie, I don't think we're in Spencerville anymore."

"What gave you that impression?"

As they walked to the door, Keith said, "They may be surprised to discover that Colonel Chandler's office is empty on Monday."

"Take the weekend to think about it. Yadzinski's one of the good guys in this administration. Give it a try. What do you have to lose?"

"My soul."

They went out into the hallway and took the small elevator down to the basement again. Charlie asked, "Do you want to find your office?"

"No."

They went to the waiting room and waited. Charlie said, as if to himself, "I think I'm off the hook. Thanks for the plug."

Keith didn't reply. He read a newspaper.

Charlie suddenly laughed and said, "So, can you get back to Ohio, pack everything, return to Washington, find an apartment, furnish it, and be at work Monday morning?"

Keith looked over the top of his newspaper but said nothing.

Charlie said, "I guess he didn't know you'd left D.C. Well, but I did tell him...maybe he wasn't listening."

Keith turned the page of the newspaper.

"I could clear that up. You can take a few weeks."

Keith glanced at his watch.

Charlie continued, "But I see your point. This place is a pressure cooker."

Keith refolded the newspaper and read a story in the metro section about rush hour traffic jams. The minutes ticked by.

Charlie said, "But to say you work in the White House...wouldn't your lady friend be proud and impressed?"

Without looking over his paper, Keith replied, "No."

"Don't tell me it's not tempting."

Keith put the paper down. "Charlie, administrations come and go, White House jobs are about as secure and longlasting as a bronco ride. Look, I don't want to be critical or judgmental, but I'm being put in that position, and I don't like it. It should be enough for me to say that I decline the offer for personal reasons. Okay?"

"Okay."

An appointments secretary came in and said, "Colonel Landry, the president will see you now."

"Good luck," said Charlie.

Keith stood, and everyone in the waiting room looked at him as he followed the appointments secretary out.

They went up the elevator again and walked down the corridor to the Oval Office. A Secret Service man at the door said, "A few minutes."

The appointments secretary reminded him of the protocols and told him not to step on the Great Seal that was woven into the carpet. Keith inquired, "Should I jump over it?"

"No, sir, walk around it to the left. The president's aide will go around to the right, then you continue on toward the desk. The president is running late and will not ask you to sit but will come around and greet you a few feet from the desk. Please be brief."

"Should I tell him I voted for him?"

The appointments man regarded him a moment, then glanced at the appointment schedule in his hand as if to reassure himself that this guy was on the list.

The door opened, and a young female aide showed him in. They walked the length of the oval-shaped office together, over the royal-blue carpet, and detoured around the Great Seal, then back toward the president's desk, which sat in front of the big south-facing windows. Keith noticed it was still raining.

The president came around the desk to greet him, smiling, and extended his hand, which Keith took. The president said, "I'm delighted to see you again, Colonel."

"Thank you, Mr. President."

"We've missed you around here."

"Yes, sir."

"Are you all settled in?"

"Not yet, sir."

"Mr. Yadzinski will see that you are. He's a tough boss, but a fair one."

"Yes, sir."

"These are difficult times, Colonel, and we value a man of your experience and honesty."

"Thank you, Mr. President."

"Is there anything you'd like to ask me?"

This was the traditional question, asked by presidents, generals, and others in positions of high authority. A long time ago, probably before Keith was born, this was a real question. These days, with everyone running a bit late, the question was rhetorical, and the answer was always, "No, sir." But Keith asked, "Why me?"

The president seemed momentarily thrown off balance, and the aide cleared her throat. The president said, "Excuse me?"

"Why did you ask specifically for me, sir?"

"Oh, I see. Well, I remember you as a man who impressed me with your knowledge and good insight. I'm delighted to have you here." He put out his hand and said, "Welcome to the White House, Colonel."

Keith shook hands with the president and said, "Thank you for inviting me, sir."

The aide tapped Keith on the shoulder, they both turned and walked the length of the oval, avoiding the Great Seal on the floor, and a man opened the door as they reached it.

Keith found himself in the hallway, minus the aide. The appointments man said, "Thank you for coming, Colonel. Please meet Mr. Adair in the lobby."

Keith went to the lobby where Adair was standing, looking, Keith thought, a bit anxious. Adair asked, "How did it go?"

"Sixty-seven seconds, counting the detours around the Great Seal."

They were shown out of the West Wing, and their driver hurried over to them with an umbrella. On the way to the car, Adair asked, "What did he say?"

"Nothing."

"Does he think you accepted the job?"

"He does."

"What are you going to do?"

"I'll think it over."

"Good. I've made a reservation for lunch."

They got into the car, and Adair said to the driver, "Ritz-Carlton."

They left the grounds of the White House, and the car made its way through the rain-splashed streets heavy with lunch hour traffic. Adair said, "You showed just the right amount of reserve and reticence. They don't like people who seem too eager or too self-promoting."

"Charlie, this was not a job interview. It was a draft notice."

"Whatever."

"Would you take that job?"

"In a heartbeat."

"You should take some time off to evaluate your life, my friend."

"I have no life. I'm a federal employee."

"You worry me."

"You worry *me*. You in love?"

"That's irrelevant. I don't want to return to Washington."

"Even if there were no Annie Baxter?"

"This subject is closed."

They rode in silence, and Keith watched the city go by outside his window. He'd had some good times here, he admitted, but the extremely rigid structure and pecking order of official Washington went against his democratic instincts, which was one of the paradoxes of the place.

Each administration that he'd served had started out with its own unique style, its own vision, energy, optimism, and idealism. But within a year, the entrenched bureaucracy reexerted its suffocating influence, and about a year after that, the new administration began getting pessimistic, isolated, and divided with internal conflicts and squabbles. The man in the Oval Office aged quickly, and the Ship of State chugged on, unsinkable and unsteerable, with no known destination.

Keith Landry had jumped ship, or more precisely been thrown overboard and washed ashore in Spencerville. A lady on the beach had been very good to him, but now his shipmates beckoned him to return. The lady could go with him if he wished, but he was reluctant to show her the real nature of this gleaming white ship, or introduce her to his crewmates for fear she'd wonder what type of man he really was. The ship would not wait much longer, and the native chief of the island, the lady's husband, just ordered him off the island. He said to Charlie, "Sometimes you get into one of those situations where, even if you wanted to take the easy way out, there isn't one."

"Right. But you, Keith, have always had a unique knack for finding just that situation."

Keith smiled and replied, "You mean I do these things on purpose?"

"The evidence seems to point that way. And you usually do it all by yourself. Even when other people put you in tough situations, you find ways to make it tougher. And when people offer to help you out of a bad situation, you turn them down."

"Is that so?"

"Yes."

"Maybe it's my background of self-reliant farming."

"Maybe. Maybe you're just a contrary, stubborn, and ornery prick."

"There's that possibility. Can I call you on the phone now and then when I need more analysis?"

"You never call anyone. I'll call you."

"Was I difficult to work with?"

"Don't get me started." He added, "But I'd take you back in a second."

"Why?"

"You never let anyone down. Not ever. I guess that's the situation you find yourself in now. But your loyalties have changed."

"Yeah . . . somewhere on the road between Washington and Spencerville, I had a conversion."

"Try to take shorter drives. Speaking of which, here we are."

CHAPTER TWENTY-FIVE

They entered the Ritz-Carlton Hotel and walked into the Jockey Club, where the maître d' welcomed Mr. Adair by name. As he showed them to a table for two near the far wall, everyone else checked them out.

This was one of the power restaurants in Washington, Keith knew, and had been for over thirty years since it opened and Jackie Kennedy was one of the first customers.

It was a masculine, clublike place, but the women seemed to like the food and the attention, he recalled. Washington, in fact, was a masculine town despite being the foremost equal opportunity employer, the spiritual home of politically correct and nonsexist language and laws. Some women here had power, to be sure, but it was a town whose fundamental attitudes toward females had lagged far behind the public utterances. For one thing, Keith knew, young, good-looking women outnumbered their male counterparts by some unhealthy ratio. For another thing, power was an aphrodisiac, and the men had it. The women who came to Washington from the hinterlands to work as government secretaries and aides were often the type who were content to bask in reflected power. In other words, the women in official Washington were furniture and happy to be polished and sat on once in a while. Everyone denied this, of course, and in Washington that meant it was true.

There were changes in the air, to be sure, but aside from a handful of rich and powerful old Washington dowagers, there weren't many women dining with other women in the Jockey Club.

Keith hadn't come here often, but when he did, he'd noticed that the place was fairly nonpartisan in regard to politics. Barbara Bush and Nancy Reagan were as likely to be at the corner table as were black civil rights leaders Vernon Jordan and Jesse Jackson. The place was heavy with media stars as well, and on this afternoon, Keith spotted Mike Wallace and George Will at separate tables. People seemed to be taking mental notes of who was dining with whom. Keith asked Charlie, "Will anyone important be joining us? We're disappointing these people."

Charlie lit a cigarette. "You could be here in a few weeks, wearing the uniform of a general."

"Generals are a dime a dozen in this town, colonels are office boys, and I don't wear my uniform anyway."

"Right. But you could have your secretary call and say, 'This is the White House. I'd like to make a reservation for General Landry.'"

"Hey, that's almost as important as actually doing the job."

"Well, then, think about this—with a promotion and thirty years' service, your retirement pay will be nearly double, and you can live comfortably. You'd still be a young man when you retire."

"What's it to you, Charlie?"

"I'd like to have you around again."

"I won't be around *you*. I'll be across the street."

"I'd like to have a friend in the White House."

"Ah. The motive."

"I'm also thinking of your best interests."

"That's two of us." He added, "I appreciate that."

The waiter came, and Keith ordered a double Scotch on the rocks. Charlie had his usual vodka with a twist.

Charlie said, "I've booked you at the Four Seasons tomorrow. I figured you'd want to be in Georgetown."

"Who's paying for all this?"

"White House."

"Including tomorrow night with my married girl-friend?"

"Anyway, if you take the two-fifteen out of Toledo tomorrow, you should be in your room by five. I'll call you, and we'll all have dinner in Georgetown."

"Fine."

"We'll do a nice tour of the city on Monday, and by Tuesday, you'll have talked it over with her and come to a decision."

"In other words, I don't have to be at work on Monday morning?"

"I'll take care of that. We'll get you a residency hotel until you find something. I'll get that approved."

"Thank you."

Keith studied the menu.

Charlie said, "With a promotion, you can afford a town house in Georgetown."

"I doubt it."

"What's a brigadier general make these days? About eighty-five thousand?"

"I guess. I'll give it my full consideration."

"But how are you leaning?"

"Forward. I'm trying to read the menu. This conversation is closed."

The drinks came, and Charlie proposed a toast. "To all of us who serve, past, present, and future."

"Cheers."

The waiter took their order.

Charlie asked, "Did you speak to your lady last night?"

"She lives with her husband."

"Oh, right." He chuckled and said, "Ted almost dropped his dentures when you said that. That was pretty funny. I didn't know you were going to say that." He added, "Why did you say that?"

"I felt like it."

They reminisced about old times, talked about the post–Cold War world, guessed about the future. The food came, and they ate. In truth, Keith was enjoying himself. He liked Charlie Adair, he liked to discuss the real issues, he liked his Scotch, and he liked his steak. He could not imagine living here again, but he could imagine getting back into intelligence work, out of the country, maybe someplace where he could actually do some good, but he couldn't think of where that could be. The irony, however, was that he was too far up the ladder to do the fieldwork any longer, and if you said no to the president, you didn't ask for another job. And even if he could wangle a job overseas, it wouldn't be fair to Annie. She had two kids in college in Ohio, and a family in Spencerville. He had to start thinking like a private citizen with private responsibilities and commitments. He said to Charlie, "Why do we still think we have to police the world?"

Charlie replied without hesitation, "Because we still have millions of people on staff and millions of square feet of office space and billions of dollars allocated by Congress. It has nothing to do with idealism, it has to do with office space. If we withdrew from the world stage, this would be a ghost town, and the Jockey Club would close."

"That's a little cynical. People could work in domestic programs. The heartland is dying."

"That's not for people like us. Do you want a job with the Department of the Interior, or Health and Human Services?"

"No."

"There you go. Even if they offered me more money and a higher position at HHS, I'd say no. The glamour jobs have to do with helping foreigners or fucking foreigners." Charlie lit another cigarette and exhaled. "You remember the peace dividend? They fired you so we could have more peace dividend. We were going to rebuild America with that money. It's not happening. We're still trying to run the world. We *want* to run the world."

"The world can do fine without us."

"Maybe." He looked at Keith and asked, "If the Soviets were still a threat, would you come back?"

"If they were a threat, I wouldn't have been fired."

"Answer the question."

"Yes, I would."

Charlie nodded. "You see, Keith, secretly you're unhappy because the Cold War is over—"

"No."

"Listen to me. You dedicated your life to fighting godless commies, and a lot of people shared your sense of mission. You were a product of the times you grew up in and a product of small-town USA. To you, this was like a holy war, and you were on the side of God and the angels. You *were* one of the angels. Now Satan and his legions are defeated, we've invaded hell itself and freed the imprisoned souls. Then...what? *What*? Nothing. Your country doesn't need you to protect it from the forces of evil. You were happier when the devil was alive and the White House was ground zero on a Soviet missile map. You woke up each day in Washington knowing you were on the front lines and were protecting the weak and frightened. You should have seen yourself stride into the office every morning, you should have seen the fire in your eyes when I told you you were going overseas on assignment." Charlie stubbed out his cigarette and said, "The last few years, you looked like a knight who killed the last dragon, sitting around with a bad attitude, refusing to kill the rats in the cellar because it was beneath your manly dignity to do so. You were born and raised for the Battle of Armageddon. It's over now. It was a good war, a lousy victory, and nobody gives a shit anymore. Find something else to excite you."

Keith stayed silent a moment, then replied, "Everything you say is right. Even if I don't want to hear it."

"I'm not telling you anything you don't know. Hey, we should form a government-funded support group called Men Without a Mission."

Keith smiled. "Real men don't join support groups. They keep their problems to themselves."

"My wife wouldn't agree with that." He thought a moment and added, "Sometimes I really think we do need post–Cold War counseling. Like the Vietnam guys. Where's *our* parade?"

Keith said, "I call your attention to the Cold Warrior's Monument in the Mall."

"There is no Cold Warrior's Monument in the Mall."

"Which is why I call your attention to it."

"Right." Charlie seemed to be thinking, then said, "It's a letdown. But we have to deal with it. Hey, you know what knights did between battles? They perfected the concept of romantic and courtly love. It's not unmanly to be in love, to be chivalrous, to court a woman."

"I know that."

"Does she excite you?"

"Yes."

"Then go for it."

Keith looked at Charlie a moment, then asked, "And the job?"

"Forget it. You have dragons painted on your shield. Don't kill rats in the cellar. That's what they'll remember you for."

"Thanks, Charlie."

They had another drink. Keith asked, "How long does it take an important person like yourself to secure a passport for another party?"

Charlie stirred his fourth or fifth vodka, and replied, "Oh, maybe a few hours if everything's in order. I'll call a friend at the State Department and get it banged through. This is for your lady friend?"

"Yes."

"Where are you going?"

"Don't know. Probably Europe."

"If you're going anyplace strange that needs a visa, let me know. I can get those processed within a day."

"Thanks."

They ordered coffee, brandy, and dessert. It was almost three P.M., but half the tables were still full. It was amazing, Keith thought, how much of the nation's business was done at lunch, cocktails, and dinner. He hoped everyone's head was a lot more clear than his and Charlie's.

Charlie swirled his brandy and said, "I would have resigned for the same reasons, but I have a wife, kids in college, a mortgage, and an expensive restaurant habit.

Eventually, though, we'll all be gone, the guys with the hard-gained knowledge of the world will be gone, and the domestic weebs and wonks can move into the NSC offices and run a prenatal-care program for drug-dependent immigrants from Eastern Europe."

"That's better than empty office space."

"Right." Charlie drank his brandy and ordered another.

They finished their meal and Keith said, "I'll take a taxi back to the Hay-Adams."

"No, take the car, and tell the driver to meet me back here at five. I feel like drinking. Can you take a taxi to the airport?"

"Sure." Keith stood. "I'll see you and Katherine tomorrow. I enjoy her company. Yours too, sometimes."

Charlie stood unsteadily and said, "Looking forward to meeting Annie." He added, "The Four Seasons is still on us. Go through the motions, don't feel obligated, and by midweek write Mr. Yadzinski a nice letter of refusal, and you're off to Europe."

"That's the plan."

They shook hands, and Keith left. It was raining harder now, and the doorman went out with his umbrella and found the car and driver around the corner. The driver opened the door and said to Keith, loud enough for the doorman to hear, "Back to the White House, sir?"

"No, the president is meeting me at the Hay-Adams."

"Yes, sir."

Keith got in, and the car pulled away. This town was nuts, he thought. "Nuts."

"Sir?"

"Mr. Adair would like you to go back for him at five."

"Yes, sir."

Keith sat back and watched the windshield wipers. Charlie, of course, was trying some reverse psychology on him. The thing was that Charlie was so convincing with the dragon and rat analogy that Keith was firmly convinced he was making the right decision for the right reasons. "Right."

This town had seduced him like the world's greatest whore, and every time he saw her, touched her, smelled her, he got tingly. She had made him take off his uniform and screwed him until he had nothing left, and he enjoyed every minute of it. She screwed other men, too, and this excited him even more. He knew she was corrupt to the core, heartless, and cold. But she was beautiful, so well dressed and made-up and clever, and she smiled at him, and he loved her in the flesh but hated her in his soul.

CHAPTER TWENTY-SIX

At six P.M., Keith checked out of the Hay-Adams and carried his own bag to the front door.

"Taxi, sir?"

"Please."

Keith waited with the doorman under the marquee. The doorman said, "Taxis are scarce with this rain."

"I see that."

"Airport?"

"Right."

"Flights are delayed. Jack's coming through Virginia Beach."

"Excuse me?"

"Hurricane Jack. Tracking up the coast. It'll miss us, but we'll have gale-force winds and heavy rain all night. Did you check your flight, sir?"

"No."

"National or Dulles?"

"National."

The doorman shook his head. "Long delays. You might want to try Dulles, if you can."

A taxi pulled up, and the doorman opened the door. Keith got in and said to the driver, "How's National?"

"Down."

"Dulles?"

"Still open."

"Dulles."

The ride to Dulles, normally forty-five minutes via the Dulles access highway, took over an hour, and the weather didn't look much better inland. As they approached the airport, Keith saw no aircraft landing or taking off.

The driver said, "Don't look good, Chief. You want to go back?"

"No."

The driver shrugged and continued on into the airport.

Keith said, "USAir."

They arrived at USAir departures, and Keith noticed lines of people waiting for taxis. He went into the terminal and scanned the display monitors. Nearly every departing flight was delayed or canceled.

He tried the ticket agents at several airlines, looking for a flight to any city within a few hundred miles of Spencerville, but no one was hopeful.

At seven-thirty, Dulles Airport was officially closed until further notice.

Keith saw that the crowds were thinning out as people left the terminal. Other people were settling in for a wait.

He went to a bar in the terminal concourse. It was crowded with stranded travelers, but he got a beer and stood with a few other men and watched the TV mounted over the bar. Jack had made landfall at Ocean City, Maryland, and was stalled there, and the effects of the hurricane could be felt over a hundred miles from the eye. The general consensus seemed to be that nothing would be flying until dawn. But you never knew.

This was not the first time in his life he'd been unable to catch a flight, and he knew it was no use worrying or getting angry about it. In other times and places, the situation had sometimes been critical, sometimes life-threatening. This time, it was important.

It was now eight-fifteen P.M., and he had a rendezvous at ten A.M. the next day in western Ohio. He considered his options. It was about three hundred air miles, less than a two-hour flight to Columbus, slightly longer to Toledo, longer yet to Dayton or Fort Wayne, Indiana. In any case, if he could get on a flight anytime around five A.M., he'd be in Spencerville in a rental car about ten A.M., but, with a stop at his farm, he wouldn't be at his rendezvous until a few hours later. Still, he could call Annie's sister Terry's house from a public phone, at some point, and say he'd be delayed.

But there was the likely possibility that air traffic would be stacked up in the morning and it might be much later before he could actually fly out of Dulles. Also, he wasn't ticketed out of Dulles.

He left the bar and went to the car rental counters, where there were long lines of people. He stood on the Avis line and eventually got to the counter. The young man behind the counter asked him, "Reservation, sir?"

"No, but I need a car. Anything will do."

"Sorry, we have absolutely nothing here and nothing coming in tonight."

Keith had already figured that out. He asked, "How about your car? I'm going to Ohio. It's a ten-hour drive. I'll give you a thousand dollars, and you can sleep in the backseat."

The young man smiled. "Tempting, but—"

"Think it over. Ask around. I'll be at the pub in the concourse."

"I'll ask around."

Keith went back to the bar and had another beer. The place was half-empty now as people gave up on the possibility of the airport reopening and as the airlines bused ticket holders to nearby motels.

At ten P.M., the young man from Avis walked in and spotted him. He said, "I asked around, but there aren't any takers." He added, "I called our other locations around the area, but there's nothing available. Probably the same all over. You might try Amtrak."

"Thanks." Keith offered him a twenty-dollar bill, which he wouldn't take. Keith went back to his beer. In most parts of the world, greenbacks could buy you the prime minister *and* his car. In America, money still talked, but not as loudly. Most people actually did their jobs without being bribed or bought and sometimes wouldn't even take a tip. Still, there had to be an inventive and enterprising solution to the problem of getting from point A to point B.

He thought awhile. There were many ways to get out of a city, as Keith had learned over the years. But when the airport was closed because of weather, artillery fire, or rebels on the tarmac, it put a strain on ground and sea transportation.

He considered calling Terry and explaining the situation, but that would be premature and an admission of defeat—or worse, a failure of the imagination. "Think." He thought. "Got it."

He left the bar and went to the public telephones. There were lines there, too, and he waited.

At ten-thirty, he got to a phone and called Charlie Adair's home number but got the answering machine. He said, "Charlie, I'm stranded at the airport. There's a hurricane outside, in case you haven't noticed. Send a car to take me back to the hotel. Page me here. I'm at Dulles, not National."

Keith read a newspaper in the waiting area so he could hear his name paged. He knew that Adair would get the message, because in that business you checked your answering machine by remote from wherever you were at least once an hour. The free world depended on it. Or once did.

At ten fifty-five, the public address system informed Mr. Landry to pick up a courtesy telephone. He'd already located the closest one and picked it up. A man's voice said, "Mr. Landry, this is Stewart, your driver from this morning. I got a call from Mr. Adair to—"

"Where are you now?"

"I'm here, at Dulles. I can meet you right outside of the USAir departures area."

"Five minutes." Keith walked quickly to the USAir departures doors. He saw Stewart, a gray-haired man in his fifties, standing beside the Lincoln and went over to him. Stewart put Keith's bag in the trunk, and Keith got in the front seat. Stewart asked, "Wouldn't you be more comfortable in the back, sir?"

"No."

Stewart got in, and they pulled away from the curb and down the ramp.

Keith said, "Thanks."

"My job, sir."

"Are you married, Stewart?"

"Yes, sir."

"Is your wife an understanding woman?"

He laughed. "No, sir." The driver proceeded slowly through the driving rain and followed the airport exit signs.

Keith asked, "What are your instructions?"

"To take you to the Four Seasons, sir. They're holding a room for you. Everything's filled up because of this weather, but Mr. Adair got you a room."

"He's a great guy."

"Mr. Adair sent me out to National as soon as he heard it was closed down, and I paged you there."

"I appreciate that."

"Then I got a call at home, and Mr. Adair said you'd gone to Dulles, so I came here."

"Modern communications are a miracle. Everyone's in touch."

"Yes, sir. I have a beeper, a car phone, and a radio."

"Did Mr. Adair say where he was calling from?"

"No, sir. But I have to call his answering machine and tell him I found you."

"I can do that." Keith picked up the cellular phone, punched in Adair's number, and said into the answering machine, "I'm in the car, Charlie. Thanks. I'll try to be there tomorrow night, but I'll go back to Ohio first. Call me on this phone." He gave him the number and said, "Talk to you later." He hung up and asked Stewart, "You ever been to Ohio?"

"No, sir."

"The Buckeye State."

"Yes, sir." Stewart glanced at him but said nothing.

They approached the entrance to the Dulles access road, and Keith said, "Take 28 north. We have to make a stop before we go back to D.C."

"Yes, sir." Stewart got onto Route 28.

Keith looked at the dashboard clock. It was a quarter past eleven P.M. He looked out the windshield. "Nasty weather."

"Yes, sir."

"I guess we knew this hurricane was on the way."

"That's what they've been saying all week. This morning they said it would touch Virginia Beach, then hit the Eastern Shore, and we'd get gale-force winds and rain by tonight. They were right."

"They certainly were. Hey, when you get to Route 7, go west."

"Okay." A few miles later, Stewart asked, "How far west are we going, Mr. Landry?"

"Oh, about . . . let's see—about five hundred miles."

"Sir?"

"Stewart, you're finally going to have the opportunity to see the great state of Ohio."

"I don't understand."

"It's real simple. I have to be in Ohio. No aircraft are flying out of Washington. We are driving to Ohio."

Stewart glanced at Keith, then at his radio and telephone, then said, "Mr. Adair didn't . . . he said to . . ."

"Mr. Adair is not on top of the situation, but he will be when I can speak to him."

Stewart stayed silent. In his many years as a government driver, Keith knew, Stewart had learned to do what he was told, regardless of how inconvenient or bizarre it may have seemed to him. Still, Keith thought he should say a few words to the man. Keith said, "You can call your wife and explain."

"Yes, sir. Maybe I should speak to Mr. Adair first. I don't know if I'm authorized—"

"Stewart, I just had a chat this morning with the secretary of defense and the president of the United States. Would you like me to call either of them now and get authorization?"

"No, sir."

"I'll speak to Mr. Adair in due time. You pay attention to the road. I'll dial your wife. What's the number?"

Stewart gave him the number, and Keith dialed. It took him several tries to get through because of the weather, but finally a female voice came on the line, and Keith said, "Hello, Mrs.—"

Keith looked at Stewart, who said, "Arkell."

"Mrs. Arkell, this is General Landry of the National Security Council, and I'm afraid I've imposed on your husband to work a little overtime tonight...Yes, ma'am. Let me put him on." Keith handed the phone to Stewart, who took it without enthusiasm.

Stewart listened for a full minute, then got a few words in. "No, I don't know how late—"

Keith said, "Figure this time tomorrow night, to be safe."

"Yes, dear, I—"

Keith watched the rain out of the side window.

Stewart said to his wife, "I'll call you later," and hung up, grumbling something.

Keith said, "Everything okay?"

"Yes, sir."

"Here's Route 7. We take this to I-81, northbound."

"Yes, sir."

"Take it slow. We'll try to make up the time later, when we get out of this weather."

"Yes, sir. I can't go over the speed limit. That's the rules."

"Good rules. Long day?"

"Yes, sir."

"I'll drive later."

"It's not allowed, General."

"Colonel. Sometimes I say general. For the ladies."

Stewart smiled for the first time.

As they traveled slowly west on Route 7, the phone rang, and Keith took it. "Hello, Charlie."

"You're still in the car?"

"No, I'm running alongside."

"Stewart found you okay?"

"Yes, I'm in the car now. That's where you called me."

"You should have been in the Four Seasons by now. Where are you?"

"Still in the car."

"*Where* in the fucking car."

"Route 7."

"Why? What's wrong with the Dulles road?"

"Nothing, as far as I know."

There was a silence, and Keith could hear music and talking in the background. Charlie asked, "Where are you headed, Keith?"

"You know where I'm headed."

"Jesus Christ, man, you can't hijack a government car and driver—"

"Why not? I've hijacked other governments' cars and drivers. Why not my own?"

Charlie took a deep breath and asked, "Is Stewart with you?"

"He is. We took care of his wife, you take care of the authorization. I'll try to get back tomorrow night. Enjoy your party or dinner or whatever. Thanks, bye—"

"Wait. Listen, can't you just call her and tell her you'll be flying out of D.C. tomorrow?"

"No. I have a morning rendezvous."

"Tell her to fly here in the morning."

"We're eloping together."

"You're being difficult, Keith."

"*I'm* being difficult? You shanghaied me to Washington. You knew about the hurricane."

"No, I didn't. Well, it was supposed to blow out to sea. Look, why can't she just fly—"

"Charlie, you met her husband. This is a bad guy. She'd like me to be there when she breaks loose. Also, I've got things I have to get from my house. Okay?"

"Okay. No use arguing with a man who's following his dick. You going to make it?"

Keith looked at the dashboard clock. It was twelve-ten A.M. He said, "Close."

"Good luck, buddy. Tell Stewart I owe him one. Call tomorrow."

"Will do." He hung up and told Stewart, "Mr. Adair owes you a big favor."

"He owes me lots of them."

"Me, too."

They drove another half hour and picked up I-81 north. Keith said, "Pay attention to the route. You're coming back alone."

"Yes, sir.

Keith settled back in his seat. "So, what did you think of the Orioles this year?"

"Not much. The only way they'll get to the Series is if they buy tickets."

"You follow college football?"

"Sure."

"The Buckeyes look great again."

"They sure do."

They drove and talked sports. The rain tapered off as they moved away from the hurricane activity, and Stewart agreed to do ten miles an hour over the limit after they crossed into Maryland.

At Hagerstown, Keith told him to pick up I-70 westbound. It was a good road, almost devoid of traffic at that hour, but it wound through the Appalachian Mountains, and Stewart, who had been an aggressive urban driver, became very timid.

Keith asked him to pull over at a rest stop, where Stewart made a quick trip to the john and returned to find Keith behind the wheel. "Sir, you're not authorized to drive this car."

"Except in an emergency, which is you nodding off

behind the wheel. Lie down in the back, Stewart, and get some rest, or I'll leave you here."

"Yes, sir." Stewart got into the rear and lay down on the wide seat.

Keith continued on. Within fifteen minutes, he heard snores coming from the rear. He played the radio at a low volume and listened to country music from a Wheeling, West Virginia, station. There was a funny song about a divorced guy who sang, "She got the gold mine, I got the shaft," that Keith found a welcome break from all the heartache-and-misery songs.

South of Pittsburgh, on I-70, Keith stopped for fuel. It was four-twenty A.M., and Columbus was about five more hours, he knew, then another two hours on secondary and country roads to Spencerville and about an hour to Chatham. He wasn't going to make his ten A.M. appointment in Chatham County, or the two-fifteen flight out of Toledo. But he should be close enough to go ahead with the plan in some modified form.

At seven A.M., still a few hours out of Columbus, Keith tried to dial Chatham County information to get Terry's number, but he had no luck getting the car phone to connect. He pulled over at a rest stop and went to a pay phone. Stewart woke up, got out, and stretched.

Keith got the area code operator and asked for the number of Terry or Lawrence Ingram in Chatham County. A recording gave him the number, and he used his credit card to make the call.

A female voice answered, "Hello?"

"Terry?"

"Yes?"

"This is Keith Landry."

"Oh, my God! Oh—"

"Is everything all right there?"

"Yes. Where are you? Are you coming? What time is it?"

"Terry, listen to me. I'm on the road, east of Columbus. I'm going to be late. I won't be there until... sometime early afternoon. Okay? I have to go to my place first. You got all that?"

"Yes...Annie will be here at ten. What should I tell her?"

Keith took a deep breath. Clearly, not everyone in the Prentis family was sharp. "Tell her what I just said."

"Oh. Okay. Keith, I'm so excited for both of you. You don't know how unhappy she's been. This is wonderful. like a dream, I can't believe this is happening."

Keith let her go on for a while, then interrupted. "Terry, *do not* call her. Listen, I think her phone may be tapped. Your call may wind up at police headquarters. Understand?"

"Yes...but she'll be coming here at ten—"

"Fine. Tell her in person. Have lunch. I'll be there as soon as I can. We'll catch a later flight. Okay?"

"Yes, I'll tell her. What time—?"

"About one. I won't call again. Just tell her to wait."

"I can't wait to see you again."

"Me, too. Thanks, Terry. Thanks for being the middleman all these years. Just this one last time. Okay?"

"Where are you now?"

"Near *Columbus,* Ohio. I'm driving in from Washington. There was bad weather, and I couldn't get a flight back. When Annie gets there, tell her I'm on my way and I apologize. Also, tell her *not* to call my house. My phone may also be tapped."

"Your phone?"

"Yes, my phone. By her husband."

"He's a bastard. I hate him."

"Right." Keith went through it one more time,

then said, "See you later." He hung up and got back in the car. He said to Stewart, who was now sitting in the front passenger seat, "You want to call home? I'll give you my credit card."

"No, thanks. I'll call from Ohio."

"We're *in* Ohio."

"Oh . . . I'll call later. It's too early."

Keith started the car and got on the road, taking the circular highway north around Columbus, then headed north and west on Route 23.

It was a sunny day, cool, with scattered white clouds. There was some early Saturday traffic, mostly campers and recreational vehicles, heading up to the lakes, probably, or to Michigan.

Stewart seemed fascinated with the countryside. "It's all farms. What's that stuff? Corn?"

"Yes, corn."

"Who eats all that corn? I eat corn maybe once a month. You eat a lot of corn out here?"

Rather than explain about field corn and sweet corn, cattle feed and people food, Keith said, "We eat corn three times a day."

Stewart was wide awake now and enjoying the scenery. He pointed out barns, cattle, and pigs to Keith.

They made good time, but not great time, and it was almost eleven A.M. when they crossed into Spencer County.

Keith slowed down and took it easy the last fifteen miles. He saw no county or municipal police on the roads, and they wouldn't recognize this car anyway, but he didn't want a problem this close to the end.

Keith pulled up to his driveway and took a few pieces of mail out of his box, flipping through it as he pulled up to the house. It was mostly junk mail, but there was also a summons for him to appear in Spencerville traffic court for a variety of parking violations that he didn't recall getting tickets for. Petty harassment, but he realized he could be pulled over by the police anytime if he didn't answer the summons by the appearance date, which was Monday. He'd be long gone by then.

Stewart asked, "You live here?"

"I do." Keith stopped near the front porch and got out. Stewart got out, too, and was busy looking around, so Keith got his bag from the trunk and said, "Come on in and wash up."

They entered the house through the front door, and Keith led Stewart up the stairs. "Bathroom's there. Meet you downstairs. Help yourself to anything in the refrigerator."

Keith went into his room and threw his garment bag on the bed, then took the packed suitcase out of the wardrobe cabinet. His overnight bag was always packed with toiletries and underwear, a habit from two decades of unplanned travel. His briefcase was already packed with his important papers, and he slipped his passport in his suit jacket pocket.

The bathroom was empty now, and Keith cleaned up, then took his things downstairs.

Stewart was in the kitchen having a glass of orange juice, and Keith poured the last of the juice into a glass for himself. He said, "Sorry I have nothing to offer you for breakfast, Stewart."

"Oh, that's okay." He looked around. "This is a real old house."

"About a hundred years old. Can you find your way back to Washington?"

"I think so."

Keith took four hundred dollars out of his wallet and said, "This is for gas, food, and tolls. Stop at a farm and get some fresh produce. Mrs. Arkell will love it."

"Thank you, Colonel. I had a good time."

"I knew you would. We'll do it again sometime."

"Can I use your phone, sir?"

"No, it's tapped. No one knows I'm here. Call from the road."

Stewart had been around long enough not to be surprised or to ask questions. Keith steered Stewart toward the door, and Stewart carried the suitcase out to the porch. Keith gave Stewart directions to Route 23 and said, "The cops in this county are tough. Take it easy."

"Yes, sir. Hope I see you in Washington again."

"You never know." They shook hands, and Stewart left.

Keith ran through a mental checklist, then closed and locked the front door, and carried his luggage out back to the Blazer.

There was a note on the front seat, and Keith read the printed message: *You was supposed to be gone by Friday, and I see your car still here. I'll be coming around Monday to see if you're gone.*

The note was unsigned and not written in words that could be construed as threatening in a court of law. But Keith had no intention of going to the county prosecutor. He was either going to kill Baxter or let him live. The choice was actually Baxter's.

Keith wondered why Baxter was waiting until Monday, then realized that Baxter was away on his Saturday hunting or fishing trip. And tomorrow being the Sabbath, even Police Chief Baxter might want a day of peace and rest. It didn't matter. Keith would be gone before Monday. In fact, by tonight, when Cliff Baxter returned home and didn't see his wife there, he might figure it out and realize that indeed Keith Landry was gone, and so was Mrs. Baxter. Keith wondered if she would leave him a note.

Keith got in the Blazer and turned the ignition switch. Nothing happened. Completely dead. He popped the hood release, got out, and lifted the hood. The battery was gone, and in its place was a note that said, simply, "Fuck you."

Keith took a deep breath. The man was making it difficult for Keith to keep his promise to Annie. All in all, the last few days hadn't been good days, starting with Charlie Adair driving up to his house. The White House was no treat, either. Neither was Hurricane Jack. Now this. "Okay, Landry. A new transportation problem." He thought a moment, then walked to the barn. The garden tractor had a 12-volt battery, and it should have enough amps to kick over the Blazer.

He slid open the door and sat on the tractor. He was going to start it, ride it over to the Blazer, let it charge awhile, then put the tractor battery in his car. He pushed the starter button. Dead. But he heard a clicking sound and looked at the dashboard. Someone had turned on the headlight switch, and the battery had run down. "Cliff, you're getting on my nerves."

He got off the tractor and looked out across the road at the Jenkins farmhouse. He could borrow a battery from them, but he noticed that both their vehicles, the car and the pickup truck, were gone. He could borrow their tractor battery, with or without their knowledge, but you didn't do that around here.

He went inside and tried the Jenkinses' number, but, as he thought, no one was home. The Muller farm was about a half-mile walk down the road. "Damn it."

He looked through the phone directory and called a service station out on the highway, and they said they'd be there in half an hour with a new battery. The man added, "Damn kids probably stole it. You ought to call the cops."

"I will." He gave them directions to his farm and hung up. "Maybe I should have called Baxter Motors because that's where my battery is."

He considered calling Terry. Annie was there now, waiting, and Cliff Baxter was presumably out of town. But what if his calls did actually go through police headquarters? No matter how guarded he tried to be with Terry, or whoever answered, the call would be like a four-alarm bell ringing at police headquarters. All his instincts, as well as his tradecraft, said, "Do not use the phone."

He used the time to shave, shower, and change into casual clothes, all the while trying to put these bad omens into a happier context. *The course of true love never did run smooth.* "Tonight, Washington, dinner with the Adairs, Sunday, maybe the National Cathedral, Monday, Charlie's tour of Washington, then submit a written turndown of the job offer, get the passport, and fly to Rome no later than Wednesday." Sounded good. "Where's the damned battery? For want of a nail, the king sat in Dumferling Town." Something like that.

About forty minutes after he'd called, a pickup truck came into the driveway, and within ten minutes, he had a new battery. He started the Blazer while the serviceman was still there, and everything seemed to be all right.

Keith pulled out of the driveway, and within a few minutes was heading south on a straight country road toward Chatham County. It was one thirty-five P.M., and he'd be there in less than an hour.

A blue and white Spencer County sheriff's car fell in behind him. At this point, Keith couldn't care less. There was only the driver in the car, and Keith decided that if the sheriff pulled him over, the sheriff would find himself hog-tied in the trunk of his own car.

At the southern end of Spencer County, Keith got

onto an eastbound highway, giving the impression he was heading to Columbus and points east, in case the man was wondering why Keith Landry was taking the rural road to Chatham County.

The sheriff's car kept following, but as they approached the Dawson County line to the east, the sheriff's car turned off. Keith continued on, out of his way, for another ten minutes, then turned south, then west again toward Chatham. He suspected that the Spencer sheriff had radioed to his Dawson counterpart to track the Blazer, but Keith didn't pick up any tails. The rural sheriff's departments were small, and the counties were big. Compared to the drives he used to make from the West German border across East Germany to Berlin, this was easy. But when you were avoiding the police, whether they were rural sheriffs in the American heartland or the Stasi on the prowl in East Germany, luck played a big part in the game.

Within fifteen minutes, he crossed the county line into Chatham. He didn't know exactly where he was, but it was easy to navigate the grid squares of roads, which ran almost true to the cardinal points of the compass.

Eventually, he found himself on County Road 6 and continued west, reading the road markers of the intersecting township roads numbered in descending order until he got to T-3, the road where Terry lived, where Annie was waiting. He didn't know if he should turn left or right but flipped a coin in his mind and turned left. He drove slowly, looking for the red brick Victorian house, which he saw up ahead on the right. Truly, he thought, some sixth sense had gotten him here without a wrong turn, and he remembered with a smile what Charlie had said about following his reproductive organ, though Keith believed he was following his heart, which was beating rapidly now.

He slowed down and turned into the gravel drive. The first thing he noticed was that there was only one vehicle in the driveway, and it was a pickup truck. The next thing that disturbed him was that the side door of the house was opened, and the woman who came out to meet him, though she looked like Annie, was not Annie.

CHAPTER TWENTY-SEVEN

Terry stood at the door a moment, then walked over to Keith, who had gotten out of the Blazer.

Keith already knew by the look on Terry's face that Annie wasn't there, but he didn't know why.

Terry said, "Hi, Keith."

"How are you?"

"Okay...Annie's not here."

"I know that."

"She was here, but she left."

He nodded. "Okay."

"She...had to go."

Neither of them spoke for a while, then Terry said, "You want a cup of coffee?"

"Sure."

He followed her into the kitchen, and she said, "Have a seat."

He sat at the round kitchen table.

As Terry poured two mugs of coffee, she informed him, "Annie left you a note."

"She's all right?"

"Yes." Terry put the mugs on the table, with cream and sugar, and said, "She was upset."

"Well, I don't blame her."

Terry sat and stirred her coffee absently. "She wasn't angry. But when she got here, she was all…sort of excited…then, when I told her you'd be late, she was disappointed. But then she was okay again, and we had a nice visit."

"Good." Keith looked at Terry. She was about three years older than Annie and had Annie's good looks, but not Annie's sparkle or bounce. Terry had graduated high school two years before Keith and Annie had started going together in their junior year. She'd gone to Kent State, so Keith hadn't seen much of her except for summers and holidays, but as Annie had reminded him, Terry sometimes covered for them when she was home. Terry was one of the romantics. He recalled that Terry had met her future husband, Larry, in college, and they'd married and left school before either of them graduated. Keith and Annie, freshmen at Bowling Green by that time, had gone to the wedding together. He recalled now that Terry had given birth about seven months after her wedding, and Annie had said to him, "We will graduate, marry, and have children, in that order."

Terry said, "We had lunch. I haven't seen her so happy in years." She added, "A guy from down the road pulled in to drop something off, and when she heard his truck in the driveway, she jumped out of her chair and went out the door." Terry looked at him and smiled. "I guess I shouldn't give away family secrets."

"I appreciate your honesty. You can tell Annie I looked like an unhappy, lovesick puppy."

She smiled again. "You look tired. Drive all night?"

He nodded.

"I know the look. Larry comes in from the road, looks like hell, not hungry for food, but hungry for love." Her face flushed, and she added, "You guys."

Keith smiled in return. Larry owned some sort of trucking business according to one of Annie's letters of some years back, and Terry kept the books. He imagined that they did well, the house was nice, the pickup truck was new. They had three children in or graduated from college, he remembered. Keith had seen Larry a few times when he and Annie were home from college, and Keith recalled that Larry was a big, quiet sort of guy. Larry was either working this morning or playing weekend sheriff, or was lying low somewhere, as men did when affairs of the heart were being discussed.

Terry said, "She waited until one, then all of a sudden she said, 'I'm leaving,' and she wrote you a note." Terry took an envelope out of her jeans pocket and put it on the table.

Keith looked at it and saw his name in Annie's familiar handwriting. He sipped his coffee, which he needed.

Terry said, "I tried to keep her here, but she said it was okay, she'd see you another time." Terry added, "She's always so bubbly, you know, and you can't tell when she's hurting. I don't mean this morning, but with that bastard she's married to. Oh, God, I want so much for her to be happy. Really happy again."

"Me, too." Keith said, "So how are you? You look good."

She smiled. "Thank you. You look terrific, Keith. I recognized you as soon as you got out of your car."

"It's been a lot of years, hasn't it?"

"Oh, yes. They were good times back then."

"They were, weren't they?"

She nodded, then said, "Larry had to go in to work. He hung around awhile to see you. Said to say hello."

"I'll see him next time."

"Hope so. So you've done okay for yourself. I always knew you would."

"Thanks. This is a nice house."

"Oh, these old places are a pain, but Larry likes to fix things. You're back on the farm?"

"Yup. Lot of work. How are your parents?"

"They're fine. Getting on, but healthy, thank the Lord. Yours?"

"Enjoying Florida. They can't believe they have a son who's retired."

She smiled. "You look too young to retire."

"That seems to be the consensus."

"So you were in Washington?"

"I had to finish up some business. Thought I'd be back in time."

They talked awhile, the letter lying on the table between them. Keith thought it was important to reestablish a relationship with Annie's sister, and in fact he liked Terry, and he wanted her to like him, as a person, not as her sister's lover or white knight. She turned out to be a lot more lucid than she'd sounded at seven that morning, and he had the sense she had a lot she wanted to tell him, but he kept the conversation general for a while, but then said to her, "I only want the best for your sister. You know we've never stopped loving each other."

Terry nodded, and a tear ran down her cheek.

Keith took the letter and said, "Mind if I read it here?"

"No, go ahead..." She stood and said, "I have to go throw some stuff in the dryer." She went down into the basement.

Keith opened the envelope and read: "Dear Keith, No, I'm not angry, yes, I'm disappointed. I know that whatever took you back to Washington couldn't be helped, but it gave me a few hours this morning to think. Oh, no, Prentis! You're not thinking again!"

Keith smiled, remembering that he used to say that to her in college whenever she preceded a sentence with, "I've been thinking—"

He knew this wasn't going to be an amusing letter, however, and he read on. "What I was thinking is that this is a big step for you. For me, it means getting out of a situation that I can't stand any longer. But for you, it means taking on a big responsibility—being responsible for me. Maybe you don't need that burden. I know my husband has made life difficult for you, and I know that you can deal with it fine. But I'm starting to feel guilty about all of this. I mean, Keith, I don't think you'd be here, or be in this situation, if it weren't for me, and I appreciate that. But without me, you could do what you want, which, by now, after all that's happened, is probably to go back to Washington, or to Europe, or wherever without trying to fit me into your plans. No, I'm not being sulky, I'm finally thinking about what's best for you."

Keith was pretty sure he knew the gist of the next paragraph, but read it anyway. "Maybe we both need some time to think and to let things cool off. We waited this long, so maybe we can wait a few more weeks. It would probably be a good idea if you left—not that I want you to leave, but, with the situation with Cliff, it might be best. As we've done for twenty years, you can contact me through Terry, and we'll work out a time and place to meet and talk it over—but not for a while. I know, you're probably angry that I didn't wait, but I couldn't handle it—sorry. And yes, I'm a lousy letter writer, and I can't write what I feel, but you know how I feel, Mr. Landry, and I'll tell you again when we meet. Love, Annie."

Keith folded the letter and put it in his pocket.

Terry came upstairs into the kitchen and glanced

at him as she got the coffeepot off the counter. "Another cup?"

"No, thanks." He stood. "Well, thank you again. When you see Annie, tell her I'll be leaving Monday."

"You're leaving? Where are you going?"

"I'm not sure yet, but I'll contact her through you, if I may."

"Okay...hey, let me call her. She's got a car phone, and maybe she's on the road, and I'll tell her you're here."

"That's okay. It's getting late." Keith moved to the door.

"You want to leave her a note?"

"No, I'll write and send it here."

Terry walked out with him. She said, "I don't know what she wrote, but I know what she feels. Maybe you shouldn't pay a lot of attention to that letter."

"The letter was okay."

"I don't think so. Hey, what's wrong with you two?"

Keith smiled. "Bad luck, lousy timing." He got into the Blazer and rolled down the window. "We'll work it out."

"You came real close to doing that this time." She put her hand on the car door and said, "Keith, I know my sister, and I wouldn't tell this to another soul except you...she's frightened. She had a bad week with him."

"Do you think she's in any danger?"

"She didn't think so, but...I think it got to be too much for her this morning. She started getting worried about you...so she called up at their lodge in Michigan, and he answered the phone, and she hung up. She felt better knowing he was there and not around here. Just the same, about an hour later, she said she was going home. That was about two hours before you got here. I'm surprised you didn't pass each other."

"I took another route."

"She probably went past your place."

"Maybe."

"Try to speak to her before you leave. She needs to hear from you."

"That's not easy."

"I'll drive out to see her tomorrow. I know I can't call her on the phone. But I'll stop by after church and get her alone somehow. I'll work out a meeting for you two."

"Terry, I really appreciate what you're doing, but she and I both need time to think."

"You had over twenty years for that."

"And another few weeks won't make a difference."

"They could."

"No, they can't. Let's let it slide for now. I'll contact you in a few weeks. By then, everyone will be thinking clearly, and we can take it from there."

Terry stepped back from the Blazer. "Okay. I don't want to interfere."

"You've been very helpful." He started the car.

"You're angry."

"No, I'm not." He smiled. "If I tell you you're as good-looking and sexy as your sister, will you be a real mid-western lady and slap me?"

She smiled. "No, you get a kiss." She leaned through the window and gave him a peck on the cheek. "Take care of yourself. See you soon."

"Hope so." He backed out of the drive and headed back to Spencer County.

Being an intelligence officer for twenty years had its advantages. For one thing, you learned how to think differently than most people, you played life like a chess game and thought six moves ahead, and you never gave away your game plan and never gave out more information than the other person needed to have. He could trust Terry, of course, but he didn't trust her judgment. It was best for her to think he was angry or whatever she was thinking. He wasn't trying to manipulate her, and through her, Annie. But Cliff Baxter had to be reckoned with, and the less Terry knew, the better.

Annie's letter. He didn't have to read between the lines—it was all there in her own words. She was disappointed, perhaps hurt. She was concerned about his safety. She didn't want to be a burden to him. He took all this at face value. What she wanted from him was a reassurance that it was still okay—the trip to Washington was nothing to be concerned about, Cliff Baxter didn't worry him, she wasn't a burden, she lifted his spirits.

Still, she asked him to wait, and no doubt she meant it. Even if he wanted to wait, which he didn't, Cliff Baxter's actions were unpredictable. *She had a bad week with him.*

He recalled what Gail had told him about a firearm incident at the Baxter house, and it occurred to him, not for the first time, that Annie was going to kill her husband. He couldn't let that happen. It didn't have to happen. But if it was going to happen, she'd wait until Keith Landry was gone, so Keith had some time to make sure it didn't happen. If Keith had played his cards right with Terry, she'd tell Annie that Keith Landry was going to leave, and, by the looks of him, he might not be back. That may have been a little manipulative, he admitted, but it was necessary. "All's fair in love and war." Maybe not all, but a lot.

He crossed the line into Spencer County, and, within twenty minutes, he was in Spencerville. He drove past Annie's house on Williams Street, but there was no car in the driveway. He went downtown and stopped at the bank, hitting the cash machine for the maximum, which was four hundred dollars in these parts. He drove around town for a while, but didn't see her white Lincoln.

Keith headed out of town, got on Highway 22, and stopped at Arles's self-service gas station.

Keith got out and pumped.

Bob Arles ambled out of his office and waved to him. "How you doin'?"

Keith replied, "Fine. How about you?"

"Okay." Bob Arles walked over to Keith. "Got yourself a new Blazer."

"Sure did."

"Like it?"

"I do."

"You got rid of that other thing?"

"Made a chicken coop out of it."

Arles laughed, then asked him, "Hey, did Chief Baxter ever look you up?"

Keith glanced at Arles and said, "He stopped by last week."

"Yeah, he said he might. I told him you was in here one day."

"Thanks." Keith finished pumping and put the nozzle back. He and Arles went into the office, and Keith paid for the gas. Keith inquired, "Does he come in here much?"

Bob Arles's expression changed. "Well...he did. We get a lot of city and county business here. But...uh... we had some problems."

"I think I might have heard about that."

"Yeah...a lot of people heard about that."

Keith went through the door into the convenience store, and Bob Arles followed him. There was no one behind the counter, and Keith asked, "Where is Mrs. Arles?"

"She's away for a while." He added, "I guess you know why, if you know about that church meeting out by Overton."

"But why did Mrs. Arles leave?"

"Uh...well...I guess she felt kinda...maybe a little nervous after she went and shot her mouth off."

"Was she telling the truth?"

"Hell, no. I mean, you got to give a little to get a little in this here world. Women don't understand how business is done." Arles shook his head and added, "The chief and his cousin, Don Finney, who's the sheriff, came in here and told me they was gonna get the city and the county to switch accounts to someplace else. You know how much of my business that is? I'll tell ya. Damned near fifty percent. You know what's gonna happen now? I'm out. Because she shot off her damned mouth."

"So you don't see Chief Baxter anymore?"

"Oh, he comes in, just like he used to, 'cause this is where the city has to charge it until the city council changes it. But he don't say much to me, and what he says ain't nice." Arles added, "He says he got a bone to pick with Mary. I told him he won't be seeing her around here for a while."

"Does he still help himself to whatever he wants?"

"Hey, he never did that. He always paid. And if I wanted to give him a few things to munch on, so what?"

Keith threw a few items on the counter, things to tide him over for the weekend. Arles went behind the counter and rang up the items.

Keith said, "I'm leaving Spencer County. Monday."

"Yeah? For good?"

"Yes. No work here."

"Told ya. Too bad, though. Need more people. That'll be twenty-one dollars and seventy-two cents."

Keith paid him, and Arles bagged. Arles said, "Next time you come through, you'll see this place closed."

Keith said to Bob Arles, "Your wife did the right thing. You know that."

"Yeah, maybe. But I don't need Chief Baxter for an enemy, and I don't need to start over again at my age."

"I wouldn't count on Baxter being chief much longer."

"Yeah? Ya think?"

"You read the transcript of the St. James meeting?"

He nodded.

"What do *you* think?"

"Well . . . the man ought to have better control over his dick." Arles smiled. "Hey, you know why men give their penises names? 'Cause they don't want a total stranger makin' ninety percent of their decisions." Arles laughed and slapped the counter. "Get it?"

"Sure do."

Arles got serious again and said, "But this other stuff they's sayin' he did . . . like fillin' up his private car here for free . . . hell, even if it was true, which it ain't, nobody got hurt. Now, the thing about him and those women, well, my wife says that makes him unfit to be police chief. I don't know, because I don't know if them women is lyin', or what. But I do know that those kinds of charges ain't doin' much for his home life. Hey, you know Mrs. Baxter?"

"We were schoolmates."

"Yeah? Well, that's a fine, fine woman. She don't have to hear that kind of crap from those sluts what got up in church, brazen as can be, and told all."

"Try to make the next meeting. My regards to Mrs.

Arles. You should be with her." Keith picked up the bag and left.

From a pay phone around the side of the convenience store, he called Charlie Adair's house and got the answering machine. He said, "Charlie, my plans are postponed. I'll get back to you in a day or two. Sorry I can't make it tonight. Regards to Katherine. Meantime, if you call my home phone, assume it's tapped by Police Chief Baxter, who has this crazy idea that I'm interested in his wife. Stewart did a great job. He should be back before midnight. I'm still thinking about the job offer. Can I have a grow-light in my basement office? Tell the president I said hi. Speak to you."

At about nine o'clock that evening, Keith figured he'd been up for about thirty-six hours straight, and he got ready for bed. He opened the drawer of his nightstand and saw that the Glock was missing.

He thought a moment. The Porters knew where the key was, but they wouldn't help themselves to the pistol. He looked through his wardrobe cabinets and noticed now that things were slightly disturbed.

Obviously, Baxter had gotten into his house, which, for a policeman with at least one or two locksmiths on call, was not difficult.

Nothing seemed to be missing except the pistol, and there was nothing compromising in the house for him to be concerned about. He'd burned Annie's last letters to him, and her past letters of two decades had gone through one government paper shredder or another. He wasn't much of a saver, and he was glad now that he wasn't.

Letters aside, the Glock was gone, and Baxter had been through his things. That was reason enough to kill the man, and he would have except for his promise, and except for the fact that Baxter was about to lose his wife, his job, his friends, and his town. Death, as the expression went, was too good for him.

Keith found his old K-bar knife and put it on his nightstand. He turned off the lights and went to sleep.

He awoke at dawn, showered and dressed, and went downstairs. It was a cool, crisp Sunday morning, and when he went outside, he could see his breath. He walked to the cornfield and peeled back the husk on an ear. The color was about right, and so was the dry, paper-thin husk. Almost but not quite ready. Another week or two, weather permitting.

He walked around the farmyard, surveyed the buildings, the fences, the grounds. All in all, he'd done a good job, and all it took was some money, a lot of time, and backbreaking labor. He didn't know, really, why he'd done it, what the objective was, but he felt good about it. He knew he'd touched things, fixed things, that his father and uncle had touched and tinkered with, as had his grandfather. There weren't many physical remains from his great-grandfather's day, or his great-great-grandfather, the original settler, but he was walking the same ground they walked, and in the early morning and in the evening, when the countryside was quiet in half-light, he could feel their presence.

He went to church. Not St. James, but St. John's in Spencerville. This was a different congregation, to be sure—better dressed, better cars. The big brick and stone church was the best building in Spencerville, aside from the courthouse. If the county had an establishment church, it was St. John's Lutheran, firmly connected to the early settlers and the present power structure. Even the Episcopalians dropped in now and then, especially if they were running for office or had a business in town.

Keith looked for the Baxters but didn't see them as he walked in. Even if he'd literally bumped into Mr. Baxter's ample body, there wouldn't be a problem; it was Sunday, this was a church, and Spencerville's God-fearing gentry wouldn't tolerate discord or disharmony in or around the Lord's house on the Lord's day.

Keith went inside. The church was large and held about eight hundred people. Keith scanned the backs of the congregation in the pews, but still he didn't see Mr. and Mrs. Baxter. If they were there, however, he'd see them coming out if he stood at the bottom of the steps after the service.

Keith took a seat on the left toward the rear, and the service began with Pastor Wilbur Schenk, Mrs. Baxter's confessor, officiating.

It wasn't until about halfway through the service that he realized that Annie was in the choir, sitting on the far right side of the altar, so he had a good view of her.

The choir rose to sing, and she looked at him as though she'd noticed him long ago and was impatient with him for not seeing her. They made eye contact for a moment, and he winked at her. She smiled as she began singing "Rock of Ages," then looked down at her hymnal, still smiling. She looked angelic, he thought, with her red choir robe and her eyes that sparkled in the candlelight. When the hymn was finished, she folded the hymnal and glanced at him again as she sat.

Before the service ended, Keith left and drove out of Spencerville.

He stopped at the Cowley farm and knocked on the door, but no one answered. It was unlocked, so he went in and called out for Billy Marlon, but the house seemed to be empty. He went into the kitchen and found a pencil and an envelope from a piece of junk mail and wrote: "Billy, leaving town for a while. See you next time. Stop the boozing. Go to the VA hospital in Toledo for a checkup. That's an order, soldier." He signed it, "Landry, Colonel, U.S. Army, Infantry." Keith didn't know how much good the note was going to do, but he felt some sort of need or obligation to write it. He put a hundred dollars on the kitchen table and left.

He considered going to the Porters' house, but he'd said his good-byes and didn't want to alarm them with a change of plans; another case of the less they knew, the better for them. Cliff Baxter and his cohorts not only had to be reckoned with, but they were setting the agenda for a while.

Next call was Aunt Betty's. On the way, he stopped at a big indoor farm stand and bought jams, home-made candy, maple syrup, and other sugar products that would have put most people into sugar shock, but which Aunt Betty seemed to thrive on.

She was home, ready to go to Lilly and Fred's house for Sunday dinner, she informed him. She invited him in, but like most elderly people he knew, especially his German relatives, she didn't know how to handle a small change in her day. She said, "I have to be there in an hour."

Lilly and Fred lived about twenty minutes away, and Keith recalled with a smile Aunt Betty's theory of time relativity as it applied to herself and to other people. He said, "I'm only staying a minute. If you hurry, you can make it. Here, I brought you a few things." He put the bag on the dining room table, and she emptied it, item by item.

"Oh, Keith, you didn't have to do that. You're such a sweet man." And so on.

He said to her, "Aunt Betty, I'm leaving for a while, and I wonder if you'd be good enough to keep an eye on the place."

"You're leaving again?"

"Yes. I don't do it often. Once every quarter century or so."

"Where are you going this time?"

"To Washington to take care of some leftover business. I've asked some other people to keep an eye on the place, as well. Jeffrey and Gail Porter. Jeffrey is an old schoolmate of mine."

"Which Porter is he? The one with the three sons?"

"No, his father had three sons. Jeffrey is one of them. Jeffrey is my age. Anyway, I just wanted you to know."

"Wait here. I have something for you." She went into the kitchen and returned with his bottle of French red Burgundy, cold from the refrigerator. "This will just go to waste, so you should take it."

"Thank you."

"Why don't you come to Fred and Lilly's with me? I'll call. They can put out another plate. She always makes too much. Wastes food, that woman. I told Harriet, that daughter of yours wastes—"

"I have another engagement. Aunt Betty, listen to me. I know you don't listen to gossip, spread gossip, or believe gossip. But in a few days or so, you're going to hear some gossip about your favorite nephew, and about Annie Baxter. Most of what you hear will probably be true."

She only glanced at him a moment, then turned her attention to the items on the table.

Keith kissed her on the cheek. "Don't speed. I'll write you."

He left Aunt Betty in the dining room, probably

worried about getting to Lilly's on time with less than an hour to spare. Keith smiled. Well, he'd gotten his wine back, which was a good trade.

He headed home, back to the farm. It was midafternoon now, and the October sun was in the west, clouds had appeared, along with a north wind, and the countryside seemed dark, cold, and lonely on this Sunday afternoon.

He had a sense of loneliness himself, a feeling of closure, but also an assurance that he'd done things right. He would leave in the morning, with or without her, but she would be with him in his heart, and he'd be with her. Next week, or next month, or even next year, they'd be together.

CHAPTER TWENTY-EIGHT

At about six P.M., Keith was in the living room, reading and drinking his Burgundy, which was at room temperature now. He'd found a box of his old college books in the attic and had chosen Edith Wharton's *Ethan Frome*. He'd enjoyed Wharton in college, as well as other American writers from that period, including Henry James, Theodore Dreiser, and Ohio's native son, Sherwood Anderson. He suspected, however, that no one read these people any longer. He made a mental note to ask the Porters if Anderson was still required reading at Antioch.

His reading since college had been mostly current affairs and political nonfiction, the sort of stuff that appeared on the *Washington Post* best-seller list and probably nowhere else. He looked forward to spending the next twenty-five years reading things that had no immediate relevance whatsoever.

He had the radio tuned to a Toledo station that played oldies, and Van Morrison had just finished "Brown Eyed Girl," which he liked, and Percy Sledge was now crooning "When a Man Loves a Woman," which Keith considered one of his favorite songs to make love by.

It was dusk, made darker by the rolling clouds, and

he saw the headlights of a vehicle turn into his driveway before he saw the car. A few seconds later, he heard the tires on the gravel.

He put down his book, shut off the radio, and looked out the window. A white Lincoln passed by the house and went around to the side.

Keith went into the kitchen and out the back door as the Lincoln came to a stop. The driver's-side door opened, and Annie got out, wearing a white turtleneck, brown tweed skirt, and matching jacket. With her was an energetic gray mongrel who jumped out of the car and began running around the yard.

Keith and Annie stood a few feet apart, and she smiled. "You made me lose my place in the hymnal."

He said, "You looked and sounded like an angel."

"Some angel. You should know what I was thinking up there. I must have turned as red as my robe."

He walked over to her, and they kissed, not passionately, but tentatively, neither knowing where this was going.

She said, "My Aunt Harriet says you send me your regards."

"I do. I like her. I want you to send her a postcard from Rome."

Annie didn't respond to that directly but said, "She told me she had Sunday dinner with you at your aunt's. She went on about what a handsome, cultured man you were." Annie added, "She even used the word sexy."

"My goodness. *I'll* send her a postcard from Rome."

She wasn't smiling, Keith saw, and looked as though she had a lot on her mind.

Keith happened to notice a blue and white bumper sticker on her car that read, "Support Your Local Police."

She saw where he was looking and said, "You want one? I have extras."

"Let me think about it."

She smiled, then frowned. "I don't have much choice."

"I know that."

There were a few seconds of silence again, then Keith asked the obvious, unromantic question. "Where is your husband?"

"He's still at the lodge on Grey Lake. He called yesterday afternoon and said he was staying overnight. He'll be back around midnight, he said." She added, "He doesn't give me much notice. He probably knew he was staying over."

Keith nodded to himself, recalling Baxter's note to him indicating he'd be coming around on Monday. Keith asked, "And are you sure you weren't followed?"

"I didn't see any police cars, city or county, and I know the unmarked cars. Anyway, I'm leaving in a few minutes, and we can stand here behind the house."

"Okay." He asked, "Should I explain about Washington?"

"No. No need." She said, "I heard about the hurricane on the car radio after I left Terry's. I just got myself upset, then I was going to come back, but I thought Cliff would be home, and I figured you and I needed a running start." She added, "Then he calls and says he's staying over. I could have killed him...I cried myself to sleep last night, thinking about you and what could have happened yesterday."

"It's not too late."

She looked at him a moment, then said, "My sister told me you're leaving tomorrow."

"You asked me to leave."

"Oh, and you do what I ask you to do? Since when?"

He smiled. "I used to do about half the things you asked me to do. That's not bad."

"Depends on which half."

"You're tough."

"No, I'm a pushover. That's my problem."

"I know a good assertiveness-training course for women in Washington. Every woman I knew in D.C. took it. I'll get you a brochure."

"Poor Keith. Did they give you a hard time?"

"Are we having a fight?"

"Not yet." She stayed silent a moment, then said, "Okay, I *do* want to know about Washington."

"All right. On Thursday, my old boss, Charlie Adair, came here—right here to the farm—and informed me that my former employers wanted me back. I said, 'No, I'm madly in love with the girl next door.' He said, 'Fine, bring her along.' I explained about your small-minded husband not letting you travel with former lovers—"

She suppressed a smile and said, "So this was business?"

"Yes. What did you think it was? A Washington holiday before my elopement to Washington?"

"I didn't know what...well...you know...I just got myself..." She looked at him. "It had nothing to do with a woman?"

"Oh...I see...no, it didn't. Do we have a jealous streak?"

"You know I do. But only with you."

"Well, all the more reason for me to turn down this job, then. They wanted me to fly around the world seducing female heads of state."

"Don't tease. I was a wreck. I don't know what's wrong with me. I've never felt like this...well, once. I used to be insanely in love with this guy years ago."

"Was he faithful?"

"Faithful as a puppy."

"Was he good in bed?"

"Best lay in Ohio."

"Who dumped who?"

"We'll never really know."

"That's a sad story."

She nodded, then looked at him. "So the government wants you back?"

"They do, and I had to go there in person to say no—"

"Keith, if you want to go back to Washington, don't let me stand in your way—"

"I don't want—"

"Listen. You can go back, and if we decide to be together, if you want me there and if I want to come, then I'll come to Washington."

"You wouldn't like it. Believe me."

"I might."

"Annie, if I'm asking you to leave your world, then I have to leave mine. I have no regrets, and I hope you won't, either."

"No, Keith, you listen to me—this was your world here, and it could have been again. But you can't stay here because of me, and I won't be responsible for you not going back to Washington."

"Are we both through being noble? Good. Let's be selfish, because I think we both want the same thing."

"Maybe. I have to go."

"Where are you supposed to be?"

"Nowhere. He could be home anytime. He does that. Whenever he bothers to tell me when he'll be home, he always shows up a few hours earlier, like he expects to find me in bed with the milkman or something."

"How about a farmer? Let's go to your house and give him something to get annoyed about."

Again she suppressed a smile, then said, "I just stopped by to see you before you left, and I wanted you to meet Denise."

"Who?"

She called out to the dog, who came running, licked Annie's hand, then sniffed at Keith and put her paws on his knee. Keith knelt down and played with the dog, who was friendly and who looked like a wire-haired terrier.

Annie watched a moment, then asked, "Do you remember?"

He looked at her, obviously not remembering.

She said, "This is actually Denise number four."

Then it came back to him—he had given her a mongrel puppy in the summer of '63, and they'd named her Denise after the Randy and the Rainbow's hit song of that summer. He stood and looked at Annie. "This is...?"

"This is Denise's great-granddaughter. Denise died about 1973, but I'd kept one of her pups and named her Denise Two, then *she* had a litter, and so on...I...it was just sort of a connection, I guess...really sentimental and silly...you know how us country girls are..." She looked at the dog, who was pulling on Keith's shoelaces, then at Keith, and she said, "A dog's life is short, but...they don't make problems for themselves."

Keith contemplated the dog awhile, realizing that this dog represented an incredible display of love and loyalty, faith and remembrance over the years. "I can't believe you did that."

"I didn't have much else..." She tried to smile and said, "If only Cliff knew...he has dogs of his own, but this one is mine, and this one *hates* him. In fact, they all hated him. Old Denise bit him once." She laughed.

"The dogs all had good judgment."

She smiled again. "He asked me once where I'd gotten Denise, and I told him my guardian angel gave her to me."

Keith nodded but didn't reply. The dog bolted off in chase of something she smelled or heard near the barn, and as Keith watched, a flood of memories came back to him, and he couldn't trust himself to speak.

He recalled the day when he'd first noticed Annie Prentis in school, then remembered the summer they'd begun courting, the long walks, sitting with her family on their porch, ice cream sodas in town, holding hands in the movies, the feel of her skin and hair, the smell of her, the first kiss. The sexual tension had almost driven him out of his mind, and in those days the chances of actually doing it were somewhere between nil and zero. Yet, one night, when her family was out of the house and he'd come over, they sat on the porch together, and she said almost nothing for about half an hour. At first he was annoyed at her distraction, then somehow, in some manner that to this day he didn't quite understand, without a word or a touch or an obvious look, she let him know she wanted to have sex. He recalled being so frightened by the thought that he almost went home. But he didn't, and he'd said to her, "Let's go to your room." His world and his life were never the same after that night.

He recalled, too, his decision to take a puppy from a friend's litter and give it to her a few days afterward. He didn't know about flowers after sex then, and since then his gifts to women had been more substantial, as had his gifts from women. But the puppy was the first thing he'd ever given to a girl, and more important, what she'd given to him—herself—was as good a gift as he'd ever gotten.

He said, "You never wrote to me about Denise."

"I was...I couldn't think of a way to mention Denise without sounding like I was being soppy and lovesick." She took a breath and looked at him in the fading light. "So...these dogs were a daily reminder of you." She smiled. "Are you insulted?"

"No, I'm speechless."

"I'm too sentimental for my own good...I'll tell you another secret—at my sister's house I have a trunk full of Keith Landry...love letters, prom photos, our high school and college yearbooks...valentines, birthday cards, a teddy bear...I had some other things, too, and I was stupid enough to keep them with me when I got married. He found the box of things—no letters or photos or anything like that, but little gifts and souvenirs that you'd bought me, and I guess he figured they weren't from my girlfriends, and he threw them out." She added, "I didn't say anything to him, because I wanted to be a loyal wife. But I knew then, if not before then, that I'd married the wrong man." She stayed silent a moment, then said, "I have to go now."

"Did you leave your things at your sister's house?"

She looked at him. "Yes...I was afraid to bring anything home in case he was there. Why?"

"Good. Let's go."

"Where?"

"To your sister's house. We're leaving. Now."

"No, Keith—"

"Now, Annie. Not tomorrow, not next week or next year. Now. Does your sister like dogs? She just got one." He took her in his arms and kissed her.

She pulled away. "Keith, no...I mean...are we really going? Now?"

"Within the minute. Leave your car here. My car is still packed. Call the dog. Sit in my car." He went into the house, got his keys, and turned off the lights. He took a piece of paper from a pad in the kitchen and wrote, "Cliff, Fuck you." He signed it, then went outside to the Blazer and asked Annie for her keys, which she gave him. He asked, "Do you want to leave him a note in your car?"

She glanced at the paper in his hand and replied, "No. He doesn't leave me notes."

"Okay." He jumped into her car and drove it to the barn, got out, slid open the doors, and drove the Lincoln inside. He left his short explanatory note to Cliff on the driver's seat, slid the barn doors closed, and went back to the Blazer. He handed her keys back to her and started the Blazer. As he pulled down the driveway, she asked him, "Did *you* leave a note for him in my car?"

"Yes. It was petty and childish."

"What did it say?"

"Two words, not 'Happy Birthday.' "

She smiled but said nothing.

He pulled out of the driveway, Annie beside him, Denise in the backseat, and his luggage in the rear.

Keith turned south, toward Chatham County. Neither of them spoke for a while, then Annie said, "I can't believe this is happening."

He glanced at her and saw she was staring straight out the window, looking a little dazed, or perhaps frightened. He asked her, "Are you all right?"

She nodded, then looked at him. "This is really happening."

"Yes, and there's no turning back."

Again she nodded, then slipped off her wedding and engagement rings and threw them out the window. "There's no turning back." She leaned over and kissed him on the cheek. "I love you."

He felt her tears on his face. He said, "I've missed you."

CHAPTER TWENTY-NINE

A little past seven-thirty P.M., Annie and Keith drove up to the red brick Victorian house, and Annie jumped out of the Blazer as Terry came out the side door. Without a word, except for some squeals and exclamations that Keith couldn't make out, they ran to each other, hugged, kissed, and jumped around like schoolgirls. Although Keith felt he was the proximate cause of this joy, they ignored him for a while, then Terry ran to him and embraced him. She said, "Well, look who's back."

"Yeah, we got it together this time."

"Oh, Keith, I *knew* you would."

Annie stood beside him with her arm around him, and Keith had the feeling he was posing for a trophy photo. Annie said to Terry, "We're going—" She looked up at Keith. "Where are we going, darling?"

"To New York," he replied. That wasn't where they were going, but, in Keith's mind, this wasn't the end of a covert operation; it was the beginning of an escape-and-evasion out of enemy territory.

Annie added, "Then we'll go to Rome. Right?"

"Right."

Denise, still in the Blazer, began barking, and

Annie said to Terry, "It was all such a last-minute...
would you mind keeping Denise for a while?"

"I'd love to. We haven't had a dog since the kids
left." Annie opened the car door, and the dog bolted
out and began running around as if she knew the place,
Keith thought.

The side door opened again, and Terry's husband,
Larry, came out. He was bigger than Keith remembered, over six feet tall, and he'd gained some weight
and lost some hair, but still looked like a force to be
reckoned with. He greeted his sister-in-law, then shook
Keith's hand and said, "Nice seeing you again."

"Same here."

Larry was the strong, silent type, Keith recalled,
and like a lot of men around these parts, he didn't
waste words. In fact, he didn't use many of them. Keith
remembered drinking beer with Larry Ingram one
night at someone's house in Spencerville, about a million beers ago, and, except for Larry saying, "I'll have
another," Keith couldn't recall much else that the man
had said. Larry also never asked questions, so Keith volunteered, "Annie and I are leaving together."

Larry nodded.

"I don't think this will cause you any problems with
Cliff Baxter, unless he knew about Annie and me being
here."

Larry shrugged.

"Somehow I feel you can handle that."

"Yup."

"I thought so."

Terry said to Annie, "Can you stay awhile?"

Annie glanced at Keith, who said, "We really should
get moving."

"Okay." Annie's eyes met Keith's, and he thought
she looked like she wanted reassurance.

Keith said to Annie and Terry, "We'll be fine. We don't have to drive through Spencer County."

Terry nodded. "Good."

Keith noticed that Larry had disappeared, then he came out the side door carrying a suitcase and an overnight bag and put them in the rear compartment of the Blazer without a word.

Annie thanked him, then said to Keith, "I brought my stuff here in shopping bags, but Terry is lending me her luggage."

Keith asked, "Is that all of it?"

"That's it. I pack light."

"I think I'm going to like traveling with you."

She smiled and said, "I can buy what I need on the road."

"Right."

Terry said to Annie, "I have the two letters for the kids, and I'll go see Mom and Dad tomorrow morning. I'll stop by Aunt Louise's, too."

Keith wanted to get on the road, but he said to Annie, "Why don't you take something from your memorabilia trunk?"

She smiled at him. "You're such a romantic." She looked at Terry. "Isn't he a doll? Can I get to that trunk?"

"Sure. Come on in."

The two women went in the house, and Keith turned to Larry. "You're a Chatham County deputy sheriff."

"Honorary."

"Do you have a police radio in the house or car?"

"Both."

"Can you monitor the Spencerville police here?"

"Sometimes. Weak signal."

"How about the Spencer County sheriff's office?"

"Yeah. Better signal."

"Can you do that tonight?"

"Sure will."

"Can you call the Chatham County sheriff later and see if there's an all-points out for my Blazer or her Lincoln?"

"Will do."

"I'll call you from the road."

"Okay." He added, "Tell you what. You take my car."

"No, I can't do that."

"Sure can."

"Larry, listen, I know you can handle that guy, but I don't want him to know there's any connection between what's happening tonight and you and your wife."

"Don't matter."

"If I get pulled over in your car, there's going to be trouble for you. That bastard will be out to get you even if it takes him twenty years."

"Don't worry about it."

"I *am* worried about it. Look, like it or not, he's your kin. His children are your niece and nephew, and your children are his children's cousins, and you have the same in-laws for now. You don't need that kind of bad blood in the family. I'm okay in my own car."

Larry didn't reply.

Keith added, "And to tell you the truth, I don't want to alarm the women."

Larry nodded.

Keith said, "I don't think there'll be an all-points out for a few hours, anyway, and they're going to look for Annie's car first, then maybe mine. That's all the time I need."

Larry thought a moment, then said, "Keep to the interstates as much as possible. Shouldn't be any county police on those roads." He added, "I don't think the state highway patrol will get any all-points unless Baxter has some specific charge."

Keith replied, "He's got no lawful charges against me."

"Well ... you never know what he can come up with. It don't take much for a pull-over. Then they got you, and they'll call him."

"I understand."

"Where's her car?"

"Why do you ask?"

"Well, if it's just sitting on the side of the road, or in some parking lot, and she isn't around, Baxter damn sure will call the state police and say his wife's been abducted."

Keith nodded.

"If her car's at home, and she's not, or if no one can find her car, then a lot of cops think domestic problem, or no problem, until they get more information. Understand?"

Keith nodded again, then said, "The car is hidden."

"Good."

Not good, Keith thought, *if the car is hidden in my barn, and they find it.*

Larry said, "You'll be okay in Chatham County. I'll see to that."

"Thanks."

Annie and Terry came outside, and Keith saw that Annie was holding a teddy bear. Annie looked at both men and asked, "Is everything all right?"

Either she was too perceptive, Keith thought, or very nervous, or Keith and Larry weren't the poker-faced studs they thought they were. Keith replied, "Everything's fine. What did you find?"

She threw him the teddy bear, and he examined it. "I didn't give you this. Wrong boyfriend's trunk."

Annie smiled and said to Terry, "I told you. He's sarcastic, and he thinks he's funny."

Keith said, "Well, we should be heading out." He shook Larry's hand. "Thanks again."

Annie hugged her sister. "You've been wonderful. Thank you. We'll call you from New York. Oh, I think I'm going to cry."

She hugged Larry, and he said, "You take care now. Don't worry about anything here."

Keith was about to take Terry's hand when the phone in the kitchen rang. They all stood still, and the same thought passed through everyone's mind.

Keith said, "Maybe you should get that."

Terry nodded and hurried into the house. Keith, Annie, and Larry followed.

Terry picked up the wall phone and said, "Hello?"

Keith could tell by the expression on her face that it wasn't her kids calling to say hello.

Terry looked at the three of them as she listened, then said into the phone, "No, Cliff, I haven't seen her."

Annie took Keith's hand, as though, he thought, just her husband's presence on the telephone made her uneasy.

Terry said into the phone, "No, she was here yesterday morning and stayed for lunch. I stopped by your place after church today, and I saw her...No, she didn't mention she was going anywhere...Well, she did say she had a lot of food shopping to do...No, I don't know why she didn't do it yesterday—" Terry stuck her tongue out at the mouthpiece, and, despite the situation, everyone smiled.

Terry said, "How would I know if her car phone is working?" Terry listened, then, to everyone's surprise, she said, "Look, Cliff, why don't you stop checking up on my sister? I'm tired of—" She listened, then said, "Cliff, go to hell." She hung up and said, "That felt good." She looked at Keith, Annie, and Larry and said, "Well, you know who that was."

Larry asked his wife, "Did he cuss you?"

"Sort of."

Larry frowned.

Annie said to Larry, "You don't have to consider him your brother-in-law any longer."

Larry nodded, and Keith could only imagine what those sweet words meant to him. Keith asked Terry, "Where was he calling from?"

"He said he was home. Got home earlier than he thought."

"How did he sound?"

She shrugged. "Same. Annoyed."

Annie commented, "He's finally got something to be annoyed about."

Keith glanced at the kitchen clock and saw it was seven forty-five P.M., and Cliff Baxter was in Spencerville, missing his wife. They didn't have much time now. He said, "All right, we should head out."

They all went outside and again said their good-byes, but this time with some sense of urgency.

Within a minute, they were in the Blazer, backing out of the driveway and waving, the teddy bear sitting between them.

Five minutes before, Keith would have given himself and Annie very good odds of getting away without mishap. Now the odds had dropped to about fifty-fifty, and that wasn't a gamble he normally took.

CHAPTER THIRTY

County Road 6 was straight and flat, and there was very little traffic on a Sunday night, so Keith kept his high beams on and pushed the Blazer up to seventy miles per hour.

Annie asked, "*Is* everything all right? Don't humor me."

Keith replied, "I didn't want to worry your sister."

"Everything is not all right."

"Well, the question is—how long will it take Cliff to figure it out? Maybe you can answer that question."

She thought a moment, then replied, "It's nearly eight o'clock, and I've never been out this late without him knowing exactly where I was."

Keith didn't reply.

She said, "I guess we really needed that running start."

"Takes the fun out of it."

She looked at him and saw he was smiling, so she smiled, too, but both of them knew it wasn't funny. Finally, he said, "Fun aside, this is more risk than you had to take, and I'm responsible for that. If I could get you to my farm without being seen, I'd do it and tell you to go home tonight."

"No. Even if I could, I wouldn't. I'm with you,

and I'm never going back there again. And you're not responsible for me saying yes tonight. Okay?"

"Okay."

They continued east and left Chatham County, crossing into Dawson County. Keith asked her, "What will your trusting spouse do next?"

"You mean Peter, Peter, the pumpkin eater? Well, he'll call my car phone every two minutes—that's why he was so generous about having Baxter Motors install it. In between those calls, he'll call my parents, relatives, and friends, including Pastor and Mrs. Schenk, for instance. He's absolutely shameless when it comes to tracking me down, and he's not very subtle when he gets people on the phone."

Keith smiled and said, "They must all think you fool around."

"No, they think he's nuts." She added, "He thinks he's embarrassing me and punishing me for not checking in with him every time I go somewhere. But he makes a fool of himself."

"Better yet, it takes time to make those calls...what order is Terry on the list?"

"Usually second, after my parents. So he's got about a dozen more calls to make."

Keith nodded.

Annie smiled. "Terry finally did it." She mimicked Terry's deeper voice and said, "Cliff, go to hell." She laughed. "That will put him into a rage for about half an hour. He doesn't like women who back-talk him."

"Who does?"

"You do. And you love to give it right back. But you're not mean—you're funny." She added, "You still make me laugh." She put her hand on his cheek and gave him a pinch.

He smiled. They were making good time, and he figured that Interstate 75 was about ten more miles.

She picked up the teddy bear and put it on his lap. "Do you remember this?"

He glanced at the brown and white stuffed animal. "State fair," he guessed.

"County fair."

"Right."

"Shooting gallery. You were very good. Do you still like to shoot?"

"No. I think I got it out of my system."

"I can imagine."

She asked him, "Are you armed?"

"No."

"Why not?"

"Well, I don't intend to have a shoot-out with the police."

"But what if it's *him*?"

"We're not going through his little kingdom."

"He'd go anywhere, Keith, if he was looking for us."

"Well, are *you* armed?"

She didn't reply immediately, then said, "I was yesterday morning. Tonight was sort of a surprise."

He thought a moment, then asked her, "Would you have used it?"

"If he tried to stop us from being together, I would."

"Well... I would, too. To tell you the truth, I might have brought my pistol, but it's missing. I think your husband burglarized my house."

"What? You mean he went into your house?"

"I can't be certain it was him, but he's on a real short list of suspects." He added, "We don't need a gun. We'll be fine."

"All right..."

He glanced at her and said, "About two months ago, about the time I arrived, there was a firearm incident at your house, in the early morning hours. Do you want to tell me about that?"

She put her head down and stared at the floor a long time, then replied, "No, I don't."

"Okay."

"I will...but not now."

"Fine."

"How did you know?"

"It's a small town."

"People talk about the Baxters, don't they?"

"You know they do. You're always the saint. He's always Satan."

"And you're my guardian angel."

"Thank you. I'll try." He still needed more information, and he asked her, "What will he do after he harasses everyone with phone calls? Would he call his own police force?"

"He might...that's a last resort. But he's done it. What he's probably doing now is cruising in his police car, looking for my car—motels first, as if I'm going to use a local motel to have an affair. Then, at the same time, he'll be calling everyone he can think of. When he gets frustrated enough, he'll call headquarters—he wouldn't stop in because he doesn't want to face his own men with some idiotic story about being worried about me having an accident or something. I mean, I think the hospital, or the EMS, or his own police might notify him if I had an accident. He's such an idiot, and his men know it."

Keith observed, "You seem to know his modus operandi fairly well."

"After all these years, I think I do. There used to be an older sergeant on the force, a real good friend to me, and he'd tell me about Cliff's craziness. Cliff got rid of him and all the good old guys as soon as he could. Did you notice that most of those guys were young? Cliff handpicked each one. He told me once that it was like training dogs—get them young, hand-feed them, make them afraid of you, and loyal only to you." She added, "He said it was the same with wives."

Keith didn't reply.

She continued, "He's also tried to make them as vicious as he is. But I don't believe you can make people vicious unless they have it in them to begin with. Most of those guys are okay—they like me, but they have to play the part for the boss."

Keith wasn't entirely sure about that, but since he had no intention of traveling through Spencer County, he wasn't going to find out. Unless, of course, some other police force picked them up and turned them over to the Spencerville police department. Keith said to her, "Okay, after the phone calls, he finally calls the Spencerville P.D. and, I suppose, the county sheriff."

"Yes. That's his mother's cousin."

"So, at that point, the whole county is looking for your white Lincoln."

"Yes. Before I had a car phone, they'd pull me over and very politely ask me to call my husband at work, or go home because he needed to tell me something." She added, "A lot of them smirked—not *at* me, *with* me."

"Sounds like fun being married to the local police chief."

"Actually, sometimes it was. God forgive me, but I used to love seeing him make a jackass of himself." She added, "I'm sorry. That's not me."

"It's okay." He said to her, "I'll be honest with you—a lot depends on how long it takes him to decide to drive out to my place, then decide to come onto my property, then to open the barn door."

"I know."

He tried to put himself in Cliff Baxter's position. He thought about what Annie had told him about her husband's usual wife-searching routine, and he also considered the fact that Baxter didn't really believe there was any recent connection between his wife and Keith Landry. Yet, eventually, Cliff Baxter would be drawn to the Landry farm. Then what? If he came onto the property, he'd see the house was dark and the Blazer was gone. He would think that Keith Landry had taken Chief Baxter's threat seriously and run away, which was a logical conclusion for Baxter, considering the man's overblown ego. Or Baxter could think something else, based on his jealousy and paranoia, which in this case was well founded. If Baxter thought to go to the barn, all his questions would be answered. The "Fuck you" note wouldn't improve his mood much. Keith processed all this and figured they had about another hour or less before the police radios started crackling in the surrounding counties.

A half hour after they'd left Terry and Larry, they approached the intersection of Interstate 75. Southbound led directly to Dayton or to Route 15, which would take them to Columbus. Northbound led directly to Toledo. Keith considered the problem. If he went south, to Columbus, it would take about two hours, and to Dayton, close to three. The airports in both cities were bigger than Toledo Airport, and they'd have a better chance of getting a flight to Washington, or even Baltimore or Richmond. It didn't matter where at this point. But that was a very long time to be on the road in this situation.

Toledo Airport was only about a half-hour drive,

but Keith didn't know if they could get a flight east, or a flight anywhere for that matter. Yet there had to be some flight out of Toledo that they could get on. The main consideration as he saw it was to get off the road as quickly as possible. He said to Annie, "I think we should go to Toledo because it's a shorter drive."

She nodded in understanding.

He added, "But I don't know what's flying out of there, where, or when."

"I don't care what, where, or when."

"Okay." He swung onto Interstate 75 northbound. It was a good, fast road with two lanes in either direction and not much traffic. He kept his speed at seventy miles per hour. They were heading back toward Spencer County, but Interstate 75 would not go through the county. He tried to determine how much territory a police search would include and asked her, "When was the last time you saw or spoke to anyone today before you came out to my place at six?"

She thought a moment, then replied, "I called both of my children at about five...just to hear their voices...Tom was out, but I spoke to Wendy."

"Would Mr. Baxter call his daughter?"

"Not usually, but this time he might. Yes, I think he would, because he might think I drove up to see her. I told him I wanted to do that, but he didn't like the idea."

"So Wendy would fix your time at home at about five-thirty."

"Yes. And I left a message on Tom's answering machine about that time."

Keith glanced at the dashboard clock. It was eight-thirty P.M. If Baxter had done his detective work well, he'd figure his wife was unaccounted for since five-thirty, or for the last three hours, which meant about a

180-mile radius from Spencerville by car. That included Toledo, of course, and also Fort Wayne, Indiana, which had an airport about the size of Toledo's. And with each passing half hour, the search radius would be automatically increased. That was assuming there *was* a search in progress, or about to begin.

Annie watched him awhile, then said, "Keith, you don't need this."

"No, I *want* this."

"But you don't have to run if I'm not with you. Let me off at the next rest stop, and I'll call Spencerville police headquarters and say—"

"Say what? You lost your car in my barn, and you need a ride home?"

"I don't care what I have to say, or what he does, or what happens. I won't put you in this—"

"Annie, I have my own grudge against Cliff Baxter going back a lot of years. I'm not doing this for you."

"Oh…"

"I just want to steal his wife and annoy him. I'll go to Washington, you go to Rome. Send me a postcard. Okay?"

"I guess you're joking."

"I'm being sarcastic and not funny. And you're being much too decent. But I appreciate your concern." He said, "Annie, you threw away your wedding ring. We agreed there is no turning back. Subject closed. Forever."

"Okay." She observed, "You handle this well. I guess you did things like this in your job."

"I used to abduct a wife a week."

"I mean dangerous things. Was it dangerous?"

"Not if you did it right." He added, "I spent the last five or six years mostly behind a desk. I'm rusty."

"I'm shaky."

"You have every right to be." He took her hand and squeezed it. "You're doing fine."

"I feel safe with you."

"Good. So your sister looked great. Good genes in the Prentis family."

"My mother hasn't aged much either. You're getting a good deal, Mr. Landry."

"I know." He added, "It sounded to me like you gave Larry the green light to go a few rounds with Mr. Baxter."

"Cliff won't come within fifty miles of him now, and Larry would never go looking for trouble." She said, "Larry and Terry have a great marriage. The Prentis women also make good wives." She added, as if reading his mind, "Right. One of them didn't know how to pick a husband."

Against his better judgment, Keith asked, "Did you ever love him?"

"No. Not ever."

"But he loves you."

"He does. But it's not the kind of love I want or need. It's the kind he wants and needs, and it kept me feeling obligated. It kept me around too long." She added, "With Wendy at school, I was going to do something, with or without you. Do you believe that?"

"I do. You hinted as much in your letters." He added, "Maybe that's what made me come back."

"No maybes about it, Keith. This was our last chance. You knew that."

"Yes, I did."

"We're going to make it this time, aren't we?"

"We are."

"If I wasn't so frightened, I'd be bouncing in my seat."

"You can bounce on the airplane seat." He put a

tape in the deck and said, "Sixties stuff. Mixed album. Okay?"

"More than okay."

The Lovin' Spoonful sang, "Do You Believe in Magic," and Annie said, "Nineteen sixty-five. We're in our freshman year. Right?"

"Right."

She said, "My kids love this stuff."

The Casinos sang, "Then You Can Tell Me Good-bye," and Keith said, "That's...maybe sixty-seven. We're juniors."

"That was fast."

They listened to the tape and, about ten minutes later, Annie touched his arm and pointed to the exit sign up ahead. "Bowling Green."

He nodded. It was odd, he thought, how certain place names could be so evocative in a person's personal history. He felt a little twinge in his heart and turned to say something to her and saw a tear run down her cheek. He put his hand on her neck and massaged it.

She said, "You know...if my daughter is half as happy there as I was with you, she'll have good memories to last her for the rest of her life."

"I'm sure she'll be happy, if she's like you."

"I hope so...this country has changed so much... I can't tell if it's better or worse than when we were kids."

"I can't either, but to tell you the truth, I don't care anymore. I'm ready to live a private life, and I hope the world leaves us alone."

"You must have seen too many bad things in the world, Keith."

"I have. And to be honest, I've contributed my share to the world's problems."

"Have you?"

"Maybe not on purpose."

"Tell me a good deed that you've done on purpose."

"Oh, I don't know offhand...I've seen good deeds...it's not a bad world, Annie, and I don't mean to suggest it is. For all the bad things I've seen, I've also seen the most extraordinary acts of courage, kindness, honesty, and love." He added, "And miracles— like finding you again."

"Thank you. It's been a long time since I've heard words like that." She glanced at him and said, "Keith, I know your life wasn't all glamour and excitement, and that there must be some scars, some heartbreak, some disappointments, and some things you'd like to forget, or maybe need to talk about. Tell me as much or as little as you want to. I'll listen."

"Thanks. Same here."

A big, overhead green and white sign came into view: *Toledo Airport—This Exit.*

Annie said, "We're close."

"Yes." They just needed one or two more miracles.

CHAPTER THIRTY-ONE

Keith drove into the small airport, which lay southwest of Toledo. He hadn't seen any aircraft coming in or taking off as he approached, but this didn't overly concern him because it wasn't a busy airport, and he seemed to recall there were only six gates.

They pulled up to the terminal entrance, which was both arrivals and departures.

There were no skycaps around, and in fact Keith saw no other cars, no taxis, no people. He said to Annie, "Wait here a minute."

He went inside the small, modern terminal and saw it was nearly empty and all the concessions were closed except the coffee shop. This didn't look promising.

He found the departure monitor. Seven airlines serviced the airport, mostly commuter links, according to the monitor. He kept staring at the departure schedule, refusing to accept the information that the last flight, an American Eagle to Dayton, had left over an hour ago. "Damn it."

He went to the nearest ticket counter, which was USAir. A solitary woman stood at one of the stations doing paperwork, and he asked her, "Do you have any flights leaving for anywhere?"

"No, sir."

He looked at the other six airline counters, all of which were deserted. He asked the woman, "Are there any flights leaving here tonight?"

She looked at him quizzically and replied, "No, sir. Where did you want to go?"

He didn't want her next phone call to be to the security police, so he said, "I thought there was a late flight to Washington."

"No, sir. The last flights out of Toledo are usually about seven forty-five. Can I book you to Washington in the morning?"

"Maybe." He thought a moment. "Are the rental car companies open?"

"No, sir. The last arriving flight landed forty-five minutes ago."

He was stuck with the Blazer, and he wasn't going to get too far with it.

She said, "I have a seven-fifteen A.M. to National Airport. Arrives at eight fifty-five. Seats available. Can I book that for you?"

Keith knew better than to leave a paper trail, and, in any case, by morning they'd have Annie Baxter's photo, if not his, in the hands of every ticket agent.

"Sir?"

"No, thanks. Is there an air charter service here?"

"Yes, sir. Over there. They're closed, but they have a phone."

"Thanks." He went to the charter service counter, picked up their telephone, and dialed the indicated number. It rang, and a recording told him to leave his name, number, and his message. He hung up, remarking to himself that getting out of Saigon with communist tanks approaching the American embassy had been easier than getting out of Toledo on a Sunday night.

He went to a pay phone and called the Ingrams. Terry answered, and Keith said in his most upbeat voice, "Hi, Terry."

"Keith! Where are you? Is everything—?"

"Everything's fine. We're about to fly out. Annie is at the gate, and I just wanted to say thanks again and goodbye."

"Oh, that's so sweet of you. I'm so happy we could help, and—"

"Hold on...okay, they're announcing our flight. I just want to say a quick good-bye to Larry."

"Sure. He's right here."

Larry came on the line, and Keith said, "Larry, without worrying your wife, can you tell me if you've heard anything?"

"I did. Hold on."

Keith heard him say something to Terry, then Larry came back on and said, "Okay, I can talk. I heard about ten minutes ago—they broadcast an all-points bulletin, and I got a call to see if I wanted to go out on patrol tonight."

"All right...what and who are they looking for?"

"Green Chevy Blazer, this year's model, your plates. They're looking for Annie Baxter and Keith Landry."

Keith nodded to himself. Obviously, they'd found her car in his barn. He asked, "Anything about possible locations?"

"Well, the usual—car rental places, airports within a two-hundred-fifty-mile radius of Spencerville to be increased each half hour, bus terminals, train stations, all roads and highways—like that."

"Why are they looking for us?"

"Kidnapping. Major-league. Seems they found her car in your barn."

"Would you advise me to go to the police and explain?"

"Nope. Don't do that. They'd hold you until he arrives and tells his side. He's a cop, they're cops."

"But if she signs a statement saying—"

"I spoke to Baxter. He says he's got his kids on the way in from college. I don't know if that's true, but if it is, and if they all wind up at some station house with you two, it could get real messy and emotional. If you can get away, do it."

Keith considered this. Annie would never go with Baxter—but why put her or her children through that? He had other, cleaner options. Or he thought he did. He said to Larry, "Okay. Thanks again."

"You okay?"

"Yeah. We're about to fly out."

"Do that. Good luck."

Keith hung up. *Ten minutes ago.* That gave him about no minutes to get out of the airport.

He walked quickly through the empty terminal, wondering if he shouldn't have tried for Dayton or Columbus airports. But if he had, he'd still be on the road, and even if he'd gotten to one of those airports, they'd be looking for him and Annie by the time they arrived. In fact, they'd be looking for them here within minutes.

So there was no use second-guessing decisions; you made them based on what you knew and what your experience and intuition told you. Plan A hadn't quite worked; Plan B was simple. Hide.

He went outside and saw an airport security man standing at the curb near the Blazer. The man looked at him and walked over. "This your car?"

"Yes."

"The lady says you're flying to New York. I don't think so."

Keith saw Annie get out of the Blazer and walk toward them. Keith said to the security man, "I guess not."

"Nope. I told her the last flight left over an hour ago."

"Right. I just found out."

Annie stood beside Keith and said to him, "This gentleman says we missed the last flight."

"Yes. Let's go home." He took her arm and walked her back to the Blazer.

The security man followed and pointed to the license plate. "I see you got this car in Toledo."

Keith glanced at the plate, whose frame had the name of the dealer advertised on it. "That's right."

"Lady says you drove in from Chatham County."

"Right. I bought the car in Toledo." He opened the passenger-side door, and Annie got inside.

Keith noticed the two-way radio on the man's belt and didn't want to be around when it broadcast an all-points bulletin. He went around to the driver's side and opened his door.

The security man followed and said, "You should have called for reservations before you made that drive."

Keith had faced too many of those kinds of questions around the world, and he knew the mentality of the people that asked them. He had no idea what Annie had already told the guy, except that they wanted to go to New York and were from Chatham County. Meanwhile, Keith had already inquired about a flight to Washington.

Keith glanced at Annie, and in his best midwestern accent, he said, "I told you we should have called up ahead for reservations."

She nodded in understanding and leaned toward the open window, addressing the security man. "Like I said, it was a spur-of-the-moment thing to go to New

York. Like you see people do in the movies." She added, "We never flew before."

The security man advised them, "You can get a motel and stay over. There's a USAir flight to New York in the morning."

Keith replied, "The hell with it. We're going home." He opened the door, got in the Blazer, and drove off. He watched the security man still standing at the curb. Keith said, "He was a little too nosy."

"You've lived in Washington too long. He was trying to be helpful. He was very concerned when I spoke to him."

"I guess." Either way, the man would remember them and the car.

Annie asked, "What are we going to do now?"

"Get a motel."

"Can't we just drive to New York?"

"I don't think so." He glanced at her and said, "I spoke to Larry. There's an all-points bulletin out on us and this car."

She didn't say anything.

Keith left the airport and turned east on the airport highway road, toward Toledo.

She said, "Could we rent a car?"

"I thought we could before I heard about the all-points. We have to be careful where we go and what we do."

She nodded.

There was an Airport Sheraton up ahead, and Keith pulled up and parked out of sight of the lobby. "Wait here."

She tried to smile and said, "Just like old times."

"Sort of." He went into the lobby. Near the front desk, sitting on a shelf, he found the 800-number reservation telephone. He picked it up, got the reservation operator, and made a late-arrival reservation for the Sheraton at Cleveland Airport and confirmed it with his American Express card. He then went to a pay phone and called the 800 number for USAir. He reserved two seats on the eight-fifteen morning flight from Cleveland to New York and gave his card number. He wasn't used to escape-and-evasion in his own country, but he was reasonably sure his toll-free calls couldn't be traced back to the Toledo area. And even if they were, the police would be looking for him on the interstate to Cleveland, or more likely waiting for him at the Airport Sheraton in Cleveland. Red herrings were so stupidly simple they sometimes worked, and only two things were necessary for success—a police force efficient enough to pick up on the reservations, but gullible enough to think it was real. As for the latter, he assumed the police thought they were looking for John A. Citizen, not someone who'd once done this for a living.

He left the lobby, went to the Blazer, took his briefcase out of the rear, and got back behind the wheel. "Could you hold this?"

She took the briefcase, and Keith pulled out of the motel parking lot, continuing east on the highway.

Annie asked, "Aren't we staying there?"

"No." He explained what he'd done.

She looked at him and asked, "This was your vocation or avocation?"

"Vocation." He added, "And I thought it had no application to civilian life. Goes to show you."

He continued east, along the highway toward Toledo, whose downtown skyscrapers he could now see. Traffic was heavier here, and the commercial strip was more built-up.

He considered switching license plates. That meant

finding a car that he thought would be parked all night and/or whose owner wouldn't notice that his plates had been switched and report it. Meanwhile, they could drive all night with the switched plates and be in Washington before dawn. But you never knew if the plates had been reported stolen. Also, even if the plates weren't reported stolen, the police were looking for a green Blazer, and if they saw one and the license plate on the Blazer didn't match the all-points bulletin, they'd still run the license number through the computer to see if it matched up. Basically, switching plates was a sucker's bet.

She asked him, "What are you thinking about?"

"Options. Run or hide?"

"Why don't we just go to a police station and explain?"

"That is not an option."

"Why not?"

He told her why not and asked, "Are you up for that domestic scene?"

She thought a moment and replied, "If it was just him, I could handle it. If my children were with him... I don't know..."

"Why don't we just lay low overnight and think about it in the morning? These all-points bulletins tend to get a little stale after a while, and maybe by morning, the state police will have had a few conversations with the Spencerville police chief and maybe with the security guy at the airport. They may very well conclude that Mr. Baxter is not telling it like it is."

She nodded. "Maybe..."

"And to tell you the truth, it's not a good idea to be in the hands of the police at this hour of the night without a judge or lawyer available."

She tried to laugh and said, "You think like a criminal."

"I *was* a criminal in many countries, never my own. But the rules are the same." He added, "I think time is on our side if we lay low. But I won't do anything you're not comfortable with."

"I haven't heard those words in a while." She thought a moment, then said, "Maybe we should stop for the night...and in the morning, even if I have to see him and to explain to the police, I'd rather do it then."

"With luck, you won't have to see him tomorrow or ever again."

"Good."

"All right, so now we're looking for a hot-sheet motel. Know any?"

She smiled. "I know six or seven."

"One will do. Open my briefcase." He gave her the combination.

She opened it, and he said, "This is going to make you laugh. There's a false bottom." He explained how to open it and said, "I need the eyeglasses and the small brown envelope."

She retrieved both items without a word.

He took the glasses and put them on, then said, "Open the envelope. No laughing."

She opened the envelope and took out a mustache the color of Keith's light brown hair. He said, "Peel off the cellophane and stick it on me."

She did what he said, and he checked himself in the rearview mirror. "What do you think?"

"I'm speechless."

"That's a treat. Keep looking for a motel." He took a comb out of his windbreaker and restyled his hair.

She said, "How about that place? Up ahead on the right."

Keith saw the small motel sign, a portable lighted

signboard, actually, that said *Westway Motel—$29* with an arrow that pointed to the right. He recalled that the airport highway had once been a meandering two-lane road, but had been widened and straightened many years ago, leaving some of the old motels hundreds of yards away from the side of the new road. Keith turned onto a narrow lane that took him to the parking court of the motel. He stopped out of view of the lobby. "Okay. *This* is like old times. Two minutes."

"You used to have the key in forty-five seconds."

He smiled and got out of the Blazer, noticed a Ford Escort in the parking lot, and went inside the small lobby.

The desk clerk, a young man, looked up from a television behind the counter.

Keith adopted a manner of sexual urgency and said. "Need a room."

The clerk put a registration form on the desk.

Keith said, "How much for a few hours?"

"Same."

"Hey, I just bought her a Sizzler steak, buddy. Can you do better?"

"How long you staying?"

"Maybe midnight. You get off at midnight? You can check."

"Yeah, I'm off at midnight, but I'm not rushing you."

"Tell you what—I might be longer. I'll give you twenty-five for all night."

"Okay."

Keith filled out the registration form with some creativity, listing a Ford Escort as his car. He'd discovered that the clerk, who could possibly identify him despite the disguise, would be gone at midnight. So far, so good. He gave the young man twenty-five dollars in cash, took the key to room 7, and left.

He got into the Blazer and pulled up to a parking spot several places away from room 7. There weren't too many cars there on a Sunday night, and none of them could be seen from the highway. But he had no intention of leaving the Blazer there anyway.

They took the luggage, and Keith also took all his personal possessions out of the car, including his audiotapes, the registration, and other odds and ends.

Keith opened the door to the room, and they carried everything inside. Annie turned on the lamp and said, "It's lovely."

Actually, it was very shoddy. Keith found the telephone book under the nightstand and flipped through the yellow pages.

"What are you looking for?"

"I need...here it is." He closed the book and said, "I'll be back in about fifteen or twenty minutes."

"Where are you going?"

"To get the car out of here."

She put her hand on his arm. "I'll go with you. If they come, I don't want to be here without you."

"All right."

They went outside and got into the Blazer. Keith drove up the lane and stopped at the lighted signboard near the highway. He got out and pulled the light plug out of the electrical outlet, leaving the signboard in darkness, then got back in the Blazer and said, "Enough customers for one night."

Annie glanced at him but said nothing.

Keith pulled back onto the highway and made a right, toward Toledo. He said, "We're going to have to walk back."

"Okay."

A police cruiser came toward them from the opposite direction and passed them. Keith looked in his
sideview mirror, but the cruiser kept going. He said
to her, "There's a Chevrolet dealership on this road,
according to the phone book. Odd number, so it'll be
on the left-hand side."

She nodded. "That's a good place to leave a Chevy.
You're smarter than you look, Landry."

"Thank you."

"Do you still need that mustache and glasses?"

"For your fantasy, later."

She smiled and punched his arm. "*You* are my
fantasy."

The Chevrolet dealership came into view on the left
side of the road, and Keith slowed down and took the
left into the lot. The place was closed, as he thought it
would be at this hour, and he found space in the used-
car lot.

They got out, and Keith went around to the rear,
got two screwdrivers from the toolbox, and they
took off the license plates. "There. They'll wonder about the good car fairy in the morning. Let's
walk. It's exactly one-point-four miles, if you're
interested."

They began the walk back to the motel, along the
commercial highway. Keith stuck the license plates in
his waistband and zippered his windbreaker over them.

She asked him, "Will we come back for the car in
the morning?"

"It's an option."

They came to a Burger King, and Keith asked,
"Hungry?"

"No, my stomach is in knots."

"You need a belly-bomber. Come on."

They went into the Burger King, got hamburgers,

Cokes, and fries, and sat at a table. Keith asked, "Is this as romantic as you thought it would be?"

She smiled. "When I'm with you, the airport highway looks like the Via Veneto."

"I think I'm going to throw up."

She laughed, and he put his hand on hers. "It's okay now."

She nodded.

They ate, and he found he was hungry and so was she. He glanced at his watch. It was always a good idea to put in some time outside of the room you just booked. The police sometimes got sloppy about their stakeouts when they were waiting for you to return.

She said, "Don't swallow your mustache."

He smiled. "I like you."

At ten P.M., he said, "Let's walk off the fries."

They left and crossed the highway at a light. There were absolutely no other pedestrians on this highway, and in some parts of America, pedestrians were a rare enough sight to attract attention. He picked up his pace, and she kept up with him.

They approached the dark motel sign near the lane, and Keith slowed down and took her arm. There was an all-night convenience store next to the lane that led to the motel, and he directed her into the parking lot. They stood in the lot and kept watching the motel. He asked, "Do you want to go in there and get some snacks for later?"

"No. I'm not leaving your side."

"Okay. We'll wait here a few minutes."

Keith gave it five minutes, then they walked to the motel, through the parking lot, and went to the door of room 7. If the police were here, or somewhere out there, it was already too late, so he just walked in, noting the lights were still on and nothing seemed disturbed.

Annie locked and bolted the door behind them.

Keith threw the key on the nightstand and the license plates on the bureau and looked at her. "You're a real trouper."

"You're amazing." She took his glasses off, peeled off his mustache, and kissed him.

In fact, he was basically happy with his tradecraft, which was at one time second nature to him. Now he had to think about it, but at least he knew what he was supposed to be thinking about.

Annie was unpacking her overnight bag in the bathroom, and Keith parted the blackout curtains and looked out into the parking court. Everything seemed all right, but he had this sense of déjà vu, like he was in East Berlin again, looking out at the street from a window in a safe house that wasn't so safe.

So far, he thought, he'd done the best he could. Even picking Toledo because it was closer was the right decision, notwithstanding the small problem of having missed the last flight. The only thing he'd done wrong, his only true mistake, was his spontaneous decision to run off; to act on his emotions instead of his intellect. But maybe that's what the entire last two months were about. To let go, to lose control, to want someone so badly that a quarter century of doing things by the book—what they called the right combination of D&D, discipline and daring—was suddenly transformed into desire and daring, just like that. It felt good. But there was a price to pay. After his first impulsive act, all his cleverness—all of Plan B—was just damage control. He looked out into the parking lot again. "It *looks* okay. It *is* okay…"

There were no chairs in the room, so he sat on the bed and pulled off his shoes. He let himself think about the morning. There was no way they were going to Toledo Airport, of course, or any other airport. An all-points bulletin for kidnapping a police chief's wife, mother of two, and so forth was sufficiently serious to keep every cop in the state and surrounding states on full alert, unless, of course, as he'd suggested to Annie, the state police got onto Baxter. But Keith wouldn't know that immediately.

His best bet, the thing that appealed to him most, was to just get out of the state. And the best way to do that would be to wait until about seven or eight A.M., a normal, busy workday, then take a taxi into Toledo, which was a big enough city to blend in. He couldn't rent a car, as he knew, and he didn't want to steal one and compound his problems.

Trains and buses were not an option, but he had several other options—hire a limousine, charter a plane, or charter a boat to take them to a Great Lakes port someplace out of state. Charter and hire places were cash up front, didn't require identification, were not normally watched or even notified by the police, and the only question a charter or hire service usually asked was, "Where do you want to go?"

He had three other options—call the police, as Annie suggested, call the Porters, or call Charlie Adair. But none of those options seemed palatable at the moment. He might call the police in the morning, but the Porters didn't need any more problems at any hour, and lastly, Charlie Adair had a string attached to everything. Nevertheless, these were options, too, and Keith would decide in the morning.

Annie came out of the bathroom, and he stood. He said to her, "Is it your birthday?"

"No. Why?"

"You're wearing your birthday suit."

"Oh! I forgot to put on my pajamas. I'm so embarrassed. Don't look."

He smiled, and they walked to each other, embracing and kissing.

She said, "Keith, no matter what happens tonight or tomorrow, we're going to have this time now."

"We have all the time in the world."

CHAPTER THIRTY-TWO

Cliff Baxter sat alone in his office at Spencerville police headquarters. The entire fifteen-man force was on duty, some at headquarters, the rest on the road.

He drank a Coke, staring off at the opposite wall. He took some perverse satisfaction in the knowledge that he'd been right. His wife was a liar and a whore, Keith Landry was a low-life, wife-fucking prick. "I knew it."

What bothered him was the fact that they'd somehow gotten together over the past weeks, right under the noses of his stupid men, and had made their plans and gotten away. He couldn't blame himself; he'd been right on top of this from day one.

It had been relatively easy to find Annie's car. One of the options she didn't know the car had was a radio transmitter, a homing device bought by the Spencerville police for its high-tech fight against crime, and in Baxter's car was the radio receiver.

Baxter remembered walking into the Landry barn, seeing the white, gleaming Lincoln sitting there beside the tractor, and opening the car door. *Cliff, Fuck you,* signed Keith Landry. "No, fuck *you,* asshole."

He'd pocketed the note before his men could see it—not out of embarrassment, he told himself, but because it was a purely personal note and wasn't a clue to the kidnapping.

Of course, it wasn't a kidnapping, and he guessed his men knew that, but no other cop in the state knew it.

The intercom buzzed, and Sergeant Blake said, "Chief, it's Captain Delson from the State."

"Okay." Cliff Baxter picked up the phone, and Captain Delson, of the Ohio state police, said, "Chief, we got something."

Baxter sat upright in his chair. "Yeah?"

"About half an hour ago, the state police were checking out Toledo Airport, and a security man there tells them he saw the subjects. Right car, right description, and he even remembered part of the license plate, which matches."

"They get on a plane?"

"No, they missed the last flight and told the guy they were going home."

"Okay, okay. Good. You got them fixed in the Toledo area, so—"

"Right...thing is, Chief, the guy said that the woman, who he identified from the photo you sent as Mrs. Baxter, didn't look like she was under duress or being forced—"

"Ah, bullshit. The son-of-a-bitch had a gun on her—"

"Well, the male suspect—Landry—was away from the Blazer for some time, and the female was sitting alone in the vehicle."

Baxter cleared his throat and said, "Well...who was this airport guy? A security cop? How the hell does a square-badge guy know about—?"

"Chief, the subjects appeared to be wanting to board an aircraft together. This doesn't look like a kidnapping or an abduction in the strict legal sense."

Baxter didn't reply for a few seconds, then said, "You're gonna take that chance? If she winds up dead, you want to be the one that called off the search?"

"Chief, we turned this state upside down for you, and I don't respond well to threats. Look, cop-to-cop, I have to tell you, it looks like your wife ran off with this guy."

Baxter stayed silent.

Captain Delson continued, "Based on the Social Security number you gave us for Keith Landry, we faxed the FBI, but we can't seem to get much information on him. What we have seems to indicate that he's a retired colonel in the United States Army, assuming this is the same guy. No criminal record, no previous anything. We're still checking."

"Yeah...a colonel?"

"That's right."

"What's the bottom line? What are you telling me?"

"Well...I don't know. You want to fax us a deposition with the whys and wherefores and your signature?"

"Well...why don't you make the state of Ohio the complainant?"

"The state of Ohio has no complaint against this man or Mrs. Baxter."

"No? You mean you have no complaint against kidnapping?"

"Yeah, we would, but it seems you were *mistaken*. Look, Chief, I know this is tough, but I had that security guy on the phone myself for twenty minutes, and I have to believe that these two people he saw were the subjects of the all-points, and further, that Mrs. Baxter, whose photo he identified, was a willing companion of the male she was with. Now, we can keep looking for them, as a professional courtesy—and that's between us and not for the taxpayers to discover—but I have to put out a new bulletin that says locate and maintain observation, await further instructions, and do not question unless subjects are about to leave the jurisdiction, and do not detain or arrest unless there's probable cause. We don't need a lawsuit, and you don't need the embarrassment. Okay?"

Baxter thought a moment, then took a deep breath and said, "Landry is wanted here in connection with traffic violations, obstructing justice, harassment, and trespassing."

There was a silence on the phone, then Captain Delson said, "Well, fax us the particulars." He added, "But don't reach for things that won't stand up."

"Hey, I'm gonna send you a bench warrant, signed by the local judge here, and we will extradite. All you got to do is hold them. Spencerville will come get them."

"I'm not holding them, but if we locate them, we'll let you know. Here's something else—a Keith Landry made reservations at the Airport Sheraton in Cleveland and booked a USAir flight to New York from there." He gave Baxter the details and added, "We're watching the roads between Toledo and Cleveland, and there will be Cleveland police at the Sheraton." Captain Delson added, "We'll leave that in place for you. Also, because they were spotted at Toledo Airport, as standard operating procedure, the state and local police are checking the area motels, boardinghouses, and so forth. The subjects might not be going to Cleveland if they get wind of an all-points bulletin."

Baxter nodded. "Yeah...okay. You'll let me know as soon as you get a lead or something."

"We will." Captain Delson stayed silent, then said, "You might want to handle it yourself, man-to-man."

"Yeah...whenever and wherever you get a fix on them, you let me know." Baxter added, "I want to talk to her...I want to see if she knows what she's doing before she runs out on a husband and two kids. Hey, if you're right, and she's going with this guy willingly, then the hell with her. But I want to hear it from her own mouth. You understand."

"I do."

"Yeah...hell of a thing. Married twenty years...son and daughter in college...they're home now," he lied, "real upset...her mother almost had a heart attack. Sister can't stop crying, father is mad as hell at her. What the hell's wrong with these women today?"

"I don't know."

"Well, I appreciate all that's being done. I just want to talk to her."

"We'll keep you posted."

"I'll be right here all night." He blew his nose into the phone and said in a cracking voice, "I just want to see her again. Please, God—"

"Okay. Take it easy."

Baxter hung up and slammed the desk. "Goddamnit! I'll fucking kill her! I'll crucify that cocksucker—"

The door opened, and Sergeant Blake stuck his head in. "Everything okay, Chief?"

"Yeah. Get the hell out of here—no, wait." He thought a moment, then said, "Have Schenley fix up a bench warrant for Landry—obstructing justice, trespassing, some other shit—and tell him to go wake up Judge Thornsby and get it signed, and send it out."

"Yes, sir."

"Wait! Then get two cars, three men including you, and the homing device. We're going up to Toledo."

CHAPTER THIRTY-THREE

As he undressed, she sat on the bed, cross-legged, the teddy bear in her lap, and said to him, "I'm not on the pill. Did I tell you that?"

"No. We didn't get around to the preliminaries last time." He said to her, "I should have told you I had an exit physical before I left D.C. I'm okay."

"I assumed...but I guess I was supposed to ask beforehand...I'm not used to...I mean, I don't do this."

"No, *you* don't."

She nodded in understanding. "When I realized that he...that he had other women, I had some tests done, then I had my gynecologist tell him I couldn't take the pill, and I couldn't wear a diaphragm, so he had to wear a condom. It was humiliating. He got very annoyed, but he understood what it was really about... do we have to talk about this?"

"I think that about covers it." He smiled. "Did I get you pregnant?"

She smiled, too. "I hope so. Do you want to try again?"

Keith got into the bed, moved the teddy bear away, and they sat face-to-face, their legs wrapped around each other, and they fondled, kissed, and massaged, drawing out the foreplay as if they truly had all the time in the world, as if there were no possibility of a knock on the door.

She moved closer to him, raised herself up, and came down on him, never taking her mouth off his.

For the next half hour, without acknowledging it, they were adolescents again, without prior experience—feeling, exploring, touching, probing, experimenting with oral sex, mutual masturbation, and pretending to discover new positions for intercourse. She said, "I haven't been fucked like this since that guy I told you about. Where'd you learn this stuff?"

"From a sixteen-year-old. I was seventeen."

"I'm glad you haven't forgotten any of it."

"No, and I never forgot her."

They lay on the bed, on top of the sheets, holding hands. There was a mirror on the ceiling, and they both made jokes about it, but Keith thought she'd been a little embarrassed. He stared up at the mirror and saw her beside him, her hair fanned out on the pillow, her eyes closed, looking very contented with a smile on her face. Her image in the mirror was like a quiet dream, he thought, her breasts rising and falling, the thick bush of pubic hair, the slightly parted legs, and her toes wiggling, which was something he remembered from long ago. In fact, this was how he remembered her on the morning he left, and he recalled saying to her then, "See you later."

Keith sat up slowly and looked around the room. It was sparsely furnished, and what there was, was bolted down, including the TV set and the wall-mounted bed lamps. He'd have liked to put something against the door, but there wasn't even a chair in the place. It occurred to him that, if the Westway Motel customers were the sort who would load tacky motel furniture on their pickups, they were also the sort who needed more identification

and security than twenty-nine dollars up front. With
that in mind, it also occurred to him that the clerk probably went outside and took down license plate numbers,
which rarely, or never, matched the ones on the registration form. He hadn't parked the Blazer in front of the
door, but there weren't that many vehicles parked outside
to begin with. In the plus column, the Blazer hadn't been
there more than ten minutes before they'd gotten rid of
it. There was no use worrying about it. He'd been taught
two mutually exclusive things: never underestimate the
police, and never overestimate the police. The bottom
line on this situation was not life and death, or the end
of the Free World—it was a trip to the local police station, some messiness and embarrassment, and eventually
a reasonable and hopefully happy resolution. Keith didn't
want a trip to the police station to be part of their memories, but if it happened, it happened. Meanwhile he rather
enjoyed outsmarting Baxter and wanted *that* as part of
their history. He looked at his watch on the nightstand. It
was eleven thirty-five. So far, so good.

She said to him, "This is the happiest I've been since
our last summer together in Columbus."

"Me, too."

"Do you mean that?"

"I do. I really do."

"Do we live happily ever after?"

"Yes, we do."

She stayed silent a moment, then said, "But we have
to get through tonight and tomorrow, don't we?"

He didn't reply immediately, then looked at her and
told her, "No matter what happens tonight or tomorrow, even if we're separated for a short time, remember
that I love you, and know that we'll be together again.
I promise."

She sat up and kissed him. "You remember that, too."

"I will."

She put her head on his chest. "I feel like a kid again, like it hasn't been twenty-five years, but twenty-five hours, and everything that happened between that morning you left in Columbus and now, didn't happen."

"That's a nice thought."

"Good. Let's pretend. There's no world outside that door, it's just us again, like it used to be."

"How in the name of God did I let you go?"

"Shhh. You didn't. I'm here. I've always been here—" She patted his heart. "Here, where it counts. I never left your heart, you never left my heart."

Keith nodded and started to reply, but couldn't find his voice, then, for the first time in over two decades, a tear formed in his eye and ran down his cheek.

Cliff Baxter sat in the front seat of the two-car convoy. Sergeant Blake drove. In the car behind them were Officer Ward and Officer Krug.

Sitting on the dashboard in front of Cliff Baxter was the location finder. It wasn't a state-of-the-art device—the city council hadn't liked the price of the big model that had to be mounted in a van with a big rotating thing on the roof and all kinds of screens and gadgets. This was a simple line-of-sight, VHF radio receiver that just beeped within a mile or so of the planted transmitter and got louder as you got closer. Still, it worked for what he bought it for—keeping track of his wife. The unit came with two small transmitters, and he'd used the second one a few times as sort of a fun thing to keep track of other people, but mostly the spare sat in his desk until he got the idea of putting it in Landry's car on Friday.

Of course, he'd cruised past the Landry farm early in his search for the Lincoln, and since each transmitter had a different channel, he knew long before he pulled into Landry's driveway that the Lincoln was there and the Blazer was not. At that point, he knew exactly what had happened.

They drove into Toledo Airport. This was the logical place to start, he thought, and they cruised the parking lots, but they didn't need the location finder because the place was nearly empty. They drove to the rental lot and cruised up and down the rows of parked cars.

Blake said to him, "I don't see his car."

"Nope. Okay, we go out on the highway and turn right, toward Toledo."

"Right."

The two Spencerville police cars headed east on the airport highway.

Cliff Baxter picked up his mobile phone and called headquarters. Officer Schenley was acting desk sergeant, and Baxter said to him, "Hear anything?"

"No, sir. I would've called—"

"Yeah. You would've called. I'm making a goddamned communications check."

"Yes, sir."

"And like I told you, if anybody calls from the state police, or anyplace, you don't mention where I am."

"Yes, sir."

"Just call me, and I'll get back to them. Don't bullshit with them."

"Yes, sir."

"Stay awake." He hung up and said to Blake, "Hey, pull into that Sheraton."

Blake pulled into the Sheraton parking lot and commented, "We're not getting a sounding here, Chief."

"Shit, I don't trust this thing. I trust my eyes and my ears. Pull up to the lobby and let me off, then cruise the lot."

"Yes, sir."

Baxter got out and went into the lobby. He approached the desk clerk, an attractive young woman, and said, "How're you tonight, darlin'?"

She smiled. "Pretty good. Yourself?"

"Could be better. Lookin' for a bad guy, ran off with a woman. You know about that?"

"Sure do. Seen it on TV."

"That's good. I hope you seen it come across your fax, too."

"I did." She rummaged around and found a piece of paper behind the counter. "Got the descriptions here, names, make and model of the car—"

"And you ain't seen them."

"No, I told the state trooper that about an hour ago. I'll keep an eye out."

"You do that, sweetheart."

She looked at his uniform and asked, "Spencerville? Isn't that—?"

"Sure is. That's where the kidnapping took place. Hey, if you ever get down there, you look me up."

"You're...you're the Chief Baxter whose wife—"

"That's right."

"Hey, I'm real sorry. I hope she's all right—I know she's going to be okay—"

"She'll be fine as soon as I find her. She'll be real fine. See ya."

Baxter went outside and met the cars. He got in, and Blake said, "Negative here."

"Negative there. Let's roll."

They continued on down the highway, passing several motels. Blake asked, "Want me to stop?"

"No, we're gonna cruise right into Toledo and see if that damned noisemaker goes off. If it don't, we'll double back and start checking motels. Jesus Christ, I never seen so many motels."

"You think they're here?"

"Don't know. But if I was him, and I just missed a flight, I might hole up in the area, especially if I was listenin' to the radio and found out there was a bulletin out on me. And if he don't know that, then he'll find out when he gets pulled over. He ain't gettin' too far either way."

"Right." Blake thought a moment, then said, "I don't understand how he thought he could get on a plane with her, without somebody noticing that she was being held against her will."

"Why don't you just fucking drive?"

"Yes, sir."

"He had a gun on her. That's how. And probably got her drugged up."

"Yeah, that's it."

That wasn't it, and just about every cop in the state knew that by now, Baxter thought. The truth was, he didn't see a real good future for himself or his career after this. But for the time being, he had the power, he had the law on his side, and he had the balls to do what he had to do as a man. By morning, it would start to come apart, so he had to find them before then. And because he was finished as a cop, he could do whatever he wanted to do to them when he found them.

They continued on another few miles and saw the highrise buildings of downtown Toledo in the distance.

The receiver on the dashboard beeped, a faint sound, followed by silence.

Blake and Baxter glanced at each other but said nothing. False readings, especially in built-up areas, were common. A minute later, the receiver beeped again, then again, then got louder and more continuous, until the beeps ran into one another and made a continuous electronic squeal. "Pull over."

Blake pulled onto the shoulder, and the police car behind them did the same.

Blake and Baxter sat listening to the electronic noise. Baxter looked around outside, then said, "Go ahead. Slow, on the shoulder."

Blake drove slowly on the inside shoulder. The intervals between the beeps decreased, then the sound itself grew fainter.

Baxter said, "Make a U-turn and go back."

"Right."

They swung onto the highway, then turned at a break in the median. The beeping got louder and steadier.

Baxter looked up ahead and saw it. "Well, I'll be ... hey, Blake, where do you hide a needle?"

"In a haystack."

"No, in a box of needles. Pull in there."

It took them a few minutes to locate the dark green Blazer, and even then they couldn't be sure it was the right one because it had no license plates. Baxter reached under the right rear fender and pulled off the magnetic transmitter. He looked at the rectangular device, about the size of a pack of cigarettes with a short antenna projecting from it, and smiled. "Well, well, well..." He shut it off, and the beeping from the car's receiver stopped. "How about that?"

Blake was beaming, and Krug and Ward stood looking at their chief with admiration. Everyone would have been a lot happier, of course, if the Blazer had been found at a motel, a rooming house, or a restaurant. Obviously, Keith Landry and Annie Baxter were not at the Chevy dealership. Blake was the first one to point this out and asked his chief, "Where do you think they went?"

Baxter looked around, up and down the highway, and said, "Not far."

Blake pointed out, "They could have stolen a car here, Chief."

"They could have . . . but they took the plates off this one. Now, why'd they do that if they was in another car hightailing it to Cleveland or someplace? No . . . I think they're close by, walking distance, and they didn't want this car connected to them." He looked at his three men. "Anybody got any other ideas?"

Krug said, "They could've gotten a taxi or bus from here, Chief. Could be in Toledo."

Baxter nodded. "Could be." He looked around again at the immediate area. "Taxi or bus. Could be. But I don't think so. I think they got a motel, one of them fuck places, dumped their shit, then went out to dump the car. The guy got lucky and smart when he saw this Chevy place. Yeah. They're a little walk from here. Maybe campin' out, but most likely a fuck place, or a roomin' house, where they don't need to use a credit card. Yeah. Okay, Krug, you and Ward take this side of the highway and start checkin' the motels back toward the airport. Blake and I'll start back near the airport and do the eastbound side of the highway. If you get anything, you call me and nobody else. Use the mobile phone. Let's roll."

Blake and Baxter began at the airport, drove past the Sheraton, and approached a Holiday Inn. Baxter said, "Keep goin'. We're only gonna stop at the small ram-it-inns."

"Right."

They continued on.

Baxter thought about things. Keith Landry was an asshole, but a lot smarter asshole than Baxter had figured. But maybe not smart enough. Baxter realized that he'd been out of touch with real police work for too long, but after almost three decades on the force, he'd learned a lot, remembered some, and recognized, grudgingly, that he was dealing with a pro. He wondered what Landry had done for the government and decided it had nothing to do with the U.S. Fish and Wildlife Service. But what Landry hadn't reckoned with was Chief Baxter's innate predatory instincts. What Baxter lacked in formal training, he made up for in intuition. Out in the woods of Michigan, Cliff Baxter was the best hunter of any of his friends. He had a sixth sense for locating an animal, for smelling its blood and reading its mind, for guessing if it was going to break and run, go to ground, turn and fight, or simply stand frozen, waiting for its fate. Humans, he'd decided, were not much different.

He thought next about his wife, and tried to figure out how she'd pulled this off without him really knowing about it. He had suspicions, but he always had suspicions. Somehow, she'd completely outfoxed the fox. And he knew, deep down inside, that she had an understanding of him, a result of twenty years of living with him and having to survive on her wits. When he complained about her to other women, one of the things he never said was, "My wife doesn't understand me."

He didn't want to think about his wife and Keith Landry, but in a way, he did. He sometimes pictured Annie—Miss Perfect, Miss Choir Lady, Miss Goody-Goody—having sex with another man. This had always been his worst nightmare, and it was happening now—Landry and his wife were somewhere close by, naked, in bed, laughing, having sex. Landry was on top of her, and she had her legs wrapped around him. It made him crazy to think about it. It also made him hard.

They cruised past the dark sign of the Westway Motel, still traveling east, then Baxter said, "Wait! Slow down. Pull onto the shoulder."

Blake pulled over.

Baxter sat a moment. Something had registered in his mind, but he didn't know what it was. He said, "Back up."

Blake put the cruiser in reverse, and when they came abreast of the dark signboard, Baxter said, "Stop."

Cliff Baxter got out of the car and walked over to the plastic sign with the red plastic letters and read, *Westway Motel—$29.* He got closer to the sign and saw that the battery plug was disconnected. He plugged it in, and the lights went on. He pulled the plug out, leaving the sign in darkness again.

Baxter got back into the car and said, "Back up to that side road and turn in."

"Right." Blake got onto the narrow lane, and the Spencerville police cruiser pulled up to the Westway Motel at five minutes past midnight.

Baxter said, "Wait here." He took a cardboard file case with him and went into the small lobby.

The young man behind the desk stood. "Yes, sir?"

"Lookin' for somebody, son." He put the file case on the counter. "You hear about an all-points bulletin tonight?"

"No, I didn't."

"What the hell you watchin' on TV?"

"A videotape."

"Yeah? Okay, how long you been on tonight?"

"Since four. Waiting for my relief—"

"Okay, you're my man. Now listen good. I'm lookin' for a guy drivin' a dark green Blazer. He had a woman with him, but I don't reckon she'd come in here. He's about mid-forties, tall, medium build, light brown hair, kinda gray-green eyes...and I guess not too bad-lookin'. You seen him, didn't you?"

"Well..."

"Come on, son. Man's wanted for kidnapping, and I ain't got all night, and I got fifty bucks for your time."

"Well, I had a guy in here...did this guy have glasses and a mustache?"

"Not the last time I saw him. Give me the registration card."

The clerk flipped through a stack of cards and found the one he thought the police officer wanted. "Here. This guy came in about—"

"Let me read, son." Baxter read the card. "John Westermann of Cincinnati, driving a Ford Escort. You seen his car?"

"Well, after he checked in, I poked my head out the door and there was a Ford Escort there, but that one had been there for a few hours. I'm supposed to take the license numbers—"

"I know how you run a fuck place. Did you see a green Blazer?"

"Don't know...I saw a dark four-wheel-drive outside, but it was hard to see, and it wasn't in front of the room I gave this guy Westermann. I hadn't seen it before, and I was going to go out later and get the license number, but when I went out about ten minutes later, it was gone."

Baxter nodded. "Okay, what room did you give this guy?"

"Room seven."

"He still there?"

"I guess. He took it for the night. I just checked the key drop, and it isn't there."

"Okay..." Baxter rubbed his chin. "Okay...and you never saw a woman?"

"No. Never do."

Baxter opened his file case and took out a book. It was his wife's high school yearbook, one of the few things he'd allowed her to keep, mostly because it had a picture of him in it, in his junior year, at a dance. He turned to the graduation photos and said, "Flip through this, son, and keep in mind it's over twenty years old, and imagine a mustache and glasses on the guys who don't have any. Take your time, but be quick."

The young man flipped through the pages of the small graduating class, then stopped.

"You see him?"

"I..."

Baxter took a pen out of his pocket and gave it to the man. "Draw the glasses and mustache you saw."

The man took the pen and drew glasses and a mustache on the photograph of Keith Landry. The clerk said, "Yes...that's the guy...I think that's the guy..."

"I think you're right, son. Give me the key."

The clerk hesitated, and Baxter leaned over the counter. "The fucking key."

The clerk gave him the key to room 7.

Baxter said, "You just sit tight and everything's gonna be fine. Be outa here before you know it."

"Yes, sir...uh, you mentioned—"

"Check's in the mail."

Baxter went outside to the patrol car and leaned into the window. He said to Blake, "Call the boys. We got him."

"Jesus..."

CHAPTER THIRTY-FOUR

Keith Landry and Annie Baxter lay in each other's arms. They were half-asleep, but every now and then she'd say something to him, and he replied.

He was fighting off sleep, and he suspected she was doing the same. Finally, she turned on the lamp and rolled over on top of him, nestling her head beside his neck, and bit his ear. She said, "Am I getting on your nerves?"

"No. I like that." He put his hands on her buttocks and massaged.

"Feels good." After a minute, she said, "Keith, I can't sleep."

"Try."

"I can't." She reached between them and fondled him until he got hard, then put it inside her. "That's my pacifier. Can you keep it hard until I fall asleep?"

He smiled. "I guess. Never tried it before."

"I love you."

"I adore you."

"I snore."

"Me, too."

"I drool. I absolutely drool all over everything. I'm going to drool on you."

"You're funny."

"I eat barbecued chicken and potato chips in bed, and I wipe my mouth on the sheets, and I burp."

He laughed. "Stop it."

"I have wet dreams and screaming orgasms all night.'

"Good—"

She moved her hips up and down. "I'm about to have one now."

"Oh, that feels—" He heard something at the door, then, before he could react, he heard the door crashing in, the bolt splintering through the wood.

A second later, Cliff Baxter was charging into the room with a shotgun in his hands.

Annie screamed as Keith pushed her off him. He jumped out of bed and, at the same time, grabbed his K-bar knife, which was lying under the phone book on the nightstand.

Baxter rammed the rubber-padded butt of the shotgun toward Keith's face, and Keith deflected it with his forearm, but it grazed his forehead and left him momentarily stunned. Baxter raised the stock of the shotgun again and brought it down hard on Keith's shoulder, paralyzing his arm and causing him to drop the knife. Baxter was about to swing again when Annie sprang from the bed and landed on Baxter, her arms and legs encircling him and causing him to stagger backward.

Keith, still dazed, his right arm hanging limp at his side, retrieved the knife with his left hand. His vision was blurred from the blow to his head, but he could see Annie hanging onto Baxter while Baxter tried to break her loose. Keith lunged along the floor and plunged the knife upward at Baxter's femoral artery, but the man was still staggering around, with Annie hanging onto him, and Keith didn't see the gush of arterial blood where the knife penetrated.

Baxter bellowed in pain, Annie was screaming, and before Keith could plunge the knife again, two other men were in the room, guns drawn. "Freeze! Freeze!"

Keith stood unsteadily, the knife still in his hand, and one of the cops—Keith thought it was Ward— swung his nightstick, catching Keith's wrist, and the knife flew out of his hand.

Baxter had disengaged himself from his wife, and Annie was lying on the floor, crying. The two cops still had their guns pointed at Keith, but their eyes were on their chief's naked wife.

As Keith moved toward Annie, Baxter swung the butt of the shotgun again and buried it in Keith's solar plexus. Keith doubled over and fell to his knees. He could hear Baxter screaming to his men, "Get out of here! Get the fuck out of here!"

Keith was aware of the two cops leaving, then felt the shotgun butt hit him again, this time on his back, sprawling him forward on the floor. He heard Baxter's voice, "So—fuck *me*? No! Fuck *you*! Fuck *you*!" Keith felt Baxter kicking him in the ribs, he heard Annie scream again, then felt her fall on top of him, covering him with her body, her arms wrapped tightly around his chest and her face buried in his neck. He heard her shouting, "Leave him alone! Leave him alone! Go away!"

There was a silence in the room, and Keith fought to remain conscious. He could see Baxter's legs in front of him, blood running down the man's pant leg and into his shoe.

He heard Baxter's voice again. "Get off him! Get off of him or, so help me God, I'll kill you."

"No!"

Keith heard the pump-action shotgun cocking, and

he caught his breath and said to her, "Get off...Annie, get off..."

"No!"

A voice from outside the door called into the room, "Chief! We got to get moving! Got people out here now. Police on the way!"

Baxter stuck the muzzle of the shotgun under Keith's nose. "I'll count to three, and if this bitch isn't up and getting dressed, your fucking brains will be laying on your ass. One—"

"Annie...get off..."

"Two—"

"It's okay...remember what I said—"

"Three."

He felt her arms loosen around his chest, then felt her weight lifting off him.

Baxter gave her a shove, then stepped back, but kept the shotgun pointed at Keith's face. Baxter said to him, "When I get through fucking her, there's not gonna be any fucking left in her."

Keith tried to raise himself up, but Baxter kicked him in the head, and he fell forward on his face. He heard someone shout from the doorway, "Chief! State police on the way!"

Keith kept passing in and out of consciousness. His vision was blurred, and sounds seemed to reach him from far away. He could see Annie's bare legs, then saw her legs again with jeans and slippers on, then the legs of uniformed men walking away with her, and heard her voice calling him, but couldn't make out what she was saying, except for his name.

He heard Baxter's voice more distinctly, and the voice said, "Look at you, lying there, naked as a skinned buck."

He opened his eyes and saw that Baxter was kneeling

in front of him and that Baxter had the K-bar knife in his hand. Baxter said, "You're mine now. All mine."

"Fuck you."

Baxter spit in his face and brought the heavy pommel of the knife down on Keith's head.

Keith was vaguely aware of hands on him, then his body rolling so that, when he opened his eyes, he saw the ceiling. He saw Baxter squatting over him, the knife in his hand, and he heard Baxter saying in a soft voice, "I'm just gonna relieve you of those things that got you in trouble." Keith could feel a tug at his scrotum and thought he felt Baxter's hand fondling his testicles, but he might have been imagining that, then realized he wasn't, and Baxter's voice was still droning on in a soothing tone. "So, we're just gonna take these home with us, and for the rest of your life, you can think about who's got 'em, and about who's fucking my wife and who's never gonna fuck her again—"

Keith jabbed two fingers into Baxter's right eye, and the man howled and tumbled backward, covering his face with his hands.

There were hurried footsteps in the room, the sound of urgent voices, and the image of Baxter being half dragged, half carried away by Ward and another policeman.

Keith couldn't feel any pain, except for the heavy pounding in his head, and the feeling that his eyes wanted to burst out of their sockets. A wave of nausea came over him, and he was on the verge of blacking out, but he knew he had to get on his stomach so he wouldn't drown in his own vomit. Somehow, he managed to get on his side, then got sick and felt well enough to let himself go, slipping into unconsciousness.

CHAPTER THIRTY-FIVE

What day is this?"

The nurse replied, "First tell me your name, then I'll tell you what day it is."

Keith thought that was a fair deal, so he said, "Keith Landry."

She smiled. "Today is Tuesday. You got here Sunday night—Monday morning, really."

Keith looked at the sun outside the window. "Is it morning or afternoon?"

"My turn. Who is the president of the United States?"

Keith told her and added, "He's a delightful man. I had a chat with him last week."

She frowned.

Keith realized this was not what she wanted to hear from a head injury patient, so he added, "Just kidding."

She nodded.

He tried to sit up, but she put her hand on his shoulder. "Lie still, Mr. Landry."

He regarded her a moment as she hovered over him. She was about mid-thirties, plump, friendly face, but with enough experience, he guessed, to be stern if he got frisky. He asked her, "What time is it?"

"It's eight-fifteen A.M. You've been unconscious for about thirty-six hours."

"Oh . . ." He felt a little foggy, and his head and body ached, but otherwise he thought he was all right. He tried to remember exactly what had happened, and he recalled parts of it, but it was like a piece of broken china whose fragments had to be fitted together.

The nurse asked him, "What is your address?"

He told her, and she kept asking those kinds of questions, and he saw now that she was marking a sheet of paper as he responded. He wanted to think about what happened, but she was going on and on with the questions. Finally, he remembered the last minute or two before he blacked out, and his hand went down beneath the covers and between his legs. He said, "I'm okay."

"You're fine. Good vital signs, good responses, good—"

"Good. I'm out of here." He sat up again, and again she put her hand on his shoulder.

"Lie down, Mr. Landry, or I'll have to call an attendant."

"Okay. When can I check out?"

"When the doctors sign off on you. The neurologist is making his rounds now."

"Good. Where are my things?"

"In that closet."

"Does this telephone work?"

"No. Do you want me to have it turned on?"

"Yes, please." He asked her, "Do you know what happened to me?"

She didn't reply immediately, then said, "I understand you were assaulted."

"That's right. I was with my girlfriend. Do you know anything about her?"

"No, except that there are a few items of women's

clothing in your closet." She added, "A police ambulance brought you here, and the police inventoried all the personal items that were found with you and brought everything here. I can go through it with you later, if you're concerned."

"No. I just need my wallet. Can you get that for me?"

"Later."

He thought a moment, then asked her, "Do the police want to question me?"

"Yes, they've asked that we notify them when you're up to it."

"Okay. But not today."

"We'll see."

"What is my prognosis?"

"Well...favorable."

"Did they do a CAT scan?"

"Yes. You have a hairline fracture, some internal swelling...I should let the doctor speak to you about that."

He questioned her further, but she was reluctant to give him specific medical information and only described his injuries in general terms—trauma to the midsection, the right shoulder, the left forearm, and to the head, no internal bleeding, a few contusions, lacerations, and so forth. He concluded that, if he could stand and get dressed, he was well enough to leave.

He asked her, "Where am I, exactly?"

"The Lucas County Hospital, outside of Toledo."

He nodded to himself. He was in the hands of the local government, and that included the local police, who considered him either a victim or a fugitive, or both.

She said to him, "I'll ask the doctor if you can have solid food. Do you want breakfast?"

He did, but it was time for him to play sick and

feeble. In fact, he felt weak, but not too bad otherwise except for the headache. He said, "I just want to sleep."

"All right. I'll be back later with the neurologist."

"Fine. But I need some sleep now."

She left, and Keith sat up. At some point, the police would ask the hospital to sign a fit-for-confinement slip, and he'd be transferred to a prison sick bay or similar facility. He didn't know his legal status and wasn't completely clear on his medical status, but he had no time to waste finding out or straightening it out to other people's satisfaction. Headache and fogginess notwithstanding, he knew he had to get out of where he was, and get to Spencerville and find Annie.

He pulled out the two IVs, and his veins bled. There was gauze and tape on his bed stand, and he quickly wrapped the punctures. He put his legs over the side of the bed and stood slowly. He knees buckled, but he raised himself up and took a few tentative steps around the room.

There was an elderly man in the next bed, and Keith saw he was sleeping. Keith pulled the curtain around both beds to partially block the view from the open door. He could see the nurses' station off to the left.

Keith opened the wall locker and saw his suitcase and overnight bag wedged inside, along with his briefcase and a large plastic bag filled with assorted pieces of male and female clothing and toiletry items. He pulled his suitcase out, took off his hospital gown, and dressed himself quickly in his blue Italian silk suit.

Inside the plastic bag that the police had used to gather loose items, he found the jeans, shirt, and windbreaker he'd been wearing on Sunday, but couldn't find his wallet or his license plates. Obviously, these items were in the hands of the local police. At the bottom of the plastic bag, he saw the brown and white teddy bear. He held it a moment, then dropped it back in the bag.

Keith opened his briefcase, which was still unlocked from when Annie had opened it. The police had undoubtedly looked inside, but everything that was visible seemed innocuous enough. He pushed down on the false bottom of the case, and it sprung loose. He lifted the bottom and saw that his passport was still there, as well as several hundred dollars in various denominations. He put the money in his jacket pocket, then stuffed everything except the briefcase back inside the locker and shut it. Keith carried the briefcase and walked quickly and purposefully into the hallway, glanced left and right, and located the elevators to his right. He went directly to an open elevator, stepped inside with hospital staff, and rode down to the lobby.

In the lobby, he saw a uniformed policeman sitting in a chair, reading a magazine, and across from him a man in a suit who Keith figured was a detective.

Keith went outside and spotted a taxi dropping someone off. He got into the rear of the taxi and said to the driver, "Airport, please."

The driver got onto the airport highway. It was still rush hour in both directions, Keith noticed, but they were making decent time heading away from Toledo. The commercial strip looked different in the daylight, and he noticed the Chevrolet dealership on the right, but didn't spot his Blazer. Further down, on the opposite side of the highway, he saw the sign for the Westway Motel.

He wasn't certain how Baxter had found them, but he assumed that the manhunt had been intense enough to finally turn up the only two clues he had left: the conversation with the security man at the airport, which led to an area search and eventually to the Westway Motel, the dark sign notwithstanding. America was, by no means, a police state, but it had far more policemen with far more advanced gadgetry, mobility, and resources than any police state Keith had ever been in. Nevertheless, it was only a bad break at the airport that changed the outcome of that evening so quickly and completely.

Keith knew that if he dwelled on it too much, if he let the rage and the guilt take over, he wasn't going to be able to do what he had to do. He put it out of his mind and considered his next moves. He wasn't going to get many more shots at this, if any. But all he needed was one more.

The taxi arrived at the airport, and the driver asked, "Where to?"

"Just stop over there near the USAir sign."

The driver stopped at the terminal and said, "That'll be twelve seventy-five, please."

Keith gave him a twenty, took the change, and tipped him.

He went into the terminal, turned around, and came out another door twenty feet away. He stood at the curb, looking at his watch, and seeming for all the world like a businessman who just got off a morning flight. He'd been to this airport many times over the years, and he knew the ropes. He ignored the line of taxis and said to a skycap, "Anyone around who wants to take a long ride?"

"Sure. Where you headed?"

"Lima."

"Okay." The skycap signaled to a customized van parked in the lot across the ramp. The skycap asked Keith, "Luggage?"

"No." Keith gave the skycap two dollars as the van pulled up. A skinny kid of about twenty jumped out and asked, "Where you headin'?"

"Lima. How much?"

"Oh...let's say...that's about two hours, so we got gas and the return...is fifty too much?"

"Sounds okay." Keith opened the passenger door, and the driver got in the van, and they were off. As they drove out the airport, the young man stuck out his hand. "Name's Chuck."

Keith shook his hand. "John."

"Good to know you."

"Nice van."

"Ain't she, though? Did it all myself." Chuck gave Keith a complete rundown of the customizing done on the van, a late-model Dodge. Chuck was currently unemployed and supported his expensive chroming habit by undercutting the fixed taxi rates at the airport. By the time Chuck was finished with his monologue, they were on Interstate 75, heading south.

Keith was going to tell Chuck to step on it, that he was late, but Chuck already had the van cranked up to seventy-five. Chuck saw him looking at the speedometer, laughed, and said, "Route 75, I do seventy-five. Lucky we ain't on 106." He added, "Hey, if this is too fast for you, let me know."

"It's fine."

"Yeah? Good. I got the best fuzz-buster made— right here." He tapped the radar detector on the dashboard. "Fuck them."

"Right."

He nudged it up to eighty and asked, "Where you from?"

"New York."

"Yeah? You like it?"

"It's okay."

"Never been there myself."

Keith felt a headache coming on, and his stomach heaved. He didn't know if it was because of the ride, or the beating he'd taken. Maybe it was Chuck.

Chuck glanced at him and said, "Don't mean to

be personal, but it looks like somebody whooped you upside the head real good."

Keith hadn't seen himself in a mirror, which was just as well, but he put down the visor, and there was a vanity mirror on it, surrounded by pink lights. He looked at himself. His left temple was black-and-blue and slightly swollen, and he had a cut under his right eye that was smeared with iodine, but not sutured. He also looked very pale, and there were dark circles around his eyes.

"You get mugged?"

"No, had a car accident."

"Jeez. Hey, you here on business?"

"Yes."

"No luggage?"

"No. Going back tonight."

"Thought so. You want me to wait for you? Five bucks an hour to wait."

"Maybe."

"Want to listen to the radio? Tapes?"

"Radio."

Chuck turned on the radio, a hard-rock station.

Keith hit the scan button, and a succession of stations came on for about ten seconds each, then Keith locked in an all-news station from Toledo and listened to the world news, which interested him about as much as it interested Chuck. Finally, the local news came on.

The newscaster said, "The state police announced this morning that they expect to question Keith Landry, the suspect in the Spencerville kidnapping case. Landry, of Spencerville, is currently in Lucas County Hospital suffering from head injuries resulting from an assault committed by an unknown assailant or assailants in an airport highway motel. Landry was the subject of a statewide manhunt Sunday night and early Monday morning, after the Spencerville police charged that he kidnapped Annie Baxter, the wife of the Spencerville police chief. Mrs. Baxter was not found at the motel, but the state police have been informed by the Spencerville police that Mrs. Baxter is safe and is now back with her family. The investigation will continue, according to authorities who hope to discover the identity of the assailant or assailants, and to determine what charges will be filed against Landry."

Keith hit a button, and a country-western station came on.

Chuck said, "That's something, ain't it?"

"What?"

"That kidnapping. They found the guy right near the airport back there." Chuck gave his opinion of the incident. "Like, they got all kinds of stuff on the radio, on TV, and all, and I'm thinkin', hell, if that was my girlfriend or something, the cops wouldn't go jumpin' through their asses like that. But it's another cop, you know, and this woman was like an upstanding member of the community and all, two kids, and the husband is a police chief. So, anyway, they find them...well, like they said, they never found her, which is weird, but the state police get to this motel and all, like some kind of hourly place, you know, and so they find the guy who kidnapped her, and he's all beat to shit, but nobody knows where the wife got to—when the cops got to the motel, everybody who was checked in are long gone, you know, because they don't belong there in the first place, and the only witness is this motel manager or something, and the cops ain't saying what he said. Now, I think there was two of them, two guys, Landry and another guy, and they get into an argument about who's gonna fuck her first and all that, and one of them slam-dunks the other guy, then cuts out with the wife. And they was all white people. Can you believe that shit?"

"Incredible story."

"You said it. And now they're sayin' the wife is back with her family. And the state police says the husband, the chief, is in...some word..."

"Shock?"

"Yeah, that, but...*seclusion*. In seclusion. Like layin' low. You know?"

"Yeah."

"What do you think? Two guys, right? That explains it. Cops say they don't know what happened. Big mystery. Hell, they got the motel guy, and they got the guy who got the shit beat out of him. They know, but they're not letting on. They do that sometimes. Something weird here. How did the wife get away? You know what I think? The husband paid a ransom. The cops don't want to say that another cop paid a ransom. Right?"

"Could be."

"I should be a cop. Hey, you want coffee? There's a stop up ahead."

Yes, he wanted coffee, he wanted food, he wanted to get rid of a three-day stubble and brush his teeth and wash the stench off him, but he said, "No, I'm in a hurry."

"Sure thing."

About a half hour after they started, Keith saw the exit for Route 15, westbound. He said, "Let's get off here."

"Here?"

"I have to pick up some papers at a lawyer's house."

"Okay...where's that?"

"Not sure. I have directions. If it takes a long time, I'll give you a few bucks extra."

"No problem."

They traveled west on Route 15, and Keith directed Chuck onto a series of roads that he figured the man wouldn't recall later if it ever came up.

Chuck said, "Hey, you got all this memorized, right?"

"Sure do."

"What town is it?"

"It's a farm. Lawyer lives in a farmhouse."

"Okay."

They got onto County Road 22, and as they approached his farm, Keith realized there was something wrong. What was wrong with the skyline—there was no house there.

Keith stood in front of the charred ruins of what had once been his home, his father's home, his grandfather's home.

Chuck said, "Jesus...you think everybody got out all right?"

Keith didn't reply. He looked at the other buildings, which still stood, then out at the endless fields of corn, the deep blue sky, the distant tree line.

Chuck asked, "What do you want to do now?"

What he wanted to do was sit on the ground and look at the house until the sun went down. What he had to do was something else.

It had been a little over an hour since he'd walked out of the hospital. The staff would not have discovered that immediately, and when they did, there'd be an in-hospital search, some confusion, and finally the police in the Toledo area would be notified. Keith figured there would be some lag time before the state police were notified, and more time before someone thought to notify the Spencerville police, who in turn were undoubtedly not famous for their reaction time. Still, the first place they'd look for him was here. He jumped back into the van.

Chuck got behind the wheel. "Where to?"

"Spencerville."

CHAPTER THIRTY-SIX

They drove into Spencerville, and Chuck commented, "Hey, there's the police station. This is some coincidence, ain't it? I mean, you comin' all the way from New York and windin' up here where this kidnapping happened. Not a bad-looking little town. Where's this lawyer's office?"

"In his other house. Turn over here."

Keith directed Chuck to the north side of town, and, within a few minutes, they were on Williams Street. Keith had no expectation that Annie and Cliff Baxter would be there, sitting around trying to iron out their differences. They were in seclusion, and Williams Street was not seclusion. The van passed the house, and Keith saw the white Lincoln in the driveway, but there was no other sign that anyone was home, and no obvious sign that the house was being watched. He said to Chuck, "Pull over here."

Chuck pulled over to the curb.

Perhaps by now, the Spencerville police knew that Keith Landry had escaped from the hospital, and if they did, their first thought would probably be that Landry was fleeing the state. But their second thought might well be that Landry was headed back to Spencerville, though they'd think that was a long shot. Still, they'd be on some sort of alert and would probably stake out the farm. But Keith knew there would be two places they wouldn't expect to see him: the police station and the Baxter house.

Keith got out and said, "Be about ten minutes." He took his briefcase and walked to the Baxter house. It was a cool morning, and there was no one on the porches, and no one visible on the street at all. He walked up the driveway and headed toward the rear. If anyone was watching from a window, the blue trust-me suit and briefcase gave off a message of respectability and legitimate purpose.

There was a kennel at the end of the yard, but Keith couldn't see or hear any dogs.

Keith walked up to the rear porch, opened the screen door, and tried the knob on the back door, but it was locked. He looked in both neighboring yards and at the windows of the surrounding houses, but didn't see anyone through the high hedges. Holding the screen door open with his leg, he drove the corner of his briefcase through one of the windowpanes, reached inside, and unlocked the door. He slipped quickly inside, closing the door behind him.

Keith looked around the kitchen, noting its cleanliness and orderliness. He opened the refrigerator and saw that it was nearly empty, which was probably not the way it usually was. Clearly, the Baxters were gone and were not coming back for some time.

He opened the basement door and went down the stairs. He found the den and turned on the lights. A few dozen animal heads were mounted on the walls, and he noted the gun rack that could hold twelve rifles or shotguns. It was completely empty.

He went upstairs again and glanced into the dining

room and living room, again noting how clean and tidy everything was. He opened the coat closet in the foyer and saw that there was only one man's civilian trench coat and one police uniform topcoat and two ladies' overcoats. All the casual and cold weather outerwear was missing.

Keith went upstairs and glanced into a boy's bedroom and a girl's bedroom, then into a room that was a home office. He went into the office and rummaged around, pulled some Rolodex cards, then left. He found the master bedroom and opened the two closets. Again, only dress clothes hung on the poles, and whatever casual and outdoor clothes and footwear there may have been were gone. In Cliff Baxter's closet were four neat police uniforms—two summer and two winter, along with the accessory shoes, hats, and belts. The bureau drawers were pulled open, and most of the underwear was gone. Keith had a pretty good idea where they had gone, and by the looks of what they'd taken, Baxter intended to be away a long time, perhaps forever. Most important—if her missing clothes were a true indication, it appeared that Annie was alive and that he intended to keep her alive.

Keith went into the master bathroom and saw that the medicine cabinet was open. There was a bloody towel on the sink, blood in the washbasin, and on the counter were a box of gauze, a bandage roll, and a bottle of iodine. On the floor was Baxter's tan uniform, the trousers stained with dried blood.

An inch or so to the left or right, Keith thought, maybe a half inch deeper, and he'd have severed the femoral. Better yet, if he'd reached Toledo Airport an hour earlier, they'd be in Washington now. And if he hadn't gone with Adair to Washington on Thursday, he and Annie would be in Rome by now. And so on and so forth. It didn't do any good to dwell on the bad timing; the important thing was that he and Annie were alive and fate had given them one more chance to be together.

He picked up Baxter's bloody trousers from the floor and went back into the master bedroom. Like most of the house, it had sort of a country look—oak furniture, hooked rugs, chintz curtains, and dried flowers. It struck him that Annie, despite her bad marriage, or perhaps because of it, had taken a great deal of time and trouble with the house, the small details, the touches of hominess and warmth. He supposed she did it out of pride, or out of a need to present a normal setting for her children or her friends and family, but also out of a longing for a life and a marriage that in some small way reflected the surroundings she'd created of home and hearth, peace and caring. Keith, for some reason, found it all very sad and troubling.

There was no great need to be here, he knew, and the risk probably outweighed whatever information he could gather. But he knew he had to come here, to be a voyeur and peek into the lives of Cliff and Annie Baxter, two people who, more than any others, had so profoundly changed and influenced his life.

Cliff Baxter, who as a schoolmate had never been invited into the Landry home, had very recently broken into it and, in some way, Keith reflected, that violation was more flagrant than Baxter's burning of the house, or even what had happened in the motel room. Keith had no intention of burning the Baxter house down, because it was filled with Annie's things and her children's things. But he felt that he had to leave behind some evidence of his presence, some mark of contempt—though not, he thought, for Cliff Baxter to see, because Keith had decided that Baxter would never see this house again. But he wanted to do something for himself, and for the record.

Keith examined his handiwork in the living room. Sitting in the wing-back chair was Baxter's bloody uniform, stuffed with towels and linens, and protruding from the neck of the uniform shirt was the stuffed head of a wolf.

Keith told himself he wasn't crazy, that the blow to the head had not affected his judgment. But neither was he the same man he had been before Cliff Baxter came crashing through the door of the motel room. Keith stared at the wolf head atop the uniform. The white teeth and the glassy eyes mesmerized him for a moment, and he knew that to kill that thing, he would have to become that thing. Clearly, his better angels had been chased away, and he felt the dark wolf rising again in his heart.

"You get what you needed?" Chuck asked.

"Yes."

"Off to Lima?"

"A few more stops first."

Keith directed him out to the commercial strip and into the parking lot of a 7-Eleven. Keith took sixty dollars out of his pocket and handed it to Chuck. "Take this for now."

"That's okay, John. I know you're good for it."

Keith put the money on the dashboard. "You just never know, Chuck. Go get yourself something to eat. You have some change?"

"Sure." Chuck handed him a pocketful of loose change, and Keith got out and went to the phone booth, while Chuck went into the convenience store. Keith took one of the Rolodex cards out of his pocket and dialed. He wasn't feeling appreciably better physically, but mentally he was much better, sure she was alive, though not letting himself think of what she was going through.

"Hello?"

"Terry, it's me."

"Oh, my God! Keith, Keith, where are you?"

"I'm on the road. Where is Annie?"

"I don't know. They came back to Spencerville, she called me and said they were going away to spend time together and talk it out. She said they were going to Florida."

Keith knew they hadn't packed for Florida. "How did she sound?"

"It was all a lie. Damn him, he probably had a gun to her head. That bastard. I called the police here in Chatham, but they said they can't do a thing without proof, and I should call Spencerville—"

"I know. Terry, listen, I'm going to find her and bring her back. Tell me where you think they really went."

"Grey Lake."

"I think so, too. Did she give you any clue on the phone?"

There was a silence, then Terry said, "Yeah, she said something...something about driving through Atlanta on the way, and afterward I remembered that Atlanta is also the name of the county seat in Montmorency County in Michigan on the way to Grey Lake. I think that's where they really went, but I called up there a few times and only got the answering machine. So I don't know..."

"Okay. I think that's it."

"Larry wants to drive up there—"

"No. Baxter is armed and dangerous. I'll take care of it through the local police up there."

"The police won't do anything, Keith. She's his wife. That's what they keep telling me."

"I'll take care of it."

"What happened? I thought you were about to get on a plane?"

"It's a long story, but basically we were stopped by the police."

"Damn!"

"Right. But she was all right when they took her away."

"I don't think she's all right now. My father has been hounding the state police, and he's gotten a lawyer, but . . . I can't believe that bastard could just kidnap her—"

"When did she call you?"

"Monday night, about six. She said she changed her mind about going with you and that she and Cliff were home and they'd spent the day together at home, packed, and were about to drive to Florida. She said she'd called the kids at school and told them everything was fine, and that she and their father were going on vacation. But I called her kids after I heard from her, and they said they never heard from their mother—it was their father who called early in the morning. So then I called Annie back, but the damn call rang at police headquarters, and I asked them what the hell was going on, and they said the Baxter calls were being automatically forwarded . . . so then my father went to the police station, and they told him Cliff and Annie went to Florida. It's all a lot of bull."

"Okay, do me a favor—don't rock the boat anymore, and tell everyone the same thing. I don't want to spook him if he's up there. Okay?"

"Okay . . ."

"What does the house look like, Terry?"

"Oh, jeez...I was only up there a few times...it's an A-frame, dark wood, set back a ways from the lake."

"What side of the lake?"

"Let's see...north side. Yes, north side of the lake, and you can only get to it by a single-lane dirt road through the woods."

"Okay. Tell Larry I said hello. I'll call you both tonight from Michigan."

"Promise?"

"You know I will, Terry. Hey, I'm sorry—"

"No, don't apologize. You did the best you could. That bastard is the devil—I swear he is."

"I'll bring his tail and horns back for you."

She tried to laugh. "Oh, God...I'd kill him myself if I could...Keith?"

"Yes?"

"If she can't be with you, she'd rather be dead than be with him. I'm frightened for her."

"I told her we'd be together again. She knows that."

"I pray to God you're right."

"Speak to you tonight." He hung up and took another Rolodex card out of his pocket and dialed.

The operator gave him the charge, and he put the coins in and heard it ring.

An answering machine picked up, and Cliff Baxter's voice said, "You reached Big Chief Cliff's lodge. Ain't nobody here. If you know where the fish is bitin', or the deer is hidin', leave a message."

The machine beeped, and Keith was tempted, but hung up.

Keith took another Rolodex out of his pocket on which were the mobile phone numbers of Spencerville's ten police cars and the beeper page numbers of all fifteen officers. He dialed a beeper number, hung up, and waited.

The phone rang, and he picked it up. "Officer Schenley?"

"Who is this?"

Keith could tell that Schenley was calling from his mobile phone. Keith replied, "This is Keith Landry."

There was a pause, then Schenley said, "How'd you know my beeper number?"

"Doesn't matter. Are you alone?"

"Yup. Cruising. Looking for you, as a matter of fact."

"Well, here I am."

"Where?"

"Let me ask the questions. Do you have a friend on the city council?"

Again, there was a pause, then Schenley said, "Maybe."

"That's my friend, too."

"I know."

"I need some help."

"I guess you do. I'm surprised you're alive."

"Do you want to help?"

"Hold on. Let me pull over." A minute later, Schenley said, "Okay. Listen, Landry, there's a warrant out for your arrest."

"For what?"

"Well, this and that. All bullshit. Signed by Judge Thornsby here, who'll sign anything Baxter shoves under his nose. But there's no state warrant for kidnapping. On the other hand, we just got a message that the state police are looking for you as a witness."

"Witness to what?"

"You know to what. To what happened at that motel."

"Were you there?"

"No. Baxter wouldn't take me on that kind of thing,

and I wouldn't go. But I was on the desk that night."
He added, "I didn't like what I saw."

"What did you see?"

"Well...damn, I'm a cop, Landry, and you're a
fugitive—"

"Are you sleeping well?"

"No."

"Schenley, you understand that Baxter has broken
the law, and that when it hits the fan, everybody goes
down with him. He doesn't care about you or the men."

"I don't need convincing."

"How do the men feel?"

"Scared. But happy he isn't here."

"Does he call?"

"Maybe. If he does, he only calls Blake."

Neither man spoke for a few seconds, then Schenley
said, "Okay, about two A.M. Monday, I'm on the desk,
and Baxter gets in from Toledo with the three guys he
took with him—no names, okay? And with them is...
her. He brings her into the station house, in cuffs for
God's sake, and puts her in a cell. He's got blood all
over his pants, down his left leg, and he's limping, and
you can tell he's in pain, and his right eye's got blood
in it, too, like somebody smacked him or poked him,
and he's swearing like a trooper. Anyway, then he leaves
with one of the guys, and the other two stay there. One
of the guys tells me you tried to knife the chief in the
balls. Then, about an hour later, Baxter comes back
with his Bronco, and he's in civvies now, and he takes
her away in cuffs. I saw that the Bronco was packed
with clothes and stuff, and Baxter's three dogs were in
the back."

Keith nodded. "Where did they go?"

"I don't know. I heard something about Florida.
But I know I saw him turn south on Chestnut Street,

and I remember wondering why he wasn't heading east to pick up a highway."

"Because he made a stop at my place first."

"Yeah...I know. Sorry."

"Has anyone gone out to the Porter house to look for me?"

"Yeah. Ward's out that way. The Porters aren't home, but Ward cruises by once in a while."

"How many men in a car?"

"One. We got to cover a lot of ground. They think you're heading back this way. They got all the honorary deputy sheriffs out, too, and they also called out the mounted posse. They haven't done that in about five years since a kid went missing. There's about twenty deputies out in their private cars, and maybe twenty mounted posse. Hey, if you're not in Spencer County, don't come."

"Thanks. I won't." Keith asked, "Did she look all right?"

Schenley didn't reply immediately, then said, "As well as can be expected." He added, "She had a bruise on her face...you know, when she was in the cell, I wanted to talk to her, but the other two guys were there, and I felt about as bad as I've ever felt. She just sat there, no crying, no screaming, just sort of, like, above it all—very classy lady—and when she looked at me and the other two guys, there wasn't any, like, hate or anything, just sort of like...she felt sorry for *us*—"

"Okay...thanks. I'll remember the favor if it ever comes up in court."

"Thanks, Landry. This is a damned mess. I can't understand how these three guys, who I thought I knew, could do what they did."

"When we know that, we'll have solved most of the world's problems." He added, "I'll put in a good word for you with Pastor Wilkes."

Schenley laughed, then said, "Hey, for your information, Baxter had a homing transmitter on your Blazer."

Damn it. He asked Schenley, "What color is his Bronco?"

"Black." He gave him the license plate number and added, "Hey, let it go, Landry. Stay away from here. They're looking for you, and Baxter's long gone."

"Yeah, but maybe I'll head for Florida, too."

"He'll kill you next time. The other guys with him say they had to pull him off you before he killed you."

"Thanks again." Keith hung up and got back into the van, where Chuck was drinking a Big Gulp and eating a donut.

Chuck said, "Got extra donuts here."

"Thanks. Make a left."

"Sure thing." Chuck pulled out of the 7-Eleven and made a left on the commercial strip. He said, "This ain't the way to Lima."

"No. Make another left at the light."

"Sure thing. Don't mean to be nosy, John, but I get the feeling something's bothering you."

"No, I'm fine, Chuck. In fact, that phone call just restored my faith in the human race."

"Yeah? Sorry I missed that."

"But don't miss your turn. Left here."

They headed south into the country.

Keith thought about what Schenley had said and what Terry had said. Obviously, the call that Annie had made to Terry on Monday night was not made from Spencerville, but from Grey Lake if Schenley's chronology was correct, and it probably was. If Baxter had left Spencerville about three A.M., he'd have been at Grey Lake about nine or ten A.M., with a side trip to burn down the Landry house. Baxter had called his children from Grey Lake in the morning, then made Annie call her sister much later, probably after he realized that all the news reports about the Baxters being reunited and in seclusion needed to be verified by Annie to at least one family member. Also, the Florida story had to be put out. Again, Keith thought, Baxter was not only vicious but cunning. A bad combination.

Keith had no idea what was going on at Grey Lake, but he knew it wasn't a reconciliation. He tried to take some comfort in Annie's assurance that she could handle Cliff Baxter. But in truth, after what Baxter had seen—his wife and her lover naked in bed together—Keith was certain that Baxter had snapped. If he was even halfway rational, he wouldn't have kidnapped his own wife and left such a mess behind; he would have stayed around to protect his job, his power, and his reputation. But obviously the man knew he was finished, and with that knowledge, whatever social control he'd managed to maintain up to now was gone.

But he wouldn't kill her. No, but he'd make her wish she were dead.

Keith directed Chuck to an intersecting highway, then gave him a few other directions. Chuck asked, "How do you know this place so good?"

"I was born here."

"No shit? Hey, you're a Buckeye! Give me five, John!"

Keith felt compelled to solidify the camaraderie, and they did high fives.

A few minutes later, they approached the Porter house. Keith could see for a good distance in all directions, and he didn't see any police cars, or in fact any vehicles, not even the Porters' car in their gravel driveway. "Pull in here, Chuck."

Chuck pulled into the drive, and Keith said to him, "Thanks, buddy. This is it."

"This ain't Lima."

"I guess not. There's the sixty, and here's twenty more. See you next time I'm in Toledo."

"Hey, thanks."

Keith opened the door and got out. He said, "I love this van."

"Ain't she somethin'?"

Keith moved quickly to the back of the house. There was no one in the herb gardens, but the back door was unlocked, and he went inside. He called out, but no one answered. Keith put his briefcase on the counter, locked the back door, then went around to the front door and bolted it.

He went back to the kitchen, opened the refrigerator, and took a bottle of orange juice and a bran muffin, which he ate as he drank the juice straight from the bottle. He finished both and felt his stomach heave, but managed to keep it all down. He was definitely not well and was operating on pure adrenaline and hate.

He had no idea where the Porters were, or when they'd be back, but he was actually glad they weren't around.

At some point, the Spencerville police, or the sheriff, or the posse, or the deputies, or somebody would come around again, and he had to get moving. It was nearly three hundred miles to northern Michigan, and he needed a rifle, a car, clothing, and the other odds and ends of the killing game.

He went into the front foyer and started up the stairs, then heard a knock on the front door.

Keith went quickly to the living room and peered out the window. Parked in front of the house was a Spencerville police car.

There was no one in the car, so the question was, How many cops were around the house? Schenley said only one in each car. There was another, more insistent knock.

Keith didn't have to answer it, of course, but if it was one of the men who had accompanied Baxter to the motel, Keith wanted to say hello and maybe borrow the car and the shotgun in the car.

He peered sideways out the window and saw Kevin Ward, his thumbs hooked in his gun belt, not looking very alert.

Keith went to the front door and opened it. "Hi."

Before Ward could react, Keith delivered an uppercut to Ward's groin, then as Ward doubled over, Keith pulled him inside, kicked the door closed, and delivered a powerful handchop to Ward's neck. Ward crumpled to the floor, semiconscious.

Keith took Ward's handcuffs and cuffed his right wrist, then snapped the other cuff to the radiator's steam pipe. Keith unbuckled Ward's gun belt and pulled it off.

Ward was coming to now, and Keith said to him, "You looking for me?"

Ward lay on his side, and it took him a few seconds to realize he was tethered to the steam pipe. He stared up at Keith and said, "You fucking..."

Keith drew Ward's service revolver, aimed it at Ward's head, and cocked it. "Where's your boss?"

"Fuck you."

Keith fired into the wooden floor in front of Ward's face, and the man actually levitated off the floorboards.

Ward shouted, "Florida! He's in Florida!"

"Where in Florida?"

"I don't..."

Keith fired again into the floor near Ward's head, and again Ward bounced, then yelled, "Stop! He went...I think he went to Daytona. Yeah, to Daytona."

"Where in Daytona?"

"I...he never told us."

"Okay. She with him?"

"Yeah."

"Did you have fun at the motel?"

"No."

"Looked like you were having fun."

"I was scared shitless."

"Not as scared as you are now."

"No. Hey, Landry, I just follow orders."

"Every time I hear that, I want to kill the guy who said it."

"Give me a break. You got me down. I told you what I know. Hey, for all I care, you can go down to Daytona and kill the son-of-a-bitch. I hate him."

"And he's not real happy with you either. You saw his wife naked. You better hope I kill him, or you have a career problem."

Keith holstered the revolver and climbed the stairs before Ward started to think about that. With any luck, Ward knew that Baxter was at Grey Lake and would call Baxter to say he'd been a good boy and sent Landry off to Florida. It didn't matter that much either way, but you never passed up an opportunity to play the great flimflam game.

Keith found the master bedroom, which had a very lived-in look, with clothes strewn around, the bed unmade, and every object out of place. He got down on the floor and reached under the bed, hoping that Gail had taken him literally and put the rifle there, but he couldn't feel the carrying case. He looked around the room. In truth, the rifle could be on the floor, and he wouldn't see it amidst the junk. He went around to the other side and looked under the bed, but aside from the clutter, there wasn't anything resembling a canvas carrying case.

A voice said, "Looking for this?"

Keith straightened up and saw the muzzle of the M-16 rifle resting on the edge of the mattress. Keith stood and said, "Hello, Charlie."

Charlie Adair dropped the rifle on the bed and said, "You look like shit."

"Thank you. You, too."

"Did I hear you assaulting and abusing an officer of the law downstairs?"

"He was that way when I found him."

"That was very clever—getting the Florida story out of him, and you know that's not where they went. You're very good in the field. I always thought your real talents were wasted behind a desk."

"That's what I've been saying." Keith had no idea how Charlie Adair knew that Baxter and Annie had not gone to Florida. For that matter, he had no idea how Charlie had wound up in the Porter house.

Adair looked around the room. "With friends like these, you don't have to raise pigs."

"They're good people."

"They're left-wing radicals."

"Don't check out my friends, Charlie. I don't like that."

"These are the kinds of friends I have to check out."

"No, you don't."

"Actually, they *are* nice people."

"How'd you get onto them? Or should I ask?"

"You shouldn't. You should tell me."

Keith thought a moment, then said, "Telephone records."

"Bingo. You haven't made many calls since you've been here, so it was easy. Don't be impressed."

"I'm not." He asked, "Where are the Porters?"

"Running errands. Hey, I never saw a man in an Armani suit step out of an iridescent van. Who was that guy?"

"Chuck. From Toledo Airport."

"Ah. Good. He coming back?"

"No."

"You're without transportation."

"I have a police car. Where's your transport?"

"I just clicked my heels, and here I am."

"Charlie...I already have a headache. What can I do for you?"

"That's not the question, Keith. Ask not what you can do for your country, but what your country can do for you."

"That's not how it goes."

"Unfortunately, Keith, that's exactly how it goes in Washington, the big tit of the world. Your country is here to help you."

"With no strings attached."

"I didn't say that."

"I don't really have time for this."

"A little time with me will save you a lot of time later. Hey, can we get out of this sty? I think I saw a clean spot downstairs."

Keith took the rifle off the bed, and, carrying Ward's gun belt and holster, he followed Charlie into the upstairs hallway, where Charlie picked up the carrying case with the scope and ammunition. It was just like Adair, Keith thought, to materialize out of nowhere, brandishing a rifle that could just as well have been in its case—Charlie Adair was all show, mostly drama and comedy, but one day, for sure, tragedy.

They came down into the front foyer, and Charlie went over to Kevin Ward on the floor and stuck out his hand. "Hi, I'm Barry Brown from Amway."

Keith almost laughed as Ward actually put out his left hand and shook with Charlie.

Charlie said, "I have some stuff that'll make that uniform look like new again. I'll be right back. Stay there."

Keith and Charlie went into the kitchen. Charlie washed two glasses in the sink and said to Keith, "There's fresh tomato juice in the refrigerator."

Keith got the pitcher out and poured two glasses. Charlie touched his glass to Keith's and said, "Good to see you alive."

"Good to be alive, not good to see you."

"Of course it is."

They drank. Charlie smacked his lips. "Not bad. Needs vodka. But maybe you shouldn't drink. You really look like shit. I guess Chief Baxter got ahold of you."

Keith didn't reply.

"Let's go out back where we can talk."

They went outside, and Charlie sat in a lawn chair, looking out over the gardens. "Beautiful."

Keith remained standing. He said, "Charlie, I'm on a schedule."

"Right. Okay, I won't be too cryptic. Here's what I know. You got back here from Washington on Saturday, missed your rendezvous with Mrs. Baxter, but by Sunday night you were both gone, according to what I've pieced together. By about nine P.M. Sunday, the whole fucking state of Ohio was looking for you on suspicion of kidnapping, but for some odd reason, the FBI wasn't notified of a possible kidnapping with probable flight across state lines. The next we hear from the Ohio police is that they've found your naked and battered person in some fuckarama out by Toledo Airport, sans Mrs. Baxter. You're in Lucas County Hospital with a mild concussion, and so on and so forth. Mr. and Mrs. Baxter are reunited and are on a second honeymoon in Florida. So I fly out to Toledo on Monday morning and look in on you, but you're still out cold. I get a local FBI guy to keep an eye on you so that Mr. Baxter doesn't return to retrieve your balls, which they tell me are intact, then I come out to Spencerville and do some old-fashioned snooping. By Monday night, I've had bean curd with the Porters, and we've become great buddies despite our political differences." He looked at Keith and said, "I went out to your place, of course. Sorry."

"It's okay."

"I don't think so. So you want to find him, kill him, and get her back."

Keith didn't reply.

Charlie continued, "Anyway, I'm staying out at the local mom-and-pop motel, and this morning I get a call from the FBI guy at the hospital, and he's all upset to have to tell me you gave him the sliperoo. I'm impressed. Not with the FBI guy, of course. I mean, the last time I saw you Monday morning, you looked like you couldn't get into any trouble. So I get a federal marshal to go out to the sister's place in wherever the hell that is and do a stakeout, then I get all kinds of phones tapped, courtesy of a federal judge in Toledo, and I come here to the Porters', taking a chance that you'd show up. Meanwhile, I've got a federal writ of habeas corpus in my pocket in case some of the locals pick you up. All I have to do is fill in the blanks. Isn't this wonderful? I *can* do anything I want. But I'm on the side of the angels with this one, buddy, so any minor abuse of federal power can be forgiven." He added, "We take care of our own, Keith. We always have."

"I know."

"I'm here to help."

"I know you are, Charlie. But I don't think I need your help."

"Sure you do. You need a car, clothes, and some good hunting gear."

"Why do I need that?"

"To go up to Michigan. That's what you told Terry on the phone."

Keith shook his head. "You're a piece of work. You know that? Look, I'm not going to sell my soul for a pair of boots. I can handle this myself."

"Let me apprise you of your situation. You have a cold-cocked cop in the front foyer, no car, no home, damned few friends, not much if any money, every cop in this county is looking for you, you're wearing a silk suit and tight shoes, you're walking with a slight wobble, my friend, and your only decent weapon, discounting the cop's pea-shooter, is that M-16, which is really not your property, but Uncle Sam's, and I might just take it with me."

"I wouldn't try that."

Charlie took out a pack of cigarettes. "The Porters said I could smoke here. They smoke grass." He lit a cigarette and said, "Isn't it a great feeling to be part of a big, powerful, omnipotent organization?"

"You tell me. Is that what you need to feel good about yourself?"

"Actually, yes. You, too."

"Wrong. Hey, I thought you were on my side. Remember? Dragons on my shield, rats in the cellar?"

"That was Friday. This is Tuesday, and you're vulnerable again."

"Wrong again. I'm on a pure quest, Charlie. I'm a knight again, and I'm going to rescue the damsel in distress from the monster. This is a good fight, and knights always do this alone. Fuck the king and all the king's men. That includes you."

Charlie thought a moment, then replied, "Okay. I get it. No strings attached, but I'm not letting Sir Keith go up there without the things he needs. I'll just supply what you need for the mission, and you go up to Michigan and take this guy out, then you get yourself to... let's say Detroit. The downtown Marriott. I'll book a room. If you don't show up by this time tomorrow, I'll assume it didn't go your way. If you do show up, you and Mrs. Baxter and I will celebrate. No strings."

Keith didn't reply.

Charlie continued, "I told the people in Washington you had personal matters to take care of. All they want from you is a yes or no by Friday. Gives you time to think about it, if you're alive tomorrow. If you're dead, I'll tell them you're terminally inconvenienced. Anyway, after you get out of here, you're on your own. Just like old times, when I kissed you good-bye at some fucked-up border crossing or airport. But I have to feel that I've given you every advantage before you leave. Just like old times, Keith. Let me do that for you."

"Why?"

"I like you. I didn't like Chief Baxter. I don't like what he did. I want you to be happy. A happy man makes happy decisions."

Again, Keith didn't reply.

"If nothing else, think of the Porters. They have a cop in the foyer. I'll take care of that for you and for them."

"I'll take care of that." Keith asked, "Where are the Porters, Charlie?"

"Running errands."

"*Where* are they running errands?"

"Antioch. I sent them away. Hey, they were telling me about the Antioch rules of sexual conduct. I laughed my ass off. But it's not funny." He added,

"Actually, I like them. They promised to vote Republican next time. You want another juice? I'll get it."

"No. You have to get going."

"Okay." Charlie put his juice glass on the ground and stood. He took an envelope out of his pocket and said, "I have a thousand dollars for you."

"I don't want Uncle's money."

"It's *my* money. Personal."

"No, it's not."

"Well, it's an advance on your pension check."

"Keep it."

Charlie shrugged and put the envelope back in his pocket. He said, "Self-reliance, chivalry, and knighthood are dead, Keith."

"Forgive me for sounding pompous, but they're not dead while I'm still alive."

"Then they'll be dead by tomorrow. Okay, I tried. Good luck, my friend."

They shook hands, and Charlie Adair walked away, across the yard and through the herb gardens, then disappeared into the cornfield, like some sort of ethereal nature sprite, which was the effect Charlie was looking for, Keith knew. Keith liked a man with style, but sometimes Charlie overdid it a bit.

Keith kept watching the wall of corn, and sure enough he saw the tall stalks start to move, then flatten as Charlie Adair drove out of the cornfield in a gray Ford Taurus.

Charlie went through a flower bed and across the lawn and stopped near Keith. "I'm at the Maple Motel."

"Good choice."

"No choice. Hey, she must be a hell of a lady."

"She is."

"Is she as good as what's-her-name in Georgetown?"

"I don't remember what's-her-name in Georgetown."

"Well, if she's that good, then you owe her a better chance than you're giving her."

"I have to do it without your help or any help from Uncle. Keith will learn how to handle problems on his own."

"As you wish." Charlie added, "You created the fucking problem."

Keith didn't reply.

Charlie said, "I mean, really, Keith, a guy who slipped in and out of East Germany a dozen times can't even get the fuck out of Ohio? Jesus Christ."

"Don't bait me. I'm not in the mood."

"You don't have to prove anything. You fucked up, now you need help. No big deal. Your problem is that your ego is too big. You never were a team player, Keith. I'm surprised you weren't killed or fired long ago. Well, you've cheated death all over the world for too many years—don't get iced here."

"Thank you for your concern."

"Fuck you, Keith." Charlie hit the gas and drove away, across the yard and out to the street.

Keith had the strong suspicion that he hadn't seen the last of Charlie Adair.

CHAPTER THIRTY-SEVEN

Keith drove the blue and white police car west, along a straight, flat farm road that was barely wide enough for two cars to pass. The walls of tall corn came almost up to the gravel, creating the effect of driving in a deep trench.

Keith had on Ward's hat and shirt, but so far he hadn't passed another police car or sheriff's car on the way from the Porter house. He was mindful, however, of the deputies driving their own vehicles, but he hadn't seen any uniformed deputies in private cars, nor had he seen any mounted posse. Spencer County was big, he knew, about six hundred square miles, and the distance between the Porter house and the Cowley farm was only about ten miles. With any luck, he'd get there, though he didn't know what he'd find when he did.

Keith had encouraged Officer Ward to radio headquarters and give a situation report, and Sergeant Blake had reprimanded Ward for being away from the car so long. Ward, with his own revolver being held to his head, his hands cuffed behind his back, his groin somewhat achy, and his sergeant chewing him out, was a truly unhappy man. He was less happy now, Keith suspected, bouncing around in the trunk. But that was

Officer Ward's own fault and was the least of Ward's problems and the least of Keith's problems.

The farm road ended at the T-intersection of Route 8, and Keith turned onto it.

As he approached the Cowley farm, Keith saw five mounted men with rifles and dogs coming out of a tree line and onto the road in front of him. Keith slowed down as the troop crossed the road, and everyone waved. Keith waved back. One of the mounted posse reined his horse around and came toward him. Keith didn't know if the horseman would know every cop on the force by sight, but he did know that the blue Armani trousers weren't going to pass inspection, not to mention the problem of Officer Ward, who now and then kicked and shouted.

As the horseman approached, Keith waved again and accelerated past him as if Keith didn't understand that the man wanted to speak to him. Keith looked in his rearview mirror and watched the horseman looking at him.

Keith passed the Cowley farm and noticed Billy Marlon's blue pickup truck near the house. He continued on a mile up the road, then made a U-turn and came back.

The mounted posse was in the far distance now, and Keith swung the police car into the driveway of the farmhouse, then veered off, avoiding the pickup truck, and headed straight for an old cowshed. He hit the double doors, and they burst inward. He slammed on the brakes, but not in time to avoid hitting a pile of milk cans, which toppled over with a deafening crash.

Ward shouted something from the trunk.

Keith shut off the ignition, then took off Ward's hat and shirt and strapped on Ward's gun belt. He gathered his M-16 rifle and the rack-mounted police shotgun, then went around to the trunk and rapped on it. "You okay?"

"Yeah. Let me out."

"Later." Keith walked out of the cowshed and met Billy Marlon coming toward him.

Marlon looked at the police car in the shed, then at Keith and said, "Jesus Christ."

"Not even close. Are you alone?"

"Yeah."

"Let's get in the house." He gave Marlon the shotgun to carry.

Billy Marlon was understandably agitated and confused, but he followed Keith into the farmhouse. Marlon said, "Hey, they're lookin' for you."

"Who was here?"

"That bastard Krug. Asked me if I seen you, and I told him I didn't even know who the fuck you were."

"He buy it?"

"Sort of. He reminded me that you helped me out of a scrape with the law—hey, thanks for the money. I found it. I thought you was gone."

"I came back. You sober?"

"Sure. I'm broke, I'm sober." Billy looked at Keith. "What the hell happened to you?"

"I got drunk and fell down the stairs."

"No shit? Hey, something else, there was a guy here yesterday, can't remember his name, says he was a friend of yours and that the Porters told him you might be here—"

"Charlie?"

"Yeah...kinda all spiffed-up, light hair, wiseass—"

"Charlie."

"Yeah. Lookin' for you. I showed him that note you left me and told him you was gone, but he said you might be around. What the hell's goin' on? What's all the hardware for?"

"I don't have a lot of time, Billy. I need your help."

"Anything you want, you got it, if I got it to give."

"Good. I need your pickup truck and a pair of boots. Do you have camouflage fatigues?"

"Sure do."

"Binoculars, compass?"

"You got it. You goin' huntin'?"

"Yup. Got to get moving."

"Come on upstairs."

They went up the stairs of the tidy farmhouse and into a small bedroom.

Billy pulled his hunting gear out of a closet, and Keith took off his suit pants and shoes, saying to Marlon, "Burn these."

"Burn . . . ?"

"Burn everything I leave here."

Keith tried on the tiger fatigue pants, which were a little snug and less than clean, but for a man who hadn't bathed since Sunday morning, it was okay. The boots fit fine, and so did the camouflage shirt. Billy gave him a bright orange vest for visibility, which Keith took but had no intention of using.

Billy watched him getting dressed and said, "I'll go with you."

"Thanks, but I want to hunt alone."

"What're you huntin' for?"

"Varmint." Keith tied the boots and stood. He thought about Baxter's three dogs. At the house on Williams Street, there had been a kennel, and Keith had seen no signs of dogs living inside the house. He assumed that if the dogs were outdoor animals on Williams Street, they would be outdoors all night at the lodge. He asked Billy, "You do any longbow or crossbow hunting?"

"Nope. I like the rifle. How about you?"

"Same." Despite all his exotic training, he'd never

been introduced to bows and arrows, blowguns, slings, spears, or boomerangs. The only silent way of killing he'd been taught was by knife and garrote, which wouldn't work on a dog, and he didn't have a silencer for his M-16, and Billy didn't have a crossbow. But he'd worry about that later.

Billy said, "Varmint's a real hard shot with a longbow. Seen it done with a crossbow."

"Right. Okay, thanks. I'll get the truck back to you tomorrow or the next day."

"Hey, Keith, I may be a fucked-up juicehead, but I'm sober now."

Keith looked at Billy Marlon, and they made eye contact. Keith said, "The less you know, the better." Keith moved to the door, but Marlon held his arm.

Marlon said, "I remember some of that night at John's Place and in the park and you drivin' me home."

"I have to go, Billy."

"He *did* fuck my wife...my second wife. I loved her...and she loved me, and we was doin' okay, but that bastard got between us, and after what happened, we tried to get it back together again...you know? But I couldn't deal with what happened and I started to drink, and I got like real mean with her. She left, but... she said she still loved me, but she'd done somethin' wrong and she could understand why I couldn't forgive her." Billy suddenly spun around and kicked the closet door, splintering the plywood panel. "Ah, shit!"

Keith took a deep breath and said, "It's okay." It was amazing, he thought, how much wreckage Cliff Baxter had left behind as he indulged himself in his carnal gratifications and moral corruption. Keith asked Billy, "What was her name?"

His back still to Keith, Billy replied, "Beth."

"Where is Beth now?"

He shrugged. "I don't know...Columbus, I think." Billy turned around and looked at Keith. "I know where you're goin'. I'm goin' with you. I have to go with you."

"No. I don't need help."

"Not for you. For me. Please."

"It's dangerous."

"Hey, I'm dead already. I won't even notice the difference."

Keith looked at Billy Marlon and nodded.

Keith went into the cowshed, and, with an ax that Marlon had given him, he sliced a few air vents in the trunk lid of the police car. He said to Ward through the slits, "Be thankful it's a Fairlane and not an Escort."

"Fuck you, Landry."

Keith drove the police car out of the shed and headed back on Route 8 the way he'd come. He didn't want to leave any evidence of an association between himself and Billy Marlon and Marlon's pickup truck.

Keith swung off the road onto the shoulder, then cut the car hard right over a drainage culvert and onto a tractor path between two fields of corn. Fifty yards into the corn, hidden from the road, he stopped and shut off the ignition.

He got out of the car and said to Ward, "I'll call from Daytona and tell them where you are. It'll be a while, so relax. Think about early retirement."

"Hey! Wait! Where am I?"

"In the trunk."

Keith jogged back to the road and met Billy Marlon, who was waiting for him in the pickup truck.

Billy drove the pickup, a ten-year-old blue Ford Ranger, and Keith sat in the passenger seat, a dirty bush hat pulled low on his head.

In the storage space behind the seat was the hunting gear, canvas ponchos for the Michigan cold, his M-16 rifle and scope, the Spencerville police shotgun, Officer Ward's service revolver, and Billy Marlon's hunting rifle, an Army M-14 with a four-power scope. He'd also taken his briefcase, which held his passport, important papers, some money, and other odds and ends. It occurred to him that this was about all he owned in the world, which was actually not much more or less than he'd owned when he left Spencerville for the Army half a lifetime ago.

As they drove, Keith said to Billy, "Baxter has three hunting dogs with him."

"Shit."

"Think about it."

"I will." Billy asked, "Where are we going?"

"Michigan. Northern part."

"Yeah? I do most of my hunting up that way. There's some good maps in the glove compartment."

Keith found the maps and located Grey Lake at the northern end of the peninsula. It was nearly one P.M., and they should be in Atlanta about seven and, with luck, be able to find Baxter's lodge at Grey Lake within an hour.

As they drove, Keith spotted two Spencerville police cars, saw another troop of mounted posse, and a Spencer County sheriff's car. He slid down in the seat each time, and no one seemed to pay any attention to the old pickup truck. Billy was wearing a John Deere cap pulled low over his eyes, and Keith instructed him not to make eye contact with any cops, since they all knew him from his frequent nights in the drank tank.

Keith asked him, "Do they know this truck?"

"Nah...I never got a DUI or nothin'. I drink and walk. Hardly use the truck to get to town."

"Okay...if they want to pull us over, you do what they say. We can't run the police in this thing."

Billy replied, "Fuck them. I'm not gonna lay down for those assholes anymore."

"They'll shoot. I know this bunch."

"Fuck 'em. They'll shoot you anyway. Hey, those assholes drive regular Fairlanes. When I get into the corn with this thing, there ain't gonna be no fuzz on our tail."

"Okay. It's your call." Keith regarded Billy a moment. Apparently, there was more to the man than Keith had been able to determine when Billy was drunk. Billy was on a mission now, too, and though Billy Marlon and Keith Landry had traveled different roads since high school and Vietnam, they now found themselves on the same road and with the same thing in mind.

In fact, Billy said, "I'm gonna get us to northern Michigan, Lieutenant—hey, you signed that note 'Colonel.' You a colonel now?"

"Sometimes."

Marlon laughed. "Yeah? I'm a sergeant. I made three stripes before I got out. Ain't that somethin'?"

"You must have been a good soldier."

"I was...I was."

They drove a few more minutes, and Keith said to Marlon, "They might have roadblocks at the county line."

"Yeah, I know. But there's got to be fifty, sixty farm roads that leave this county. They can't put a roadblock at each of them."

"Right. Let's pick one."

"I know the one. Town Road 18—mostly dirt and most of the time mud because of the bad drainage. Lots of cars get stuck, and Baxter's bozos got to keep their

Baxter Motors lease cars lookin' good." He laughed. "Assholes."

Marlon turned west onto a paved farm road, then a minute later turned right and headed north on a rutted gravel road, Town Road 18.

Ten minutes later, the corn ended and they were in a low-lying area of marsh grass, a vestige of the ancient Black Swamp. The road became muddy, and the truck splattered through the black silty muck.

Five minutes later, Billy said, "We're out of Spencer County."

Keith hadn't seen a sign, but he figured that Billy was familiar with the area. He took an Ohio map out of the glove compartment and said, "Let's take back roads up to the Maumee, then maybe we'll pick up Route 127 to Michigan."

"Yeah, that's the way to go."

They continued on, heading west and north on a series of intersecting town and county roads, through the rich autumn farm country, the endless fields of corn and hay, the pastures and meadows. Now that he was leaving and perhaps never coming back, he made certain he noticed everything: the road signs, the family names on the barns and the mailboxes, the crops and the animals, the people, and the vehicles, and the houses, and the whole sense and feel of this land whose whole was indeed far greater than the sum of its parts... *And the end of all our exploring will be to arrive where we started and know the place for the first time.*

They drove another half hour without much said that didn't pertain to the subject of land navigation and police.

Keith regarded the map and saw that most of the bridges across the Maumee River were located in the bigger towns on the river, and he didn't want to go through a town. He spotted a bridge near a tiny village called The Bend and asked Billy about it.

Billy replied, "Yeah, bridge is still there. Got some sort of weight limit, but if I gun it, we'll be across before it falls."

Keith wasn't sure about Billy's understanding of applied physics, but it was worth a look at the bridge.

They approached the small trestle bridge, and before Keith could see a weight limit sign or evaluate the structure, Billy was racing across the narrow span, and within ten seconds they'd crossed the Maumee. Keith said, "I think that bridge was closed to motor vehicle traffic."

"Yeah? Looked okay."

Keith shrugged.

They drove through The Bend, which took slightly less time than the river crossing and picked up U.S. Route 127 at a village called Sherwood. Keith noted it was two P.M., and it was about thirty-five miles to the Michigan state line, then another two hundred fifty miles or more to Grey Lake.

Route 127 went through Bryan, Ohio, but they skirted around the small city and returned to the highway some miles north of the town. That was the last major town in Ohio, and, in fact, after Lansing in southern Michigan, there were no major towns along Route 127 all the way up to the tip of the peninsula. Twenty minutes later, a sign welcomed them to Michigan, "The Land of Lakes." Keith was only interested in one of them.

There were no great differences in terrain or topography between northern Ohio and southern Michigan, Keith noted, but there were those subtle differences in signage, blacktop, and land surveys which, if you hadn't seen the Michigan sign, you might not notice. More important, Keith thought, whatever residual interest the state of Ohio had in him most probably didn't extend beyond that sign. This border crossing wasn't the heart-stopping equivalent of the old East to West border crossings in Europe, but he did feel a sense of relief, and he relaxed a bit.

They drove on for another half hour, and the terrain started to change from flat farmland to rolling green hills and small valleys. There were large stands of trees now, mostly oak, hickory, beech, and maple, and the autumn colors were further along than in Ohio. Keith hadn't been in Michigan since he and Annie used to drive up to see the Ohio State–Michigan game in Ann Arbor, or to see Bowling Green play Eastern Michigan in Ypsilanti. Those had been magic weekends, he recalled, a break not only from classes but from the war and the turmoil on the campus, a time-warp weekend without dissent or demonstrations, as if everyone agreed to dress, act, and look normal for a traditional Saturday afternoon football game.

He let his mind drift into thoughts about Annie, then realized this wasn't good or productive. The objective was Grey Lake, the mission was to settle the score with Cliff Baxter, not just for himself, but for Annie as well, and thinking about her meant he wasn't concentrating on the problem.

Billy asked, "Where in northern Michigan we goin', exactly?"

"Don't know exactly."

"Then how we gonna get there?"

"We'll manage. Hey, remember that old Army expression? I don't know where we are—"

"Yeah." Billy smiled and recited, "I don't know where we are, or what we're doin', but we're makin' really good time." He laughed.

Keith thought that seemed to satisfy Billy, but a few minutes later, Billy asked, "Is Baxter alone?"

Keith thought a moment, then replied, "I don't think he has any other men with him."

Billy mulled this over a minute, then asked, "Where is Mrs. Baxter?"

"Why do you ask that?"

"Well...I mean, I heard about the kidnappin' on the radio." Billy glanced at Keith and added, "The radio said you kidnapped her."

"What do you think?"

"Well, it's plain as day that you two ran off together. The whole town knows that."

Keith didn't reply.

Billy went on, "What I can't figure out is what happened next."

"What do you think happened?"

"Well...I guess he caught up with you. That explains them cuts and bruises on your face. But that don't explain why one of you ain't dead."

Keith replied, "We tried."

Billy laughed and said, "I bet you did. This is like round two, I guess."

"Two, maybe three, four, or five. But who's counting?"

"And I guess this is the last round."

"I'm sure it is."

"You gonna kill him?"

Keith thought a moment, then replied, "I'd rather not."

"Why not?"

"That's too good for him."

Billy nodded and didn't reply.

Keith said, "If I take you all the way, you're going to follow my orders. Right?"

Billy nodded.

"Can't hear you, soldier."

"Yes, sir."

They drove in silence awhile, then Billy said, "She's with him, ain't she?"

"She is."

"Right. So we got to take him without hurting her."

"That's right."

"That ain't gonna be easy."

"No, it's not."

"Three dogs?"

"I think."

"What kinda stuff is he packin'?"

"You name it, he's probably got it. He's a hunter and a cop."

"Yeah, he is." Billy asked, "He got any night-vision stuff?"

"Probably. Compliments of the Spencerville P.D."

"Okay...and I guess he's holed up in a cabin or somethin', someplace where he knows the lay of the land."

"That's right." Keith glanced at Marlon. In medical terms, a doctor would say Billy Marlon's brain had suffered prolonged alcohol insult, and in human terms, anyone who knew him would say his spirit had suffered too many of life's insults. Yet Keith had no doubt whatsoever that Billy Marlon had reached deep down inside himself today, and this was going to be his finest and most lucid hour. Keith said, "Tell me about Beth."

"I can't."

"Sure you can."

Billy sat quietly for a few minutes, then pulled out his wallet and fished out a grubby photo. He handed it to Keith.

Keith looked at it. The color photograph showed a head-and-shoulders shot of a woman in her mid-thirties, short blond hair, quite pretty in fact, with big eyes and a big smile. Keith was sort of surprised at how good-looking she was and not at all surprised that she should have come to the attention of Chief Baxter. There was certainly a normal ratio of pretty women in Spencer County, as Keith had observed, but he understood why this one had become Baxter's victim, and the reason was sitting in the seat beside him. Civilization and civility aside, a weak man with an exceptionally endowed wife was bound to lose her—perhaps on a temporary basis—to someone like Cliff Baxter. Keith handed the photograph back to Billy and said, "She's very beautiful."

"Yeah."

"How long has it been?"

"Two years."

"She remarry?"

"Don't think so. She's still in the Columbus phone book as Beth Marlon."

"Maybe you'll go look her up after this."

"Yeah, maybe."

After a few minutes, Billy seemed in better spirits and said, "Hey, time for a war story."

Keith thought not and asked, "You know this road?"

"Yeah, I take this up now and then. Good hunting up in Hartwick Pines State Park. You ever been up there?"

"No, never been this far north. You remember a gas station around here?"

"Let's see . . ." He looked out the window. "Yeah, another mile or so. Hey, how far up we goin'?"

"Near the tip of the peninsula. Another two hours, I guess." Keith added, "You don't have to come all the way. I can drop you at a motel and come back for you."

"Yeah? And what if you don't come back?"

"I'll be back."

Billy suddenly grinned. "You got your shit together,

man. Hey, tell you what—we get this fucker, we gut him, and drive into Spencerville with him tied onto the roof like a deer. Whataya say?"

"Don't tempt me."

Billy let out a howl of delight and slapped his thigh. "Yeah! Yeah! Up and down Main Street with the horn honkin' and Baxter's naked butt stickin' up in the air, and the fuckin' wolves eatin' his guts back in Michigan. Yeah!"

Keith ignored this bloodthirsty outburst, not because he thought it was disgusting, but because he thought it wasn't.

He saw the service station up ahead and pointed it out to Billy, who pulled in. Keith gave Billy money for snacks, and Billy went into the building. Keith got behind the wheel.

The attendant filled the tank, and Keith paid him while Billy went to the men's room. Keith's impulse was to leave Billy there, not because Billy Marlon was a burnout—Keith understood burned-out, and he appreciated Marlon's rising to this occasion. The problem was that the occasion that Billy had risen to included Billy's own agenda, and his presence added another dimension to the problem.

But Keith, in a weak moment, had acknowledged what it was he was hunting for, and Billy knew too much, so Billy couldn't be cut loose and left wandering around.

Billy came back to the truck and got in the passenger seat. He looked at Keith, and they both understood that Billy Marlon was a man who was used to being tricked, snubbed, and left behind. Billy said, "Thanks."

Keith got back onto Route 127.

The farms thinned out, and the hills became higher and more thickly wooded. The oaks and maples had lost most of their leaves, and the birch and aspen were almost bare. There were more evergreens, too, Keith noticed, white and red pines and hemlock, some of them reaching towering heights. The sign at the last county line they'd crossed had announced a population of 6,200, about one-tenth the population of Spencer County, which was considered rural. Truly, he thought, this place was remote and nearly uninhabited, bypassed by the great wave of westward pioneers.

The daylight was starting to fade, and the trees cast long shadows over the hills. It was very still outside the truck, and except for an occasional small herd of cattle on a hillside, nothing moved.

Billy asked, "You think she's okay?"

Keith didn't reply.

"He wouldn't hurt her, would he?"

"No. He loves her."

Billy stayed silent for a minute, then commented, "I can't think about him lovin' nobody but himself."

"Yeah, well, maybe love isn't the right word. Whatever it is, he needs her."

"Yeah. I think I know what you mean." Billy added, "She's okay."

At Gaylord, in Otsego County, Keith turned east onto Route 32, and twenty minutes later, at seven-fifteen P.M., they reached Atlanta, the principal town in the area, with a population of about six hundred souls. Keith said to Billy, "We'll stop for gas. Don't mention Grey Lake."

Keith pulled into the only service station and topped off the tank on the assumption that he would be leaving Grey Lake at some late hour, with no known destination.

The attendant made small talk, and Billy spun a yarn about going up to Presque Isle to shoot duck.

Keith went to the pay phone and dialed the Baxter

house in Spencerville. As Terry had said, the call was automatically forwarded, and a voice answered, "Spencerville police, Sergeant Blake speaking."

Keith said, "Blake, this is your old pal Keith Landry. Your missing car and man are sitting in a cornfield off Route 8, north side, about a mile west of the city line."

"What—?"

Keith hung up. He felt obliged to make the call, to get Ward out of the trunk before the harvesters found him dead. Keith doubted if his call from Michigan to the Baxter house, forwarded to the police headquarters, would be displayed on any caller ID that the Spencerville P.D. had. Normally, he wouldn't have done anything so charitable if it had even the slightest element of risk to himself, but he didn't want Ward to die, and when the police found Ward, Ward would tell them that Landry was heading to Daytona. The Spencerville police would alert the Ohio state police to look for their fugitive witness at nearby airports or in Florida. There was no reason why they would think of Grey Lake, or of Billy Marlon, or the pickup truck. He hoped not.

Keith had also wanted to see if anyone answered the phone at the Baxter house. Keith believed, based on what Terry had said and Annie's clue about Atlanta— *this* Atlanta—that Baxter was at Grey Lake. On the other hand, Keith had the nagging thought that this was a setup. But if it was, it was a very elaborate setup and probably too sophisticated for Cliff Baxter. Keith's problem, he knew, was that he'd lived too long in that wilderness of mirrors where thousands of bright boys played the most elaborate and sophisticated tricks on one another. This was not the case here. Baxter was in the only place he could be—his lodge at Grey Lake; and he was alone, except for Annie, and he didn't know Keith Landry was on his way. Reassured, Keith put this out of his mind and thought about the immediate problem at hand.

Keith went into the small office and said to the attendant, "I'm looking to buy a good crossbow."

The attendant said, "Feller named Neil Johnson sells sporting equipment. Some used, some new. Cash. He's closed now, but I'll give him a call if you want."

"Good."

The man made the call and spoke to Neil Johnson, who was apparently having dinner and wanted to know if the gentleman could wait awhile.

Keith said to the attendant, "I'd really like to get on the road. I won't take much of his time."

The attendant passed this on to Mr. Johnson, and the appointment was set. Keith got directions to Neil's sporting goods store, thanked the attendant, and got into the pickup.

Billy said, "What's up?"

"We're going to get a crossbow." He pulled out and headed east.

Billy nodded and asked, "Is there any way we can kill Baxter without killing the dogs?"

"We'll see." Of course, Keith thought, there was a chance of nailing Baxter at a hundred yards or more with the M-16 and the four-power scope. But that's not what Keith wanted to do; he wanted to look into the man's eyes.

Keith found Johnson's house, a small clapboard at the edge of Atlanta, which was to say a few hundred yards from Main Street, and pulled into the driveway.

Dogs barked, and the front porch light came on. Keith and Billy got out of the truck and were met by a tall, wiry man, still chewing on dinner, who introduced himself as Neil. Keith introduced himself and Billy as Bob and Jack. Neil glanced at the old pickup truck for a second and regarded Keith and Billy, probably trying to determine if this was worth his time. He said, "You're from Ohio."

Keith replied, "Yup. Thought I'd try my hand at crossbowing."

"Crossbowing? Hell, that ain't no sport. You want a longbow."

"I'm not an archer. I just want to shoot varmint."

"Yeah? Okay, I only got one kind of crossbow, and you're welcome to it. Come on in."

He led Keith and Billy to an aluminum warehouse-type building set back from the road that had been converted into a sporting goods store. Neil turned on the fluorescent lights. The right wall of the long building was lined with gun racks and counters laden with hunting paraphernalia and ammunition, and Keith figured that Mr. Johnson could outfit an infantry battalion. The left-hand side of the building was stocked with fishing gear, archery equipment, outdoor clothing, tents, and assorted odds and ends for the hunter. Keith didn't see any tennis rackets or running shoes.

Keith was not in a particular hurry at this point, knowing that whatever he was going to do at Grey Lake had to wait until the early hours of the morning. Still, he wanted to get moving, but you didn't show any impatience in a town of six hundred people, and each purchase had to be treated like the deal of the century.

After some polite chatter, Neil Johnson handed Keith the crossbow and said, "This here one is used, made out of fiberglass by a company called Pro Line. Pretty good."

Keith examined the weapon. Essentially, it consisted of a short bow mounted crossways on a riflelike stock also of fiberglass. A trigger arrangement released the drawn string and sent the arrow on its journey along a groove running the length of the top of the stock. "Looks easy."

"Yeah. It's too easy. No sport. You'll be as good as anyone else in a few days. A longbowman got to practice years to get good."

Keith had the feeling that Mr. Johnson was disdainful of the crossbow and of anyone who used it.

In fact, Neil Johnson informed him, "A feller told me once that crossbows was outlawed by the pope back in the days of knights, you know, because it was considered unfit and unfair for Christians to use it."

"You don't say? Did that include shooting rats?"

"Probably not. Anyway, it's real accurate. You got about a sixty-pound pull, and you cock it by putting the stock against your chest, and you draw the string back with both hands. Here, I'll show you." Neil took the crossbow and cocked the string back and hooked it on the trigger catch. He put an arrow in the groove and pointed it down the length of the room at a dusty deer head mounted on the far wall about thirty feet away. He aimed along the sights and pulled the trigger. The short arrow flew out of the crossbow and pierced the deer head right between the eyes, passed through, and stuck into the wooden wall mounting with a thud. "How's that?"

"Very good."

"Yeah. I couldn't do that with a longbow. Okay, so the arrow travels about two hundred feet a second, and if you're leadin' a animal, you got to remember you ain't firin' a rifle, and you got to lead him more. Somethin' else to remember—at forty yards, you're gonna get as much as a four-foot drop in the arrow, so you got to compensate for that." He picked up one of the arrows and said, "These here are fiberglass, with plastic vanes, and this here's a broad-tipped hunting head. They come eight to a box. How many you want?"

Keith looked at the plastic quiver on the counter and said, "Fill 'er up."

"Okay. That's twenty-four. You need anything else?"

"Can you mount a scope on this?"

"Scope? You ain't givin' them rats a chance, are you?"

"Nope."

"Let's see what I got here." Neil found a four-power bow scope and within ten minutes had mounted it on the crossbow. He handed it to Keith and said, "You want to adjust that aim?"

"Sure do."

"I'll set out a target. Step on back to the door. That's about twenty yards."

Keith took the crossbow, slung the quiver, and walked back to the door, while Neil Johnson set up a bull's-eye target against a bale of straw and stepped away. Keith cocked the bow against his chest, fitted the arrow, aimed through the telescopic sight, and pulled the trigger. The arrow hit low, and he adjusted the sight and fired again. On the third shot, he put the arrow through the inner circle. "Okay. How accurate is this at, say, forty yards?"

Neil replied, "About twice as accurate as a longbow, which is to say you ought to be able to put all your arrows inside a nine-inch circle at forty yards."

Keith nodded. "How about eighty yards?"

"Eighty yards? You ain't gonna even *see* a rat at eighty yards . . . well, maybe with that scope it's gonna look like twenty yards, but you're gettin' that four-foot drop at forty yards, and maybe a ten-foot drop at eighty yards. These things is made for forty-yard target shooting. You can send an arrow maybe seven hundred yards with that thing, but you ain't hittin' nothin', 'cept maybe Farmer Brown's cow, by accident."

"Yeah...can I hit, let's say, a wild dog, stationary, at eighty yards, no wind, with this scope?"

Neil rubbed his chin. "Well...you're gonna get a straight, true flight regardin' left and right, but you got to figure your drop. What's the point of this?"

"Dogs bothering my sheep back in Ohio. When I fire a rifle at one, the others scatter. I figure with a crossbow, I won't spook them."

"Why don't you just poison the damned things?"

"That's not real Christian."

Neil laughed and said, "Have it your way." He took a pencil and scratched some numbers on the wooden counter. "Let's see...crossbow, twenty-four arrows including the one I shot...you want that back?"

"No."

"Okay, quiver, carrying case, and scope...let's say six hundred dollars, and that includes the tax."

"Sounds fair." Keith counted out the money, which was almost all the cash he had, and he recalled Charlie Adair's thousand dollars, then thought about Adair and wondered when and how he'd see him again.

As Billy packed everything in the canvas carrying case, Keith inquired, "Do you get many folks from Ohio up this way?"

Neil counted the money and replied, "Get a lot in the summer, then during the hunting season. After that, you don't see many. Where you headed?"

"Presque Isle."

"Yeah? Ain't easy getting through them hills at night unless you know the way."

"We'll take it slow. I see you sell dog chow."

"Yup. Do a lot of my out-of-town business in ammo, dog chow, some fish bait, and like that. People's got their own rifles and all." Neil went on, then remembered the subject and asked, "You need some dog chow?"

"No, but a friend of mine comes up here with two, three dogs, and they eat like wolves. I think this is where he comes for his chow."

"Yeah, you run 'em, you got to feed 'em. Fact, a guy from Ohio was in here a few days back and bought enough chow to last a few months."

"That could have been my friend. He's up here."

"Coulda been."

The conversation seemed to be stalled, so Keith, against his better judgment, prompted, "I was thinking about maybe buying a place up here, but I'd like to talk to some Ohio guys who already got a place."

"Yeah, you can do that. Fact, that guy who near cleaned me out of dog chow, he's up at Grey Lake. Take a ride up there and look for his signpost. Name's Baxter. That your friend?"

"No."

Billy's eyes opened wide, Keith noticed, but Billy's mouth stayed shut.

Keith said to Neil, "Yeah, maybe I'll look him up on my way back, but I don't want to just pop in if he's got the missus with him."

"Didn't see no lady in his car."

Keith didn't reply.

Neil added, "But I didn't see no dogs neither, so he must've gone up to his place, then come back here." He said, "You can call ahead. He's in the book. Tell him I sent you. We do business now and then."

"Thanks. Maybe I'll call on the way back. Meantime, I got to make a call home. Mind if I use your phone?"

"No, go right ahead. Over there by the cash register."

Keith walked over to the cash register, found the phone, and dialed. Billy was making conversation with Neil, talking guns and hunting.

Terry answered, "Hello?"

"Terry, it's me."

"Keith! Where are you?"

"I'm here. Listen, your phone is tapped."

"*My* phone?"

"Yes, but not by the Spencerville P.D. By the federal government."

"*What?* Why—?"

"It doesn't matter. Call your lawyer in the morning and get the tap taken off. More important, I know he's up here, so we have to assume she's here, too." He added, to make her feel better, "I'm sure she's alive."

"Oh, thank God . . . what are you going to do?"

"I've spoken to the local police, and they're very cooperative. I just want to remind you and Larry again not to do anything that might jeopardize the situation. Don't say anything to your parents over the phone, either. Okay?"

"Yes."

"Terry, trust me."

"I do."

"I'll have her back tomorrow."

"Do you mean that?"

"Yes."

"And him? Will they arrest him?"

"I can't say. I suppose, if she swears out a complaint, they will."

"She won't do that. She just wants to be rid of him."

"Well, first things first. The police here want to wait until morning, and that's all right. I'll call you tomorrow with good news."

"All right . . . can I reach you tonight?"

"I'll get a motel and call you only if I have new information."

"Okay. Be careful."

"I will. And now a message to the people recording

this conversation: 'Hello, Charlie—I got here without your help, but thanks again. Billy helped me, and if I'm inconvenienced later, you take care of him. Okay? Meantime, one more dragon. See you around.'" Keith said, "Terry, sit tight. Regards to Larry."

"Okay."

Keith hung up. He, Billy, and Neil went back to the pickup truck, and Keith said, "See you next week on the way back."

"Good luck."

Keith and Billy got in the truck and pulled out onto the road. Billy said, "Hey, you hear that? Baxter's at Grey Lake."

"Indeed he is." Keith felt much better.

"We got him!" He looked at Keith. "You knew he was there, didn't you?"

Keith didn't reply.

Billy thought awhile, then asked, "You think he knows you're lookin' for him?"

"I'm sure he knows I'm looking for him."

"Yeah...but you think he knows you knew where to find him?"

"That is the question."

Billy examined the crossbow. He raised it and sighted out the front window through the small telescopic sight. "Aims like a rifle. But I don't know about that drop."

Billy examined the tip of the arrow, a razor-sharp, open-bladed broadhead made of high-quality steel. "Jesus, this tip is over an inch across. That'll put a big slice in the meat." He asked Keith, "You sure we got to kill the dogs?"

"You tell me when we get there."

"Okay...hey, maybe we can get Baxter with this thing."

"Maybe." Whether he killed the man with his M-16 at a hundred yards or a crossbow at forty yards, the man was just as dead as if Keith had severed his femoral artery with his knife. There was a difference, however, in the after-action report, so to speak. He mulled this over awhile, taking into account the fact that Annie was going to be right there when it happened. Keith also considered not killing Baxter at all. Much of what was going to happen before dawn was not in his power to control, but he felt he should at least think about life after death—that is, *his* life after the other guy's death. He always did this, though rarely did it work out the way he wanted it to. Mostly you just tried to avoid shooting a guy in the back or the balls. Beyond those minor concessions to chivalry, anything was permitted. Yet Baxter was a special case, and Keith really wanted to be close enough to smell the man, to make eye contact, to say, "Hi, Cliff, remember me?"

Billy asked, "You tuned out?"

"I guess. Did I miss a turn?"

"No, but you turn here. Take the left fork."

"Okay." Keith veered off to the left, and they headed north from Atlanta into a vast tract of unspoiled wilderness, hills, lakes, streams, and marsh. Billy commented, "I remember that the roads on the map don't always match the roads on the ground."

"Okay." Keith turned on the overhead light and glanced at the map. The region they were entering was mostly state land, about two or three hundred square miles of forest, most of it accessible only by logging roads, game trails, and canoe. Keith couldn't see a single village or settlement. He shut off the light and handed Billy the map. "You navigate."

Billy took a flashlight out of the glove compartment and studied the map.

Keith said, "Baxter's lodge is on the north side of Grey Lake."

Billy glanced at him but didn't ask how he knew that. Billy said, "Okay...I see a road goin' around the east side of the lake, but it don't turn around to the far north side."

"We'll find it."

"Yeah, people got these wood signs like that one over there, pointin' up these dirt roads with their names on it—see that? 'John and Joan's Hideaway.'" Billy asked, "You know what his place is called?"

"No...yes, I think it's 'Big Chief Cliff's Lodge.'" Keith added, "But I have a feeling he took down his welcome sign."

"Yeah...we might have to ask around."

"I don't see another human being around to ask, Billy."

"There's usually somebody. They'll know."

"Right, and they might call on ahead to Baxter."

"Yeah, maybe. Hey, you think about all these things, don't you? Maybe I should start thinkin' ahead once in a while."

"Can't hurt. Start now."

They continued on through the pitch-dark night, through the narrow, winding road, bordered by towering pines. Keith asked, "You ever hunt through here?"

"Now and then. You got deer, bobcat, and even bear. You get the odd timberwolf, too. But you got to know the area or you could get fucked-up in here. I mean, this ain't the end of the world, but I think you can see it from here."

After a few minutes, Billy said, "You take this here small road to the left, and it wraps around almost to the north end of Grey Lake. After that, we got to wing it."

"Okay." Keith turned onto the road, which was

barely wide enough for the truck, and the pine boughs brushed both sides of the cab. Off to the left, through the pines, Keith caught a glimpse of the lake itself. A bright, nearly full moon had risen, and the lake indeed looked gray, like polished pewter. It was maybe a mile across, totally surrounded by pine with a few bare birch at the water's edge. He saw no lights from boats or from houses in the pines.

Truly, he thought, this was a spectacular piece of the world, but it was very far removed from Michigan's other recreational areas, and Keith wondered what Annie thought of her husband buying a place in this wilderness. It occurred to him that, for people used to the endless horizons and big blue sky of farm country, this place must feel claustrophobic and nearly spooky, and it was probably hell in the winter. Baxter, however, would feel at home here, Keith realized, a timberwolf in his element.

Keith spotted a cabin through the trees that looked uninhabited, and he suspected that most of these places were probably weekend homes, and, for all he knew, there wasn't a single human being around the lake other than himself and Billy, and Cliff and Annie Baxter, which was fine with him, he thought. Before dawn, the population of Grey Lake would be zero.

The road curved around the lake, and, again, Keith caught a glimpse of it to his left, then the road turned north again, away from the lake, and Keith pulled over.

Billy said, "There's got to be a road wide enough for a truck to get through someplace back there."

"Right." Unable to make a U-turn, Keith backed up, looking for an opening in the pine trees and brush. There were utility poles along the narrow road, and Keith tried to spot an electric line or telephone wire that ran from a pole toward the lake.

Finally, Keith nudged the pickup off the road onto a narrow drainage shoulder, leaving room for another vehicle to pass. He got out of the truck, and Billy followed. It was cold, Keith noticed, and he could see his breath. It was also quiet, a typical autumn evening in the northern woods, with no sounds of insects, birds, or animals, and it was dark and would stay that way until the first snows brightened the land and the trees.

Keith and Billy walked along the road for a hundred yards, searching for an opening in the pine trees that was wide enough for a vehicle to pass though. Billy said softly, "Maybe we should just take a compass heading through the woods and get down to the lake and look around."

"That might be the thing to do. Let's get our gear."

They walked back toward the truck, and Keith kept looking up at the utility poles. He stopped, tapped Billy on the shoulder, and pointed.

Billy stared up at the dark sky. A squirrel was making its way along an electric wire that was nearly invisible among the dark shadows of the pine trees. The wire ran toward the lake. Under the wire was another one, probably the telephone line, Keith thought.

Billy said, "That definitely goes to the lake, but they always run along a road, and I don't see no road."

Keith stood near the utility pole, then walked into the woods and grasped an eight-foot-tall white pine by its trunk, shook it, then pulled it out of the ground.

Billy looked at the base of the sawed-off trunk and said, "Jeez . . . this guy must be a gook."

Keith kicked another pine, and it tumbled. Someone, undoubtedly Cliff Baxter, had camouflaged the narrow dirt road that led to his lodge with cut pine trees, each about eight or ten feet high. There were about a dozen of them implanted into the dirt road, running back about twenty feet, giving the impression of a continuous forest. They were still green, Keith noticed, and would stay green for weeks, but they were slightly tilted and smaller than the surrounding pines.

Keith also noticed that where the dirt road met the blacktop was strewn with deadwood and pine boughs to conceal the tire ruts leading into the hidden road. Not a great job, Keith thought, but good enough to keep a lost or curious driver from turning into the road that led to Baxter's lodge.

Keith looked around and found a signpost that had been chopped at the base and pushed over onto the ground. There was no sign on the post that said, "Big Chief Cliff's Lodge," but Keith was certain there had been.

It was obvious, Keith thought, that Cliff Baxter wanted no visitors, casual or otherwise. And the same laboriously transplanted pine trees that kept people out kept Baxter from making occasional forays into the outside world. So there was no chance of staking out the road, waiting for Baxter to leave for a while, and rescuing Annie without putting her in danger of a fight. Apparently, Baxter had everything he needed for a long stay. The essential questions, of course, were, Did he also have Annie and was she alive? Keith was almost certain that he did have her, and she was alive, if not well. This was the whole point of Baxter's flight to this remote lodge—to imprison his unfaithful wife and to take out his anger and rage on her without any interference from the outside world.

It occurred to Keith that ultimately, regardless of Keith Landry—or someone like him—this was where the Baxters were destined to end up, sooner, if not later, though Annie may or may not have understood the psychological subtext of this hunting lodge and future retirement home. He recalled something she'd said. *The few times we went up there alone, without the kids or without company, he was another person. Not necessarily better, and not actually worse...just another person...quiet, distant, as if he's...I don't know...thinking of something. I don't like to go up there with him alone, and I can usually get out of it.*

One could only imagine, Keith thought, what Cliff Baxter was thinking about. One could only hope that whatever he'd done to Annie in the last three days, to her mind and her body, was not permanent or scarring.

Keith and Billy went back to the pickup and collected their gear, then returned to the place where the camouflaged road began. They both knew not to walk through the camouflage or on the open dirt road beyond it, and they entered the woods to the right of the road and began walking on a parallel course to it, keeping it in view when they could. They maintained their heading with the compass and an occasional sighting of the small utility poles that ran along the road.

After about fifteen minutes of slow progress, Keith stopped and knelt down, listening to the forest. Billy knelt beside him and they stayed motionless for a full five minutes. Finally, Billy whispered, "Sounds okay, smells okay, feels okay."

Keith nodded.

Still whispering, Billy said, "I know that camouflage back there looks like Baxter's work, but how we gonna be *sure* the house at the end of those wires is his? We don't know what it looks like, and we ain't gonna knock before we shoot."

Keith said, "It's an A-frame, dark wood, set back from the lake."

"Yeah? You know more than you say, don't you?" He added, "Typical officer."

Keith replied, "I think you know everything I know now. I told you up front this was going to be dangerous."

"Yeah, you did."

"I'll tell you something else—I took you along for *you*, not for me. But I appreciate the help."

"Thanks."

"If I take you the rest of the way, I want you to promise me that you'll finish the job if I'm not able to."

Billy looked at Keith and nodded. "You know I got my own reasons, and you got yours...so if one of us is down, the other guy's gonna give it his best shot."

Keith hesitated, then said, "Okay...and if it turns out at the end that it's just you and her, you tell her... whatever."

"Yeah, I'll tell her whatever." He asked, "Anything in particular?"

There was, but Keith said, "Just tell her about today."

"Okay. You do the same for me." He added, "Maybe she don't care, but she should know."

"Will do." Keith had the distinct feeling he'd had this conversation before, in other places with other people, and he was definitely tired of it. He said, "Let's move."

They continued on through the forest. Keith tried to guess how thorough Baxter had been in his preparations. Camouflage was okay, but an early-warning device was essential. That was what the dogs were for, of course, but the thing that concerned him most was a trip flare, though he wondered if Baxter, who had no military experience, had thought of such a thing. Still, he stepped high as he walked, and so did Billy, he noticed, who had the same thing on his mind. It was interesting, Keith thought, how much old soldiers remembered, even guys like Billy. But after you'd seen your first trip wire set off by someone else—whether it led to a flare or an explosive booby trap—you didn't want to repeat the experience.

The moon was higher now and cast some light into the pine forest, but Keith still couldn't see more than twenty feet in front of him. It was colder than Keith had imagined it would be, and a wind had come up from the direction of the lake, adding to the chill.

They moved slowly, covering about half a mile in thirty minutes. Keith slowed down, then stopped and pointed.

Up ahead, they could see the beginning of a clearing through the pines, and at the end of the clearing, the moonlit waters of Grey Lake.

They moved another twenty yards and stopped again. To their right, about a hundred yards away, sitting in the large clearing that ran to the lake's edge and silhouetted against the lake, was an A-frame house of dark wood.

They both stared at the house a moment, then Keith raised his binoculars. The house had sort of an alpine look and was built on cement-block columns, he saw, so that it was elevated a full story above the ground. A raised, cantilevered deck ran completely around the house, giving Baxter a full 360-degree view from a raised vantage point. A stone chimney rose from the center of the roof, and smoke drifted toward them, so they were downwind from any dogs. Parked in the open garage beneath the A-frame structure was a dark Ford Bronco.

The house was set at an angle to the lakeshore, so that Keith could see the front of the house as well as the long north side. Light came from the dormered windows set into the sloping roofline and also from the sliding glass doors that led onto the deck, and, as he watched, a fleeting figure—he couldn't tell if it was a man or a woman—passed in front of the glass doors.

Keith lowered the binoculars. "This is it."

From the direction of the house, a dog barked.

CHAPTER THIRTY-EIGHT

Cliff Baxter strapped on his holster and put on his bulletproof vest. He went to his gun rack and took down his Sako, model TRG-21, which was his night rifle, with an Army-surplus infrared scope mounted on it. The rifle, made in Finland, had cost the taxpayers of Spencerville four thousand dollars, and the scope another thousand, and in his opinion, the rifle and scope together made about the most accurate and deadly nightsniper system in the world.

He shut off the lights in the living room so he wouldn't be backlighted and slid open the glass door that led from the living room to the elevated deck.

Baxter dropped to one knee behind the deck railing and raised the rifle, sighting through the scope and adjusting the infrared image with the focus knob. His right eye was still fuzzy from where Landry had jabbed him, but the magnification helped.

He looked out into the woods that started about a hundred yards across the open space around the house, and scanned along the edge of the pine trees, but didn't see anything.

Baxter wasn't certain which dog barked, or why, so he walked in a low crouch around the continuous deck, looking through the variable-power scope at the woods that surrounded the house on three sides, then scanned the shoreline of the lake, which, like the woods, was about a hundred yards away across open terrain. He focused on the waters of the lake itself but didn't see any boats.

One of the dogs, the Rottweiler, was tethered to a dog run parallel to the lake side of the house. The second dog, a Doberman pinscher, was on its dog run, which ran from the lake, across the front of the house, out toward the woods where the dirt road came into the clearing. The third dog, a German shepherd, was out toward the rear of the house. The shepherd wasn't on a wire run, but was on a fifty-yard-long leash, attached to a pole, that allowed it to roam at will as far as the woods and as close as the house. He was satisfied that the placement of these dogs covered the perimeter of the clearing around his house.

They were good dogs, Baxter thought, but they barked at nearly everything. Still, when they barked, he checked it out. He went back to the front deck and, again in a kneeling stance, he raised the rifle and pointed it toward the dirt road. It sounded like the Doberman pinscher who'd barked, and in fact the Doberman was at the end of its run near the wood line. But Baxter noticed that the wind was coming off the lake now, so the dog probably couldn't smell anything downwind. But it must have heard or seen something. Baxter adjusted the focus knob again and concentrated on the infrared images as he slowly scanned from left to right.

He focused on the Doberman pinscher again and saw that the dog was facing toward the woods about thirty yards left of where the dirt road began. Baxter dropped into a prone firing position, rested the rifle on the deck below the bottom slat, and sighted to where the Doberman was pointing. He aimed low at the base of the pine trees and squeezed off a single round.

The shot echoed through the trees and over the lake behind him, breaking into the silence of the night. All three dogs began barking. Baxter sighted again and fired another round, then another.

The echo died away, and the dogs quieted down. Baxter lay motionless, peering through the scope, waiting for a sound or movement in the pine, and waiting, too, for return fire. After two full minutes, he decided there was nothing out there, or if there was, it was gone or dead. "Maybe a deer." They liked to feed after dark during the hunting season, but as soon as the dogs barked, they ran. So why was the dog still looking into the woods? "Maybe a rabbit or squirrel. Yeah..."

"Okay..." He didn't want to attract attention and didn't want to kill a hunter, but he didn't think there was anyone in the few cabins around this side of the lake, and even if there were, they didn't belong out at night in the woods during the deer season; at least not this close to his house.

He waited a few more minutes, then rolled along the deck, stood quickly, and went back into the living room through the sliding door.

Baxter put the rifle back in the gun rack and locked it, pocketing the key chain. He had four other semi-automatic rifles on the rack, one with a twilight scope for dawn and dusk shooting, one with a standard four-power scope for daylight, one with a long-range twelve-power scope for distance shots of up to a mile across the lake, and an AK-47 assault rifle with open sights for close-in shooting.

Aside from the armaments and the dogs, he also had six old-fashioned bear traps set around the property, out of reach of the dogs. One of them was near the staircase that led up to the deck. He also had a few other tricks up his sleeve, in case any uninvited and unannounced visitors showed up. He wasn't expecting anyone, but somewhere in the back of his mind was the image of Keith Landry.

Keith lay flat on the ground among the pine boughs, with Billy beside him. When the firing stopped, Keith whispered, "Just probing fire."

Billy nodded. "Yeah...but damn close."

"I think the dog was pointing."

Billy whispered, "You had a clear shot at him when he was kneelin'."

"I did, but I think he was wearing a vest. I'd have to go for a head shot, and that's tough at this distance."

"Hey, did you see that red-eye lookin' at us?"

"I did." The infrared scope's major drawback was that you could see the red glow when it was pointing directly at you. He wasn't surprised that Baxter had a night-vision scope, but it made things a little more difficult.

The dog, which was about twenty yards from them, made a low, rumbling sound.

They lay quiet and motionless for another few minutes, then the dog, responding to some other sound or impulse, turned and ran off down the length of its wire run toward the lake.

Keith waited another minute, then slowly rose up into a kneeling position. He raised the binoculars and trained them on the house.

Baxter slipped out of his bulletproof vest but kept his pistol strapped to his side. He turned on a floor lamp that cast a soft light across the big, cathedral-ceilinged living room.

Along the slanted walls of the A-frame room were

trophy heads: elk, deer, bobcat, wild boar, two black bears facing each other on opposite walls, and above the mantel of the fireplace, a rare gray timberwolf surveyed the length of the room.

Sitting in a rocking chair beside the fireplace was Annie, staring into the flames. She glanced at him as he came toward her.

Baxter said, "You expectin' company, darlin'?"

She shook her head.

"I think you are." He sat in an easy chair opposite her.

She was naked but had a blanket wrapped around her to keep away the cold. Still, her feet were cold despite the fire. On her ankles were leg manacles from the jail, connected by a twenty-four-inch chain long enough for her to walk normally but too short for her to run. The chain was padlocked to a large eyebolt screwed deep into the oak floor.

The only telephone in the house was the wall phone in the kitchen, but Cliff had locked the handset in the kitchen closet, along with all the sharp knives. When he sent her to bed at night, he handcuffed her wrists to the iron headboard and released the leg manacles, "So you can spread your legs for me, darlin'."

Cliff looked at her awhile, then said, "You think he's comin' for you, but that phone call I got before was from Blake, and he tells me that your lover boy went and kidnapped Ward and tortured the guy. But Ward told him that we went off to Florida. So that's where the stupid bastard is goin', if he gets that far." He added, "If he even gives a shit about you."

Annie didn't reply.

Baxter added, "I don't think he cares, and even if he does, he don't have the balls." He laughed. "I mean, he *really* don't have the balls. But, in a way, I hope he does show up here. You ever seen a man caught in a bear trap? It ain't pretty, I'll tell you. Most of the time they can't get it open and they die of starvation and thirst. Sometimes they cut off their foot to get out. Now, if your lover boy gets himself caught in a trap around the house, we can both watch him dyin' for a week or so. They usually yell themselves hoarse, cryin' and beggin', then at the end, they want you to shoot 'em."

Annie kept staring into the fire.

Cliff said, "Never saw it myself, but I know someone who did. I think I'd enjoy that." He couldn't seem to get a reaction out of her, so he said, "Don't know what good he can do you anyhow. Last time I saw him, his balls was sittin' in my hand. You ever seen a man's testicles out of their sack? Hell, I shoulda saved 'em and showed 'em to you." He stared at her, and she glanced back at him. He could tell she wasn't sure about this, but each time he told her this story, she seemed less believing, so he decided not to repeat it again for a few days.

Cliff went on, "I hope, if he shows up, I don't have to kill him outright. If he don't get caught in one of them bear traps, then maybe the dogs'll get on him, or maybe I can wing him. Hey, I'll bring him inside here, and you can take care of him. Get him fixed up enough so I can skin him alive and tan his hide—"

"Shut up!"

He stood. "What did you say?"

"Stop! Stop it!"

"Yeah? Stand up."

"No."

"Stand up, bitch, and get it over with; or I'll make it worse."

Annie hesitated, then stood.

"Drop the blanket."

She let the blanket fall to the floor. Baxter took the key chain out of his pocket, knelt, and removed the padlock, freeing the manacle chain. He stood and said, "Go over there and bend over the arm of the sofa."

She shook her head.

He drew his revolver and aimed it at her face. "Do what I say."

"No. Go ahead and shoot."

He lowered his aim to her stomach and said, "If I gut-shoot you, you're gonna take a day to die."

Annie remained standing where she was, wanting to die, and it didn't matter at that moment how long it took. Then she thought about her children and thought of the possibility that Keith would remember what she'd told him about Grey Lake, or of Keith speaking to Terry, who she prayed understood about Atlanta.

Annie knew that they couldn't stay in this house forever, and when someone came along, there would be bloodshed, and it would probably end with Cliff killing her, then himself.

So she wavered between wanting him to kill her now, and living a little longer and hoping she could do something to end this nightmare. But she didn't know how long she could live like this, how long it would be before he broke her. It had been three days now since they'd gotten here, and already she was losing touch with reality, bending to his perverted will to save herself some pain. She was no match for him in this situation, she realized. He had all the power, and even her subtle resistance met with his sadism. Still, she wasn't going to be his willing victim, and she said to him, "Go to hell."

Baxter lowered the pistol, went to the fireplace, and stuck the poker in the flames.

Annie watched. No, he wouldn't kill her. Not yet.

But he would do what he was preparing to do. The poker tip glowed red, and he pulled it out of the fire, held it up, and spit on it. The spit sizzled, and he held the poker out a few inches from her right breast. He said, "I don't want to do this, but you ain't givin' me any choice."

She replied, "I don't want to do this either, and you're not giving *me* any choice."

He looked at her, then said, "We're gonna have it my way, either way. So?"

Realizing she'd resisted as much as she could, she turned and walked to the couch, the chain dragging over the rug, and the leg manacles chafing her ankles.

He said, "Bend over."

She bent over the upholstered arm of the couch and put her hands out in front of her on the cushions. She heard Cliff put the poker down, then unbuckle his gun belt and lay it down somewhere. He came up behind her and unbuckled his trouser belt and whipped it out of the loops. "Okay, you got to pay for your smart mouth. And you got a lot of payin' to do for a lot of smart-mouthin' over the years."

She didn't want to reply, but she knew if she didn't say anything, he'd go on and on, and she didn't want to wait for it in that humiliating position. She said, "Just get it over with."

"I want you to think about what's comin' and why you're gettin' it."

"Damn you—"

He swung the belt and brought it down hard across her buttocks.

Keith focused on one of the lit dormer windows that protruded from the sloped side of the A-frame. He caught a glimpse of something, then saw her. She was standing, and he could see her from the waist up. She was bare-breasted, and she stood motionless for a few seconds. He could see her face, but at this distance, the equivalent of about twenty-five yards with the four-power magnification, he had trouble making out her features. He thought she looked frightened, but that might have been his imagination.

Suddenly, she disappeared, and standing where she had been was Cliff Baxter. He focused as tight as he could, then watched Baxter making some sort of odd movement. It took him a few seconds to realize that Baxter was swinging something, a whip, or a belt, or a switch, and he understood what was happening. He lowered the binoculars and felt a tightening in his stomach.

Billy whispered, "What do ya see?"

"Nothing."

"You see anybody?"

"Yes...I did." He looked at Billy and said, "He's beating her. I'm going in." He grabbed his rifle and started to stand, but Billy pushed him down. "No! No! You wait."

Keith lay on the ground. He thought he could hear the sound of whatever was happening in that house, the steady slap of something against bare flesh and her crying. But, of course, he couldn't hear it, but he felt it, as if it were happening to him.

Annie yelled out in surprised pain. Usually, she prepared herself for the first blow and hardly made a sound until the pain got to be too much. Yesterday, she'd taken ten strokes without crying, and that had given her some satisfaction.

He said, "I was gonna give you only five, but now you're gettin' a full ten. You count, and if you lose count, I start over again. Ready?"

She didn't reply.

"*Ready?*"

"Yes."

"Come on, Keith. We don't want to spook him. We got to back off and wait awhile. Right? Hey, man, you okay? Get it together, Keith. This ain't a trainin' exercise."

Keith didn't reply.

"Come on. We can't stay here."

Keith got up on one knee, then stood and raised the binoculars again, but couldn't see anything through the window.

Billy reached up and pulled him down again. "Jesus! If he's lookin' through that infrared scope, you're dead. Come on."

The dog barked again.

Baxter turned away and walked back to his chair, leaving her bent over the couch. He sat down, watching her. He heard the dog bark again, but he ignored it. After a minute, he said, "Turn around and kneel."

She turned toward him on her knees.

"You fuckin' whore." He leaned forward and kept staring at her. "Look at me, bitch. You lied to me about him, didn't you?"

"Yes."

"You said you didn't even remember runnin' into him. And all the time you was fuckin' him. Right?"

"Yes."

"Maybe lover boy got AIDS, and now you got it, and you gave it to me, bitch."

She didn't reply.

"He probably fucks everything and everybody. Probably fucks goats and little boys and two-dollar whores. Whatever he got, you got. He use a rubber on you?"

She didn't reply.

"How many times you fuck him?"

"Do you mean in high school and college, or—?"

"Shut up! You make me sick. I ought to kill you, but you ain't gettin' off that easy. You're gonna pay for what you did. You know that, don't you?"

"Yes."

"And you're gonna keep payin', 'cause you can't ever make that right. I'll bet you're sorry you did it, ain't you?"

She didn't reply.

"Answer me."

"Yes."

"Yes, what?"

"Yes, sir. I'm sorry."

"You bet you are. And you ain't half as sorry as you're gonna be. When I get through with you, you're gonna be like my bitch retriever. You're gonna do what I say, when I say, eat when I tell you, curl up at my feet, lick my hand, and follow me around with your head down. Right?"

"Yes."

"Yes, what?"

"Yes, sir."

"Good. And I'll treat you just fine, though you don't deserve it after what you done. You'll get three meals, a warm place to sleep, and a whippin' only when you deserve it. Right?"

"Yes, sir."

Cliff sat back and watched her still kneeling, her head down, and her arms wrapped around her. He smiled. "Cold?"

"Yes, sir."

"Come on over here by the fire. Don't walk."

Annie hesitated, then walked on her hands and knees over to Baxter and came to a stop at his feet.

"Straighten up."

She rocked back on her haunches and sat up, facing him, her head still down.

"Look at me."

She looked him in the eye and noted with some satisfaction that his right eye still had blood in it.

"When did you fuck him? *Where* did you fuck him?"

"In his house."

"You fuck him in our house?"

"Yes."

He seemed surprised and asked, "How the fuck did you manage that? You're lyin'! You never could've fucked him in our house."

"If you say so."

"You're a fucking slut. You know that? You're a fucking whore, so I'm gonna treat you like a whore."

She noticed the gun belt on the small end table to the right of his chair. She thought she could grab it, roll away, and draw the pistol before he reacted. She could make him chain himself with the leg irons, and she could get away. That's all she wanted—to be away from him and this house. She'd only shoot if he made her, and then she'd only try to wound him. She waited for her chance.

Reluctantly, Keith moved away from the house, Billy behind him. About a hundred yards from the edge of the clearing, some two hundred yards from the house, they stopped.

Billy sat with his back against a pine tree and said, "The son-of-a-bitch could have nailed our ass with that infrared scope."

Keith nodded and looked at him in the dim light. "You don't have to stay. Go back to the truck."

"Hey, we got a deal. Right?"

"Yes, but—"

"Cool out, Keith. I know you saw somethin' that got to you, and I didn't see it. But I don't have to *see* it. I know him better than you know him. I been in his jail."

Keith got himself under control. "Okay. Thanks."

"We just sit here awhile. Let the dogs calm down. Let Baxter get settled in. We got him fixed. Remember that... how'd that go? Find 'em, fix 'em, and finish 'em." He added, "Fuck him."

Keith nodded to himself. He thought perhaps he should have taken the shot. But there were good shots and bad shots, sure shots and long shots. That definitely would have been a bad, long shot, and if he'd missed, or just hit Baxter's body armor, there was no taking the shot back. You just never knew. They told you in class that the first shot was not always the best you were going to get, but it might be the only one you'd get. You had to make a quick calculation, had to decide when to maintain fire discipline and when to go for it. Maybe if he had seen or foreseen what Baxter was going to do to Annie... but at least he knew she was alive and would stay alive as long as Baxter was getting some pleasure out of her. "Bastard."

"Yeah. But more than that. This guy needs a whole new word invented for him."

"I've got a word for him. Dead."

"I like that word."

Baxter went on verbally abusing her for a minute or two, and she kept eye contact with him as he'd ordered her to do, kneeling at his feet, but she wasn't listening, she was waiting for an opportunity to move. The gun was only about four feet away, but she had to distract him. She said, "I'm cold. May I get the blanket?"

"No, you can freeze your tits is what you can do." He went on to another subject and asked, "How many other guys did you fuck since we been married?"

"None."

"Don't lie to me. You got a hot twat, sweetheart. I see how you look at other men. All you think about is cock. Well, you're gonna get plenty of cock here, darlin'." He asked again, "How many guys did you fuck since we been married?"

"None."

"Bullshit. Before I'm through with you, you're gonna name every guy you fucked behind my back. There was other guys, wasn't there?"

She nodded.

"How many?"

"Just two."

"Oh, yeah? *Just* two?" He suddenly seemed interested. "Who?"

"You'll get angry."

"Angry? I'm pissed off now. *Who?*"

"Promise you won't hit me."

"I ain't promisin' you nothin', except another beatin' if you don't tell me. *Who?*"

She took a deep breath and said, "Reggie Blake and your brother, Phil."

He stood. *"What?"*

She put her hands in front of her face, mostly to keep him from seeing the smile on her lips.

"You...you're lyin'! You bitch, you're lyin'! Look at me!"

She lowered her hands and looked at him.

Cliff kneeled down on one knee and put his face

to hers. "You think you're gonna fuck with my head, don't you?"

"Cliff, please, this isn't fair. I did everything you asked me to do. I answered all your questions about other men a hundred times. What do you want me to tell you?"

"I want the fuckin' truth."

"I never had sex with another man since we've been married ... except him."

"You never fucked Blake?"

"No ... but he comes on to me."

"Oh, yeah? That fuck ... and my brother?"

"He comes on to me, too."

"That ... I don't believe you."

"I'm sorry."

Cliff stared at her, then nodded. "Okay, we're gonna have the real truth. Maybe not today, but little by little, you're gonna tell me everything about other men. Right?"

She knew he was obsessed with this and other subjects like this, so as long as he was interested in the subjects, she was relatively safe. "Yes,"

He didn't speak for some time, then, still kneeling on one knee in front of her, he took her chin in his hand and turned her face to him. He said softly and slowly, "You always knew you'd wind up here like this, didn't you?"

She looked into his eyes and thought about that. In one way, she thought she knew him, knew how crazy he was, but never did she think he was capable of this. Yet the thought haunted her that she did know.

"You knew, didn't you? *I* knew, so you must've known. So if you knew this was gonna happen someday, you must've wanted it to happen."

"No!"

"You love it—"

"No! You bastard—" She swung her fist at him, but

he caught her by the wrist and slapped her across the face. She rocked back, then slumped on the floor.

He stood. "Get up!"

She buried her face in her hands, curled up into a ball, and began sobbing.

"Get up!"

"Leave me alone! Leave me alone!"

Baxter didn't like it when she became hysterical because he couldn't get her to do anything he wanted, couldn't get her to listen to him, so he just had to wait it out.

Annie lay on the floor, curled into a protective ball, her face still buried in her hands. After a few minutes, Baxter said, "If you're through with your bullshit, I'll let you wrap the blanket around you, and I'll let you get something to eat. I'm waitin', but I'm not waitin' much longer before I get the horse whip. Fact, you got ten seconds. Nine." He began counting backward.

Annie uncurled herself on the floor, then slowly got up into a kneeling position again.

"That's good. Listen, darlin', this can be as hard or easy as you want to make it. The quicker you understand that I'm in charge here and that you got to learn to shut your wise mouth, and that you got to do everything I say just like I say it, the easier it's gonna be on you. There ain't no way out for you, sweetheart. You're gonna cook, clean, wash me, suck cock, fuck, and kiss my feet. The better you get at that, the better it is for you. Understand?"

"Yes, sir."

"You know, all you Prentis girls has always been stuck-up. You think I don't know you look down on me and my family? Who the hell do you think you are? What I'd really like is to have your bitchy sister here, too. Look at me, whore. I'm talkin' to you. How's that sound to you? The two bitches waitin' on me hand and foot with no clothes on—"

"Please, Cliff…I'm not feeling well…I'm going to pass out…I don't want to get pneumonia…I have to have something to eat…I'm going to faint…"

He looked at her closely, then said, "Yeah, we don't want you gettin' sick. I don't want to take care of you."

She didn't reply.

"Okay, first you get that medical kit and change my bandage. Don't bother to stand, sweetheart. You're a St. Bernard now."

Annie moved on all fours across the room and got the medical kit from a wooden storage chest, then, without him reminding her, she hung the canvas bag around her neck by its strap and went back to where he was now standing beside the sofa.

Baxter lowered his pants and his undershorts, then lay down on the couch.

Annie opened the canvas bag and took out a pair of blunt nose scissors made for cutting surgical tape. She put the lower blade beneath the tape that was wrapped around Baxter's left thigh and cut through it. She noticed that there was still blood on the tape, and when she peeled the gauze away, she saw that the wound wasn't healing properly, but it wasn't infected. She wondered if there was a way she could infect it.

She took alcohol and cotton and washed away the blood around the wound. He winced. She put iodine on the two-inch cut, and this time he let out a small groan. He lifted his thigh, and she ripped off the old bandages, which also caused him pain, then she reapplied fresh gauze and began rewrapping the wound. He never said a word, she noticed, about the wound, or about his eye. His silence on the subject was his way of trying to convince her and himself that everything in the motel room had gone his way. In fact, she knew that Keith had put up a good fight and had almost succeeded in cutting Cliff's femoral artery. At first, she'd almost believed Cliff when he said he'd castrated Keith, but it was obvious, by his unresolved rage, that he hadn't.

She noticed that he had his eyes closed, and she glanced over her shoulder at the end table beside his chair where the holster lay.

He said, "Lookin' for somethin'?"

She turned back to him.

"Now here I am, layin' down with my drawers around my ankles, and you're wonderin' if you can get to that gun belt before I do. Well, darlin', you can. But when you get there, you're gonna be surprised, 'cause"—he drew the pistol out from where he'd stuck it between the cushions—"I got it here." He tapped the barrel on her head and said, "We got a long way to go, don't we? When I'm finished with you, you're gonna go fetch my guns for me and not even *think* about usin' them on me."

She nodded, but she knew, and he knew, that time would never come. It occurred to her that he enjoyed the cat-and-mouse game; it gave him some amusement during the days and nights. It was important for him to show her he was smarter than she was, or at least more cunning and better able to survive in this world that he'd created. In one way, he wanted to break her, but in another way, he liked her spunk, liked her to present him with challenges. If she broke too easily, or too fast, he might get bored and depressed, then become more sadistic, until finally he'd just end it all for both of them. On the other hand, if she showed too much resistance, or if he believed that she was clever enough to actually get the drop on him, then he'd kill her out of rage, or out of his instinct for self-preservation. This much she'd figured out in the last three days, but she hadn't fine-tuned the balance between spunk and submission. There were moments when she didn't care, when the humiliations were so grotesque that she just wanted to give up. But each time she felt that way, she rallied herself and promised to go on for another hour, then another, until finally he would handcuff her to the bed and let her sleep.

Baxter said, "Wash the Baxter family jewels, darlin'. Use alcohol. I like that."

She poured alcohol onto a gauze pad and washed his genitals.

He said, "You know, I can fuck three times a day. I'd fuck one or two women in a day, then come home and fuck you. How about that? And you thought you was the only one foolin' around."

She never once thought he was faithful, and she didn't know why he thought this revelation was going to hurt her. But his brain was working hard to find things to do to her and say to her that would hurt, humiliate, and cause her to question her own worth and integrity. He thought if he called her bitch, whore, and slut long enough, she'd start to believe it. If he told her he'd castrated Keith, she might believe it. When he told her he wanted to fuck her sister, it did make her angry and anxious. When he used the belt on her, she felt defeated and powerless, but through the agony, she maintained whatever dignity she could, and the beatings strengthened her resolve to keep her sanity.

She said, "Can I get my blanket now and get something to eat?"

"You was naked when I found you in the motel, and you can stay naked." He got off the sofa and pulled up his shorts and trousers.

"Please, Cliff, I'm cold and hungry. I have to go to the bathroom."

"Yeah? Okay, you can stand."

She stood and, without him giving her permission, she wrapped the blanket around her.

"Let's go," he said.

"Can't I go alone?"

"No way, sweetheart. Go on."

She walked past the kitchen, down a short hallway, and turned into the bathroom.

Baxter sat on the rim of the tub, while she sat on the toilet seat and urinated, avoiding his eyes. She wiped herself with tissue paper, stood, and walked back into the hallway, the chain keeping her from taking the long strides she wanted to take. She turned into the kitchen, but he moved past her and stood in front of the refrigerator.

She said, "I'd like something to eat."

"You eat what I give you. Sit down, if your butt don't hurt too much, or you can stand, or get on the floor, and I'll get the dog dish like last time."

She went to the small table and lowered herself gently onto the wooden chair, with the blanket draped around her shoulders.

He opened the refrigerator and put two slices of bread on a paper plate, then a few slices of mixed cold cuts, and threw it on the table. "Eat."

She began eating the bread and cold cuts while he watched. She didn't eat fast, but took her time, though she was so hungry, she felt faint.

He took a beer for himself from the refrigerator and put a container of milk in front of her with no glass. He sat across from her and said, "You ain't gettin' no more, so don't ask."

Annie thought it was time to engage him in some normal conversation. He seemed calmed down, self-satisfied, and he might give her some information. She tried to adopt a pleasant tone of voice, as if nothing unusual had happened, as if he hadn't just beaten her. She asked, "How much food do we have, Cliff?"

"Enough for two or three months. Ain't gonna be much fresh stuff left after a week. But I got cans and dried food. Plenty of beer."

"Then what?"

"Then I can go into town and get more. Why? You got someplace you got to be?"

"I just want to know how long it's going to be before we can go home."

"You are home, honey buns."

"I mean to our house in Spencerville."

"Why do you want to go there?"

"I just thought we'd spend some time there."

He smiled. "Yeah? I don't think so. We're retired now, sweetheart. Gonna get that house sold."

"All right. I guess that's a good idea." She didn't want to drink from the container, but she did, then asked casually, "When can I make a few phone calls?"

He looked at her. "When you start feelin' sorry for what you did."

"I *am* sorry, Cliff. I'm sorry it happened. When will you forgive me?"

"Never. But I might decide someday to go easy on you. But we got a long way to go before that day gets here."

She nodded, knowing that day would never come. It was dangerous, she knew, to remind him that their children couldn't be put off too much longer, that they'd want to come to Grey Lake for Thanksgiving, or Christmas at the latest. Then there was her family, her sister, her parents, and his family. But to remind him that there was an outside world that had to be reckoned with might send him off the deep end. However, she'd already broached that subject by mentioning phone calls, and she could tell he was brooding over this. She said, "If I can call a few people, they wouldn't wonder where we were. I'll say we're back from Florida, and—"

"You let me worry about that. Maybe next week, or the week after. Far as anybody is concerned, we're on a second honeymoon in Florida. I don't have to report to nobody. I'm on extended leave of absence, and it's my fucking business where I am, not nobody else's. The kids ain't kids no more, and they got their own lives and don't give a shit about us. I'll call them now and then."

She nodded. "Okay." She looked at him and said, "Cliff, you really made me pay for what I did, and I got everything I deserved. So why don't we just pretend that nothing happened and go back to Spencerville? You know that you want to go back to the job, to finish out your next few years. I promise you that I've learned how to treat you, and I'm very...sorry for what I've done, and it will never happen again. You're all the man I need." She watched him closely, and she could see that she was actually getting through to him and that he was thinking about it. She continued, "There's no reason to stay here too long. Whatever I learned here, how to satisfy you and make you happy, I can do in Spencerville. If we go back in a few weeks, we don't have to answer a lot of questions. Okay?"

He stayed silent for a full minute, then stood but said nothing. He looked at her, and she stood also, drawing the blanket tightly around her. They faced each other, and she could see he was fighting some inner battle. She didn't know how much of his behavior was a result of rage and how much was psychopathic. But the fact that he hadn't gotten any calmer, and in fact had gotten worse in the last three days, frightened her.

Finally, he smiled and said in a pleasant voice, "Sounds like you want to go back to the way we were, except better."

"I do."

"That must mean you love me. You wouldn't want to do all those nice things for a man you didn't love."

"No, I wouldn't."

He asked her, "Do you love me?"

She didn't reply.

"Say you love me."

She knew she should say it, just to say it, otherwise he'd know for certain that everything she'd already told him was a lie.

"Tell me you love me."

"I don't."

"I didn't think so. But I love you."

"If you loved me, you wouldn't do this to me."

"I haven't done nothing to you that you didn't have coming. Did I ever treat you like this before you went and spread your legs for somebody else? Did I?"

"You . . . no, you didn't."

"See? You just don't like payin' the price. You don't like takin' responsibility for your own actions. That's what's wrong with you women. Always lookin' for a free ride, a pass, a way out with no sweat on your part. You pulled that shit in Spencerville. You ain't gettin' off so easy here."

"Neither are you."

"What the fuck do you mean by that?"

She didn't reply.

"You want another strappin'?"

"No."

"I'll bet not. So you don't love me. But you will. And when you finally say it, you're gonna mean it. Really mean it, from deep down inside of you. You're gonna say, 'Cliff, I love you.' And I'll tell you what—if I had my lie detector machine here, it would tell me that you're tellin' the God's honest truth. But I don't need the machine, sweetheart, 'cause when the day comes, I'll know it, and so will you."

"Never."

"Remember you said that. Meantime, be thankful I still love you, 'cause the minute I don't, you're dead. When you say your prayers tonight, pray that I still love you in the mornin'."

"When I say my prayers tonight, I'll pray for your soul, Cliff, and ask God to forgive you. I can't."

He didn't like that and said to her, "Go lock yourself to the floor."

She turned and walked out of the kitchen, into the big living room, and knelt near the rocker by the fire. He came in behind her and watched as she put the shackle of the padlock around the chain and through the eyebolt and snapped the lock shut. She wrapped the blanket around her and under her buttocks and sat.

He poked the fire and added another log, then stood watching the flames awhile. One of the dogs barked again, but he didn't seem to notice. Finally, he turned around and looked at her. He said, "I told you, when I'm through with you, you ain't gonna be you. When that happens, you won't *want* to go back to Spencerville. Get used to this, sweetheart. This is it, forever." He pointed to the gray timberwolf head, mounted above the mantel "Just me, you, and these guys for company."

Annie turned away from him and looked into the fire. A tear ran down her cheek.

He turned on the small table lamp beside his chair, then shut off the floor lamp. He sat down and began reading a hunting magazine. After a few minutes, he looked up and spoke in a normal, almost conversational tone of voice. "Tell you what, though. There's a guy out there someplace who fucked you, and if my boys get him and bring him here, or if he somehow comes here and I get him, then after he's dead, I might reconsider things. But meantime, you're stayin' here with me. You can think about that cock all you want, but you're never gonna see it again unless I got it in my hand and I'm feedin' it to the dogs."

Annie wiped the tears from her face with the blanket.

"Don't cry, sweetheart. I know you're worried about me, darlin', but I can take care of myself. You found that out, didn't you?" He laughed and went back to his magazine. "Bitch."

Annie sat in the rocker, feeling cold, hungry, violated, in pain, and exhausted. It had been a bad day, and there would be more of them. She looked at him, then closed her eyes and thought of Keith. She felt his presence inside her and tried to imagine that he was close by. She remembered what he'd said... *even if we're separated for a short time, remember that I love you, and know that we'll be together again...* "I promise."

"What?"

"Nothing."

He went back to his magazine. He said, "I bet I know what you're thinkin' about, and it might surprise you that I'm thinkin' the same thing. I hope he comes, too."

CHAPTER THIRTY-NINE

Keith found it difficult to sit and wait, but he knew that the later the hour, the more chance of catching Baxter with his guard down. The attacker, he reminded himself, always had the advantage of surprise and mobility, not to mention being psyched up for a fight. The defender had the advantage of having picked the place and prepared it to his liking, and, not inconsequentially, the advantage of creature comforts. But it was this last thing that sometimes lulled the defender into a fatal sense of security.

Billy took a cellophane bag out of his pocket and ripped it open. "You want some peanuts?"

"No."

Billy munched on the peanuts. He said, "Maybe we don't have to kill the dogs. Now that I seen his setup there, I think we can take him from a distance. We just set up firing positions at the edge of the clearing, make a noise, and the dogs bark and he comes out onto that nice high deck and we plug his ass. We got scopes, and we can get off two, three rounds each before he knows what the fuck hit him."

"He's wearing a bulletproof vest."

"Ah, fuck his vest. When those rounds start slapping

him around, he's gonna be hurt, even through the vest. And maybe we'll hit an arm or leg. Maybe his fucking head. What do ya think?"

"I like the idea that you're thinking. Okay, he's down. Then what?"

"Okay, after he's down, you move fast—a hundred yards to the house and up to the deck—that's maybe twelve, thirteen seconds, and meantime I'm still layin' down coverin' fire for you, so if he picks his fat ass up from the deck, I nail him again. If there's anything left of him when you get there, you cut his fucking throat. Then I'll come up and gut him. No, shit, Keith, I'm gonna gut him. Hey, if you want, *I'll* rush him and you lay down the fire. Your call, Lieutenant."

Keith glanced at Billy Marlon. Clearly, the man was enjoying himself, and he had every right to. He said, "Standard fire and maneuver. Not bad. Safe for us."

"Yeah. Whoever's layin' down the covering fire is safe, and the guy who's rushin' the house has to trust the other guy to know how to shoot. You a good shot?"

"Pretty good. You?"

Marlon hesitated, then said, "Used to be the best. Depends now on how steady I can get."

"How steady can you get?"

"For this motherfucker, steady as a rock."

Keith nodded. He thought about Billy's idea. The infantry school would approve. But there were other things going on. A hostage for one, and Keith's image of himself and Baxter face-to-face, for another. They didn't cover any of that in tactics classes, or even in intelligence school. Revenge and payback was something you learned on your own. He said to Billy, "There's a chance that Baxter could take cover before he's badly hurt. He could get around to the blind side of the house, or worse, he could get back *into* the house."

"Yeah...but—"

"Look, a hundred yards isn't too long a shot, but at night and with the other guy wearing protective armor, it could be a disaster. I don't want him back in the house."

Billy nodded but said, "That's why you or me has to charge across that open space like we got a hundred gooks on our ass. We'll be on top of him before he can get his shit together. Even if he gets in the house, he's gonna be hurt."

"He could kill her."

"Keith, he's gonna be hit, because we both ain't missin' at that distance with scopes, so even if he makes it into the house, he ain't got nothin' on his mind except us and him. He ain't gonna bother her."

"Maybe."

"Hey, you got something else on your mind?"

"Yes, I do. What I don't want to happen is one of us getting him with a lucky head shot." Keith added, "I don't want him to die quickly. That's where I'm coming from. You have to know that."

Billy stayed silent a moment and nodded slowly. "Yeah...I already figured that out. Look, I don't want him to be standin' there one second and the next second he's lights-out with a slug through his brain, no pain, no eye-to-eye. Hell, I want to gut him *alive*. Alive, Keith, and watch his eyes when I hold his guts up in front of him. But if you're thinkin' we got to low-crawl up to that house and catch him with his thumb up his ass, I ain't buyin' it. I don't have that kind of nerve. Do you?"

"Yes."

"Well, then you go ahead. I'll cover you from the trees. But you got to take those dogs out first."

"Right. That's why I bought the crossbow. Low-tech solution to a low-tech problem."

"I guess so." Billy added, "Hey, what we want to do and what we *can* do is two different things. I'm givin' you the safe way to take this asshole out, and you're givin' me some commando shit."

"Billy, either way, you do the same thing. Just set up a firing position in the trees."

"Hey, I ain't worried about my useless ass. But I don't want you gettin' wasted out there in the open, or gettin' into that house and findin' out he's waitin' for you. I can't help you there, buddy." He added, "My way, when we get to him, he's either dead or hurt bad. Either way, I gut him."

Keith took a deep breath and informed Billy, "I think I want to take him alive."

"No way."

"Yes, I want to tie him up and throw him in the back of the pickup truck and bring him to the law. I've been thinking about it, and that's the way I want to do it. You think about it."

"I already thought about it, Keith. I know what you mean. He'd rather be dead than face the music for what he done. But I gotta tell you, the fucking law works funny. The law fucks me around, 'cause I'm dog shit, but I never hurt nobody. That motherfucker could walk."

Keith considered that. Aside from all the humiliations that Baxter would face, in a year or two he could be loose on the world again. Cliff Baxter was sick, and the state might agree with Baxter's attorney that he needed therapy and counseling. He'd had a traumatic experience, seeing his wife in bed with another man, a slick seducer from out of town, and he did what any man would do: He beat up the boyfriend, then, instead of kicking his wife out, he took her on a little vacation and tried to work things out. Sure, he overdid it a bit, which is why he needed counseling. Keith thought about that and finally decided that, despite his promise to Annie, Cliff Baxter needed to die. He said, "Okay... we waste him. But I have to do it up close. He's got to know it was me and you."

"Okay...if that's what you need to make it right for you, I'm okay with that. I like it. Hope we can do it."

"We'll do it."

Billy said, "Hey, after we finish this shit, I'm goin' to Columbus to look her up. I couldn't do that while he was alive. You know?"

"I know."

"I couldn't look nobody in the eye, Keith. I hung around that town, and I'd see him on the street, and he'd laugh at me. He'd arrest me sometimes when he saw me drunk and take me in and make me go through a strip search, and the bastard took pictures, and he said he mailed some to Beth with him standin' next to me."

Keith didn't respond.

"And you're probably wonderin' why I hung around. I'll tell you, because I was tryin' to get up the nerve to kill him, but I never got the nerve...and I never was going to get it. Until you came along." He added, "Remember, if I don't make it—"

"Okay. Enough." Keith looked at Billy, sitting with his back to the tree, staring off into the dark. Billy Marlon, Keith thought, sober now and with the insight of all lost souls who saw things too clearly, had probably foreseen his own death, and Keith thought he might be right. But Billy had reached one of those rare moments in life, he thought, perhaps the rarest of moments, when it was equally good to live or die.

They waited, listening to the infrequent night sounds of autumn—a chipmunk, a squirrel, a hare, an occasional bird. Keith looked up at the moon, which was nearly overhead now. It would set in perhaps three or four hours. That would be the time to move, except he needed the moonlight if he was going to use the crossbow on the dogs.

Keith didn't want to think about what was going on in the house, but he thought about it. Undoubtedly, Cliff Baxter had snapped, and his possessiveness had turned to something far more ugly. Keith knew that Baxter would beat Annie, degrade her, and punish her for her unfaithfulness. In reality, Baxter was a sexual sadist who had finally found the excuse he was looking for to play out his sick fantasies on the woman he had never completely broken. Keith had every confidence that Baxter hadn't yet broken her, that when he saw her, she would be like he was—beaten and bloody, but unbowed.

He put himself in the right mind-set for what was to come. He had to act rationally, coolly, and with the same cunning that he knew Baxter was capable of. He understood that Baxter could kill her anytime, but he was fairly certain that Baxter hadn't yet finished with her. What was going on between them now was the most exquisite thing that Baxter had ever done in his life, and he wasn't going to end it, except at the very last moment. And it was in that last moment, when they were face-to-face, that everything had to come together: rescue, revenge, and redemption, all long overdue.

Billy said, "I got this feelin' he knows we're here. I mean, he don't *know*, but he knows."

Keith said, "Doesn't matter. It doesn't change a thing, for him, or for us."

"Right. He's got himself in a corner." He thought a moment and said, "I guess we're in a corner. too. We can leave, but we can't leave. You know?"

"I do."

"Hey, I wish I had a smoke."

"Do you need a drink?"

"Well...you got somethin'?"

"No. I'm asking you if you *need* a drink."

"I...do. But...it'll wait."

"You know, maybe you *can* get your life together after this, if you lay off the juice."

"Maybe."

"I'll help you."

"Forget it. We're even." Billy asked, "Did you ever think we got fucked big-time?"

"Yeah. So what? Every veteran since the first war got fucked big-time. Maybe you should stop feeling sorry for yourself. There's no war long enough or bad enough to mess up your head as bad as you messed it up yourself."

Billy thought about that awhile, then replied, "Maybe not *your* head. You was always together. My head couldn't take too much."

"Sorry."

"Tell you somethin' else, Keith—if you don't think you're a little fucked-up, too, you ain't listenin' to the bells and whistles in your skull."

Keith didn't reply.

They waited another hour, mostly in silence. Finally, Billy said, "Hey, remember that Findlay game in our senior year?"

"No."

"I was playin' that day, halfback, and we was down seven to twelve, and I take the handoff and shoot off left tackle. They nailed my ass at the scrimmage line, but I didn't go down—I spun off and flipped the ball back to you. You was playin' fullback that day, remember? The Findlay bastards were all over you, but you chuck the long bomb out to some end—what the hell was his name? Davis. Right? And he didn't even know he was in the play, but he turns around, and the ball lands in his hands, and he gets hit and falls in the end zone. Touchdown. You remember that?"

"Yes."

"Hell of a game. Goes to show you. Even when things are goin' wrong, if you hang in there, you can catch a break. I wonder if they still got a film of that?"

"Probably."

"Yeah, I'd like to see that. Hey, do you remember Baxter from high school?"

"No... actually, I do."

"Yeah, he was always a prick. You ever get into it with him?"

"No, but I should have."

"Never too late to settle a score."

"That's just what he's thinking, and that's why we're all here."

"Yeah... but we never done nothing to him in school. *I* never done nothing to him. He just gets off on fucking with people. I can't understand why somebody didn't take him down long ago."

Keith said, "He picks on weak people."

Billy Marlon didn't respond to that but said, "Hey, he's really pissed at *you*." He laughed, then added, "You know something, after I saw you in the bar, like the next day when my head was straight, I remembered about you and Annie Prentis. And I got this wild thought in my head that you and her was gonna meet and get it back together. How's that for smart thinkin'?"

Keith didn't reply.

Billy went on, "I guess he figured that out, too. You know, I used to see her sometimes on the street—I mean, I never knew her too good in school, but bein' we was old classmates, she'd always smile at me and say hello. Sometimes, she'd stop and talk a minute, you

know, askin' me how I was doin'. I'd stand there, like
not knowing what to say, thinkin' to myself, 'Your husband fucked my wife, and I should tell you that,' but
of course, I never did. And I didn't want to talk too
long, because I was afraid that if he saw me talkin' to
his wife, he'd do somethin' nasty to me, or to her."

Keith said, "Maybe I *should* let you gut him alive."

Billy looked at him and said, "I don't need your permission to do that."

This sort of surprised Keith, but it was a good sign
for Billy. Keith said, "We agreed that I give the orders."

Billy didn't reply.

Another hour passed, and it got cold. Keith looked
at his watch. It was ten P.M. He was anxious to get moving, but it was too early. Baxter would be awake and
alert, and so would the dogs.

Keith saw that the moon was in the southwestern
sky now, and he figured he still had about two or three
hours of moonlight.

Keith said, "Okay, here's the way we're going to do
this. We take out the dogs in the moonlight, we wait
until moonset, I charge across that clearing, you cover,
I get onto the deck and put my back to the wall near
the sliding glass doors. Okay?"

"So far."

"Now you have to draw him out. Can you bark like
a dog?"

"Sure can."

"Okay, you bark, he comes out, just like he did last
time, only this time I'm behind him with a pistol to his
head. Simple and safe. You see any problems with it?"

"It sounds okay...they always *sound* okay, don't
they?"

"Right. Sometimes, they even work."

Billy smiled. "Remember them chalkboard sessions

in football? Every play was a touchdown play. Same in the Army. But they never showed what happened when some of your guys got taken out, and nobody ever knew what the other side was plannin' on doin' to fuck you up."

"That's life."

"Yeah." He thought a moment and said, "I think I fucked myself up. I didn't need no bad guys." He added, "But I hung in there long enough to catch this break."

They waited in the cold dark, wrapped in their canvas ponchos. At midnight, Keith stood, dropped his poncho on the ground, and said, "Let's move."

CHAPTER FORTY

Cliff Baxter put down his magazine and yawned. He finished his can of beer and scooped out a handful of pretzels from the bag and ate them. He looked at his wife in the rocking chair and threw a few pretzels on her blanket. "Don't say I never give you treats. Eat up."

She ignored the pretzels and didn't reply.

He said, "Ready for bed, darlin'?"

Still looking at the dying fire, she replied, "No, I just want to sit here."

"Yeah? All night?"

"Yes."

"Who'm I gonna cuddle with?"

"Not me. I'm chained to the bed."

"Handcuffed, not chained."

"What difference does it make to me?"

"Hey, if I could trust you, you wouldn't be chained to the floor, or cuffed to the bed, or nothin'. Can I trust you?"

"Yes."

He laughed. "Yeah, I can trust you to blow my brains out."

She looked at him. "Are you afraid of me?"

His eyes narrowed, and he said, "I'm afraid of anybody who can pull a trigger. I ain't no fool."

Annie said, "No, you're not. But you're..."

"What?"

"You don't trust people, Cliff. Do you know how to trust?"

"Nope. Why should I trust anybody? Why should I trust you?"

"If I gave you my word that I wouldn't try to kill you, would you uncuff me?"

"Nope. Why you makin' such a big deal about bein' cuffed?"

"Why? Because I don't want to be chained like an animal. That's why."

"Oh, you ain't chained like an animal. Animals got more freedom." He laughed. "You're chained like a felon who got caught by the law. Them dogs outside never did nothin' wrong, so they can move a hundred yards or so. You fucked up, lady. Big-time. Maybe in a few weeks, I'll hook you to the dog run, then you can say you're chained like a animal and thank me."

Annie took a deep breath and said, "Cliff...I had a chance to kill you that time...it's not in me to kill anyone. Please believe that...you know that. You said so yourself. Let me sleep without the cuffs tonight. I can't sleep like that with my wrists cuffed to the headboard. Please. I swear to you, I won't harm you."

"Yeah? But that ain't sayin' I won't wake up cuffed to the bed, and you'll be long gone. Right? Right? Hey, don't bother to answer." He leaned toward her. "That reminds me. Next time you got to take a piss, you can do it right where you are."

"Cliff...please..."

"Then clean it up." He added, "But not in the bed."

He yawned again. "So you'd rather sleep in the god-damned chair all night than sleep with me?"

She shook her head. "No . . . I'm sorry. I don't want to sit here all night. I'll go to bed." She added, "I have to go to the bathroom."

"Yeah? I got a better idea. Stay here. Do you some good." He moved toward her and ripped the blanket away, throwing it across the room. "Freeze your ass off, and piss on your chair."

"Bastard."

He pinched her cheek hard. "You got ten strokes across your butt comin' in the mornin'. Think about that all night. And no breakfast. You can sit there in your own piss and smell the bacon and eggs cookin'."

He walked to his gun rack and unlocked it, taking down the AK-47, then relocked the rack. "I'd rather sleep with a rifle than you, anyway. Rifle's warmer than you ever was."

She sat in the rocker, her arms around her, looking into the glowing embers.

He asked, "You want me to throw a log on?"

She didn't reply.

"Wasn't gonna do it, anyway."

She looked at him and said, "Cliff, please . . . I'm sorry. Don't leave me here. I'm cold, I have to—"

"You should've thought of all that before you opened your mouth. You remember that Doberman I had that used to bark at me all the time and bit me once? Lots of guys said I should've shot him. Well, anybody can do that. It took me about a month to show him who was boss, didn't it? Turned out to be the best damned dog I ever had. That's gonna be you, sweetheart."

She stood. "I am *not* a dog! I am a person, a human being. I am your *wife*—"

"*No!* You *was* my wife. Now you're my property."

"I am *not!*"

Cliff pushed her back in the rocker and stood over her. He stared at her a long time, then spoke in a sarcastic tone. "Well, now, if you was my wife, you'd be wearing a wedding ring, and I don't see one on you."

She didn't reply.

"Now, if you can find your weddin' ring, we can talk about you bein' my wife. Where do you think you lost it?"

She stayed silent.

"Well, hell, you don't need a ring. You got leg irons and handcuffs. Fact is, that's what I shoulda put on you years ago. And one of them chastity belts to keep your hot twat outa trouble. God knows, you don't take your marriage vows real serious."

"You . . ."

"*What?* You gonna tell me I fucked around. So what? But I'll tell you somethin'—them women didn't mean shit to me. If you'd've done what you was supposed to do, I wouldn't've had to go stickin' it here and there. Now, you, on the other hand, you went and fell in love. Didn't you?"

She didn't reply.

He came closer to her, and she turned in the rocker. He said. "Look at me."

She forced herself to turn toward him.

He said, "You think I'm ever gonna forget what I saw in that motel? I don't mean you fuckin' him. Hell, I pictured you fuckin' guys lots of times. I mean you jumpin' on me, so he could . . . he could try to kill me. I mean you layin' on him, so I couldn't smash his fuckin' head in. You think I'm ever gonna forget that? Ever?"

"No."

"No. Not ever."

*   *   *

Keith and Billy knelt at the edge of the clearing.

While Billy scanned through his telescopic sight, Keith trained his binoculars on the house. A light was still on, but not the light Keith had seen before, which had shone nearer to the sliding glass doors. This was a weaker light, coming from the dormered window where he'd seen Annie, near the center of the house where the chimney rose through the roof. He guessed that the light came from a single table lamp. He saw no other lights on and no discernible glow of flames from the fireplace, though smoke still drifted out of the chimney, and it still came toward them, so that he and Billy remained downwind from the dogs, which was good.

He continued to look at the house through the binoculars. He saw no movements and no shadows across the window. He couldn't see the telltale, blue-white flicker of a TV set, either, which would have meant background noise in the house and which would have been helpful. There could be a radio or tape playing, of course, but Keith gave Baxter enough credit for not creating a disadvantage for himself. If Keith had to guess what was going on inside the house now—and he did have to guess—he'd say that one or both of them were still awake, sitting by the dying fire, and perhaps reading, maybe talking. He also made the assumption that Annie was physically restrained in some way, or Baxter would have to be on his guard constantly.

Keith scanned the open space around the house. He saw that the Doberman pinscher was at the far end of its run toward the lake, lying down, perhaps sleeping. He noticed another dog, further away, silhouetted against the glow of the lake, walking near the shore, and it appeared that this dog was also on a wire run, which ran along the lake. The third dog, which he couldn't see now, was somewhere out toward the rear of the house. It occurred to him that, long before Baxter had retreated to his lair, he had positioned these dog posts to provide maximum security. Keith supposed that, if he'd lived Baxter's life, he'd take precautions, too.

Keith lowered his binoculars, and Billy put down his rifle. They remained almost motionless and could speak only in low whispers into each other's ears because of the dogs. Billy whispered, "Gettin' harder to see."

Keith nodded. The moon was low over the southwest end of the lake now, barely ten degrees above the tallest pines. He'd have welcomed complete darkness and would have wanted to wait until between three and four A.M., when dogs and men slept soundest. But if he could eliminate the dogs now, while he could see them, he'd feel better about that open space between the trees and the house.

They waited, wanting the light in the house to go out before the moon set behind the pines.

Keith stared at the house without the binoculars. The longer he stared at it, the more sinister it looked, he thought, this dark triangular-shaped structure, sitting high above the ground in the middle of nowhere, bathed in moonlight, and surrounded by a purposely cleared killing zone, with a faint light glowing from somewhere in its unseen rooms. A mist rose off the lake now, adding to the spectral mood of the setting. Keith tried to imagine what was happening inside that house, what Annie and Cliff Baxter were saying to each other after all these years, what they were thinking and feeling now that both of them knew the end was near.

Annie continued to look at Cliff, and for the first time in the last three days, perhaps the first time in years, she thought, their eyes actually met. She hadn't loved him in many years, and they both knew that, and for the last few years, she hadn't even cared for him as a person. But she'd never really wanted him to suffer, despite all he'd done to her. And now, even after all the physical agony he'd caused her, she was sorry for his emotional pain, which she knew was real and deep. She felt no emotional attachment to him—he'd killed that long before this. But she did wish he hadn't seen what he saw in the motel room.

He seemed to sense what she was thinking and said to her, "You never would've done that for me. Not even twenty years ago."

"No, I wouldn't." She added, "I'm sorry, Cliff. I really am. You can beat me, rape me, do whatever you want, but all I feel for you is pity. Maybe some of it is my fault for not leaving you sooner. You should have let me go."

He didn't reply, but she could see some of this was sinking in. Her words, she knew, would only cause him more pain, but under the circumstances, with life stripped to its bare essentials, and since he'd brought it up, it was time for honesty and reality. She didn't think what she said would snap him out of his insanity, and in fact it would probably make it worse. But if she was going to die, or both of them were going to die, she wanted him to know how she felt at the end.

Keith felt that familiar pre-combat calm come over him, that almost transcendental disassociation between mind and body, as though none of this were actually happening to him. This was how most men went into battle, he knew, but later, when it began and the adrenaline kicked in, you snapped out of denial, and your mind and body got together again.

He thought about Annie. He hoped that she believed

help was on the way, and that she could hang in there and not give up and not push him over the edge.

Baxter pulled the pistol out of his holster. He held it up and said, "This is his gun. I stole it from his house. I want you to know, if I shoot you, it's gonna be with his gun."

"So what?"

He pointed the Glock 9mm pistol at her. "You want to get it over with now?"

She looked at the black pistol pointing at her. She said, "It's your decision, not mine. Nothing I say matters to you."

"Sure it does. You love me?"

"No."

"You love him?"

"Yes."

He stared at her down the length of the barrel, then raised the pistol to his head and released the safety. "You want me to pull the trigger?"

"No."

"Why not?"

"I...Cliff, don't..."

"You don't want to see my brains splatter?"

She turned away. "No."

"Look at me."

"No."

"Don't matter. If I blow my brains out, you're gonna die a slow, slow death chained to that floor. You can watch me rot. You can smell me rot, right here in front of you."

She put her hands over her face and said, "Cliff... please, don't...don't torture me, don't torture yourself—"

"It's you or me, sweetheart. Which one?"

"Stop it! Stop!"

"Bye, darlin'—"

Suddenly, a muffled shot rang out from somewhere, and Keith and Billy got lower. They waited, but there was no second shot, only the sound of the dogs barking.

Billy whispered, "Did that come from the house?"

"Don't know." But it sounded as if it did. It wasn't the distinct crack of a rifle being fired in the open, but was muted, as if a pistol was being fired indoors. Keith raised his binoculars and noticed that his hands were unsteady. He couldn't see anything through the windows, and his impulse was to rush the house, but whatever had happened was finished, and he was too late to do anything about it.

Billy whispered, "Stay cool. We don't know."

"No, but we'll find out soon."

Annie heard the pistol fire, an ear-splitting explosion that made her jump. She turned her head to him and saw him standing there, the pistol at his side, a smile on his face. He said, "Missed." He laughed. "Piss yourself?" He laughed again.

Annie put her hands over her face and sobbed.

Cliff gathered his AK-47, the bulletproof vest, and a shotgun, then turned off the table lamp, throwing the room into darkness.

She could hear him breathing not far from her, then he said, "Good night, sweetheart."

She didn't reply.

"I said, good night, sweetheart."

"Good night."

"Don't sleepwalk." He laughed.

She heard him walk out of the room.

Annie sat motionless for a full minute, then opened her eyes. The embers glowed weakly in the fireplace. She felt her heart pounding and took a deep breath. Despite his periods of irrational behavior, which truly frightened her, she could still plant a suggestion in his mind and have him act on it. He wasn't going to kill himself, or her, tonight. But he did want her to suffer, so he liked what he thought was his idea of leaving her there, naked and cold, her feet chained to the floor. So far, so good. She had one chance and one chance only. She slid off the rocker, onto the floor, and moved toward the fireplace.

As Keith watched, the light in the lit window went out, then a few seconds later, the light in the window toward the rear of the house, probably a bedroom, went on. A minute later, the light in the second window went out, and he lowered his binoculars. It didn't seem logical that someone in the house had just been killed and that the other person turned off the lights and went to bed. In hunting country, he assured himself, there were lots of shots fired, even at night, and because of the lake and the trees, it was difficult to tell where that one had come from.

He got himself under control and glanced at Billy, who was looking at him, waiting for him to say something. At this moment, as they both knew, waiting at the jump-off point, conversation was essentially reduced to three commands: go; no go; hold. "No go" was not an option, "Hold" was what you wanted to say, and "Go" was irrevocable. Keith asked, "Ready?"

"Ready."

"Let's go."

CHAPTER FORTY-ONE

Annie slid quietly across the oak floor, the chain running through the padlock until the manacle on her left ankle came in contact with the eyebolt. She reached out with her right hand toward the wrought-iron poker, which stood upright against the stone fireplace, but couldn't reach it.

She rested a moment and listened. She could hear Cliff snoring twenty feet away in the bedroom down the hallway. She stretched as far as she could toward the poker, and it was close, but her fingertips were still a half inch away.

She tried again, stretching as far as she could, but her fingertips only brushed the handle of the poker. She went limp, and the taut chain fell to the floor, making a sound against the floorboards. She froze and listened.

Cliff's snoring stopped a second, then continued. She sat up, looking around the darkened room. The embers still glowed, and moonlight came in through the south windows. She needed something to extend her reach, but there was nothing near her. Then she saw it. Lying on the hearth, illuminated by the embers, was a big, twisted beer pretzel that had fallen to the floor when Cliff yanked the blanket off her. Cliff's little treat. *Thank you, Cliff.* She picked up the pretzel and again stretched her body and hand toward the poker.

Every muscle was pulling, and she felt pains shooting up her legs and through her battered body. But she remained steady and calm, the pretzel held tight in her fingertips until she looped it around the hilt of the poker and pulled. The poker fell toward her and she caught it, then lay still, breathing hard.

Finally, sure he hadn't heard anything, she inched back toward the rocker and sat on the floor. She bent over and examined the chain, padlock, and eyebolt between her feet. She didn't think she could lever the bolt out of the floorboards or snap the shackle open. But she could unscrew the threaded bolt from the floor. She put the tip of the poker through the shackle and moved the poker counterclockwise, using it as a lever to twist the padlock so that it also turned the eyebolt to which it was connected. The threads squeaked in the oak floorboards, and she stopped and listened, then repositioned the poker so as not to tangle the chain, then turned it again. After a few turns, she could feel with her fingers that the threaded bolt was rising out of the floorboard. She recalled that it was a three- or four-inch bolt, and when Cliff had put it in the oak floor, he'd said to her, "That' ain't comin' out." *Wrong, Cliff.* But it would take some time. She continued working the poker, and within a few minutes, the bolt was about two inches out of the floor, but it still held fast.

She heard the bed squeak, then heard the floorboards squeak as his heavy body came down the hall.

She quickly slid the poker under the hearth rug and got into the rocker, putting her bare foot over the padlock and eyebolt. She slumped to the side and feigned sleep, looking at him through a narrow slit in her left eye.

The table lamp came on, but he didn't say anything,

just stood there in his boxer shorts and undershirt. His eyes darted around the room like an animal, she thought, trying to see what, if anything, was not as it should be. His eyes glanced down at her feet, but then they darted somewhere else. In many ways, she thought, he'd become like his dogs, and there were even times when she thought he had the super-sharp sense of smell and hearing of a dog, or the cunning of a wolf. His weakness, however, was overestimating his own intelligence and underestimating everyone else's, especially women, especially hers.

"Hey! Wake up!"

She opened her eyes and sat up.

"You comfortable, darlin'?"

"No."

"You piss yourself yet?"

"No . . . but I have to go—"

"Good. Go right ahead."

"No."

"You will. Cold?"

"Yes."

"I was thinkin' about letting you come to bed." He jiggled the keys that were on a chain around his neck. "You want to come to bed?"

No, no, no. She tried to look relieved and grateful. She said, "Yes, thank you. I have to go to the bathroom. I'm cold, Cliff, and hungry. And I think I'm starting my period. I need a sanitary napkin." She added, "Please?"

He thought about that awhile, and so did she. If he had an ounce of compassion left in him, she thought, he'd take pity on her and let her do what she asked of him. But she was betting that he had no pity whatsoever, and the word "please" was all he wanted to hear, and "nothing" was all he wanted to do for her.

Baxter said, "Well, I'll think about it. I'll check on you later and see how cold, wet, and hungry you are."

"Please, Cliff—"

He said, "Remember, ten strokes in the morning, and no breakfast. But maybe we can work something out. Think about that thing you never let me do to you." He winked and reached for the light switch. Before he turned it off, she glanced at the mantel clock.

Annie heard him walk away, heard the toilet flush, then heard the bed squeak again. She listened to the mantel clock ticking. For the last two nights, he'd set his alarm to go off at two-hour intervals, starting at one-thirty A.M. It was twelve forty-five, so she had time, unless, of course, he'd set it to go off at a different time tonight. She had no way of knowing, but she had to wait until she was sure he was asleep again.

She let some time go by, about twenty minutes she figured, then thought she heard him snoring. She dropped down to the floor, took the poker from under the hearth rug, then began again.

One of the dogs barked, but just once, then a wind rattled a windowpane, and a backdraft blew soot through the fire screen and the embers crackled. Every sound, every groan of the house, made her jump, and her heart was beating too fast.

As she continued to unscrew the bolt, she allowed her self to picture herself free. She'd still have the chained leg manacles on, but she could walk. She knew where the keys to the Bronco were in the kitchen; all she had to do was take them, wrap the blanket around her, slide the glass door open onto the deck, and go down the stairs. She recalled what he'd said about a bear trap, so she knew she had to climb over the stair rail near the end, go under the house where the Bronco was parked, get inside and start it. She'd be on the dirt road within seconds. She wondered if he'd shoot at the car if he had a chance. She thought about what he'd said about him camouflaging the end of the dirt road and wondered if the Bronco, with four-wheel drive, could make it through. Neither of those two questions would matter if she just went into the bedroom with the poker and smashed him over the head with it, then she could get dressed and call the police.

She felt the heft of the cast-iron poker in her hand. The act itself would be simple, simpler than running. But if she couldn't kill him that time when they were face-to-face and both armed, how could she kill him when he was sleeping? Another half an inch, another few minutes, and she'd be free.

CHAPTER FORTY-TWO

K eith and Billy made their way through the pine forest and came to a stop at the edge of the clearing toward the back of the house.

Keith braced the butt of the crossbow against his chest and pulled on the sixty-pound bowstring until it hooked into the trigger release catch. He fitted one of the short arrows into the groove and knelt beside a pine tree, using the trunk to steady his aim. He looked through the crossbow's telescopic sight.

About sixty yards away, walking in the moonlight of the clearing, was a big German shepherd. The dog was not on a wire run, Keith noticed, but was tethered to a pole with a long leash.

Keith waited, hoping the dog would come closer, or at least stop in place for a few seconds, but the shepherd continued to pace randomly. Keith waited and watched.

Billy focused the binoculars on the house and whispered, "Okay here."

Finally, the shepherd stopped pacing at about forty yards' distance and raised its head, as though listening for something. It was a profile shot, and Keith aimed at the dog's forward flank, hoping to hit his heart or lungs. He pulled the trigger, and the arrow shot out of the crossbow.

He couldn't see where it went, but it didn't hit the dog. The dog, however, heard the vanes as they hummed past and let out a short, confused bark, then began running around.

Keith recocked the bowstring and fitted another arrow.

Billy whispered, "Still okay here."

Keith stood and fired purposely short, and the arrow sliced into the ground about twenty yards away. The shepherd heard it and streaked directly toward the arrow as Keith recocked, fitted another arrow, and aimed through the sight. The dog stopped short and snapped at the feathered vanes. Keith pulled the trigger.

He could actually see the arrow pass through the German shepherd's head, and he was sure the dog was dead before it hit the ground.

Keith tapped Billy on the shoulder. "One down. Let's move."

Keith reslung his M-16 rifle and carried the crossbow at his side. Billy slung his M-14 and carried the shotgun. Together, they began moving again through the pine forest, toward the other two dogs.

It took them over twenty minutes to navigate through the dark woods around the perimeter of the clearing. They crossed the open dirt road in a quick rush, and continued on in a semicircle through the pines and toward the lake.

They stopped at a point where they could see the lake ahead. The moon was almost behind the pines now, and the lake looked much darker. Keith figured they had only a few more minutes of good moonlight left.

There were some felled pines in the area, cut down, it appeared, to expand the clearing. Keith used the sawed base of a tree trunk to steady the stock of the crossbow. He scanned through the bow sight and saw the Rottweiler on its wire run, sitting about twenty yards away on its haunches, looking out at the lake.

Billy watched the house through the telescopic sight of his rifle. He had an oblique view of the sliding glass doors on the front deck and whispered, "House okay." He shifted his aim and found the Doberman pinscher. "Third dog sleeping."

Keith lined up the bow sight's crosshairs over the Rottweiler's left flank. The dog raised its head and yawned. Keith pulled the trigger. Except for the twang of the bowstring, there was no sound as the arrow flew off. A second later, the dog jerked, let out a short, surprised sound halfway through its yawn, and rolled over. It whimpered softly for a few seconds, then became quiet.

Keith rolled over, too, on his back, and with the butt against his chest, recocked the bowstring as Billy handed him another arrow from the quiver. Keith fitted the arrow, then jumped to his feet. With two dogs gone, absolute silence was not as important as speed. He noted on his watch that it was one twenty-eight A.M.

Keith left the cover of the pine trees and made directly for the Doberman pinscher, who was curled up on the ground about fifty yards away, apparently sleeping. Keith got within twenty yards before the dog awoke and jumped to its feet. Keith fired, and before he even saw if the arrow would hit or not, he dropped the crossbow and sprinted toward the dog, drawing his knife as he ran.

The Doberman yelped and tried to run at Keith, but the arrow had pierced his rear haunch, and he stumbled. As the dog looked back over his shoulder to see what was wrong, Keith landed on him with both knees, breaking his backbone, and at the same time grabbing its muzzle and holding it closed while he slit the dog's throat.

Keith felt the dog go into spasms, its blood pouring from its slashed throat. In a few seconds, the dog lay limp.

Keith glanced up at the house a hundred yards away. There was nothing between him and the house now—no dogs to warn Baxter, but also no cover or concealment for him. Just three hundred feet of open space. The clearing was dark, but not as dark as it would be in a few minutes when the moon dropped behind the pine trees, and he knew he should wait, as per plan. But he was psyched now, the adrenaline was pumping, he'd drawn blood, and he was as ready as he'd ever be.

Billy had moved up into a concealed position among the trees behind Keith, at a slight angle from the sliding glass doors, so he could cover Keith without Keith being directly in the line of fire. Billy whispered loudly, "Keith—get back here or get moving. You can't stay there."

Keith turned to Billy and gave him a thumbs-up.

Billy said, "Okay, I got you covered. Good luck."

Keith turned back toward the house and with no hesitation began the hundred-yard sprint across the open field.

He didn't want to be slowed down, and he didn't need his rifle for this, so he carried only the police revolver and the hunting knife.

Eighty yards. Ten more seconds, and he'd be on the steps to the porch. He focused on the dark sliding glass doors.

Sixty yards. He felt very exposed, very naked, charging across the open field, and he knew that if Baxter came through that door right now with the rifle and infrared scope, Baxter wouldn't even have to rush his shot and could even take the time to smile and say something nasty. Keith hoped that Billy Marlon was a good shot.

* * *

Cliff Baxter, responding to the alarm clock, had risen from bed and, still in his underwear, came into the living room and turned on the table lamp. He had his gun belt and holster draped over his shoulder and was wearing his bulletproof vest, but didn't have his AK-47 or shotgun with him.

Annie was kneeling on the floor in front of the rocking chair, her manacled ankles behind her. The poker was squeezed tight between her thighs, the end protruding between her feet and under the rocker, not visible to Baxter.

He asked, "Why you kneeling there in the dark?"

"I couldn't sleep in the rocking chair. I'm going to lie on the floor."

"Yeah?" He walked toward the sliding glass door. "I'm gonna wake the dogs."

He drew his pistol, unlocked the sliding glass door, and opened it just enough to point the pistol in the air and fire a shot. He began to close the door but froze and listened. The dogs weren't barking.

Billy Marlon, sighting through the telescopic sight of his M-14 rifle, covered Keith's run across the open clearing, the scope's crosshairs lined up on the glass door.

Suddenly, a light went on in the house, and a few seconds later he saw a backlighted figure at the door, but he couldn't be sure it was Baxter. The door seemed to move, and Billy heard a shot, then before he could squeeze off a round, the figure was gone. "*Damn!*" He saw Keith come into the view of his scope, still running. "Okay. Okay." Then a few yards from the base of the stairs, Keith veered off and disappeared from the scope. "What the hell?"

Billy Marlon stood there a second, confused, angry with himself, and feeling that he'd somehow let Keith down. There was nothing in the world more frustrating than a shot not taken, a target not engaged. He lowered the rifle, and without much thought, he began charging across the open field toward the house.

Thirty yards. Four or five more seconds. Keith looked up and saw a light come on inside the house. He didn't slow up or break stride, but kept going.

Twenty yards. A backlighted figure was suddenly at the glass door, and Keith thought he saw the door sliding open. Keith made a snap decision and veered off, running under the cantilevered deck and bringing himself to a short stop against one of the concrete-block columns that held up the house. A shot rang out. Keith put his back to the column and aimed his revolver straight up. The light from the house cast a faint illumination through the spaced deck boards. He kept the revolver pointed up, waiting for a shadow or movement on the deck above him, but he saw and heard nothing. A second later, he heard the door slide shut with a thud.

Keith was fairly certain that it was Baxter at the door and that Baxter hadn't seen or heard him approaching the house, or he wouldn't have turned on the light. Baxter had just picked that bad moment to rouse his dogs with a gunshot, and the dogs hadn't responded. Nor would they ever respond. Cliff Baxter knew he had company.

Cliff Baxter locked the glass door and took a long step away, his back to his gun rack. He stood absolutely still with Keith's Glock 9mm automatic pointing at the door. He glanced back at the table lamp about twenty feet away. He wanted to turn it off but didn't want to move. He listened.

He kept telling himself that no one could have gotten all three dogs, that they weren't dead, that the pistol shot just hadn't woken them. But that was not possible. *Damn it.*

He looked at his wife kneeling across the room, and their eyes met.

Annie maintained eye contact with him, and she recognized that look she had seen on his face when she'd pointed the shotgun at him. She wanted to smile, to smirk, to say something, but she sensed that death was near, and she didn't know whose.

Baxter lifted the key chain around his neck and unlocked his gun rack. He took down the Sako rifle, turned on the electronic infrared scope, and flipped the safety switch to the fire position.

Keith stayed frozen against the concrete column, the revolver still pointing upward at the deck. Behind him was the open garage space where the Bronco was parked, and above the garage was the house. He listened for footsteps from the house but heard nothing.

He glanced out to where he'd left Billy Marlon near the edge of the clearing where the dead Doberman lay. The moon had slipped behind the pines now, leaving the clearing in almost total darkness.

Keith wondered why Billy hadn't gotten a shot off but was glad he hadn't. Probably it had all happened too fast for him to react, or he thought Keith was going to open fire and charge up the stairs in Billy's line of fire. In any case, Baxter was on full alert, Billy was a hundred yards away across the clearing, and Keith was under Baxter's feet, probably not ten feet from him. He would rather have been and should have been on the deck, but Keith was reasonably certain Baxter didn't know he was there. All Keith had to do now was wait until Baxter decided he had to come out with his infrared scope and deal with the problem.

Keith heard a sound and turned toward the dark clearing. It took him a few seconds to realize there was movement out there, then he saw Billy Marlon running toward the house at a high speed.

Damn him. Keith was furious at Billy for not following orders, but Keith never thought Billy Marlon would.

He watched Billy covering the open space very quickly, his rifle at his hip, ready to fire, like an infantryman assaulting an enemy position.

Keith wasn't in a position to cover Marlon, but he tried to motion him to veer off and come under the house. But Billy was intent on his charge to the deck stairs. Billy Marlon wanted Cliff Baxter, and that's all that was on his mind at this moment.

Cliff Baxter quickly took stock of the situation. He had no way of knowing when the dogs had been silenced, and no way of knowing who'd done it, but he had a real good suspect in mind. Without the dogs, he had no early warning and had no idea where Keith Landry was at that moment. He felt a line of sweat form on his forehead and run down his face. *Goddamnit.*

He was about to cross the room and turn the lamp off when he thought he heard something outside—the sound of someone running, getting closer.

Billy Marlon was less than ten feet from the bottom of the staircase and showed no inclination to veer off and join Keith under the deck. Keith had no choice now but to break cover and follow Billy Marlon up the staircase, though what they were going to do up there he didn't know, but he figured Billy would smash the glass door with his rifle butt, and they'd wing it from there.

Keith began moving out from under the deck as Marlon took a long stride four or five feet from the first wooden step. Keith saw too late the four wooden pegs driven into the ground at the base of the staircase. Billy's foot came down on what looked like solid ground, but was a sheet of canvas or plastic, secured at the corners by the pegs and covered with a thin layer of earth.

Keith watched and saw it all as if in slow motion: Billy's surprised look as the ground beneath him gave way and Billy dropping through the earth. Keith expected him to keep falling, like the men did in Vietnam who dropped into a deep punji pit and became impaled on sharpened bamboo shafts. But Marlon stopped at knee height, his feet funneled into the narrow base of a conical hole. Keith heard a sharp metallic snap, followed by the sickening sound of something crunching, followed by Billy's shrill, piercing scream. Keith froze where he was beneath the edge of the deck, a few feet from Billy. The glass door above him slid open.

Baxter heard the bear trap snap shut, followed by the scream, and he slid the door open, letting the screams into the living room. He yelled, "Gotcha! Gotcha!"

The figure at the base of the stairs was thrashing in pain, screaming, but still holding tight to the rifle.

In an instant, Baxter recognized that it wasn't Landry, and he shouted, "Who the hell—Marlon! You little shit!" Baxter, still standing inside the doorway, aimed his rifle down at Marlon.

Billy Marlon, still holding his rifle with one hand and writhing in agony, managed to get off a single shot from the hip, as Baxter fired simultaneously. Billy's shot went high and tore into the wood siding above Baxter's head. Baxter's bullet went where it was aimed, through Billy Marlon's heart.

Almost simultaneously, Keith fired three quick shots up and through the wooden planks toward where he guessed Baxter was standing in the doorway.

One shot shattered the glass door, one grazed Baxter's forearm, and the third hit him in the chest, knocking the wind out of him and throwing him back through the open door where he sprawled on the floor.

Annie screamed.

Baxter struggled to his feet, still holding his rifle.

Keith heard Baxter fall on the floor, and Keith charged out from beneath the deck, grabbed the banister post, and swung around over the hole where Billy lay dead. With his pistol aimed at the door, he took the stairs in three strides, and, not seeing Baxter on the floor or anywhere in the dim light of the room, he bounded across the deck and dove through the open door, rolling to his right behind a long sofa, his pistol sweeping the room.

He lay there, looked and listened, but saw no one and heard nothing. The single lamp still shone weakly from somewhere at the far end of the room, casting dark shadows where he lay. The sofa blocked his view of the room toward the fireplace, but he could see the stone chimney rising to the high cathedral ceiling, and noticed the gray wolf head looking across the room from thirty feet away.

He lay on his back, motionless, the pistol still sweeping, controlling his breathing and trying to get a sense of the layout of the big room from what he could see. He was fairly certain he'd hit Baxter, but by the sound of Baxter's heavy crash to the floor, Keith reasoned that Baxter was wearing his body armor and that the round had simply knocked him off his feet, and he'd scrambled away from the door. Baxter might be hurt, Keith thought, but a .38-caliber pistol round that had gone through a plank and hit body armor would not hurt him too badly.

Keith couldn't see much beyond the sofa and the other furniture, so he slid a few feet away toward the wall. His head and eyes continuously swept the room, left to right, as his pistol swept right to left, trusting his peripheral vision and his hearing to cover what was momentarily not in his direct line of sight, and trusting his instinct to snap fire at anything that moved.

Keith didn't know who was going to make the first move, but he was fairly certain that there weren't many moves left on the board now.

Images of Billy Marlon flashed in front of him— Billy at the bar in John's Place, Billy asking Keith if he could come along, Billy in the pickup truck on the way up here, Billy sitting with Keith in the dark woods... Billy writhing in agony in that hole. Billy dead.

Keith thought, too, of Annie. He knew she was here, not far away, and she knew he was here in this room.

Keith decided to make the first move, not based on rage or ego, but on the assumption that Baxter knew someone was in the room and that Baxter also knew approximately where that person was, while Keith didn't have a clue as to where Baxter was.

Keith began to rise to one knee, then heard a woman's voice from the direction of the fireplace say, "He's in the far right corner, crouched with a pistol."

Before she even finished, Keith sprang up on one knee, aimed over the back of the sofa, and fired two rounds at Baxter, who had taken cover behind a wooden chest in the corner. Keith fell back behind the sofa and rolled to the right, toward the wall, as two answering rounds ripped through the sofa.

Keith lay still behind an upholstered chair.

In the two seconds it had taken him to fire, he'd caught a glimpse of Annie to his left, kneeling on the floor near the fireplace, naked. He was sure she'd seen him.

Keith was certain that at least one of his rounds had hit Baxter, but again the body armor had saved him. Keith wasn't too happy with the six-shot Smith & Wesson Police Model 10 that Baxter's men used, especially not in this situation where, with one bullet left, he couldn't take a chance and open the cylinder, extract the used casings, and reload chamber by chamber.

He wondered if Baxter was using the Glock, which had a seventeen-round, quick reload magazine. It didn't matter anyway, because, as Keith suspected, now that Baxter knew for sure it was Landry, the round-counting game was about to be cut short.

As if Baxter had read Keith's mind, Baxter called out, "Don't shoot, Landry. I'm standing right behind her. I got a gun to her head. So you just stand up where I can see you, hands high."

Keith figured that was coming, because he knew Baxter. He noticed that Baxter's voice was steady, but not altogether calm, even though he had everything going for him.

"I want to see empty hands first."

Keith had only one option left, and Baxter had given it to him by firing. Keith played dead.

A few seconds went by, and Baxter called out, "Hey, asshole. You want her to die? Stand up like a man, or I blow her fucking head off. I kid you not."

Keith heard Annie's voice say, "Don't do it, Keith—" followed by a loud slap and a cry of pain.

Baxter yelled out again, "Hey, hero, you got five seconds, then she's dead. One!"

Keith didn't think Baxter was going to kill her,

and there were a lot of reasons for that, not the least of which was that Baxter didn't want to lose his human shield.

"Two!"

Keith knew if he stood, he couldn't expect a quick death. He held the revolver close to his body to muffle the sound, opened the cylinder, and extracted the five spent casings.

"Three!"

Keith began quietly slipping rounds into the empty chambers.

"Four! I swear to God, Landry, you stand up, or she's dead."

Annie called out, "No! Don't—"

Another slap and another cry of pain, during which Keith snapped the cylinder quickly back into the frame.

"Five! Okay, she gets it."

Keith held his breath and steadied himself. He wanted to stand, to shout, to shoot, to let Baxter take him, to do anything in that split second except what he knew he had to do, which was nothing.

There was a long silence in the room, then Baxter said, "Hey! You dead, or playin' dead?"

Keith exhaled and smiled. *Come here and find out.*

"I can wait all fucking night, Landry."

Me, too. Keith waited. One thing he thought he could count on was Annie telling him if Baxter moved toward him. Baxter's hostage, his shield, was also Baxter's problem. But apparently Baxter had also figured that out, because the light suddenly went off, and the room was black.

It was so still in the big room that Keith could hear the mantel clock ticking from thirty feet away. Then he heard Baxter say to him, "One of us got an infrared scope, and one of us don't. Guess who can see in the dark."

He heard the floor squeak across the room, then heard it again, this time closer, then the squeaking stopped.

He pictured Baxter standing in about the middle of the room now, scanning along the floor, the walls, around the furniture with his night scope mounted on his rifle. The game was almost done, and Keith had only two moves left—stand and shoot into the dark, or play very dead.

He moved his right hand with the revolver under his buttocks as though he'd fallen dead on his forearm. With his left hand, he took his knife and sliced into his hairline, then smeared the blood over his face and left eye. He slid the knife into his pocket and kept both eyes open, staring dead at the unseen ceiling above him.

He heard Baxter move again, very close now, on the other side of the long sofa. Baxter said, "Well...so you ain't *playin'*."

Keith couldn't actually see him, but he felt his presence looming over him, and, by his voice, he knew that Baxter was about ten feet away and that, at this close distance, the infrared image would be too blurry to detect a sign of life. Nevertheless, Keith didn't draw a breath and kept his eyelids frozen and his eyeballs dead in their sockets. But he couldn't keep the sweat beads from forming on his upper lip. He had a sense, a feeling, of the infrared scope boring into his face, the muzzle of the rifle pointed at about his throat. Somewhere across the room, he heard Annie sobbing.

Baxter said, "Hey, Landry. You playin' possum on me?"

Keith knew he needed a head shot, but that wasn't possible in the dark. A hit in the body armor was the best he could hope for, and that would knock Baxter off his feet, then he'd use the knife.

"I hope to God you ain't dead, shithead. I want you to feel this."

Keith understood that the next thing to happen would be Baxter firing into his leg or his groin, and he knew he had to go for it now. He yanked his gun hand free and fired three times, up and to his right where he'd heard Baxter's voice, then rolled, fired three times again, then came to a stop tight against the wall near the shattered glass door. He stared into the dark and waited.

He never heard Baxter yell out in pain, never heard the rounds slap against the body armor, and never heard the sound of a man falling. He realized that Baxter must have moved or crouched low after he'd spoken and before Keith fired. Baxter had made a smart move. Keith had made a fatal move. He heard Baxter's voice, coming from a different place, saying, "So long, sucker—"

Instead of the explosion of Baxter's rifle firing into him, he heard a dull thud. He had no idea of what that was, but it meant he wasn't dead, and he jumped to his feet, lunging toward the sofa with his knife in his hand. He collided with the sofa and slashed out with his knife, then something hit his legs and fell to the floor, making another, softer thud.

There were no more sounds in the dark room, then he heard a groan, then a floor lamp came on beside the sofa.

It took him a second for his eyes to adjust to the light, and even then he wasn't completely processing what he saw.

Baxter was kneeling on the sofa in front of him, slumped over the back, his head and bare arms dangling toward Keith. Baxter was wearing a thick gray nylon vest, and Keith saw blood running from his left arm where Keith guessed one of his bullets had grazed him. Keith looked into Baxter's eyes, which were open and were focused on him.

Keith, the knife still in his hand, glanced down at his feet and saw the rifle with the night scope lying on the floor and realized that this is what had hit him in the legs. He knew he hadn't gotten Baxter with his knife, yet Baxter was bleeding now from the mouth.

Keith was aware of Annie standing to his left, and he looked at her. She was naked, standing very rigid, her eyes a million miles away, and her right hand still on the lamp switch. Then he noticed the poker in her left hand, hanging at her side. She wasn't looking at him, but was staring at the back of Cliff Baxter's head.

Baxter groaned, and his head lolled to the side, the blood still trickling from his mouth.

Keith looked back at Annie. He said nothing and made no move but kept looking at her until finally she turned toward him.

The sofa was between him and her, but he put out his arm, reaching past Baxter, and motioned for her to give him the poker. He noticed now that she had leg irons around her ankles. He made another motion for her to hand him the poker, but she shook her head.

Cliff Baxter groaned again, and Keith looked at him. Blood was running down the sides of his neck now, and Keith said to him, but for Annie's benefit, "You brought this on yourself. You know that."

Baxter raised his head, and, still conscious, looked at Keith and said, "Fuck you . . ." Then he tried to stand and turn around, his head and eyes moving around the room. "Annie, Annie, I—"

She swung the poker in a wide overhead arch and brought it down hard against the top of her husband's head, sending him sprawling back over the couch.

Keith could actually hear the skull crack and saw

Baxter's eyes bulge out of his sockets and blood pour from his nose. Keith was not at all surprised by that second, fatal blow—he was certain she knew far better than anyone else what she was doing and why.

Annie dropped the poker to the floor and looked at Keith.

He said, "All right…it's all right…" He continued to speak softly to her as he moved around the sofa. She took a tentative step toward him, then a longer step, but the chain pulled taut and she stumbled. He caught her arms and moved her gently back into a chair, making her sit down. He took off his shirt, put it around her shoulders, and put his hand on her cheek. "It's okay."

Keith stepped away from her and picked up the poker. He took a long stride toward the sofa and brought the poker down with all his strength on the top of Baxter's already smashed skull. He noted, irrelevantly, that Baxter was in his underwear, that his skin was pale, and that his sphincter had let loose.

Keith threw the poker on the floor and turned to Annie. He said quietly, "I killed him."

She didn't reply.

He said again, "Annie, I killed him. He's dead. It's over."

She looked at Keith.

He knelt in front of her and took her hands, which were cold and clammy. He said, "It's okay now. You're going to be all right. We're going back to Spencerville now."

She nodded, and tears ran down her cheeks. She said, "Thank you."

This wasn't the time, Keith thought, to thank her for saving his life, because Keith wanted to establish a different set of events in her mind. He rubbed her hands and asked her, "Are you hurt?"

"No." She touched his face where the blood was still wet from the knife cut. "*You're* hurt."

"I'm fine." He saw a bruise on her face and bruises on her legs. Her eyes looked all right, though her skin was pale and cold. As he held her hands, he felt that her pulse was fast but regular. "You're okay. You're tough."

She ignored this and said to him, "He has the keys around his neck. I want these off." She jiggled the manacles around her ankles. "I want them off."

He smiled at her. "Okay."

He stood, went over to Baxter's body, and ripped the key chain off Baxter's bloody neck. He knelt in front of Annie again and, as he tried a few keys, he noticed the padlock hanging from the chain and the shackle running through the big eyebolt. He asked, "How did you manage that?"

"I unscrewed it with the poker."

He nodded. Keith unlocked the leg manacles and rubbed her ankles. "Okay?"

"Yes."

"Let's get you dressed and out of here."

She didn't seem to want to move, but then she looked at Cliff Baxter slumped dead over the back of the sofa and said, "Yes, I want to get out of here. Help me up."

He stood and helped her stand, turning her away from the dead body. He walked with his arm around her as she made her way toward the hallway, his shirt draped over her shoulders.

She stopped and moved away from him. "I can do this. Wait here. I'll be dressed in a few minutes."

"Okay."

She hesitated a moment, then looked at him and asked, "There was someone else outside, wasn't there?"

"Yes. Billy Marlon."

"Is he dead?"

"Yes."

"I'm sorry."

"Not your fault."

She looked at Cliff Baxter, then at Keith and said, "*I* killed him."

He didn't reply.

She put her hand on his face and looked into his eyes a long time, then said, "I knew you'd come."

"I told you I would."

"Well . . . I hope you think it was worth it."

He smiled at her and kissed her. "What are friends for?"

CHAPTER FORTY-THREE

Billy Marlon's pickup truck rolled south along Route 127. By the time Keith and Annie reached the Ohio border, the dawn was breaking over the frosty fields and meadows.

Keith glanced at Annie and said, "Why don't you try to get some sleep?"

"I want to stay awake and look at you."

He smiled. "I've looked better."

"You look fine."

"You, too," he said. In fact, he knew, neither of them looked their best, but Annie had put on some makeup and was wearing a white wool turtleneck and jeans. She had washed and bandaged his knife wound, but neither of them had wanted to stay in the lodge long enough to shower, or for her to pack anything, and he hadn't taken any of the guns. There had been a sort of silent consensus between them to leave everything behind and get out of that house of horrors.

He said to her, "I broke into your house before I came to the lodge, to look for clues. I wanted you to know that."

"That's all right." She smiled again. "You're such a gentleman. Was everything clean?"

"It's a nice house." He added, "You're still a neat freak."

"There's a pig inside trying to get out."

"Good."

They drove on in silence awhile, and when they spoke, it had little or nothing to do with the last three days.

She'd held her hand in his for most of the drive down, and even when he used the floor shift, she kept her hand over his. This reminded him of when they were in high school, on those occasions when he couldn't use the family car, and he had to pick her up in the farm truck, and she'd keep her hand on his as he shifted gears.

Keith said, "It's going to be a beautiful day."

"Yes. I like to see the sun rise." She added, "Especially this one."

"Right." A few minutes later, he said, "Billy Marlon told me you were always nice to him. He appreciated that."

She didn't reply.

Keith said, "He wanted to do what he did. He had a score to settle."

"I know. I know about his wife."

Keith nodded.

Annie said, "I always knew that, one day, all of Cliff's bad deeds would catch up with him." She added, "He *did* bring it on himself."

"That's usually the case."

She asked him, "Would you have killed him? I mean, if you didn't have to kill him in self-defense?"

"I don't know. I really don't know."

"I don't think you would have. It's all right. You're a good person. You made me a promise." She added, "I didn't make any such promise to anyone."

He didn't respond to that but changed the subject

and said, "We'll stop at a roadside place up ahead near the Interstate. I'll buy you breakfast."

"I look awful. So do you."

"I have to meet someone at the truck stop."

"Oh . . . the man you called from the lodge?"

"Yes."

"Your friend from Washington?"

"Yes."

She didn't say anything further, and, a few minutes later, Keith pulled into a truck stop off the Ohio Turnpike.

She said, "I'll stay here."

"No, I want you to meet Charlie, and I want you to call your sister."

They got out of the pickup truck and went into the coffee shop.

Charlie Adair was sitting in a booth near a window, wearing the first and only British tweed suit in the place, drinking coffee, smoking, and reading a newspaper. He stood as they approached, smiled, and said, "Good morning."

Keith and Charlie shook hands, and Keith said, "Charlie Adair, I'd like you to meet Annie Baxter."

He took her hand and said, "I'm very glad you could come."

"Thank you. I'm very glad I could be here."

They all sat, and Charlie ordered two more coffees. He said, "This is a great place. Everyone here smokes." He asked Annie, "Do you mind if I smoke?"

Annie shook her head.

Charlie lit another cigarette and said to her, "Keith and I had some words before he went up to Michigan, so we wanted to apologize to each other in person."

Annie replied, "And you wanted to get a look at me."

"Absolutely. You're beautiful."

"I am, you know, but not at this moment."

Charlie smiled, then said, "I think you are." He added, "I'm not going to take Keith away, so let's be friends."

"Okay."

Keith said to Annie, "Don't trust a word he says."

She replied, "I already figured that out."

Charlie smiled again.

The coffee came, and they sipped on it. Charlie said to Annie, "Here's something you can trust me on— Keith Landry is the finest, bravest, most truthful man I know."

She smiled, "I know that."

Keith said, "I think that's enough." He said to Charlie, "This woman saved my life."

Charlie nodded and said, "You owe her."

Annie said to Charlie, "Actually, Keith risked his life to save mine."

Keith said again, "Enough."

Charlie asked, "Can Uncle buy you breakfast? No strings attached if it's under ten bucks."

They both shook their heads.

Charlie inquired, "Do you need money?"

Keith replied, "No, we're fine."

Charlie said, "So you've known each other since you were kids. That's great. Who did better in school?"

Annie said, "I did. He has the attention span of a gnat."

Charlie smiled. "Depends on the subject. He can read Russian. Did you know that?"

"It never came up and probably never will."

Charlie laughed.

They drank their coffee, and Charlie said to Annie, "I know you've probably had a very trying experience, and I appreciate your agreeing to stop and make small talk."

"I'm sure when I get up to make my phone call, you'll dispense with the small talk."

Charlie looked at her and said, "I used to meet him when he returned from someplace—usually a small café in a small town near a nasty border. So this sort of feels like old times." He went on, "We'd have a coffee or a drink, and I'd fill him in on the latest sports news. We'd never discuss his trip until much later. But this time, since I don't think I'll see him again for a while..."

Annie stood. "I'll make that phone call."

Keith and Charlie stood as she left, and every trucker in the place watched.

They sat down again, and Charlie said, "Good woman. Good presence, good eyes, good face, good body. Bad taste in men."

"Apparently."

"You still in love?"

"Yes."

"The inconvenient husband, I imagine, is out of the picture."

"Very much so."

"You need a cleaning service?"

"Yes. He's in the lodge, Billy Marlon is outside."

Charlie nodded.

Keith gave Charlie directions to the lodge and said, "I want everything that's hers taken out of there, I want Marlon's body out of there. You may even decide to burn the place. Your call. Then I guess someone can make an anonymous phone call to the local police. Let them figure it out."

Again, Charlie nodded. "We'll take care of it. How about Marlon's body?"

"Find his next of kin in Spencerville. There's an

ex-wife and kids in Fort Wayne, and an ex-wife named
Beth in Columbus, Ohio. I want a military funeral with
honors in Spencerville."

"Okay. Hey, you feeling good or bad?"

"Both."

"She really save your life?"

"Yes, she brained him with a poker."

"Ouch!" Charlie added, "Aside from him trying to
kill you, I guess he deserved it."

"More than we'll ever know."

"How's she doing?"

"Okay."

"It's going to get a little rocky later, you know,
when it all hits her. I mean, with her kids and all."

"She'll be all right. But no one else has to know
what happened there."

"No one ever will."

"Thanks."

Charlie smiled. "So you did it yourself. But I have to
clean up the mess."

"That's what you're good at."

"Is this a free favor I'm doing?"

"Sure is."

"I don't get anything in return?"

"No."

He asked Keith, "You coming back?"

"No."

"That's final?"

"Yes."

"Good. Maybe I'll take the job."

"Serve you right."

Annie returned, and the two men stood again and
came out of the booth. Keith said to Annie, "We're
leaving."

"Okay." She put out her hand to Charlie and said,

"It was very good meeting you. I hope we see you again sometime."

"You most certainly will. I want you to be my guest in Washington."

"That's very kind of you."

Charlie took Keith's hand and said, "Good luck, my friend. We'll meet again under happier circumstances."

"I'm sure we will."

They said their good-byes, and Keith and Annie went outside and got back into the pickup truck.

Keith pulled out onto the highway and asked her, "Did you speak to Terry?"

"Yes. She's happy and relieved. She said to tell you thanks."

"Did you tell her about him?"

"Yes. She said, 'God rest his soul.'"

Keith didn't reply.

They continued south, toward Spencerville. Annie said, "Charlie is a charming man."

"He's very charming."

"He was your boss?"

"Yes, but he never took it too seriously."

She stayed silent awhile, then asked him, "Do you want to go back there?"

"No."

"Why not? I'll bet it was very glamorous and exciting. What could you possibly do after leading that kind of life?"

"Grow corn."

She looked at him and asked, "Keith...do you know about your house?"

"Yes, I do."

"I'm sorry."

"It's all right, Annie. The land is still there, and

there were two houses on that spot before the last one. I'll build the fourth."

She nodded and said, "I would offer to have you come live with me, but I don't think I can live in that house again."

"No, you can't."

"No...well...what...?" She glanced at him. "What are your plans?"

"Well, first I'm taking you to Rome, and we'll both see the Colosseum at night, together this time."

She smiled and put her arm around his shoulders and said, "Welcome home, Keith."

John Corey is back and in the middle of a
new Cold War with a clock-ticking plot that
has Manhattan in its crosshairs.

Please continue reading
for a preview of
Radiant Angel

I f I wanted to see assholes all day, I would have become a proctologist. Instead, I watch assholes for my country.

I was parked in a black Chevy Blazer down the street from the Russian Federation Mission to the United Nations on East 67th Street in Manhattan, waiting for an asshole named Vasily Petrov to appear. Petrov is a colonel in the Russian Foreign Intelligence Service—the SVR in Russian—which is the equivalent to our CIA, and the successors to the Soviet KGB. Vasily—whom we have affectionately code-named Vaseline—has diplomatic status as Deputy Representative to the UN for Human Rights Issues—which is a joke—but his real job is SVR Legal Resident in New York—the equivalent of a CIA Station Chief. I have had Colonel Petrov under the eye on previous occasions, and though I've never met him he's reported to be a very dangerous man, and thus an asshole.

I'm John Corey, by the way, former NYPD homicide detective, now working for the federal government as a contract agent. My NYPD career was cut short by three bullets that left me seventy-five percent disabled (twenty-five percent per bullet?) for retirement pay purposes. In fact, there's nothing wrong with me physically, though the mental health exam for this job was a bit of a challenge.

Anyway, sitting next to me behind the wheel was a young lady I'd worked with before, Tess Faraday. Tess was maybe early thirties, auburn hair, tall, trim, and attractive. Also in the SUV, looking over my shoulder, was my wife, Kate Mayfield, who was actually in Washington, but I could feel her presence. If you know what I mean.

Tess asked me, "Do I have time to go to the john, John?" She thought that was funny.

"You have a bladder problem?"

"I shouldn't have had that coffee."

"You had two." Guys on surveillance pee in the container and throw it out the window. I said, "Okay, but be quick."

She exited the vehicle and double-timed it to a Starbucks around the corner on Third Avenue.

Meanwhile, Vasily Petrov could come out of the Mission at any time, get into his chauffeur-driven Mercedes S550, and off he goes.

But I've got three other mobile units, plus four agents on legs, so Vasily is covered while I, the team leader, am sitting here while Ms. Faraday is sitting on the potty.

And what do we think Colonel Petrov is up to? We have no idea. But he's up to *something*. That's why he's here. And that's why I'm here.

In fact, Petrov arrived only about four months ago, and it's the recent arrivals who are sometimes sent on the field with a new game play, and these guys need more watching than the SVR agents who've been stationed here awhile and who are engaged in routine espionage. Watch the new guys.

The Russian UN Mission occupies a thirteen-story brick building with a wrought-iron fence in front of it, conveniently located across the street from the 19th Precinct, whose surveillance cameras keep an eye on the Russians 24/7. The Russians don't mind being watched by the NYPD because they're also protected from pissed-off demonstrators and people who'd like to plant a bomb outside their front door. FYI, I live five blocks north of here on East 72nd, so I don't have far to walk when I get off duty at four. I could almost taste the Buds in my fridge.

So I sat there, waiting for Vasily Petrov and Tess Faraday. It was a nice day in early September: one of those beautiful, dry and sunny days you get after the dog days of August. It was a Sunday, a little after 10 A.M., so the streets and sidewalks of New York were relatively quiet. I volunteered for Sunday duty because Mrs. Corey (my wife, not my mother) was in Washington for a weekend conference, returning tonight or tomorrow morning, and I'd rather be working than trying to find something to do on a Sunday.

Also, today was September 11, a day I usually go to at least one memorial service with Kate, but it seemed more appropriate for me to mark this day by doing what I do.

There is a heightened alert every September 11 since 2001, but this year we hadn't picked up any specific intel that Abdul was up to something. And it being a Sunday, there weren't enough residents or office workers in the city for Abdul to murder. September 11, however, is September 11, and there were a lot of people working today to make sure that this was just another quiet Sunday.

Kate was in D.C. because she's an FBI special agent with the Anti-Terrorist Task Force, headquartered downtown at 26 Federal Plaza. Special Agent

Mayfield was recently promoted to Supervisory Special Agent, and her new duties take her to Washington a lot. She sometimes goes with her boss, Special-Agent-in-Charge Tom Walsh, who used to be my ATTF boss, too, but I don't work for him or the ATTF any longer. And that's a good thing for both of us. We were not compatible. Walsh, however, likes Kate, and I think the feeling is mutual. I wasn't sure Walsh was with Kate on this trip because I never ask, and she rarely volunteers the information.

On a less annoying subject, I now work for the Diplomatic Surveillance Group—the DSG. The group is also headquartered at 26 Fed, but with this new job I don't need to be at headquarters much, if at all.

My years in the Mideast section of the Anti-Terrorist Task Force were interesting, but stressful. And according to Kate, I was the cause of much of that stress. Wives see things husbands don't see. Bottom line, I had some issues and run-ins with the Muslim community (and my FBI bosses) that led directly or indirectly to my being asked by my superiors if I'd like to find other employment. Walsh suggested the Diplomatic Surveillance Group, which would keep me (a) out of his sight, (b) out of his office, and (c) out of trouble.

Sounded good. Kate thought so, too. In fact, she got the promotion after I left.

Coincidence?

My Nextel phone is also a two-way radio, and it blinged. Tess's voice said, "John, do you want a doughnut or something?"

"Did you wash your hands?"

Tess laughed. She thinks I'm funny. "What do you want?"

"A chocolate chip cookie."

"Coffee?"

"No." I signed off.

Tess's career goal is to become an FBI special agent, and to do that she has to qualify for appointment under one of five entry programs—accounting, computer science, language, law, or what's called "diversified experience." Tess is an attorney and thus qualifies. Most failed lawyers become judges or politicians, but Tess tells me she wants to do something meaningful, whatever that means. Meanwhile, she's working with the Diplomatic Surveillance Group.

Most of the DSG men and women are second-career people, twenty-year retirees from various law enforcement agencies, so we have mostly experienced agents and ex-cops mixed with inexperienced young attorneys like Tess Faraday who see the Diplomatic Surveillance Group as a stepping-stone where they can get some street creds that look good on their FBI app.

Tess got back in the SUV and handed me an oversized cookie. "My treat."

She had another cup of coffee. Some people never learn.

She was wearing khaki cargo pants, a blue polo shirt, and running shoes, which are necessary if the target goes off on foot. Her pants and shirt were loose enough to hide a gun, but Tess is not authorized to carry a gun.

In fact, Diplomatic Surveillance Group agents are theoretically not authorized to carry guns. But we're not as stupid as the people who make the rules, so almost all the ex-cops carry. In situations like this, where I bend the rules, my personal motto is *Better to face twelve jurors than to be carried by six pallbearers.* Therefore, I had my 9mm Glock in a pancake holster in the small of my back, beneath my loose-fitting polo shirt.

So we waited for Vasily to show.

Colonel Petrov lives in a big high-rise in the upscale Riverdale section of the Bronx. This building, which we call the 'plex—short for complex—is owned and wholly occupied by the Russians who work at the UN, and it is a nest of spies. The building itself, located on a high hill, sprouts more antennas than a garbage can full of cockroaches.

The National Security Agency, of course, has a facility nearby where they listen to the Russians who are listening to us, and we all have fun trying to block each other's signals. And round it goes. The only thing that has changed since the days of the Cold War is the encryption codes.

On a less technological level, the game is still played on the ground as it has been forever. Follow that spy. The Diplomatic Surveillance Group also has a confidential off-site facility—what we call the Bat Cave—near the Russian apartment complex, and the DSG team who was watching the 'plex this morning reported that Vasily Petrov had left, and they followed him here to the Mission, where my team picked up the surveillance.

The Russians don't usually work in the office on Sundays, so my guess was that Vasily was in transit to someplace else—or that he was going back to the 'plex—and that he'd be coming out shortly and getting into his chauffeur-driven Benz.

Colonel Petrov, according to the intel, is married, but his wife and children have remained in Moscow. This in itself is suspicious because the families of the Russian UN delegation love to live in New York on the government ruble. Or maybe there's an innocent explanation for the husband-wife separation. Like they hate each other.

Tess informed me, "I have two tickets to the Mets

doubleheader today." She further informed me, "I'd like to catch at least the last game."

"You can listen to them lose both games on the radio."

"I'll pretend you didn't say that." She reminded me, "We're supposed to be relieved at four."

"You can relieve yourself anytime you want."

She didn't reply.

A word about Tess Faraday. Did I say she was tall, slim, and attractive? She also swims and plays paddleball, whatever that is. She's fairly sharp, and intermittently enthusiastic, and I guess she's idealistic, which is why she left her Wall Street law firm to apply for the FBI, where the money is not as good.

But money is probably not an issue with Ms. Faraday. She mentioned to me that she was born and raised in Lattingtown, an upscale community on the North Shore of Long Island, also known as the Gold Coast. And by her accent and mannerisms I can deduce that she came from some money and good social standing. People like that who want to serve their country usually go to the State Department or into intelligence work, not the FBI. But I give her credit for what she's doing and I wish her luck.

Also, needless to say, Tess Faraday and John Corey have little in common, though we get along during these days and hours of forced intimacy.

One thing we do have in common is that we're both married. His name is Grant, and he's some kind of international finance guy, and he travels a lot for his work. I've never met Grant, and I probably never will, but he likes to text and call his wife a lot. I deduce, by Tess's end of the conversation, that Grant is the jealous type, and Tess seems a bit impatient with him. At least when I'm in earshot of the conversation.

Tess inquired, "If Petrov goes mobile, do we stay with him, or do we hand him over to another team?"

"Depends."

"On what?"

"No, I mean you should wear Depends."

One of us thought that was funny.

But to answer Tess's question, if Vasily went mobile, most probably my team would stay with him. He wasn't supposed to travel farther than a twenty-five-mile radius from Columbus Circle without State Department permission, and according to my briefing he hadn't applied for a weekend travel permit. The Russians rarely did, and when they did they would apply on a Friday afternoon so that no one at State had time to approve or disapprove their travel plans. And off they'd go, in their cars or by train or bus to someplace outside their allowed radius. Usually the women were just going shopping at some discount mall in Jersey, and the men were screwing around in Atlantic City. But sometimes the SVR or the Military Intelligence guys—the GRU—were meeting people, or looking at things that they shouldn't be looking at, like nuclear reactors. That's why we follow them. But we almost never bust them. The FBI, of which the DSG is a part, is famous—or infamous—for watching people and collecting evidence for years. Cops act on evidence. The FBI waits until the suspect dies of old age.

I said to Tess, "Let me know now if you can't stay past four. I'll call for a replacement."

She replied, "I'm yours."

"Wonderful."

"But if we get off at four, I have an extra ticket."

I considered my reply, then said, perhaps unwisely, "I take it Mr. Faraday is out of town."

"He is."

"Why have we not heard from Grant this morning?"

"I told him I was on a very discreet—and quiet—surveillance."

"You're learning."

"I don't need to learn what I already know."

"Right." Escape and evasion. Perhaps Grant had reason to be jealous. *You think?*

Regarding the nature of our surveillance of Colonel Vasily Petrov, this was actually a nondiscreet surveillance—what we call a bumper lock, meaning we were going to be up Vaseline's ass all day. They always spotted a bumper-lock surveillance, and sometimes they acknowledged the DSG agents with a hard stare—or if they were pricks they gave you the Italian salute.

Vasily was particularly unfriendly, probably because he was an intel officer, a big wheel in the Motherland, and he found it galling to be on the receiving end of a surveillance. Well, fuck him. Everybody's got a job to do.

Vasily sometimes plays games with the surveillance team, and he's actually given us the slip twice in the last four months or so, which has earned him the name Vaseline. He's never given me the slip, but some other DSG teams lost him. And there's hell to pay when you lose the SVR resident. And that wasn't going to happen on my watch. I don't lose anyone. Well, I lost my wife once in Bloomingdale's. I can't figure out the logic of a woman's shopping habits. They don't think like us.

"So do you want to go to the game?"

Mrs. Faraday had already started the game. But okay, two colleagues going to a baseball game after work is innocent enough. Even when they're married and their spouses are out of town. No problem. Right? I said, "I'll take a rain check."

"Okay." She asked me, "You going to eat that cookie?"

I broke it in half and gave her the bigger half.

Surveillances can be boring, which is why some people try to make it not boring. Two guys together talk about women, and two women together probably talk about guys. A guy and a woman together either have nothing to talk about, or the long hours lead to whatever.

In the last six months, Tess Faraday has been assigned to me about a dozen times, which, with 150 DSG agents in New York, defies the odds. As the team leader, I could reassign her to another vehicle or to leg surveillance. But I haven't. Why? Because I think she's asking to work with me, and being a very sensitive man, I don't want to hurt her feelings. And why does she want to work with me? Because she wants to learn from a master. Or something else is going on.

And, by the way, I haven't mentioned Tess Faraday to Kate. Kate is not the jealous type and there's nothing to be jealous about. Also, like Kate, I keep my work problems and associations to myself. Kate doesn't talk about Tom Walsh, and I don't talk about Tess Faraday. Marital ignorance is bliss. Dumb is happy.

Meanwhile, Vasily has been inside the Mission for over an hour, but his Mercedes is still outside, so he's going someplace. Probably back to the Bronx. He sometimes runs in Central Park, which is a pain in the ass. Everyone on the team wears running shoes, of course, and I think we're all in good shape, but Vasily is in excellent shape. Older FBI agents have told me that the Soviet KGB guys were mostly lard-asses who smoked and drank too much. But these guys from the new Russia were into granola and health clubs. Their boss, bare-chested Putin, sort of set the new standard.

Vasily, being who he is, also has a girlfriend in town, a Russian lady named Svetlana who sings at a few of the Russian nightclubs in Brighton Beach. I caught a glimpse of her once, and she looks like she has good lungs.

I did a radio check with my team and everyone was awake.

A soft breeze fluttered the white, blue, and red Russian flag in front of the Mission. I remember when the Soviet hammer and sickle flew there. I kind of miss the Cold War. But I think it's back.

My team today consists of four leg agents and four vehicles—my Chevy Blazer, a Ford Explorer, and two Dodge minivans. We usually have one agent in each vehicle, but today we had two. Why? Because the Russians are particularly tricky, and sometimes they travel in groups and scatter like cockroaches, so recently we've been beefing up the surveillance teams. So today I had two DSG agents in the other three vehicles, all former NYPD. I had the only trainee, an FBI wannabe who probably thinks the DSG job sucks. Sometimes I think the same thing.

In the parlance of the FBI, the DSG is called a quiet end, which really means a dead end.

But I'm okay with this. No office, no adult supervision, and no bullshit. Just follow that asshole. And do not lose that asshole.

A quiet end. But in this business, there is no such thing.

VISIT US ONLINE AT

WWW.HACHETTEBOOKGROUP.COM

FEATURES:

**OPENBOOK BROWSE AND
SEARCH EXCERPTS**

•

AUDIOBOOK EXCERPTS AND PODCASTS

•

AUTHOR ARTICLES AND INTERVIEWS

•

**BESTSELLER AND PUBLISHING
GROUP NEWS**

•

SIGN UP FOR E-NEWSLETTERS

•

**AUTHOR APPEARANCES AND TOUR
INFORMATION**

•

SOCIAL MEDIA FEEDS AND WIDGETS

•

DOWNLOAD FREE APPS